THE NINTH STEP

A John Milton Novel

Mark Dawson

AN UNPUTDOWNABLE book.

First published in Great Britain in 2016 by
UNPUTDOWNABLE LIMITED

Formatting by Polgarus Studio

To Mrs D, FD and SD.

Part One

The Feather Men

Chapter One

LONDON IN NOVEMBER was cold and damp. A heavy bank of grey cloud had settled over the city the day before, and it showed no sign of moving. It had rained without pause for six hours. At first it was the icy-cold drizzle that often afflicted the city at this time of year, but it had very quickly intensified, becoming a deluge that drummed against the roofs of the buildings and rattled the windows and hissed as it crashed down onto the tarmac. Run-off sluiced into the gutters and bubbled out of swamped drains that were already overflowing. Corporal Alex Hicks had seen the forecasts. This was how it was going to be for a week.

Hicks was on the roof of a jeweller's on the corner of Green Lanes and Umfreville Road. It was a three-storey building, and he had gained access to the roof by climbing a corroded fire escape that had barely borne his weight. He had been on the roof for three hours, and although he was wearing a Gore-Tex jacket, he was soaked to the skin and freezing cold. The building was a modern construction, facing Victorian terraces on all sides. The ground level of the terrace that was adjacent to Hicks had been given over to a series of shops and businesses: a Turkish restaurant, a solicitor's office, a pub. Umfreville Road was part of the Ladder, a grid of twenty streets that connected Green Lanes and Wightman Road. It became residential once you had travelled fifty feet, with two complementary rows of terraced accommodation housing reasonably affluent families who couldn't afford the more expensive properties of Finsbury Park or Islington. Before the first house, and adjacent to Hicks, was a whitewashed one-storey back extension that abutted a shop that labelled itself as Turkish Food Market, a crude TFM logo above the childish drawings of tomatoes, peppers and other fruit that covered the windows. There were two doors. The first, offering access to the property before the extension, was guarded by a metal cage. The second, at the end of the extension, was made from a solid slab of three-inch-thick steel and set back within a recess that made it impossible to see inside unless the observer was directly in line with it.

Hicks's ear bud buzzed and he heard the voice of Joseph Gillan over the troop radio. "Eyes open, lads. We're two minutes away."

Gillan and Rafe Connolly had followed the target in separate cars after he had left his property earlier that evening. He had stopped at a café in Dalston for his dinner where, over a plate of diced lamb's liver, he had given counsel to two of his most senior lieutenants. Hicks and the others knew that the target had an important appointment after dinner, and they had continued the surveillance as he had been driven away. Hicks had been in position atop the roof for three wet hours, waiting to put their plan into action.

"We're here," Gillan said.

"Copy that."

Hicks was shielded from the street below both by the height of his vantage point and by the short parapet that marked the edge of the roof. He raised himself onto his elbows and glanced over the edge, looking to the south towards the wide green space of Finsbury Park. He saw a car slow and indicate a left turn. Gillan's Ford was three cars behind it and, rather than follow the target into Umfreville Road, he continued on. The next road to the north was one way only, so Gillan would continue to Cavendish Road, follow that to Wightman Road, and then approach the target on foot from the west.

"Unit, report."

Hicks heard Alistair Woodward's voice: "In place."

"This is Gillan. Going around."

"Connolly here. In position."

Hicks squeezed the wireless pressel that he had fixed to

the stock of his rifle, opening the channel. "This is Hicks. Ready."

"Weapons free. Take them out."

Hicks shuffled down the roof until he was in line with the second door. He glanced to the left, toward Wightman Road, and saw Woodward. He was wearing a long jacket and a beanie that was pulled down to just above the line of his brow. The coat was loose enough to obscure the Heckler and Koch 416 A5 that was supported by a length of cord that had been looped over his shoulder. The carbine was the D10RS sub-compact variation with the shorter 10.4-inch barrel. It was chambered for 5.56×45mm NATO rounds and was the assault weapon favoured by the Regiment. It was lightweight, easy to fire and reliable. Perfect for what they had in mind.

The target was a man named Mustafa Öztürk. He stepped out of the car. A second man hurried alongside and raised an umbrella to shelter him from the teeming deluge. Öztürk hobbled ahead, the man with the umbrella ignoring the fact that he was being soaked so that he could ensure that his boss remained dry.

Hicks touched the pressel and spoke into the throat mic. "Ajax is in play. Repeat, Ajax is in play."

"Copy that."

Öztürk limped ahead on his prosthetic leg. The police around here called him the Godfather of Green Lanes. He had been the leader of one of the most brutal crime syndicates in London for the last twenty years. Despite the fact that he was lame after losing a leg in a car accident in Turkey five years earlier, he had relied upon a mixture of fear and intimidation to rule the north-eastern stretches of the city. There were rumours in the cafés and bars around and about that his terraced house was equipped with a torture chamber behind a soundproof door, with meat hooks fitted to the ceiling and wired into the mains. The stories had it that Öztürk's victims would be strung up from the hooks and shocked between the frenzied beatings that he and his henchmen doled out. The police had tried for years to bring him to justice, but the man—known locally as "Uncle"—was too clever for them and had swatted their best efforts away. His impunity just added to his mystique. Uncle was quickly assuming the status of a local legend.

Hicks and Gillan had parked two stolen cars in the street adjacent to the second door. It meant that Öztürk would have to park fifteen feet away and then walk to get inside. They had timed it, taking his limp into account, and reckoned it would give them another ten seconds. It didn't seem like much, but when you were planning an operation of this nature, each additional second was a gift.

Hicks slid around just a little so that he could bring his own HK417 to bear. He had the version with a Leupold Mark 4 scope. He cradled the forestock in his left hand, pressed the butt into the cleft between his shoulder and cheek, and reached around with his right hand so that he could slide his finger through the trigger guard. He felt the cold touch of the trigger against the pad of his index finger and squeezed until he felt the resistance.

The general had wanted to get to Öztürk for months, but planning the operation had been difficult. They had scouted his property, wondering if they might take him there, but they had quickly discounted it. The front door was so well fortified that they would have had to use explosives to breach it. They had considered knocking a hole in the rear wall of the property so that they could get in, but that, too, had been discounted. Too noisy. Too slow. They would wait until he ventured out onto the street.

Öztürk was guarded by another two men. Both were shaven-headed and muscular. Both would be armed. They flanked him on either side as he hobbled down the pavement to the second door. One of the guards, the one nearest to the wall and on the other side of Öztürk to Hicks, went ahead and knocked on the door. Hicks pressed his eye to the scope and tracked him, placing the guard squarely within the centre of the targeting reticule. There was a pause, the man looking up at a CCTV camera that had been fixed above the door and then leaning forward and speaking into an intercom. Words were exchanged with someone inside the building, and then, the careful security measures satisfied, the door opened. A third man appeared from inside, stepping out into the recessed doorway.

Öztürk stepped inside the building. His men followed him, and the door was closed behind them.

Hicks reported: "They're inside."

He waited, aiming at the door. Öztürk visited this building several times a week. It was where he collected and stored the money he made from the sales of his product. He was careful, never following a routine, and they had kept him under surveillance for the last few days so that they could be sure of his plans. Hicks had camped out on the roof for several hours every night, just waiting for him to visit.

The door to the building opened.

"Stand ready," Hicks said into the mic.

He was aware of the lights of a car in his peripheral vision as it drew to a stop fifty feet along Umfreville Road. He glanced at it: an Audi. Alistair Woodward's car.

One of Öztürk's bodyguards stepped outside.

Öztürk was next.

The second bodyguard followed him, this one carrying a large sports bag.

Hicks changed his aim and spoke one word into his mic. "Firing."

He started to count.

One, two, three.

He pulled the trigger on four.

The gun recoiled into his shoulder, but he had anticipated it and was able to accommodate it easily. His 417 was chambered in 7.62mm, a heavier round that was generally used for sniping or when more muzzle velocity and penetration was needed. The man in the doorway fell, clutching his gut. Hicks had not attempted a head shot; he was confident that he would have been able to make it, even with the poor visibility in these awful conditions, but there was no need to risk a miss. That might have meant that the door would have been closed and their chance gone. Far better to plan it out this way: the man had fallen in the doorway, blocking the access point and making it impossible to shut the door.

Five, six.

Öztürk shouted in panic.

Seven, eight.

Hicks shortened his aim, placed the reticule between Öztürk's shoulder blades, and pulled the trigger. Uncle staggered against the wall as if he had been shoved in the back. He fell to his knees, one hand reaching down to prevent himself from falling flat on his face.

Eight, nine, ten.

The remaining guard was good. He realised that they were being sniped from above and immediately fell into cover behind the parked cars. Hicks held his aim, waiting for him to risk a glance up at his position, but he knew that he wouldn't be needed. Alistair Woodward was on the same side of the road as Öztürk and his men. He had been twenty feet away when Hicks had opened fire and, in the seconds that had elapsed, he had allowed his coat to part so that he could bring his own HK to bear. The man was directly in front of him; the car that he had chosen to shelter him from Hicks now prevented any possibility of him evading Woodward. He fired in two short volleys. The man was hit, and Hicks watched as he fell out of cover into the gap between two cars, toppling over onto his back, his arms splayed out wide and a pistol falling from his fingers.

Eleven, twelve, thirteen.

"Clear."

Woodward turned into the doorway, his HK raised and ready, and went inside.

The Audi raced forward. It skidded to a stop, the passenger door opened, and the general stepped out into the rain. Higgins was a man of normal height and build, unremarkable in the way that most special forces soldiers were unremarkable. He was in his mid-sixties, but he was as fit and active as a man twenty years younger. He bore the years well. He passed between the two parked cars and approached Öztürk. The Turk was on his side now, his legs lethargically scraping against the paving slabs as he tried to crawl away.

Higgins took a pistol from inside his jacket, pushed the muzzle against the top of the man's head and fired. Öztürk dropped flat to the ground and lay there, unmoving.

Nineteen, twenty, twenty-one.

Woodward appeared in the doorway again. He was carrying another bag, similar to the one that the bodyguard had been carrying. That bag was on the pavement, and the general went over to collect it. Both he and Woodward went around the parked cars and into the waiting Audi. Gillan was behind the wheel and he put the engine into first and fed in the revs. The car leapt forward, taking a sharp left into Green Lanes and disappearing quickly from view.

Thirty seconds from start to finish. Very efficient. The general would be pleased with that.

Hicks collected the two spent shell casings from the roof and put them in his pocket. He removed the rifle's bipod and barrel, put the component parts into the bag he used to carry it, and zipped it closed. Hicks crossed the roof to the ladder and descended into the empty yard below.

Chapter Two

THEY SPLIT UP and travelled back to Hereford separately. Hicks had parked his Range Rover a short walk away from Green Lanes. He put his equipment into the back and was underway as the sound of sirens could be heard from the grid of streets behind him. Hereford was one hundred and forty miles to the north-west of London, and the journey passed without incident. The M4 motorway was clear and he made excellent time, shaving fifteen minutes off the usual three-hour duration.

He was on the outskirts of the city, in sight of the illuminated spire of the cathedral, when he heard the first reports of the London shootings on the radio. The newsreader said that three men had been murdered in what the police were describing as an eruption of the violence between the Turkish and Eastern European gangs that ruled the heroin and cocaine trade in that part of north London. There was no suggestion that the police had anything useful to investigate, and Hicks was not concerned. He knew that they had been thorough in their planning, meticulous in the performance of the plan, and conscientious in the clean-up and exfiltration. The general had bestowed a sobriquet on the unit that had proven to be resilient. He called them the Feather Men, on account of their light touch during operations and the fact that they never left evidence that might later betray them.

The unit always met at the Cock of Tupsley. It was a pub to the north-west of Hereford, just off the A438 and a mile before the village of Lugwardine. It was a large white building surrounded by a broad asphalt parking area and a wide lawn. It was owned by a brewery, and, next to a sign that advertised special deals for those who booked their Christmas meals now, they had made a feature of a dray that was loaded with barrels bearing the brewer's corporate logo. Hicks would not normally have chosen that kind of pub for a social event, but this was not social, and the proprietor was an old friend of the general from the Regiment who guaranteed them privacy and discretion in return for a very small shaving of their profits.

It was just before eleven, and there were two taxis parked next to the main entrance of the pub to collect customers who had enjoyed the hospitality too much to drive. Others headed for their cars and drove back to the city. Hicks parked next to Joseph Gillan's Maserati, collected his equipment from the back, and walked around to the separate staff entrance at the back of the building. There was a flight of stairs immediately inside, and he ascended these to the first floor. There was a set of toilets up here, together with two function rooms. The unit had the exclusive use of the second of these rooms. It was the smaller of the two, with three six-person tables and chairs, a large fireplace, three armchairs and a window that looked down onto the children's play area and the pub's beer garden.

Gillan, Rafe Connolly and Sebastian Shepherd were already there, half-finished pints on the table before them. Their bulky equipment bags were on the floor next to the fireplace. Hicks placed his bag next to theirs.

"Any issues?" Connolly asked.

"None."

"You see the police?"

"Heard them as I was driving away. I left it clean."

"Sweet."

"It was on the news," Hicks said.

"When?"

"Five minutes ago. They're saying it was gang related."

"Suits us," Gillan said.

"It was clean," Shepherd reiterated. "They'll be wasting their time."

The others indicated their agreement. Hicks slumped

down in one of the vacant armchairs. It had been a long day and he realised that he was tired.

"What was it like to lose your cherry?" Gillan asked.

"I *have* done that before," Hicks said.

"In the Regiment, maybe. But not with us."

"It was fine," Hicks said. "The plan was good. You follow the plan, you don't get problems. We followed the plan."

"Listen to him," Gillan said. "Sounds like a veteran already."

"You want a beer?" Connolly asked.

Hicks was thirsty. "I'd love one."

"Bar's downstairs," he responded with a grin. "Same again for us, too."

"Come on," Hicks protested feebly. "I'm done in."

"New boy gets the drinks. Chop-chop."

There was no point in putting up a fight. He was the newest member of the unit, and, because of that, he had come to expect a little ribbing. That had certainly been the case. The Americans he had worked with when he was in the Regiment had called it hazing. It was the same the world over. No sense in letting it bother him. He levered himself out of the chair, took his wallet out of his pocket and went downstairs.

#

GENERAL RICHARD HIGGINS had arrived by the time Hicks returned with the drinks. Higgins had been driven north by Alistair Woodward, and now they had taken two of the armchairs by the fire. Hicks closed the door with his foot and brought his tray of beers to the table. He had bought six pints and distributed them to the men. No one thanked him; instead, Shepherd suggested that he had forgotten the crisps and should go back to the bar to get them. Hicks told him to piss off and get them for himself. Shepherd glared at him, daring him to repeat the suggestion, before he fell back in his chair with a chuckle and told him he was just yanking his chain. Hicks shook his head and sat down with his drink. The men were all experienced soldiers and none of them was younger than forty, but there was still an undercurrent of juvenile humour that was occasionally exposed. The operation had been stressful, and Hicks knew that it would presage a night of boozing. He thought of his wife and kids, miles away in Cambridge, and wondered how quickly he would be able to excuse himself without drawing down more of their abuse for not getting involved.

He looked around at the others. They were all ex-SAS. An observer would perhaps have said it was obvious that they had been involved with the military at some point in their lives—they all had the same firm posture and shared the same banter—but there was nothing about their appearances that would have marked them as special forces men. Joseph Gillan was the largest of them, but even he could have made his way down the high street in Hereford without drawing attention to himself. The others were much as he was: they were of solid build, they wore their hair close to the scalp, they were clean shaven. There was nothing to suggest that they were killers; nothing to suggest that they had just returned from an expedition to murder five men; nothing to suggest that they had more blood on their hands than the blood they had spilled tonight.

The general allowed them to finish their drinks before he told them to be quiet and listen. The others all deferred to him. He had a closely cropped white beard, a lined face and pouches beneath his eyes. He had the coldest and most penetrating stare that Hicks had ever seen. It was as if, when he looked at you, he could see through the deceit and mistruths and divine the pure, unvarnished truth. It was those eyes that made conversation with him so unnerving.

"Well done," Higgins said. "That was good. Quick and efficient. Did any of you have any concerns?"

They all shook their heads. Higgins nodded, seemingly

satisfied. He was an exacting commanding officer, rarely praising his men, and just the suggestion of his satisfaction was valuable. "It was a good haul. Alistair?"

Woodward picked up his bag and deposited it on one of the tables. He unzipped it and pulled out thick bundles of bank notes. Hicks counted forty bundles and guessed that each bundle must have contained five hundred notes. There would be tens and twenties and fifties in each bundle. Even on a conservative estimate, there must have been a quarter of a million on the table.

"We'll count it up and divide it tomorrow. I don't need to tell you to be careful. Nothing extravagant. Put it wherever you put it to keep it safe. *Not* the bank. All clear?"

Hicks nodded with the others until he noticed that Higgins was looking at him. He flushed; the new boy was getting special attention again. "Don't worry, sir," he said. "I'm not an idiot."

"I know you're not. But a big payday like this needs to be handled with caution. The temptation is to go out and spray the money around. Isn't that right, Shepherd?"

The men looked at Shepherd, their laughter intensifying with his discomfort. Hicks didn't know any of them well enough to know what the general was talking about, but, from Shepherd's expression, it was obvious that whatever it was, it wasn't something that he liked to have brought back up. "Very funny," he said.

Well, Hicks thought, a joke that *wasn't* at his expense. He felt like he was making progress.

Gillan leaned back in his chair and laced his fingers behind his head. "What's next, sir?"

The general nodded his head to the bags of equipment. "Get the gear put away safely."

"Yes, sir. And then?"

"There is another thing." He turned his attention to Hicks. "What are you doing tomorrow?"

He had arranged to take his kids to the cinema, but he knew he couldn't say that. "Nothing, sir."

"I need you to drive me."

"Where to?"

"Back down to London. There's someone I need to speak to."

#

HICKS STAYED for an hour before making his excuses and leaving. It was raining with a fine drizzle as he stepped outside, and he blipped the locks of his Range Rover and hurried across to shelter inside the cabin. He sat there for a moment, composing himself. He looked down at his hands. They were shaking. All that adrenaline, all that juice; now that it was gone, he was left with just the nerves that had been torturing him ever since he had agreed to take part.

He had done it now. He was involved.

He had spent the last two days searching for a way to extricate himself from taking part. But he had known that wasn't possible. He had been involved in the planning, he knew all of the men now, and the suggestion that he wanted out would have met with a hostile response. The events of the last few hours just underlined his involvement; he had committed himself as soon as he had met Higgins and Woodward and taken their offer. He had resorted to the consolation that he had taken part because he was desperate for the money and had no other choice. He wasn't driven by greed, like the others. It was fear that pushed him on. He tried to believe that that was true, and sometimes he did. But other times, he found it difficult to ignore the ache in his gut that told him that he had made a mistake, that he had bound his fate and the fate of his family to some of the most dangerous men that he had ever known.

And on those occasions, like now, there was no comfort at all.

Chapter Three

"MY NAME IS JOHN AND I AM AN ALCOHOLIC."

The meeting was held at St Leonard's, a church on the outskirts of the city of London. The building was located next to the major junction with Shoreditch High Street and Hackney Road. Milton had learned during the first meeting that he attended there that it was the church with the "bells of Shoreditch" that was mentioned in the nursery rhyme "Oranges and Lemons". It was built in grand Palladian style, with a steeple that soared high above the street and a four-columned, pedimented Tuscan portico, but the interior was shabby and in need of repair, something that seemed endemic to the venues that the fellowship used throughout the city. There were twenty other men and women in the large room, and they welcomed him with the usual, "Hello, John."

Milton took a moment. He rarely spoke at meetings, much preferring to sit quietly at the back and just soak it all up. They were the most peaceful, meditative gatherings that he had ever found, and he got more than enough by just being here, listening to the stories of the other alcoholics who turned up every Tuesday, week after week. But he *did* want to speak today. One of the most important things about the meetings was that you should share your experience, and Milton was determined to overcome his natural reticence and speak.

"I feel like it's been a good week," he said. "I didn't say anything last time, but I've been struggling more than usual the last month or so. I don't know why. Just one of those times, I know we all have them, when it all seems to get on top of us. Drink, you know. So I did what I always do and read the Big Book and came to my usual meetings. I listened, and then I went home and made myself busy. And

I think I'm coming out the other side."

The woman next to Milton, a lawyer he knew as Marcy, turned her head and smiled. He had plenty in common with her and the others who were present, and those shared experiences made it easier to be frank. There were things he would never be able to speak freely about, of course. He would never be able to tell them why he felt so guilty, the burden of the more than hundred and fifty lives he had taken and the retinue of ghosts who stalked his dreams when he was at his weakest, tempting him with the sure knowledge that the easiest way to drown out their cries was to be found in the bottom of a glass. It meant that he sometimes felt like a fraud in the face of the searing honesty of the others who shared, but that was something that he had come to terms with in the years since he had started coming to the rooms. It was obvious that he was holding back. Everyone could see it. People urged him to be completely honest every now and again, but, by and large, there was understanding. No one pressed. No one judged.

"I was in Australia until a month ago, working, working so hard that I was able to forget the voices telling me to take a drink," he went on. "It was good for a while, but then it stopped working. I was working on a sheep station. You can probably imagine what that was like. There's a lot of drink around, blokes going out and drinking every night, and I started to feel tempted. You know how it is: just one drink, that's all. I can handle it. What's the harm? I know enough about myself now to know that's the disease talking, so I left. There was a girl, too…" He paused, unwilling to go too much further down that line; he still thought of Matilda, and what he might have had with her if he had trusted himself enough to try. "I haven't been back to London for any extended period of time for months. It's where my problems started. I've been running from them. I thought about it, but I decided I was strong enough now. With the Book, with meetings, with other drunks to help me… I thought I could do it."

He had a cup of coffee held between his hands and he took a sip. He didn't want to speak for too long—he was conscious of others who wanted to share, and he didn't like the idea that his problems were any more serious than theirs—but he wasn't quite ready to stop.

"So I came back. I found a flat. Just somewhere cheap to rent. I don't have much money, hardly any at all, really, but I found a tiny place that will do very well for me. I found a job. It's nothing special, either, but I like it. Night shifts. Keeps me away from temptation. And I found the meetings I need to help me keep everything together. I feel okay about it all. I feel like I can handle it. I feel like I'm getting myself back together again."

There was a murmuring of support. Milton sipped the coffee again. He decided to tell them everything.

"I don't normally speak," he said. "The reason I am now is because this is an anniversary for me. It's three years since I took a drink. One thousand and ninety-five days. And I'm grateful. Coming to these rooms saved my life. If anyone here is new and wondering whether or not this can work, I'm here to say that it can. It's like we always say: it works if you work it—"

"—and work it 'cause you're worth it," the others finished.

Milton smiled. "That's all I wanted to say, really. Thanks for listening."

The usual chorus followed, others thanking him for his share, but Milton had said what he had needed to say, and now he felt himself drawing back into himself again.

There was a moment of silence, a pause while the others decided whether they would speak, too. Milton had been to this meeting several times, and he had already started to associate the regulars with typical AA types. There were those, much like him, who preferred to sit and listen. There were others, newer to the program, who, once they started to unburden themselves, couldn't stop. There were still others who shared every week because they liked to hear themselves speaking. Some of those were a little smug, dispensing advice that had not been requested and opining upon the shares of others. Milton tuned out whenever they spoke.

"My name is Edward and I'm an alcoholic."

The man was on the end of the same row as Milton and had been sitting quietly. Milton had seen him before and had noticed that he was friendly with the other regulars. The others welcomed his share; Milton stared down into his mug at the swirl of cheap brown coffee.

Edward looked down the row at Milton. "First of all, well done, John. Three years. That's amazing."

Milton looked back at him and gave a nod of acknowledgement.

"I feel like I might be getting to a similar place. The last month has been difficult. I've been white-knuckling it, if I'm honest. There have been days when I didn't think I could keep going, but coming to the rooms has given me the strength to stay away from booze, and I'll always be grateful for that. And things might be getting better. I've never shared the reasons why I feel the way I do, and I don't know if I'll ever be able to do that properly, but I can say that I feel like I'm making real progress now."

He paused and, when Milton looked over at him, his expression made it evident that he was considering how much he could say, just as Milton had done. He looked as if he was going to go on, but, as he started to open his mouth, he lost his nerve, shook his head and managed a rueful smile.

"I know we should be totally honest, no secrets, but I'm not ready to do that yet. There are things I might be able to say, one day, but for now I just wanted to say that I am grateful for the friendship I've found here. Like John says: it works if you work it. Thanks for listening."

Others thanked him for his share. He smiled shyly and, like Milton, returned to quiet contemplation for the rest of the meeting.

#

SOME OF THE REGULARS went out and got coffee together after the meeting had come to an end. It was eight o'clock, and Milton didn't have to be at the shelter for work until ten. He had fallen into the habit of taking a long stroll to clear his head. The quickest route to Russell Square was to follow Holborn and then turn north. It was two miles and Milton would have been able to cover the ground in just over half an hour if he moved quickly. He preferred to take the scenic route, heading south until he went by Cannon Street station and then following the river as it meandered to the west. He found it very beautiful at this time of day, with the lights glittering darkly on that wide span of water, barges and commuter craft sliding across the slow-moving tide. He would turn to the north as he reached Temple and follow Kingsway until he reached the Square. If he ambled and stopped occasionally to gaze out over the water, he could eke out two hours of peace and solitude, a useful supplementary buttress to the peace he had earned at the meeting. The walk always reminded him that there was more to London than the sordid, grubby business that was transacted from the anonymous building close to the MI5 building in Millbank from where his career had been directed. It reminded him, as he watched the city going about its business, never sleeping, that the world was larger than that, and that, perhaps, if he guarded his sobriety, he might be able to find his place in it.

He was getting ready to set off when the man who had spoken after him detached himself from the group and came over to him.

"You coming?"

"Sorry?"

"Coffee?"

"No," Milton said. "I can't. I have to get to work."

"You don't have half an hour to spare? Come on."

Milton looked at his watch. It was a superfluous gesture;

he knew what the time was. He was about to decline the invitation when something told him to stop being so foolish. He could take that walk whenever he liked. He remembered one of the most frequently repeated pieces of advice that was relayed during the meetings: you have to get involved. Sitting at the back was the taking of half measures, and, as the idiom went, "Half measures availed us nothing." He had already spoken tonight, and that was unusual. He felt better for it. Perhaps he would feel even better still if he took up the offer. He made a decision. Being sociable couldn't hurt, and maybe it would help.

"Where is it?"

"Just near Bank."

That wasn't out of his way. He had no excuse.

"Sure," Milton said. "I suppose I can."

Chapter Four

THERE WAS a commonly repeated saying in the rooms. It was that a newly sober drunk had both good and bad news. The good news was that they never had to drink again. The bad news was that the other men and women at the meetings were their new friends. Milton thought about that as he looked around the room. They were in a branch of Leon on Watling Street, near to Bank station. There were six of them and, as they filed inside, the manager acknowledged one of the women and indicated a table that had been reserved for them. Milton could see that this was a routine that had been in place for some time. They sat down and the manager took their orders. Some of them ordered cakes with their coffees. Milton declined, ordering a cappuccino with an extra shot of espresso. Caffeine and nicotine were his only vices now. He wondered afresh whether this was a good idea for someone like him. The meetings provided him with a space where he could meditate and listen to the testimonies of people with the same compulsions as he had, if not the same motivations. He took what he needed, occasionally shared something in exchange, and then returned to the comfortable cloak of his solitude. He had overheard the couple ahead of him as they had walked from the church. There was a tendency for some of his fellows to be overly enthusiastic about their recoveries, to proselytise about the program and offer critical comments about the slightest deviation from what the Big Book suggested was the best way to behave. One of the pair, a middle-aged woman, was hectoring her younger companion about the things that she was doing wrong. The second woman tried to retort, but Milton had noticed from her previous sharing that she was meek, and she quickly allowed herself to be spoken over.

The man who had invited Milton had stopped at the bathroom as soon as they had arrived. Maybe it had been a mistake to come after all. Milton decided he would stay for ten minutes. He would get the Central Line and walk from Oxford Circus.

The meek woman took the seat to Milton's right. He introduced himself and offered her his hand; she took it, her grip loose and her skin cool, and said that her name was Emma. She looked uncomfortable at the prospect of a conversation with him, and after a few awkward words, they were both rescued by the arrival of the coffees. She turned and started to talk to the other women at her end of the table. They obviously knew each other and made no effort to include Milton in their conversation. Milton made no effort to include himself, either, so he looked at his watch, preparing to make his excuses.

He stood. No one noticed.

The man emerged from the door and took the seat to Milton's left.

"What's up?" he said.

"Nothing. I—"

"You going already?"

"I was just going to—"

"We just got here," he interrupted him with a smile. "Sit down. Have your coffee. You want a slice of cake?"

"No," he said. "I'm fine."

He reluctantly settled back in his chair. Ten minutes. Twenty at the outside.

"You're John."

"Yes," Milton said. "I'm sorry—I can't remember your name."

"Edward," he said. "Eddie to my friends."

"It's nice to meet you."

Milton sipped his coffee and took the moment to indulge the curiosity that had been burned into him during the years that he had worked for Group Fifteen. Eddie was in his late thirties or early forties, a little overweight, and not blessed with the best genetic material. He spoke with a nervous cadence to his sentences and perhaps the residue of a stammer that he had, for the most part, managed to conquer. His fingernails were chewed down to the quick, and he took a napkin from the dispenser and started to fret at the edges. He was a nervous man. That wasn't unusual. Many of the men and women Milton had met in the rooms were nervous. Many of them, especially the ones who were new to sobriety, were still running from their memories. Eddie was effeminate, occasionally speaking with a slight lisp, and Milton wondered whether he was gay.

"Three years," Eddie said. "Congratulations."

"Thank you."

"Practically makes you a veteran."

Milton allowed a small smile. "It doesn't feel like it sometimes."

"What's your secret?"

"I don't really have one. Just determined I'm not going to drink again. How long have you got?"

"Clean and sober for nearly six months. Well, I say six months. There was a relapse. A small one. I'm back again now."

"One day at a time," Milton said.

"You've been going to the meeting for a while." It wasn't a question.

"This one? I don't know—a month, maybe? Six weeks?"

"And this is the first time you've come out afterwards?"

Milton nodded. "It is."

"It's weird to start with. Most people would head to a pub for a drink. We come out for coffee. Not very glamorous."

"But better than the alternative."

"Amen to that."

Milton put his cup to his lips and sipped the coffee.

"You said you were in Australia?" Eddie said. "Never been there. I'd love to go."

"Amazing place."

"Shearing sheep? How'd you get into that?"

"I've got a friend who runs a sheep station near Broken Hill."

"Hard work?"

"You wouldn't believe it."

He finished the coffee and put the cup on the table. Eddie seemed like a nice man, but Milton was not good at small talk and he knew that it would only be a matter of time before he said something that would betray his impatience.

If Eddie had noticed, he didn't say. "What's your story? What do you do now?"

"I work in a café."

"Where?"

"Russell Square. It's not really a café. It's a cabmen's shelter. It's—"

He was ready to explain his unusual place of work, but Eddie cut him off. "I know it," he said with a grin. "I've been in it before."

"I doubt it," Milton said. "Only cabbies can use it."

"I am a cabbie," he said.

"Black cab?"

"What else is there? I haven't been there for a while. Does Cathy still run it?"

Milton smiled. "Yes. She does days; I'm on nights."

"Well, look at that. What a coincidence."

Milton allowed himself to relax. He had never met anyone outside of the shelter who knew what it and the other buildings around London like it were. He felt a moment of connection and empathy that was not unpleasant. They spoke a little longer. He found that he started to enjoy Eddie's company. He was easy-going, with a wry and self-deprecating sense of humour that occasionally broadened out with good-natured quips at the expense of the others who had been present in the room that evening. Some of his observations were very amusing, and, as Milton's laughter provided him with more confidence, he became more opinionated, more like the stereotypical London cabbie. His diction became more natural, too, and he became more tactile.

"What did you do before you went to Australia?" Eddie asked.

"I've been travelling," Milton said.

"Before that?"

"I worked for the government."

"What as? A civil servant?"

"Something like that." Milton had no interest in continuing this line of questioning and quickly changed the focus back on to Eddie. "How do you like being a cabbie?"

"There are worse things to do. But there's a lot of free time when you're driving. Easy to take an hour off. Finish early if you want to. Can be quite boring. One of the reasons I used to drink. I have to be careful." He paused. "Why did you drink? You didn't say."

"Same as all of us. Trying to forget."

"Bad memories?"

Milton nodded. He didn't say anything else, but Eddie raised his empty mug and touched it to Milton's. "I'll drink to that. Cheers."

Milton was surprised to find that he was still smiling. "Cheers."

Eddie was silent for a moment. "Memories," he said at last, with an introspection that hadn't been there before. "That's why I drink. The things I remember. I mean, things I wish I *didn't* remember."

"What things?"

"When I was younger. I—" Eddie paused, wondering, perhaps, whether he should continue. "It stays between us, John?"

Milton was about to extricate himself; he didn't want the responsibility of being someone's confessor, but Eddie continued anyway.

"I had a difficult childhood. Things happened to me, when I was a kid, bad things that stayed with me all my life."

Eddie paused and Milton could see that he was thinking again about how much he was comfortable disclosing. "Ah, fuck it. It'll be better once I've got it off my chest." He inhaled deeply, then let out a long sigh. "My folks died when I was little. Car crash. I didn't have any brothers or sisters, no grandparents or aunts and uncles. It was just me. They put me in a children's home in Jersey."

"I lost my parents the same way," Milton offered.

He brightened. "There you go. Listen to the similarities, not the differences, right?" That was one of the main teachings of the program. It was repeated in every meeting. You listened to the things you had in common. You figured out that others were like you, that you were nothing special. They said drunks tended to be grandiose. Finding out you were just like everyone else made it difficult to hold on to the notion that you were special.

Eddie continued. "The home was an awful place. Haut de la Garenne. Heard of it?"

"No."

"Wouldn't wish it on my worst enemy. They had special rooms they used to discipline the kids. They called them punishment rooms. I was a bit wild, very unruly, so I got to spend a lot of time in those rooms. Lucky me, right?" He paused again and Milton could see that he had reached the point where he would either speak about what was tormenting him or he would not. "They abused us. Not just beatings. Sexual. People came to visit from the mainland because they could do whatever they wanted there. What were we going to do? We had no one to talk to. They were brazen about it. Sometimes they took us to the mainland. Little holidays, they called them. They took us to parties in London. There were men there. They did… things to us."

Milton felt awkward. He didn't know how to respond to Eddie's story, so he said nothing and just listened.

"I didn't say anything," Eddie said. "Didn't report it. We were orphans. No one cared. What were we going to do? Nothing."

Milton heard the deep rumble of an engine as a bus went by outside.

Eddie leaned back in the chair. "I got out eventually. Adopted. I was one of the lucky ones; there were others there who didn't get out. I knew at least one boy who died there, and I'm sure he wasn't the only one. They had me for eighteen months. What happened to me then is one of the reasons I am how I am now. It made me who I am. It made me want to kill myself. I nearly did, more than once. And then, when I realised I didn't have the guts to do that, it led me to the drink. It gets bad, sometimes, the memories, the pain of remembering it all, and I can't feel anything when I'm drunk."

"I know that feeling."

Eddie paused, and Milton regarded him. He hoped it was helpful for him to talk. He found, to his surprise, that he liked him and wanted to help.

"One of the reasons?" Milton said.

"What?"

"You said it was one of the reasons you drank. There was another one?"

Eddie exhaled and shook his head. "Can't talk about that yet. Family shit. Much more complicated. One step at a time."

Milton let it go. "But the program is helping?"

Eddie nodded. "It took me a lot of time and a lot of therapy to realise that none of what happened to me was my fault. The rooms have helped me to work that out. And then, when I had that fixed, I decided that I was going to take an account of my life. I was owed some justice for what happened to me, and there are people I've hurt who deserve the same. The eighth and ninth steps, right? Make a list of the people you've hurt and then make amends. I know it'll help me, and maybe it'll help others, too."

The time had passed without Milton really noticing it, and, when he did check his watch, he saw that it was time to go. He stood.

"Off to work?"

"Yes. It was nice to meet you, Eddie."

"You too. Thanks for listening."

"My pleasure."

"Maybe I'll see you at the shelter. If I get a fare out west, I'll pop in and get a cuppa."

"I'll be there. Every night."

He said goodbye to the others around the table, zipped up his leather jacket, and went outside. It was dark and damp, and, although the rain had stopped, the roads were slicked with water. Milton took out his packet of cigarettes and put one in his mouth. The weather was cold. He zipped the jacket all the way to the top, lit the cigarette with his Ronson lighter, and set off for the entrance to the underground.

Chapter Five

MILTON TOOK THE TUBE to Oxford Circus, walked from there to Russell Square, and arrived with five minutes to spare. His place of work was a building that looked nothing more than a large green shed with a shingled roof that was equipped with a ventilation chimney. A line of black cabs was parked alongside it, and steam piled out of one of the windows. Milton approached, and, as he drew nearer, he began to smell the distinctive atmosphere. The place was redolent with conflicting scents. Fried bacon was the most prevalent, with fried onions and tobacco beneath it. There was the smell of tea and coffee, too. Damp clothes and sweat.

Milton had found the job online and had Googled it. The sheds had been built all around London in the middle of the eighteenth century. They were intended to serve horse cabmen as somewhere they could have a meal or a drink, shelter from the elements and chew the fat with their colleagues. They were built on the road, and, because of that, the regulations stipulated that they could take up no more space than a four-wheel horse cab. There had been dozens at their peak, but there were only thirteen left now. The entrance to this one was next to the black rail that had once been used for tethering horses and ran along the outside of the structure. The shelters were less exclusive now, and this one advertised that fact with a chalked sign that read TAXI DRIVERS ONLY INSIDE—WINDOW OPEN TO EVERYONE ELSE. A second sign, older and more weather-beaten, announced that the shelter was supported by the Cabmen's Shelter Fund and that there were a number of regulations that had to be observed.

Milton stepped off the pavement and up through the open door. The interior was a little more spacious than might have been assumed from the outside, but it wasn't large. Half of it was taken up with bench seating that could accommodate ten drivers. There was a narrow window smeared with trails from greasy fingers. A sign on the wall offered full English breakfasts all day and the spare space had been decorated with paintings of modern black cabs. The guitar suspended from a hook was often brought down in the early hours by one of the regular drivers who thought he had talent, leading anyone else who was around in song. There were shelves filled with second-hand books and a rack for newspapers and magazines. The other half of the space was for the tiny kitchen. There was a small stove, double racking for shelves on both walls, and a sink. A refrigerator was placed against the wall between the kitchen and the open dining area.

"Hello, John."

The woman's name was Cathy. She was the owner of the shelter, and, as she had proudly announced to Milton when he responded to her ad, the business had been in her family for sixty years. Her grandfather had purchased the business after the Second World War, her father had taken it over when his father had passed away, and now it was hers.

"How are you?" she said.

"I'm good," Milton said. "How's business?"

"Brisk. It was a good day. Always busy when it rains, and it's going to rain again tonight."

"It's going to rain all week."

"Lucky us. Lots of drivers out. I think you're going to have your hands full."

"Not a problem," Milton said. "I like it better that way."

"Makes the time go a little faster?"

"That makes it sound like I don't enjoy it."

"You don't have to pretend you do, darling."

He smiled. "I'm not pretending. I do. Seriously."

"You're a strange one."

Milton had explained during their interview that he had

experience in catering. He might have overplayed that a little, but it was at least partially true. He had held down a job as a chef in a restaurant in Ciudad Juarez for a night before it had been attacked by members of one of the more dangerous cartels that rendered that city so dangerous, and he had found himself plunged into an attempt to keep a young journalist safe from harm. But he was a decent if rudimentary cook and, having been single for most of his life, had taught himself the basics. He was confident that he would be able to handle the beans on toast and bacon sandwiches that made up the staples for the mainly male customers who patronised the shelter. It had been enough for her to offer him the job.

Cathy opened the door and glanced outside. The first fat droplets of rain had started to fall. "Bloody wonderful," she said. She took her coat, put it on, and turned to Milton. "I'll see you tomorrow," she said, laying a hand on his arm. "Have a good night."

"And you."

She stepped down onto the pavement, raised a large pink umbrella, and headed off toward the station. She lived in Essex, all the way out in Theydon Bois near the end of the Central Line. "Excuse me, mate," one of the customers said as he stepped around Milton and hurried through the rain to his cab. Milton watched as the cabbie drove away, honking his horn as he passed Cathy. She was popular among her clientele. Milton envied her that.

He closed the door and went to work.

#

MILTON LOVED THE SHELTER. This was the end of his first week, and he had enjoyed each shift. He arranged the bottles of sauce on the windowsill of the exterior serving hatch, replacing an empty bottle of ketchup with a fresh one. Cathy had arranged two potted plants on the corners of the sill, decorating the window, and two stools were placed outside when the weather was good.

The atmosphere was always lively. The customers were drawn from a small collection of regulars who had obviously known each other for years. They pretended to flirt with Cathy—she made no effort to hide how much she enjoyed the banter—and took a little while to warm up to newcomers. Milton had replaced a man who had worked nights for ten years before he had fallen ill with cancer, and he knew it was going to take them a little time to come around to him. The first couple of nights had been awkward, the atmosphere clearly more reserved than it had been during the day. He knew that he would have to persevere.

The shift progressed without incident. The rain started to fall more heavily outside and, as Cathy had predicted, the weather persuaded more cabbies to take to their cabs to cater to the increased demand for their services. That, in turn, meant that there were more of them who wanted refreshment. He was busy, and the time passed quickly.

It was gone three when he heard a commotion from outside. He glanced out the window and saw, through the cloud of steam, two drunken lads from one of the local nightclubs. He eyed them for a moment, saw that they were going to be a nuisance, and wiped his hands on the tea towel that he wore in his belt. There were three drivers inside, enjoying a lively discussion about football while they filled up on hot tea.

The two young men staggered up to the front door, opened it and came inside.

"You can't come in here," said Jack, one of the drivers. He was an older regular who was particularly fond of the fact that the shelter was exclusive.

"Says who?"

The men were both rolling drunk, reeking of alcohol and looking for trouble. Milton knew that the drivers could sort them out themselves if he left them to it, but they did not; they looked to him first, and he realised that they were giving him the chance to prove himself.

"Says me," Milton said. "Drivers only, lads. Outside, please. I'll serve you through the hatch."

"Who are you to tell us what we can and can't do?" the other man said, slurring his words even more than his friend.

"I've asked you nicely. Let's be civil."

"Or what?"

"Or I won't ask nicely," Milton replied, a little more iron in his voice. They were too drunk to realise that it would have been in their best interests to retreat and decided, instead, to resist.

"It's pissing down outside. Get us a bacon sandwich. We're going to have them in here."

Their attitude was a mistake. If Milton had a choice of how to deal with them before, now he did not.

The two of them were in their early twenties and both reasonably large. But the drink had imbued them with a sense of confidence that had robbed them of their caution. Without it, they might have recognised that Milton was not the sort of man it would be wise to annoy.

The room was small and the two of them were cramped between the cabbies who were sitting at the table and Milton. He approached until he was an arm's length away and then warned them, one final time, that they needed to leave. They started to respond with another volley of slurred abuse, but he did not let them finish. One of them, the larger of the pair, was a little farther ahead of his friend and closer to Milton. There was no room for an expansive punch or a kick, so Milton opened his hand and pushed out a palm strike that ended just above the man's abdominals. He stepped into the blow and shoved forward, transferring his body weight, his arm relaxed and pushing ahead as if he was pressing through to the man's spine. The fact that his arm was relaxed meant that he hit harder and faster than if he had tensed his muscles. The impact was painful and immediately rendered the man breathless. He doubled up, and Milton took the opportunity to knock him down with an abbreviated elbow strike to the side of his head.

The man dropped to his knees, and Milton stepped around him to square up with his friend.

"Sorry," the second man said. "I didn't… we didn't…"

"Pick him up and piss off," Milton said, gesturing to the first man, who was gasping for breath on the floor at his feet. "And don't come back."

The man reached down, slipped his hands beneath his friend's shoulders, and hauled him to his feet. He was still struggling for breath, and the elbow to the side of his head had sliced open a cut in his brow. Blood was running down his face and down his neck. Milton stepped around the pair, reached for the door, and held it open as they stumbled out into the rain.

The three cabbies who had observed Milton's display broke out in spontaneous laughter.

"Where did you learn to do that?" Jack asked as Milton went back to the kitchen.

"Army," he said.

"Which regiment?"

"Infantry. Green Jackets."

"You're kidding."

"No. Did a decent stint."

"I did four years. Territorial army. Fourth battalion. Get any action?"

Milton shrugged. "Enough for my taste."

The man clenched his fist and mimed a right-handed swing. "You haven't forgotten much."

Milton shrugged.

"Remind me to leave you a generous tip."

"Who wants a cup of tea?" Milton said. "On the house."

Chapter Six

MILTON'S SHIFT finished at seven and, after taking one of the first busses of the new day, he arrived home in Bethnal Green at eight. The streets were beginning to show the usual bustle and clamour. The activity only ever seemed to draw breath, never really stopping, and he passed queues of men and women at the bus stops, waiting to go into work.

He had rented a small flat in an old local authority block in Arnold Circus. A series of blocks had been constructed around a central area that was raised up from the road that ran around it. The island had been built from the spoil that had been collected from the razing of the notorious Victorian slum that had once occupied these streets. The mound had been furnished with a bandstand, and, although local benefactors had refurbished it recently, no music was played there any longer. Instead, young boys would congregate around it, smoking and listening to music and peacocking for the girls who idled by. The blocks that surrounded the bandstand were all the same: designed in the Arts and Crafts style, large hulking buildings that were constructed from red and yellow brick that had been dirtied by the passage of time. The estate had provided the first social housing in London and at one time, perhaps, it might have been something. It was grubbier today and, despite the influx of tenants working in the nearby Square Mile, it still had a rough edge to it. But its grubbiness meant that Milton could afford it. He had neither the desire nor the means to choose a more exclusive address, and this served him well enough.

The front door to Milton's flat was accessed through a darkened vestibule that accommodated another three doors. The space was gloomy. The light bulb had popped, and Milton had forgotten that he had decided to get a new one and change it himself. The landlord was supposed to maintain the common parts, but the graffiti on the walls, the occasional discarded syringe and the smell of human waste were evidence that those obligations were not treated seriously.

He reached into his pocket for his key and paused. He heard the sounds of life from the other flats that opened out into the same space. There were families here, mothers and fathers with two and three children somehow crushed into apartments not much larger than his own. Ten years ago, he would not have envied them the chaos and disorder that seemed to comprise their days. But that was then, and he had changed. Now, especially when he was alone in his flat, a book laid out on his lap and music playing quietly, he often found himself wondering what it would be like to have a life like theirs. He wondered, sometimes, whether he would be prepared to exchange his Spartan existence for the noise and clamour and vigour of a family. Would he be prepared to swap his solitude for companionship? He had always enjoyed the peace of his self-imposed exile, but he was beginning to find that the benefits were less and less attractive the older he got.

He felt it now, that new longing, and quickly suppressed the sensation. Loneliness was weakness and a luxury that he could not afford. He had made his choice. By choosing to follow the career that had been presented to him, Milton had abjured his right to a normal life. The blood on his hands disqualified him from it. He did not deserve domesticity, and no amount of baring his soul at meetings would change that. And there were practical reasons why he could not allow himself to be drawn too close to another. There were people in the world who would have given much to know where he was. Some of those people—intelligence agencies, criminals, government officials—would have paid for him to be killed. They would have paid a lot. To bring another person into his life would be to expose her to danger. She would be leverage that could be used against him. And an untethered life meant that he could leave as soon as he smelled danger. Anything that moored him to a place or a person would be dangerous. That had been the reason he had left Australia, as well as his sense that he had been slip-sliding towards taking a drink. He was unable to deny that he had feelings for Matilda, and it was patent that she felt the same way. Being with him had already exposed her to real danger, and he couldn't take the chance that she would be dragged into his affairs again.

After a selfish life, now he would be selfless. He wouldn't risk someone else in order to allow himself happiness. That would be unfair.

He was brought out of his self-absorption by the sound of raised voices from the flat next to his. That was unusual: the mother and father of the two small children who lived there were quiet and respectful, and he rarely heard them save for a warm burble that was muffled by the wall that separated them. Their children, both young, were quiet and well behaved, too, and, as he paused, he realised that the voice he had heard was from someone else. There was another volley of angry conversation, the sound of a woman protesting, and then the sound of furniture falling to the floor.

Milton stopped, caught between staying where he was and investigating: he didn't know whether he should do something, offer his help, or whether that would be overstepping a mark. He hadn't decided what to do when the door to the flat was yanked open. There was a man in the hallway whom Milton had not seen before and, behind him, a second man. They were both in early middle age, dressed in cheap suits and cheap shoes. The first man was big, maybe six three, but padded out with fat rather than muscle. The second man was short and wiry, with tattoos that were visible on the skin of his neck above the collar of his shirt.

The fat one glared at Milton. "What you looking at?"

Milton glanced beyond him and into the flat. The door to the sitting room was open and Milton could see that the crash he had heard was from a set of bookshelves that had been pulled over. The floor was littered with disturbed books, photographs and the fragments of shattered ornaments.

The fat man stepped out into the vestibule. "I said what you looking at?"

Milton shortened his focus and regarded the man. He had a large face, with folds of fat that hung down beneath his chin, and thin stripes of whiskers that he had missed while he was shaving. He had hair in his nostrils and ears, and his skin had an unhealthy pallor, washed with a light sheen of sweat. Milton looked down, saw that the man had a large ring on the pinkie of his right hand and another on the index finger of his left. He noticed that his hands were bunched into fists and noticed that he favoured his right.

Milton felt the familiar tickle of adrenaline. He clenched his own fist, his right.

The man stepped up, raised a hand and pushed Milton on the shoulder. Milton took a step back. He let it happen. It wasn't a bad thing. The extra space would be useful for generating extra force when he retaliated.

The man was oblivious to the danger he was in. "What is matter with you? You don't talk?"

His accent was harsh and guttural. Eastern European. Polish? Russian, maybe. Milton felt the twitch in his arm. He had noticed that the man held his jaw loosely, and knew that if he struck him with even half of his usual force, he would be able to shatter the bone. The man had raised his hand to him, had pushed him; that would normally have been the trigger for Milton to respond. But he glimpsed the couple who lived in the flat. They were in the hallway, both rigid with fright, the mother in her colourful hijab clasping their young son against her legs. They were looking at him with big eyes, with faces that were full of fear, and he knew then that they did not want him to get involved. They wanted these men to leave them alone, to go away with no reason to return. Milton could have taken them both out, and he was sorely tempted to do that, but that would have been indulging himself. The family would have paid for his indulgence.

"I live here," Milton said. "I don't want trouble."

"Then get into the flat," the man said, "and stop looking at me like that."

Milton did as he was told. He closed the door behind him, but watched through the spyhole. He waited twenty seconds, opened the door a crack, and saw the two men heading out of the vestibule and down the path to the street. He waited another moment and then followed them outside. They were at the end of the path and, as Milton watched, the fat man blipped the locks on a black BMW 5-series with tinted windows and they both got in. The engine revved loudly and the car pulled out into the road and drove away. Milton watched it, remembering the plate, and then went back inside.

Chapter Seven

THE GENERAL ordered Hicks to collect him from a pub outside Hereford railway station the next morning. Hicks knew that, as the most junior member of the Feather Men, it would fall upon him to chauffeur the old man around until he had proven his worth. He was happy enough with that, even if it meant that he had to get up at five in the morning, as he had done today. Leaving his wife in their warm bed was tough, and the certainty that he wouldn't see his children today was difficult, but what he was doing was for them. He reminded himself of that as he let the water from the shower play over him, scouring away the sleep until he was fully awake. He dressed, prepared toast for a cursory breakfast, and went through into the garage.

He had allowed himself three hours for the one-hundred-and-fifty-mile drive back to Hereford from Cambridge and had added another hour so that he could make sure that his Range Rover was clean and tidy. Higgins was fastidious about cleanliness and appearance, a hangover from the military that they all shared. He took a vacuum cleaner to the car and spent twenty minutes working the nozzle over the upholstery. He polished the wooden accents, wiped the dirt from the mats and washed the windows. The car was spotless when he was finished.

The journey was straightforward until he ran into traffic just before Junction 7 of the M5. There had been a collision on the opposite carriageway, and drivers on his side of the road had slowed to gawp, causing a bottleneck that took an additional twenty minutes for him to negotiate. He made up a little time on the A4440, but he was still a little late as the buildings of Hereford appeared around the final bend.

The railway station was an old Victorian building and had probably been grand at one point in its life. These days, it was clogged with parked cars and ugly red industrial refuse bins, the walls pocked by fly posters for a travelling circus and advertisements for local bars. Hicks drove onto the one-way approach, looped around an island that had been carved out for cyclists to leave their bikes, and stopped outside the entrance. Higgins was sheltering from the wind inside the main building. He saw Hicks and came outside. He was dressed impeccably, as ever. His charcoal suit was newly dry-cleaned, with sharp creases running down his trousers. His shirt was freshly laundered and his shoes so polished that the sun's dim light gleamed against the caps. His face was distorted by a dark frown. Hicks looked at the clock on the dash and saw that he was two minutes late. He gripped the wheel a little tighter.

Higgins opened the rear door and lowered himself inside. "When I say to pick me up at ten," he said, "I mean ten. I don't mean a minute past ten. I don't mean two minutes past ten."

"I understand, sir. Traffic was—"

"No excuses. You wouldn't stand for it in the Regiment, would you?"

"No, sir."

"I won't stand for it now."

"I'm sorry. It won't happen again."

"See that it doesn't."

Hicks put the car into first and pulled away. It would take around three hours to drive to London from here, more if the traffic was poor. He had never spent that much time in Higgins's company and he found the prospect a little daunting. The general was quiet as Hicks drove them out of Hereford and onto the M50. Hicks glanced in the mirror and saw that the old man had opened his case and was reviewing a paper file. He set his eyes to the road and concentrated on the light traffic.

They had just passed the exit for Newent when Hicks heard the sound of the briefcase's clasps snapping shut.

"You did well last night, Corporal."

"Sir?"

"With Öztürk. It was good work."

Praise from Higgins was a rare occurrence. "Thank you, sir."

"How did you find it?"

"The operation, sir?" Hicks wasn't sure where Higgins wanted to take the conversation. "It was fine. It was very well planned. I don't think they had much of a chance."

"You had no issues?"

"Issues?"

"Ethical considerations."

"No, sir. None." Hicks had done a little of his own research on Öztürk and had satisfied himself that the man deserved his fate. He had been involved in extrajudicial killings before—IRA chieftains, foreign agitators—and, since those men had deserved to die, too, it was something with which he had been able to make peace.

"How many men did you kill in the Regiment?"

The number was at the front of his mind and easy to recall. It was the same with most soldiers that Hicks knew. "Twenty, sir."

"There'll be more, Corporal, now that you're working with us. As long as you're comfortable with that, you'll do well."

Hicks didn't answer, and the general fell silent again. "Doing well" meant making money, and perhaps a lot of it. That was the only reason he was doing what he was doing. It wasn't because of greed, either. It was because of necessity.

They approached Gloucester and slowed into a clutch of slow-moving traffic. Hicks glanced up into the mirror and saw that the general was looking ahead. Their eyes held for a moment. Hicks felt awkward again and spoke to break the silence.

"Who are we going to meet, sir?"

"Leo Isaacs. Have you heard of him?"

Hicks tried to remember the name. "It's familiar."

"He was an MP. He was Secretary of State for Defence, too, back in the eighties. He used to be a very influential man."

"So why are we seeing him?"

"Because we are protecting him."

"From what?"

Hicks glanced into the mirror and saw the old man clench his jaw. "From some unfortunate personal weaknesses."

"Sir?"

The general folded his arms and looked back out at the grey morning. "Keep driving."

The drizzle kept falling, the wipers swiping it from the glass. Hicks concentrated on the road ahead.

Chapter Eight

WATSON SQUARE was a grand and imposing building. It was built in the 1930s, was seven storeys tall and took up almost the entirety of Chichester Street. There were 1,200 apartments within its walls, and the grounds extended all the way down to the banks of the Thames. It was a short walk to the Houses of Parliament from here, a proximity that meant that the building had always been popular with MPs and peers. Hicks parked the Range Rover in a vacant bay and went around to open the door for the general. The old man got out, buttoned up his jacket, smoothed down his trousers and crossed the street to the entrance. The main door was found beneath an impressive marble portico, the doors sliding aside as they approached.

There was a man waiting for them in reception. He was old, too, older than the general, and dressed in a slate grey suit, a black tie decorated with white stars, and a red pocket square. His hair, once a shock of blond, had turned white with age. His brow was furrowed and there was a restiveness in his eyes as he rose from the chair in which he had been sitting and crossed the space to meet them.

Higgins took the man's hand and shook it firmly. "Leo," he said.

"Richard." He turned his head and looked at Hicks. "Who's this?"

"One of my men. He's just joined us."

"I didn't—"

Higgins interrupted him. "Shall we go somewhere private?"

Isaacs took the hint. "Yes, of course. My apartment."

The old man led the way through the reception and into an elevator lobby. They stepped into the first vacant car and rode it all the way up to the seventh floor. Hicks watched

Isaacs in the mirrored wall of the car. The man was nervous, the fingers of his right hand toying with the cufflink that fastened his left sleeve. Higgins, on the other hand, was impassive. His face was severe and he stood straight as an arrow, all business.

The doors opened and the three of them exited the car into a luxuriously furnished lobby. Isaacs led the way along a quiet corridor, their feet sinking into deep pile carpeting that muffled the sound of their progress. They reached the door to number eleven; Isaacs opened it and led the way inside. It was a two-bedroom apartment. Hicks assessed it as he passed through the small hallway. There were two doors that he assumed were bedrooms. They went through into a large sitting room containing pieces of furniture that looked as if they had been in place for decades. One wall held an old-fashioned serving hatch through which the kitchen could be accessed.

Isaacs went over to a large French door that offered access to a narrow balcony beyond. He laced his fingers behind his back and looked outside, his back turned to them. Hicks noticed that the man was nervously squeezing his hands together.

Higgins looked over at Hicks and gave a slight shake of his head. "What's happened, Leo?" he said.

Isaacs turned back to them. He pointed at Hicks.

"This man. I don't know him."

"His name is Corporal Hicks. He'll be helping with this."

"I'd rather just—"

"I've vouched for him, Leo. That should be enough for you. Move on. What's the issue?"

It was even clearer now that Higgins was in the position of authority here. Isaacs might well have had the glittering parliamentary career and the lordship that denoted it, but, between the two old men, Higgins was in control. There was something about the relationship that made Hicks feel uncomfortable. He would have been very happy to have been sent outside, but, instead, he stood quietly at the edge of the room, his arms folded across his chest.

Isaacs cleared his throat. "I've been approached by someone who claims to have known me during the eighties."

"In what capacity does he know you?"

The older man shuffled in his chair and clasped his skeletal hands together. "He says he met me here."

"The parties, Leo?"

Isaacs coughed. "Yes. The parties."

"What's his name?"

"I have no idea. It's all very random. He's a taxi driver. He picked me up in Westminster after a session at the Lords and drove me here. He was looking at me in the mirror as if he knew me the whole way, but he didn't say anything. But then I saw him again a couple of days later. He was waiting for me outside the building in the morning. In his bloody cab. He got out and came over to me. He told me he remembered who I was. He said he remembered the building." His voice trailed away. "The parties."

"And what do you think?"

"Well, I didn't recognise him, if that's what you mean."

"Why would you? He would've been a boy."

The retort was delivered with just enough scorn to condemn Isaacs, and it provided enough context for Hicks to fill in the blanks. He felt a sudden blast of disgust.

"Well, yes..." Isaacs said, his voice falling away.

"Do you believe him?"

"How else would he have known to say that?"

Higgins didn't answer. He walked across to the coffee table and picked up a paperweight that was anchoring a pile of papers.

"What am I going to do?" Isaacs pleaded.

Higgins replaced the paperweight. "First things first, Leo. What did he say? What exactly?"

"He said he was going to go to the press."

"With what? Does he have any proof? Did he say?"

"I don't see how he could."

"Then it's just rumours and innuendo."

"But what if he's believed? You know how it is. What if he gets someone to publish what he says? There's no smoke without fire, that's what they'll say, especially with what happened before."

"Yes," Higgins said. "That would be unfortunate."

"You said you'd look after me."

"And we will." Higgins looked over at Hicks again and then turned back to Isaacs. "This man—what else do you know?"

"His taxi badge. I remembered the number."

"That's better. Corporal—take a note, please."

Hicks took out his phone and opened the note application.

"56381."

Hicks tapped the numbers and saved the note.

"Anything else?" Higgins said.

"He's late thirties, early forties. Overweight. Not much hair. Looked nervous. That's all."

"Very good, Leo. You can leave it with us."

"What will you do?"

"Take care of it. You don't need to worry. That's what you pay me for, isn't it? Peace of mind."

Payment. The politician paused, confusion wrinkling his brow before it was replaced by understanding and then a brief moment of resentment. Higgins noticed, and Hicks saw the anger that flashed in his eyes; Isaacs quickly mastered himself. He walked to a bureau and opened the lid. He took out an envelope and, telling them to wait a moment, went through into the bedroom.

Higgins didn't speak. He allowed a little of the distaste he so obviously felt for Isaacs to manifest itself on his face and went across to the window and gazed out. Hicks waited where he was, thinking that it would be a simple enough matter to find out the name of the man who had been given that taxi licence number. The thought of it, and what might follow, made him feel uneasy.

Isaacs returned. The envelope had been filled, and it bulged in the middle. He handed it to the general. The end was unsealed, and Higgins made a show of reaching inside and withdrawing the contents. There were several bundles of bank notes secured with elastic bands. Higgins examined one of the bundles. The top note was a fifty, and Hicks estimated that there must have been thirty or forty notes in the bundle, with at least one other bundle in the envelope.

"Thank you."

"Do you need anything else?"

"I don't think so. Stay here for the next day or two. I'll let you know when it's handled."

Higgins turned his back on the old man and left the room without a word.

The old man looked at Hicks with anxious eyes.

"Goodbye," Isaacs said to Higgins' retreating back.

The general didn't answer.

#

HICKS FOLLOWED THE GENERAL out of the apartment and caught him up as he stalked to the elevators. Higgins said nothing as they descended to the reception, and nothing as they passed through the space and onto the street beyond. It was only when they were both in the Range Rover that he provided his summation of the awkward twenty minutes that they had spent with Isaacs.

"Pathetic."

"Sir?"

"Drive, Corporal."

Hicks started the car and pulled away.

Higgins shook his head. "What did you make of it?"

"This man Isaacs is worried about. He knew him when he was a boy?"

"Yes."

"And when you said he had 'personal weaknesses,' is it

what I think it is?"

"What do you think it is, Corporal?"

"He's a paedophile?"

"Him and plenty of others. Be frank, Hicks: is that a problem for you?"

"I don't understand why you would want to help him. I think he's disgusting."

Higgins waited a moment before agreeing with a terse, "Undoubtedly. Him and the other men who were involved. They're all scum, Hicks."

"And so why are we protecting them?"

"Because the damage that would be caused, were the details of what they did to be released, would be catastrophic. Isaacs was a very senior politician. But it isn't just him. He was involved with senior men from the military. The civil service. The police. And politicians who were even more senior than he was."

"How senior?"

"The *most* senior. I'm sure I don't have to spell it out."

There was no need to ask; Hicks knew what he meant. The clouds had cowled the sky again, and he stared into the glowing red lights of the car ahead until he had to blink to clear them from his vision. It was very likely true, but that didn't make what Higgins was suggesting any more palatable. It felt as if he was taking steps out into deeper water, knowing that at some point, without warning, the seabed would fall away from beneath him and plunge him into the depths.

"It is our duty to protect them," Higgins said.

Hicks glanced across at the envelope in the general's lap and looked away again before Higgins could notice. Duty? Hardly. The motive was baser and more venal than that.

Higgins had reached a decision. "Whoever was bugging Isaacs—find out whatever you can about him."

"And then?"

"And then I'll give some thought about the best course of action. Don't worry, Corporal, I'll be sure to let you know."

"Where to now, sir?"

"Hatton Garden."

The general was silent as Hicks drove them to the northeast. He followed the line of the Thames until they reached the junction for Blackfriars Bridge, then he turned to the north and passed along Farringdon Street until they reached their destination. Hatton Garden was one of the most famous streets in London, a district with an unusually dense collection of shops and merchants concerned with jewellery and the diamond trade. The shop frontages advertised everything and anything that could be associated with jewellery: there were watchmakers, jewellery manufacturers, a dozen shops that specialised in engagement rings, and diamond traders. It was a little shabby, the bright displays shining out from shop windows that were set into bleak concrete buildings.

"Straight ahead," the general said. "On the left."

The London Vault Company was just to the north of the junction of Hatton Garden and Greville Street. It had jewellers' businesses on either side of it. Hicks followed Higgins's directions and parked the car in a space on the other side of the road.

"Wait here. I won't be long."

"Yes, sir."

The general opened his case and put the envelope that Leo Isaacs had given him inside. Hicks glanced across and saw that the case was full of money. He saw it only briefly, turning away as the general looked up at him, but he saw the neat rows of banknotes. The money was from last night, Hicks guessed. The money that they had taken from Öztürk.

The general closed the case, stepped outside and crossed the road. Hicks watched as he went through the plain double doors that were evidently the main way to get inside the business. The London Vault Company. He took out his phone, navigated to Google and searched for information. The business had a website, and Hicks flicked through the pages. It had been established sixty years earlier and offered safe deposit boxes to clients who wanted to store valuable items. It had a variety of different-sized boxes, together with walk-in safes, and the copy declared proudly that the vault had never been breached and was considered to be impregnable.

It must be where the general kept his wealth.

Hicks switched on the radio. He found that his mind was racing, and he wanted to distract himself from the thoughts that were starting to develop.

Higgins came out after fifteen minutes. He crossed the road and slipped into the back of the car.

"Where to, sir?"

"Euston station."

He put the car into first and pulled out. He took Gray's Inn Road and started to the west. The satnav suggested that the drive would take twenty minutes if the traffic was kind.

Hicks watched in the mirror as the general reached into his jacket pocket and withdrew a bundle of notes. He reached forward and dropped the bundle onto the passenger seat.

"What's that for?"

"You have kids, don't you?"

The reference to his children made his skin prickle. "Yes, sir. Two boys."

"You'll get your cut from last night soon. This is an advance. Treat them. Treat your wife. You're not going to be going home until we've fixed this mess."

"Yes, sir."

Chapter Nine

MILTON SLEPT UNTIL MIDDAY and, finding he was still a little sluggish, allowed himself an extra hour in bed. He woke again before one, got up and dressed for a run. The streets outside were wet, and, although the rain had stopped, another thick black cloudbank had collected over the city with the promise of another downpour.

Milton set off. He had always been a runner. It was his favourite exercise, an hour or so when he could switch off his consciousness and relax into the cadence of his stride, the sound of his shoes as they slapped against the pavement. Outside of the meetings, running was the best form of meditation that he had ever found.

He ran for an hour, east along the Old Bethnal Green Road until he could break into the open green spaces of Victoria Park. He ran hard, circling the large old boating lake with the fountain in the middle, then the café that served as a shelter for locals who had nowhere else to go. He kept running, all the way to the derelict bandstand, and then turned and started for home.

He ran back to the flat, showered and shaved, and dressed in a pair of jeans and a black sweatshirt. He looked around his little place. There was a lounge just big enough for a second-hand sofa and a table and chair. He had purchased the furniture from a charity that recycled pieces and sold them to those on low incomes. There was a tiny kitchen that was little more than a cupboard and a bathroom and a single bedroom. Milton had very little in the way of possessions. He had his well-thumbed copy of the *Big Book of Alcoholics Anonymous*, a phone and a set of Bluetooth speakers that he used to play his music, the oxidised Ronson lighter that his father had owned and a collection of books that he had bought from Oxfam. It was an ascetic kind of life and one that suited him very well.

Next, he attended to the making of his bed. There were many routines and habits that he had developed during his years of service, many of them so deeply ingrained now that he would have been unable to alter them even if he had wanted to. Presenting a neat and tidy bed was one of the more important ones. It was something that set him up for the rest of the day. That one small routine, the knowledge that it had been done to his satisfaction, was an excellent foundation for what was to come. It developed discipline and fostered attention to the smallest of details. He had seen it too many times for it to be a coincidence: men who struggled to get their lives together often went straight to the most challenging goals while the rest of their lives were left in a disorganized mess. Milton had always drilled it into the soldiers under his command: get the little things under control, and the sense of confidence and satisfaction will help you address the bigger ones.

He had followed the same routine for years. Fitted sheets were a lazy compromise, and he preferred a normal sheet. He stood at the foot of the bed and spread the bottom sheet evenly across it. He tucked the top and bottom edges of the sheet between the bottom of the mattress and the box springs, fashioning perfect hospital corners. He smoothed out the creases and wrinkles with brisk strokes of his hand, then spread out the top sheet and the blanket, making identical hospital corners for those, too. He folded down the tops of the blanket and the top sheet and then placed the pillows. When he was done, he took a fifty-pence piece from the pot on his bedside table and bounced it off the bed. It sprang back up into his hand. Perfect.

He prepared his breakfast. He had recently taken to starting his day with a large iced smoothie: he would prepare the fruit, add ice, protein powder and powdered vitamins, then blitz it in a blender that he had picked up for thirty pounds on eBay. The process took five minutes, and he found that repeating the same steps again and again was almost as calming as his running. He took the smoothie into the lounge and drank it while he flicked through the copy of *Time Out* that he had found on the seat of the bus this morning. There was a matinee showing of Casablanca at the Rio in Dalston. Milton had decided that he would like to see it.

Milton stepped out into the vestibule, locked the door and immediately heard the sound of arguing from the next-door flat. He stopped, his hand resting against his door, and listened. The words were muffled and difficult to discern, but it was obvious that the mother of the family was upset. Her voice was drawn and tight, her sentences broken up, and Milton could soon hear the sound of her sobbing. The father, the woman's husband, was trying to console her. Milton couldn't make out the words.

"Mister?"

Milton found that he had been standing with his eyes closed. He opened them, turned, and saw a young boy looking at him. He recognised him. He lived in the flat. He thought, from overhearing them as he passed them playing on the swings at the foot of the building, that the boy's name was Ahmed. He had a football under his arm and he was regarding Milton with confusion.

"Are you all right?" the boy asked him.

"I'm fine."

"You were just standing there."

"I was a million miles away."

The boy shuffled forward awkwardly.

"You're Ahmed, aren't you?"

"Yeah."

"I'm John."

The boy shrugged.

"Been playing football?"

He nodded.

"Who do you like?"

"What do you mean?"

"Which team?"

"Arsenal."

"No," Milton said with a smile. "Don't say that."

"What about you?"

"West Ham."

"West Ham are rubbish," the boy said.

Milton smiled. "I can't argue with that." Ahmed had lowered his defences a little. "Who's your favourite player?" Milton asked him.

"Sanchez."

"He's good," Milton conceded. "You don't like Özil?"

"He's all right. Sanchez is better."

Milton could see that he was making progress. He decided to change tack just a little.

"Are your mum and dad okay?"

The wariness returned, and Milton doubted he would get anything out of him.

"What do you mean?"

Milton gestured to the door. "Some men came around the other day. I think they made a mess inside your flat. They pulled over your bookcase."

The boy's eyes hardened and, for a moment, Milton thought he was going to rebuff him. He bit his lip and grasped his football a little tighter to his chest.

"You don't have to tell me about it," Milton said. "I'm sorry."

Ahmed shook his head. "My dad says I don't need to worry about it. He gets angry when I ask, but I've heard him talking to my mum. They want money, but I don't think my dad has enough. My mum says we might have to live somewhere else, but I don't want to live anywhere else. I like living here. My friends live here."

There came a loud sob from the flat. They both heard it. The boy flinched and looked as if he was very quickly going to become upset. Milton decided not to push things any more.

"Well, nice to meet you, Ahmed."

He shuffled. "Yeah."

"If there's anything I can help you with, you just need to let me know. Okay?"

Ahmed shrugged and went to the door, but waited to open it. Milton realised that he wanted him to leave before he went inside. He took the hint, checked that the door to his flat was locked, followed the stairs down to the ground floor, and waited for a bus to take him to Dalston.

Chapter Ten

THE OFFICE that housed Transport for London's customer service department was on Blackfriars Road. Hicks drove there and parked the Range Rover on a quiet side street. He took the bundle of notes and peeled off two twenties. He put them in his pocket and put the rest into the glove compartment. He stepped out, shut and locked the door, and went to the office.

It was a simple space with a row of chairs facing a smeared screen. A bored-looking clerk was chewing the nails of her left hand as she pressed a telephone receiver to her ear with her right. She saw Hicks and waved at him to sit down, mouthing that she would be with him soon. He did as he was told, sitting in one of the plastic chairs and looking at the posters that had been stuck to the walls.

Hicks found his thoughts returning to Isaacs. The old man disgusted him, and the thought of helping him was something he was finding very difficult to accept. No one had mentioned that the unit was engaged in work for clients like that. He realised that perhaps he hadn't researched the opportunity that Higgins had presented with enough diligence. He could have said no then, before involving himself last night, but now that would be a difficult thing to do. No, he corrected himself. Not difficult. Impossible. And it would be similarly impossible to specify to the general which work he would accept and which he would decline. It didn't work like that in the Regiment, and it wouldn't work like that in the unit, either. Orders were orders. Work was work. You did as you were told. If you didn't like it, you kept your mouth shut and did it anyway.

"Yes, darling?"

Hicks got up and went to the window.

"I'm looking for information on a taxi driver?"

"Not much I can give you, I'm afraid."

"I have his number."

"All I can do is tell you whether or not he's registered."

"Really? I left my luggage in the back of the cab. I was hoping I might be able to get in touch with him."

"You need to go to the lost-property office. Baker Street. I can give you the number if you like."

"I really need his address."

She shook her head. "Can't do that."

"It's very important," he said.

She shook her head again.

Hicks took out the two twenties and slid them into the tray that was set into the counter beneath the screen.

"Please?"

She looked at the notes, paused, and, looking behind her to ensure that she wasn't overlooked, nodded. "What's the number, love?"

Hicks took out his phone, opened the note he had taken and recited it.

She tapped it into her computer. "His name is Edward Fabian. Ready to take his address?"

#

HICKS STEPPED outside into the gloomy afternoon and went back to his car. Edward Fabian's address was listed as Wallwood Road in Leytonstone. He drove east. It was rush hour and there was a lot of traffic along the route. The drive took ninety minutes and it was early evening and already dark by the time he finally arrived.

The address was five minutes away from Leytonstone underground station, in the middle of a terrace in a rather downtrodden part of the district. Each house had a narrow slice of garden that separated it from the pavement, but none of the inhabitants seemed to be particularly interested in keeping them in good order. Weeds had been allowed to grow tall, and Fabian seemed to have used his garden as a depository for an old freezer and a sofa that had, at some point, been slashed with a knife so that the yellowed stuffing spilled out. A taxi was parked in the road; that, at least, was kept in good order, and the raindrops that rolled off the black paintwork glistened like little jewels in the dim light that filtered down through the angry clouds overhead.

Hicks stepped out of the car and approached the taxi. There was enough light from a streetlamp to read the licence number that had been fixed to the glass partition that separated the driver from the passengers. The number was the same as the one that Leo Isaacs had taken down. Hicks was satisfied: he was in the right place. He went back to the Range Rover and took out his phone. He dialled and waited for the general to pick up.

"Higgins."

Hicks could hear the sound of a train in the background. The general was heading back to Hereford.

"I'm at the cabbie's address, sir."

"Where?"

"The East End. Leytonstone."

"What's his name?"

"Edward Fabian."

"Is he at home?"

"His cab's outside. There's a light on inside the house."

There was a pause.

"Sir? What do you want me to do?"

"Stay outside. I'll call you back."

Chapter Eleven

HICKS WAITED. He had moved the car twenty feet down the road so that he wasn't directly in front of the house. He had no idea whether Fabian was a particularly observant man, but there was no point in making his vigil an obvious one. His new vantage point offered an oblique view of the house, but it was still sufficient to see the lights, and there would be no way that Fabian would be able to leave without Hicks noticing him.

He spent the first hour getting a feel for the street and the surrounding area. It was quiet, residential, with very little passing traffic.

Ten o'clock came and went, and then eleven.

Hicks took out his phone and searched on Leo Isaacs's name. A lot of results came back. There were articles on his ministerial career and others that suggested that he still had influence on policy from his position in the upper house. He went to the second and then the third page of results and found something else: a series of articles from several years earlier. They reported on a court case. Isaacs was alleged to have been found on Hampstead Heath with another man, engaged in what one of the more salacious newspapers described as an "unnatural sex act." There had been a trial, but it had collapsed. Hicks looked for more, but that was as much as he could find.

The lights in the house remained lit.

Midnight.

The lights on the ground floor were extinguished and, after a pause, a light was turned on in a room on the floor above. A bedroom, perhaps. Eddie Fabian was turning in for the night.

Hicks stared up at the window. He was uncomfortable. He knew very little about Fabian, but he did know that Leo

Isaacs was a deeply unpleasant man with an unpleasant past, and he would not have been disposed to help him under normal circumstances. Hicks had two boys, and if the things that Fabian had said about him were true, then he was a vile predator who deserved to rot in prison.

But then Hicks thought of the money that the general had so insouciantly dropped onto the seat of the car. Thousands of pounds, just like that. He thought of the money that they had taken. Tens of thousands, maybe more. He thought of his wife, Rachel, and the cancer. It had changed everything. It had bent his principles and twisted his morals until he didn't recognise himself any more.

The cancer. He didn't want to think about it, but he couldn't stop himself. It had started with a melanoma on her back. He had seen it one morning after she had come out of the shower. The National Health Service had removed it, but the disease had already spread. The MRI discovered a five-centimetre growth under her left breast that had burrowed deep into her chest wall. There was another growth on her right lung. The doctors were talking about surgery and then aggressive chemotherapy, but Hicks had been able to tell from the way that they delivered the prognosis that they were not hopeful of being able to do very much at all.

Hicks had immediately started to research their options. Foreign treatment seemed like the best hope. The Memorial Sloan Kettering Cancer Center in New York was offering an experimental combination of two drugs: Opdivo and Yervoy. They were among a vanguard of new medicines that worked by bolstering the immune system so that it attacked the tumours. Patients who had taken the cocktail had reported incredible results. There was a story in the press that Hicks had fastened onto. One patient, a woman of similar age to Rachel, had returned for a follow-up examination to be told that her tumour had gone. The melanoma cells had simply been dissolved. Hicks spoke to Rachel's oncologist and suggested that they try the treatment. The man shook his head. It wasn't available on the National Health Service. Hicks called the clinic in New York. Treatment was possible, but the drugs were expensive. Two courses would cost over a hundred thousand pounds.

They didn't have that. Not even close.

Hicks had no choice. He had to find the money.

If he couldn't find it, or if he was too slow, then Rachel would die. He would be widowed. His children would lose their mother.

And that was not going to happen.

Hicks wouldn't let it.

He had served with Gillan in the Regiment and they had kept in touch afterwards. The two of them met for a drink once or twice a year, and the last time Gillan had suggested that he had been getting extra work with a group of other ex-SAS men. Hicks had been working in private security, body guarding for rich Arabs who treated London like their own private playground. They showered money around like confetti, yet they were parsimonious when it came to paying their staff. Gillan had asked whether Hicks would be interested in learning more about the opportunity, but he had said he wasn't interested. It was before the diagnosis, and he hadn't needed to know any more to suspect that it wasn't completely legitimate. But then came the cancer, and Hicks's priorities had changed. He would never be able to make the money he needed by working for the Arabs. He was open to alternatives.

He called Gillan and said that he might be interested. They had met again and, this time, Gillan had brought the general with him. Higgins explained the kind of jobs that they undertook: they targeted serious criminals, robbing them at the same time as they removed them from the street. He made it sound as if it was a public good.

Hicks saw that for the fig leaf that it was, but he said that he was interested.

Öztürk had been his first. That operation had been just

as advertised. A bad man had been taken out. The fact that he had a lot of money was a useful side benefit.

But now this.

Isaacs.

Fabian.

It was not the job that had been advertised at all.

The reality of becoming a member of the Feather Men was not what he had been sold.

He was jolted out of his reverie by the ringing of his telephone.

"What's going on?" It was Alistair Woodward.

"Fabian's still inside. No sign that he's awake. Where are you?"

"London."

"What are we doing?"

"Not we—you. The general wants you to break in and give him a warning."

"What kind of warning?"

"He needs to know that it's not a good idea to threaten people we're looking after. Be persuasive."

"How persuasive?"

"Use your imagination. But make it good."

Chapter Twelve

HICKS PUT the car into first and pulled out, driving down the road until he was completely out of sight of Fabian's house. He had no desire to make it easy for the man to spot his registration plate after he had done what he was going to have to do. He waited until the only other car he had seen in the last hour had rolled past the window and then opened the glove box. He pulled a pair of latex gloves onto his hands and checked that his Browning was easily accessible in its shoulder holster. It was. He took off his jacket, slipped the holster on, and then replaced his jacket.

He got out of the car, leaving the door unlocked, and quickly walked back to the house. The gate to the front garden was unoiled and it opened with a creak that seemed much louder than it actually was. He paused on the step for a moment, assured himself that all was well, and then crossed the garden in three paces. The front door was made of wood, thin and flimsy enough that it would have opened with a firm kick. That was not an option, though. Hicks had to be quiet. He knelt before it and flipped aside the hinged lid that obscured the keyhole. The lock was a simple mortice. He took out his lock pick, slipped it into the keyhole and then followed it with the long L-shaped tension wrench. He used the wrench to apply torque to the pins to prevent them from being pushed back down into place and, once he had found the correct alignment for the pins, he turned the handle and gently pushed the door open.

He slipped inside and closed the door quietly behind him.

He stood there for thirty seconds and just listened. As far as he had been able to ascertain, there was no one else in the house. Hicks closed his eyes and acclimatised. He heard the tick of water falling into a metal basin from a leaking tap. He heard the creak of a pipe. He heard the sound of a cat mewling in the back garden and then the louder screech of a fox. He held his breath and strained his hearing, concentrating on the first floor, listening for anything that might suggest that Fabian was awake. He heard nothing until, after a moment, he heard the unmistakeable sound of snoring.

Good.

He opened his eyes and took a balaclava from his pocket. He put it on, settling the woollen garment so that only his eyes were visible. He took a pair of thin latex overshoes and slipped them over his boots. Finally, he took out a small shielded flashlight, switched it on and cast the light around so that he could survey his surroundings more thoroughly. The hall was a mess. There was a pile of mail on the floor just behind the door, surely several weeks' worth, and another stack that had been precariously balanced on a small table that also held a telephone and a bunch of keys. He reached out and took an envelope from the pile, holding it between gloved thumb and forefinger. It was a bill, angry red showing through the envelope window, addressed to Edward Fabian. He put it down again.

Hicks reached into his jacket, released the clip on his shoulder holster, and withdrew the pistol. It was a Hi-Power, the model favoured by the Regiment, and one that had never let him down before.

He walked ahead and quickly checked that the rooms downstairs were empty. There was a sitting room, kitchen and bathroom. They were all untidy, with mismatched furniture, abandoned clothing, and discarded newspapers and food packaging, and they were all empty.

Hicks returned to the hall and ascended the stairs. The boards beneath his feet were old and they creaked; he stepped on the outsides of the steps, closer to the stringers, and minimised the noise.

He reached the landing. The snoring was much louder here, and it was easy to locate. There were three doors off the landing: two bedrooms and a second bathroom. He checked the other rooms first, confirmed that they were empty—and thus that the house was empty apart from the sleeper—and approached the final room. He pushed it open with his fingertips. The hinges were in good condition and the door swung back noiselessly.

Hicks stepped inside.

The window was uncovered and it admitted a little indirect light from the streetlamp outside. There was enough for Hicks to be able to look around without the flashlight, so he switched it off and put it back in his pocket. The room was as untidy as all of the others. There was a bed and the shape of a recumbent figure beneath a duvet that was pulled all the way up. There was a pile of clothes at the foot of the bed. There was a set of drawers with an old-fashioned clock radio sat atop it, the red figures glowing.

He approached the bed.

Eddie Fabian was sleeping on his side, his face turned toward Hicks. His head rested on his arm, and his right foot protruded out from underneath the cover. Hicks drew the Browning, rested his finger against the trigger guard, and then slowly lowered himself onto the bed so that he was sitting next to Eddie's body. The man exhaled and shifted position a little. Hicks let him settle again and then pressed the barrel of the pistol against the side of his head.

"Edward," he whispered.

The man jerked in his sleep, and his breathing came a little faster.

"Edward, wake up."

Fabian's eyes flicked open. There was a moment of dumb incomprehension, then confusion, and then fright. His body stiffened and his arm jerked up, catching against the duvet. Hicks placed his left forearm across Edward's shoulders and pushed down, pinning him to the bed. He kept the muzzle of the gun pressed square against his temple.

"Lie quietly. Don't try to shout. I'm here to deliver a message. If you listen to me and do what I tell you to do, you'll be all right. Understand?"

Fabian's eyes went a little wider. He didn't speak.

"Edward, you need to tell me that you understand."

Fabian managed to nod his head.

"Very good."

When Fabian spoke, his voice was thin and raspy. "Who are you?"

"It doesn't matter who I am. I'm here to give you a message."

Fabian tried to raise himself from the bed, but Hicks pushed down harder. Fabian gave up and fell back down against the mattress. He lay still, his body rigid with tension.

"You threatened a man the other day, Edward. You told him that you remembered him from years ago. When you were a boy. Do you know the man I mean?"

Fabian didn't respond. He stared up at Hicks, his eyes bulging with fear and his larynx bobbing as he swallowed down on a dry throat.

"Do you remember him, Edward?"

"Yes," he said, his voice a parched gasp.

"You are not to speak to that man again. Under any circumstances. Do you understand?"

"Yes."

"And you are not to repeat any of the things you said to him to anyone else. Do you understand?"

"Yes."

"If you do, I'll be back. I know where you live. I know the cab you drive. I know everything there is to know about you. And if I have to come back, it won't be to talk. Is that clear?"

"Yes."

"Be sure that it is. I'm going to go now. If you call the police or try to come after me, it'll go badly for you. I'd stay in bed. Think about what I've said and what you're not going to do. Understand?"

"Please—just go. I won't do anything."

Hicks stood and stepped back from the bed. Fabian did not move. Hicks backed away, keeping the gun visible, reversed through the door and pulled it closed after him. He holstered the Browning and made his way quickly down the stairs. He took off the overshoes, the gloves and the balaclava and stuffed them back into his pocket. He opened the front door a little, looked out to confirm that the street was quiet—it was—and then stepped outside. He closed the door, made his way through the garden and then the gate and onto the pavement.

Hicks walked briskly back to his car and got inside.

He waited there for fifteen minutes, using the mirrors to look back down the road toward Fabian's house. There was nothing to see.

He took out his phone and called Woodward. "Hicks here. It's done."

"And?"

"It's done."

"He'll do what you said?"

"I scared him, like you wanted. He won't—"

Hicks saw the glare of headlights in the rear-view mirror. He looked up and squinted as a vehicle closed on him and then went by. It was a black cab. It slowed at the junction with Grove Green Road and Hicks could read the registration in the light from a streetlamp.

It was Edward Fabian's cab.

"Hicks?"

"Problem. Fabian just drove past me."

He started the engine and pulled out.

"What?"

"He's in his cab."

"Where's he going?"

"How would I know?"

"Follow him."

"I already am."

Fabian pulled away from the junction and turned onto

the southbound A12, toward central London. Hicks followed. It was a dual carriageway and it was quiet, with excellent visibility. Hicks could afford to stay a good distance behind.

He didn't like the way things were going.

"Where are you?" Woodward said.

Hicks glanced up as a road sign flashed by him. "Coming into Leyton. Headed south. He's going into the city."

Hicks felt uncomfortable at the way events were unfolding. He forced himself to remember his wife, reminding himself that he was only doing the things that he was doing for her.

But that didn't make him feel any better.

Chapter Thirteen

MILTON ENJOYED the film. He stayed in the area, taking an early dinner in one of the Turkish restaurants that lined Kingsland High Road, and then took the bus toward the city. He changed onto the underground at Bethnal Green and arrived at Oxford Circus at a quarter to ten. Cathy was just leaving, and there was just time for a quick conversation before Milton got down to work. A few of the regulars popped in over the course of the first couple of hours. He shared a few words with them and then concentrated on cleaning the kitchen. He found his thoughts wandering to his neighbours in Bethnal Green and how he might be able to help them.

There was a quiet period just after midnight when the shelter was empty. It wasn't unusual for a Sunday. He took his cigarettes and his Ronson lighter and sat down on the sill of the door, arranging himself at an angle so that he could look along the rain-slicked pavement to both the left and the right.

He hadn't even had the opportunity to take out a cigarette when he saw the man walking toward the entrance.

"Hello, John."

It was Eddie Fabian, and he looked terrible. His eyes were red-rimmed and, when he put out his hand for Milton to shake his fingers were quivering. Milton took his hand and grasped it, looking into Eddie's face. His first thought was that he had fallen off the wagon.

"Are you all right?" Milton asked.

"Anyone inside?"

"No. It's Sunday. It's empty."

"Do you mind if I come in?"

"Of course not."

Milton held the door open and followed Eddie into the

shelter. People fell off the wagon all the time. Milton heard at least one share every week from someone who had returned to the fellowship after going back to the bottle. They were welcomed back with kind words and warm embraces, with talk of the slate being wiped clean, and Milton had sat at the back and observed and doubted that he would ever have enough empathy to help someone in that situation. Once, he would have seen such weakness as a sign of failure, but that was before he had admitted his own failings to himself. Now, while he did not judge those men and women—and while he could sometimes empathise with them—he still did not know how he would react if he were asked to help someone in that situation. It would require sensitivity and tact. He doubted that he would be very good at it. He wasn't blessed with an abundance of either quality.

"I hope you don't mind," Eddie said as the door swung shut behind them.

"What?"

"Me turning up like this. I know you're working. If you need to serve anyone, you know, you can just leave me here, it's fine…"

"It's quiet tonight. Sundays are always quiet."

"I haven't had a drink, if that's what you're thinking."

Milton started to retort, but Eddie shushed him with a wave of his hand.

"I can tell. The way you're looking at me." Milton tried to protest, but Eddie cut him off again. "It's all right. You wouldn't be far wrong. I might as well be honest with you. I've got a bottle of scotch in the cab. Just bought it ten minutes ago from the off-licence I used to use. Camden. They must've thought they'd seen a ghost, or thought their profits were about to go back up. I was going to find somewhere quiet and get into it, and then I thought of you. I thought maybe we could have a talk. Maybe you could persuade me why having a drink is a bad idea."

Milton was finding the conversation uncomfortable.

"Look—do you want a cup of tea?"

Eddie nodded.

Milton went into the kitchen, took down a clean mug and dropped a tea bag into it. He looked back out into the shelter as he poured hot water from the urn. Eddie was sitting quietly by himself, his hands on the table. He clenched and unclenched his fists, and then he clasped them together, one hand kneading the other. He looked anxious. Milton had seen this before. Alcoholics on the cusp of taking a drink looked like this. He took a deep breath. He found that he was frustrated that Eddie had come here, imposed himself in the middle of his own comfortable routine, until he checked the thought. That wasn't how the fellowship worked. Milton had reached out for help more than once and had always been given it. Milton didn't know why Eddie had chosen him, but he wasn't about to turn him away. He might not know what to do, but at least he could give him a drink and listen. He'd work out the rest as they went along.

Come on, Milton, he said to himself. *You can help. Just listen to him. How hard can that be?*

He took the tea and set it down on the table. "Here."

Eddie took a long sip, his eyes closed, and then set the mug down on the table and wrapped his hands around it as if using it to keep warm.

"I'm sorry about this," he said. "Coming in here."

"It's fine. What is it?"

"I'm in a bit of a state, John, if I'm honest. I haven't been this close to taking a drink since I stopped. I need someone to talk to. I know I should speak to my sponsor, but I don't have one. I did have—I've had several—but we always fall out in the end. I don't do well when I'm told what to do. You know what I mean?"

"I don't have a sponsor, either." The reason was different. Milton had no problem with accepting advice on how to live a better life. But he did have a problem with the unflinching honesty he knew that any sponsor would expect from him. It was easy to hide his history if all he had to do was stay quiet at the back of the room. He didn't think he would be able to manage that in a relationship with a sponsor, so he had avoided getting one.

"How far are you through the steps?" Eddie asked.

"I'm working through them," Milton said.

"Which is the hardest for you?"

"The ninth."

Eddie nodded enthusiastically. "Same for me. You remember what I said after the meeting?"

"You said you were doing well."

He laughed humourlessly. "Who was I kidding? What a joke."

Milton sat quietly and left Eddie the space to choose what to do next: to talk or, if he preferred, to sit quietly with his drink. He talked.

"What I told you about when we had coffee, the things that happened to me when I was a kid? I had tried to put it out of my mind. For years, I almost managed it. Then something happened that brought it all back to the surface again."

"What?"

"The weirdest coincidence. I told you I'd been thinking of telling my story. Naming names."

"Yes. You said."

"I spoke to a journalist a while ago. Some of the men who abused me were well known. Politicians. Men from the establishment. It would be a big deal if I told it and people believed me. I mean—really big. This journalist, she wanted me to go on the record, but I'd been putting it off. Too scared. Story of my life." He laughed bitterly. "I'd almost decided that I wasn't going to go through with it when I was out driving one day a couple of weeks ago. It'd been a long day. I'd been up since five, it had been raining heavily all morning, and there was a lot of business. I was up by Westminster, at the lights in front of Big Ben. This chap came out of the crowd, tapped on the window and asked if

I was free. I was, so I unlocked the door and let him in. I looked in the mirror. It was an old man. Looked like he was ex-military. He wanted me to take him to his place. He wasn't a talker—he spent most of the trip looking at papers—but there was something about him that I couldn't get out of my head. It was like I had an itch inside my skull. Couldn't scratch it. It was only when we got there that I realised what it was. I recognised the place. There was no doubt about it. The place where they had the parties. And then I recognised him, too. This man—there was no doubt about that, either. I was staring at him in the mirror when he noticed and asked me if everything was okay. It hit me, all at once: the voice, the way he spoke, like he was superior to you, his eyes. Everything. He was one of the men. I'd bet my life on it."

"What did you do?"

"Nothing—not then, anyway. I dropped him off, took his money and left. Then I went and got drunk. That was when I fell off the wagon. A massive three-day bender. I don't remember any of it." He laughed bitterly. "I'd been making progress, too. Pissed all that away. It suddenly seemed stupid."

He put both hands around the mug and clasped it. Milton said nothing and let him gather his thoughts.

"But then I sobered up and the memories came back. I thought about it. Couldn't stop thinking about it. That man got into my cab rather than all the other cabs in London that day. What are the odds of that? There has to be a reason. A purpose. I thought about it, and I knew it had happened so that I could do something about what happened to me. I had decided not to do anything, and then that happened. It's a sign. A message from my Higher Power. And I thought about it some more. He shouldn't have been allowed to get away with it, what he'd done to me and the other boys. I couldn't just forget about it."

"What did you do?"

"I went back. I went back after work, parked up outside

the block and waited for him. Every day I went back there, round about the same time. Every day I waited. It was a week before I saw him again. I took photos. Here. This is him."

He took out his phone and slid it across the table. Milton looked. The shots had been taken from inside a car, and he could see a glint of reflection on the glass of a window and the line of the dash. There was a building opposite the car, a substantial one with numerous windows in the floors that were visible in shot. There was a man coming out of the building's entrance. He was dressed in a tweed suit and he walked with a stick. His hair was white, a counterpoint to the gloom of the street and the bricks that were spoiled black by years of pollution. Eddie encouraged Milton to swipe, and he did, glancing through another dozen pictures, all similar to the first. The last one was the best: the man was looking straight into the lens. He was twenty feet away, on the other side of the road, but the likeness was clear and crisp.

"I don't recognise him."

"His name is Leo Isaacs."

Milton shrugged.

"He was an MP. Used to be a government minister in the eighties. Defence. He's still involved in politics. He's a Lord now. That's why he was at Westminster when I saw him."

"What happened?"

"After I saw him? I got out of the car. I went over and spoke to him. I told him who I was, and I asked him if he remembered me. He said he didn't, but you could tell by the look on his face that he was scared. I don't know if he recognised me or not, but he knows what he did. That was it. Made up my mind there and then. I called the journalist and told her I'd speak to her. We were going to do it tomorrow."

The door opened. Milton looked up and saw a man that he didn't recognise. He was of average height and build, with close-cropped blond hair and steely eyes.

"Sorry," Milton said, "are you a driver?"

The man gazed around the room and then looked from Milton to Fabian and then back again. "No, guv, I'm not. Why? Is that a problem?"

"Drivers only in here, I'm afraid. No exceptions. If you want something, I can serve you through the hatch."

The man shook his head and smiled. "I'm sorry. I had no idea. Sorry to bother you."

"You don't want anything?"

"No. I'm good. Good night."

The man closed the door again. Milton felt uncomfortable. It didn't feel like a random encounter. He went to the door, opened it, and looked out. The man was ambling away, his hands in his pockets. Milton watched him for a moment.

"What?" Eddie said from behind him.

"Nothing," Milton said, shutting the door again. He turned back. "You said you were going to see her tomorrow. Have you changed your mind?"

"Maybe. I don't know." He took another sip, and when he looked back up at Milton, his eyes were fearful. "Someone threatened me tonight. A man broke into my house, came into my bedroom and woke me up. He put a gun to my head and told me that if I spoke to anyone about it, I'd be killed."

"When was this?"

"An hour ago."

"Have you called the police?"

"He told me not to. I didn't want to take the chance."

"What did he look like?"

"It was dark. I couldn't really see his face."

"What did he say?"

"What I just said. I wasn't to talk to anyone about Isaacs or anything else. I wasn't to go to the papers. I've never been so scared in my life. I thought he was going to kill me. I needed a drink to calm my nerves, so I went out and bought one. And then I thought you might be here. If you hadn't been… I don't know, I'd probably be pissed out of my mind now."

"Go to the police."

Eddie shook his head. "That's what he told me not to do."

"The police can look after you. And if you let them have your evidence—"

"I don't have any evidence."

"Well, you tell them what you know."

"And nothing will happen. It was a long time ago. I've tried the police before. They ignored me. They don't believe me."

There was certainty in Eddie's answer.

Milton drummed his fingers on the table. "So you've got two choices. Do what they say and shut up, or speak to your journalist and put it out there."

"What would you do?"

"It's not easy. I'd ask myself how I would feel about keeping quiet."

"Terrible. He needs to pay for what he did to me."

"So go public and tell your story. It's going to look very strange if anything happens to you after that. It's up to you, Eddie, but that's what I'd do. You might make yourself safer if more people know about it."

"You're right. I know. I know that's what I've got to do."

"So the meeting is tomorrow?"

"Tomorrow."

"Then do it."

"Yes," he said. "I will."

Eddie looked away as he said it, his hands clenching again, and Milton doubted that he would go through with it. He knew, too, that it was the best way for Eddie to find peace. If he did nothing, there was no way that he would be able to stay sober. Milton thought about the twelve steps to recovery. They were never far from his thoughts, especially the eighth and ninth steps. They required an alcoholic to make a list of all the persons he had harmed, and then to make amends to them all. Milton couldn't do that, because most of the people that he had harmed were dead, so he had adapted the steps to suit his circumstances. His way of meeting the requirements of the program was to help others. He had made his first attempt in London, and it had not turned out the way that he had hoped it would. A man had died and a woman had been almost burned to death. He had fled to South America, working his way north through Mexico until he reached Texas. Events, and his own bloody history, had intervened along the way, but he still meant to do good whenever he could.

Eddie, for better or worse, was a chance to do good.

Milton would help him.

"I tell you what," Milton said. "Maybe you'd like someone to come along with you. Moral support."

"I can't ask you to do that," Eddie replied. "I've already imposed enough."

"I'd like to help. I'm not being completely altruistic—it's a little selfish. It helps me stay with the program, too."

Eddie looked at him hopefully. "If you're sure."

"I am. What about tonight? Do you need somewhere to stay?"

"No," he said. "I'm good."

"You'd be welcome to stay with me."

"Thanks, but I'll call my sister. God knows I have enough problems with my family, but I've always been able to rely on her. She's out of London, too."

"Where?"

"Withington."

Milton shook his head; he didn't know where that was.

"The Cotswolds. It's two hours from here. I better get off."

Milton handed Eddie his coat. "Where are you meeting the journalist?"

"Piccadilly Circus. Ten."

"I'll be there."

Milton could see that his offer of help had given Eddie some momentum.

Eddie stood and zipped up his jacket. "I better go."

Chapter Fourteen

HICKS HAD followed Eddie Fabian all the way to Russell Square and had parked in a position where he could watch his cab and the unusual building into which he had disappeared. He had called in his location and had had to wait only fifteen minutes before Joseph Gillan's Maserati pulled into a space a few cars ahead of him. Shepherd stepped out of the car and went over to the shelter. Hicks watched as Shepherd stood at the open door, the warm light from inside framing him in a golden rectangle. He had a short conversation with someone inside the shelter and then returned to the car.

Hicks's phone rang.

"It's Woodward. Shepherd's had a look inside. Fabian is talking to the man in charge of the place. Shepherd didn't recognise him. You have any idea what's going on?"

"No. None."

"It doesn't matter. We're not going to take a chance."

"Meaning what?"

"I've spoken to the general. He wants us to take him out."

"What?"

"You couldn't persuade him to keep his mouth shut. We'll do it for him."

"Kill him?"

"His choice, Hicks. If he'd listened, this wouldn't be happening."

He felt panic bubbling up. "Let me try again."

"What's the point? I'm sure you were very persuasive." There was sarcasm in his voice.

"I'll be *more* persuasive."

"No. It has to be this way."

"I'll rough him up. Do it properly this time."

There was a harshness in his voice when Woodward spoke again. "What's the problem? You lost your nerve?" Hicks started to speak, but Woodward spoke over him. "Because you didn't have a problem with Öztürk."

"That was different. He was scum. He had it coming. But this guy—"

"—is threatening someone we are protecting."

"A paedo!"

Hicks regretted the outburst almost as soon as the word had left his lips.

"We are going to deal with him tonight, Hicks. *Tonight.* That's the general's decision. If you think you'll have difficulty following that very simple order, I'd like you to say so now. You can take it up with him."

Hicks felt the cold grip of panic. He wanted to start the car and drive away. But you couldn't do that. You couldn't leave the unit. No one left.

"I didn't say that."

Hicks knew the general would rid himself of him with as much emotion as if he were a speck of lint on the shoulder of his jacket. What about his family? What would happen to his wife if he was gone? What would happen to them then?

The passenger-side door of the Maserati opened and Shepherd got out again. He followed the pavement to Hicks's Range Rover.

"When?" Hicks said into the phone.

"Now," Woodward responded. "There's no one else in there. Just the two of them. Shep's going to assist."

"And the other man in there?"

"Wrong place at the wrong time. Tough luck."

Shepherd opened the passenger door and slid into the car. He didn't speak. Hicks glanced over and saw that Shepherd had his own Browning in his right hand. Hicks stared out of the window to the Maserati. He felt sick. There had to be a way out of this.

"Ready?" Woodward said.

Hicks tried to swallow on a dry throat.

"Hicks?"

"Yes. Ready."

"Do it."

Hicks sat there for a moment, just staring out into the rain, until he accepted that the notion that he had any choice here was illusory.

"He wants *you* to do it," Shepherd said. "You go in and take them out. I'll cover the outside."

Hicks opened his jacket and reached in for his holstered Browning. His stomach turned over as his fingers closed around the butt, the metal cold against his clammy skin. The pistol was unsilenced, and it was going to make a lot of noise. He would do it quickly, in and out, two shots each for the men inside. There was no other choice. Woodward and Gillan were watching. Shepherd would be behind him. If he didn't do it, they would. And then Hicks would be next.

He opened the door and stepped out into the damp night. He started across the road toward the shelter. Shepherd followed him.

Hicks's phone buzzed. "Wait," Woodward said.

Hicks stopped. Shepherd stopped, too.

"He's coming out."

Hicks watched. He saw Edward Fabian as he stepped down from the shallow step onto the pavement and walked to his cab. If Fabian turned, he would see him, and then this brief possible reprieve would be irrelevant, but he looked distracted and he did not. He got inside the cab, started the engine, and pulled away.

The Maserati's lights flicked on and it, too, pulled out.

Woodward spoke again. "We'll follow him and wait for the right moment."

Hicks felt a wave of relief, although he knew it would only be temporary. "What about the second man?"

"Leave him."

"Copy that."

Hicks turned back and got into his Range Rover once again. Shepherd was already back inside. Hicks drove off in the direction that Woodward and Gillan had taken and, as he passed the shelter, he looked across at the entrance. There was a man there, standing in the light of the open door. He was watching the Maserati and, as Hicks passed, the man turned his gaze to take him in, too. Hicks looked at him and for a moment their eyes locked.

Hicks frowned. The man was average in appearance, the kind of man who would be difficult to remember, but there was something about him that he recognised.

Shepherd was looking at the cook, too. "Jammy bastard," Shepherd observed. "He doesn't know how lucky he just was."

Hicks drove on, trying to think what it was about the man that bothered him. Suddenly it came to him. He couldn't stifle a gasp.

"What?" Shepherd said.

"Nothing."

"It was *something*. You had a fright?"

"Forget it."

Hicks drove on, willing the surprise from his face.

It *was* something.

It was Number One.

He was certain.

It was John Milton.

#

MILTON TOOK out a cigarette and watched as Eddie crossed the road to his cab. He lit the cigarette and drew on it, then exhaled. It was a cold night; his breath mingled with the smoke. He heard the cab's engine turn over and then saw the headlights flick on. Eddie pulled away, raising his hand as he went past the shelter.

Milton was about to go back inside when he heard the sound of a second engine. He looked back. There were a handful of cars parked near the shelter, and, as he watched, he saw a black Maserati pull away from the kerb outside the Hotel Russell on Bernard Street and drive forward, turning right into the Square. Its lights were still off as it drove by the shelter. The windows were darkened, but Milton could see the silhouettes of the driver and a passenger in the front seats. The car picked up speed, the lights finally coming on.

He heard the sound of a car door closing and, as he turned in its direction, he saw another set of headlights snap on and a second car pull out. This one was bigger. It rolled slowly away from the kerb, turned in the same direction as Eddie's cab and the Maserati, and went by the shelter. It was a Range Rover. Something about the car bothered Milton. He didn't know what it was—and knew that it could very well be paranoia on his part—but as it passed through the pool of light thrown down by the streetlamp outside the School of Oriental Studies, Milton looked for the registration plate and memorised it.

The big car rolled slowly by and Milton could see the shapes of two figures in the front. The streetlamps reflected off the windscreen, making it impossible to see inside, but he thought that the two figures were male and it felt as if they were looking at him.

Milton waited in the doorway as the car disappeared to the south-east, following the same route that Eddie and the Maserati had taken.

He went inside, closed the door, collected a dirty plate—sticky with the residue of baked beans—and took it to the sink to be washed. He ran the water and looked out into the night. He felt uneasy.

Chapter Fifteen

HICKS FOLLOWED the black cab at a reasonable distance. Fabian had turned onto Gordon Street, following it until he reached the junction with Euston Road and then turning left, headed to the west. They passed Warren Street and Great Portland Street tube stations, continued through Regent's Park, and then picked up speed as the road merged into the Westway.

Shepherd had two radio units with him and he handed one of them to Hicks. They both put them on, clipping the receivers to their belts and pushing the ear buds into their ears. As Hicks dabbed the brakes to allow Fabian to gain a little on them, the radio crackled into life.

"Woodward to Hicks and Shepherd, come in."

Shepherd reached for the pressel on his receiver and thumbed the channel open.

"Shepherd here."

"Status?"

"We're behind him. Just going through White City. Where are you?"

"We've gone ahead. Connolly is engaged, too. We'll box him. Stay in formation."

Hicks tapped his fingers against the wheel. So it was a three-car pursuit, operating in a "floating box" pattern. It was a standard SAS tactic designed to ensure that the pursuit cars could be interchanged to minimise the possibility that the target might realise that he was being followed. Hicks had been involved in surveillance operations with as many as ten cars, enough assets to ensure that the target would never see the same tail car twice. They didn't have the manpower for that tonight, but the three vehicles that they did have would be more than enough for the job.

"A little closer," Shepherd said.

Hicks gripped the wheel just a little tighter.

"Closer. He's pulling away."

"I know what I'm doing," Hicks said in as even a tone as he could manage, doing his best to mask his discomfort and irritation. Shepherd had provided a constant stream of unwelcome advice ever since they had started the pursuit. Hicks was more than capable of tailing a single vehicle through the streets of London.

Shepherd was oblivious. "What do you reckon that was all about back there?"

It was the second time Shepherd had asked him that. "He was thirsty. Fancied a cup of tea. I don't know, Shepherd. What do you think?"

Shepherd tapped his fingers against his knee and then turned to look at him across the cabin. "That's not what you think, though, is it? What was it?"

"What do you mean?"

"Something bothered you back there. When Fabian came out with the other man. What was it? You recognise him?"

Hicks stared dead ahead at the lights of the cars ahead of them. "I don't know..." He started to speak, then shook his head. "I thought I did, but I was wrong."

"Who'd you think it was?"

"Someone from the army."

"And it's not? You're sure about that?"

"Yeah," he said. "I'm seeing things."

But that was a lie. He had recognised Milton at once. He hadn't seen him for years, but there was no mistaking him. So why didn't he say something? Why didn't he admit that he knew who Milton was?

Shepherd changed the subject. "The general told you what Isaacs gets up to?"

"I know. He's a pervert."

"That's an understatement. He's a pervert, all right. A rapist, too. Kids. Boys, mostly. Higgins has evidence that proves at least some of it. Photographs and videos."

"He didn't say that. He said it was just protection."

"One thing you need to know about the general," Shepherd said. "He doesn't do anything unless he can get something out of it. And I'm fine with that. I paid my mortgage off with his money. I bought my Lexus, cash. I took my woman to the Maldives, first class all the way. I'm not going to rock the boat."

The taxi slowed for a red light and rolled to a stop. They stopped, too, three cars behind it.

"Where did he get the evidence?" Hicks asked.

"He had a brother. He's dead now, got shot during some funny business the old man will hint at if you get him drunk enough. The brother used to be in the Met. Head of the Diplomatic Protection squad. Top brass. Most of this is gossip, but Isaacs made his money in Saudi during the '70s. I heard that the company got into hot water, and there was a suggestion that the regime wanted him dead. Higgins's brother was Isaacs's personal protection officer when he was a minister. Followed him around, drove him to meetings, the usual. From what I heard, Isaacs had this idea that he could trust him to keep quiet about the things he got up to in his private life. That was crazy, obviously, and, I'm just guessing here, but it sounds like the Higgins boys decided they'd get some evidence on what a nasty little shit he is just in case it might be useful later."

The lights changed and Fabian pulled away.

"Blackmail, then," Hicks said as he squeezed down on the accelerator.

"Of course it's blackmail, but you can dress it up any way you want. The way I heard it, they told Isaacs and the others that they had seen the evidence. They said they'd make sure it never came to light if they paid them. Think about it: these men, the longer it went on and nothing came to light, the more they trusted Higgins and his brother. The more they felt grateful to them. The more they felt like they were keeping them safe."

The taxi picked up speed.

"Where is he going?" Shepherd said.

"How long's it been going on?" Hicks asked, not finished with the subject yet.

"The thing with Isaacs and the old man?" Shepherd took out his Browning and ejected the magazine. "Years. Once him and the others started paying, anyone who came along and threatened the arrangement had to be dealt with. Isaacs got into trouble on Hampstead Heath. You remember that? It was in the news."

"I read about it tonight."

"Higgins made the evidence go away. The case collapsed. And then, when it was safe, he offed the man who was making the threats. Made it look like it was suicide. Put yourself in Isaacs's shoes. How's he going to feel after that? It must feel like Higgins is his guardian angel."

"Even though it's Higgins who's threatening him the most."

Shepherd laughed bitterly. "I know. It's Stockholm syndrome. Classic."

"How much are they getting?"

Shepherd used the heel of his palm to drive the magazine back into its slot. "I don't know. A lot. Isaacs is a millionaire. The other men are richer than he is. They're golden geese. They have to be looked after."

The traffic thinned out now, and Fabian continued to head west.

"Have you seen it?" Hicks asked. "The evidence?"

"No."

"Where does he keep it?"

"What is this? Twenty questions?"

"I'm just curious."

"Same place he keeps everything else: he's got a safe deposit box. God knows what else he has there."

Hicks thought back to the drive to Hatton Garden yesterday, the general disappearing into the anonymous building with the imposing security doors.

He nodded toward the taillights of the black cab. "And this guy? Fabian? He was involved?"

"You tell me," Shepherd said. "You went to see Isaacs. What did he say?"

"Just that Fabian accosted him. Said that he remembered him. Said he remembered being taken to his apartment and abused. Isaacs said that he threatened to go to the papers."

"Whatever he said, it wasn't smart. The old man says he's involved, he's involved. The old man says he has to go, he has to go. You don't ask questions; you just do it."

Hicks clenched his jaw.

"What's wrong with you now?" Shepherd asked.

"Nothing."

"You know we're not following him so we can have a little chat, right?"

Hicks clasped the wheel a little tighter. "It doesn't bother you?"

"That he's got to go?" Shepherd leaned all the way back in his seat and stared out the windscreen. "No, Hicks, it doesn't bother me. Life can be a real bitch. It's just tough luck."

Their radios crackled into life again. "Woodward to Shepherd."

"Shepherd here. Go ahead."

"We're at Hanger Lane underground. We'll pick him up here. You can drop back."

"Affirmative."

Hicks saw the circular station building, the illuminated London Underground roundel glowing red and blue. He saw the Maserati pull out of the parking lot of the Crowne Plaza. It accelerated, pulling into the outside lane, and quickly overtook them.

"Drop back," Shepherd said.

"Jesus, Shep, I know."

He touched the brakes and reduced his speed to fifty, allowing the black cab to increase the distance between them until they lost sight of it as the road wound its way through Perivale.

Hicks maintained a steady sixty, his eyes losing their focus as he stared ahead at the red lights of the cars ahead and the glare of the headlamps from those approaching on the other side of the road. He found his thoughts returning to the purpose of the night's operation. The realisation that he knew John Milton had distracted him from it, but not any longer.

He didn't know where Eddie Fabian was going at so late an hour, but he knew that he wouldn't be returning this way again.

Chapter Sixteen

THEY FOLLOWED the cab west until they were on the outskirts of London. Woodward dropped back and handed Fabian off to Hicks and Shepherd again, and they passed through Uxbridge and Beaconsfield and High Wycombe. The M40 was quiet at this late hour. There were trucks rumbling along in the slow lane; Fabian had moved over into the middle lane and was maintaining a comfortable seventy miles an hour. The rain had started to fall as they passed out of London. It had been apologetic at first, just a few spots, but it was coming down heavily now, and the wipers were working hard to keep the windscreen clear.

"Where's he going?" Shepherd said, as much to himself as to Hicks.

They had just passed signs for Junction 8 when the left-hand indicator of the taxi started to blink.

"Here we go," Shepherd said, reaching for the radio on his belt. "Shepherd to Woodward. Come in."

"Go ahead."

"We're coming up to Junction 8. He's turning off."

"Stay with him."

"Where are you?"

"A mile behind. We'll catch up and you can hand off to us."

"Affirmative."

There were fields on either side of the motorway. Hicks could see for twenty or thirty yards before the darkness absorbed the glow from the lights of the passing cars. Junction 8 was for Oxford and Cheltenham. He took the slip road off the motorway and joined the A40, continued past the turning for Wheatley services, and then indicated again as they passed a sign advertising a turning for Wheatley and Tiddington.

Hicks slowed down to forty, allowing the cab to pull farther away from them. There was no other traffic now, and if Fabian was being vigilant, they would have to be careful for fear of spooking him.

"We need to hand off," Shepherd said. "He's going to make us if we follow much longer."

Fabian turned onto a smaller road that was marked on their satnav as London Road. They followed the cab through Littleworth, and then, as they exited the village, they continued onto Old Road. It was a narrow lane, only just wide enough for two vehicles, and, as they continued to the west, it narrowed even more. The vegetation grew taller and thicker on either side of them, reaching up and touching above them in a dark green roof.

Hicks had allowed the cab to draw perhaps half a mile ahead of them and, as the road turned to the left, they lost sight of it.

"We should turn back," Hicks said. "There's no reason why we'd be out here, too. He'll make us."

He glanced over at Shepherd and saw he was chewing the inside of his lip, working out what they should do. The satnav showed that the road continued for another mile before it fed into the Eastern Bypass that led north to south along Oxford's eastern boundary.

"Stay on him," Shepherd said.

They turned the corner and came upon a house. It was bounded by a stone wall, with a pair of cast-iron gates that had opened to admit Eddie Fabian's cab. There was another car inside the gates. Both it and the cab had their lights on.

Hicks dabbed the brakes. "What the fuck?"

"Keep driving," Shepherd said.

He was right. They couldn't stop.

Hicks maintained a careful pace and glanced out of the blackened window as they passed the two cars. The door to the taxi was open and Fabian was standing behind it. The other car was a Jeep, its registration plate lit up in the glow of the taxi's lights. Hicks memorised it. He looked in the mirror and saw the house's front door open and three figures step out. They were all male, but that was all that he could tell before the Range Rover turned the corner and the house was out of sight.

Shepherd spoke into the radio. "Abort," he said.

"What's happening?" Woodward said.

"Target is meeting someone. There's a house here, another car waiting for him. Three males. Some kind of rendezvous. The road is too minor. If you come down it too, they'll know he's been followed. Suggest you stop in Littleworth."

"Copy that."

Hicks drove to the end of Old Road.

"Pull over," Shepherd said.

Hicks did as he was told.

Woodward radioed again. "Do we know who he's meeting?"

"Didn't get a good look," Shepherd said. "We couldn't stop."

"Three males, like I said. That's all I saw."

Woodward cursed. "Higgins is going to hate this. What about the road ahead of the house? Is there any other way on or off?"

"No," Shepherd said. "Fields on either side. No other roads."

There was a pause as Woodward considered their options. Hicks found his stomach was turning over. Nerves.

"Shepherd," Woodward said at last, "is there anywhere you can park up out of sight?"

"We're at Eastern Bypass. There's a lay-by."

"Park there. How far back to the meet?"

"A mile."

"Go back and check it out. Find out what he's doing, who he's meeting. We'll stay at this end. When Fabian drives out, whether he goes east or west, we tail him again."

"Copy that."

"And get whatever you can about the other car."

The radio went dead.

"Go on, then," Shepherd said.

"What?"

"You heard what he said. Go back and check it out."

"Why me?"

"Look at the weather," he said, flicking a finger toward the window. "I'm not going out in that."

There didn't seem any point in arguing with him. Shepherd was a loudmouth, and Hicks had no interest in getting into a dispute with him. Hicks had only been a member of the Feather Men for a short time, just long enough for the one operation, and that meant that he was more junior than all of the others. He shared the same rank as Shepherd, but there was another layer of authority within the unit and he knew that he was lacking. And he was already fearing for his position after the situation that had developed with Fabian. He had no choice.

Hicks unclipped his belt, opened the door and stepped out into the rain. It was sheeting down now, a steady deluge that had created broad puddles across the pitted surface of the lay-by. The road ahead was empty, the only noise the steady hiss of the water as it sluiced onto the tarmac. Hicks reached a hand into his jacket, touched his fingers against the butt of his Hi-Power, and zipped it up again. He cast a quick look back at the car—he saw Shepherd's shadow as he moved across to take his place in the driver's seat—and went back in the direction from which they'd come.

Chapter Seventeen

HICKS JOGGED back to the junction with Old Road and, once he was satisfied that the way ahead was empty, turned down it and set off. The lane was particularly narrow here, and Hicks was painfully aware that he would have very little time to hide should either the taxi or the Jeep come in this direction. He hurried on, passing the driveway to a large house and then the house itself as he worked back to the east. There were trees on either side and thick hawthorn hedges that offered little in the way of cover.

The rain continued to slam down onto the surface of the road, rivulets running down toward him as he ascended a gentle incline. The water plastered his hair to his scalp and soaked through his dark denim jeans. He was wearing a jacket with a waterproof double membrane, the sort of garment he would have been equipped with in the Regiment, and that, at least, kept his upper body, his radio and his weapon dry.

He reached up with his hand and sluiced the rain from his eyes just as the glare of headlights approached from around a turning.

It was a hundred yards away. Hicks saw the glow of the high beams just before the car turned the corner, and used that tiny moment to his advantage. He flung himself onto the verge and rolled to the left. There was a narrow cleft, more of a trough than a ditch, and he wedged himself down into it, muddy water running around his body. He pressed down as hard as he could, hoping that the depression and the abundant vegetation around him would offer enough cover. He hoped, too, that he hadn't been seen as the car turned the corner.

He squinted up into the glow of the lights. The car was silhouetted behind their powerful glare, but he could see from the shape that it was the Jeep and not the cab. The car was travelling quickly, and Hicks held himself still as it rushed by. The wheels threw up parabolas of spray from the standing water, but Hicks was already soaked through and ignored it. Instead, he turned his head and looked back at the car, now fast retreating toward the bypass and, beyond that, Oxford. The Jeep bumped and bounced down the road, the red of the brake lights flaring against the overhanging greenery as it slowed for the turn that preceded the main road.

He took the radio and toggled the pressel to open the channel. "This is Hicks. The rendezvous car just went past me, heading west."

"I've got it," Shepherd said.

"Hold position," Woodward reported. "What about the target? Was he in it?"

"Couldn't see," Hicks said.

"His cab?"

"Not yet."

"Proceed," Woodward ordered. "Check it out."

"Copy that."

#

HICKS RAN ON. He was covered in thick mud and slime from the ditch, his hair was bedraggled, and even the waterproof jacket had failed him. He reached the corner from behind which the car had emerged. He recalled the geography, remembering that the house where the two cars had stopped was a quarter of a mile farther along the road. He turned the corner onto the straight beyond it and saw the gate and the glow of headlamps.

Hicks pulled his pistol and continued his approach, staying close to the edge of the road. He closed on the gate. It was open. He could hear, above the drumming of the rain, that a car engine was still turning over.

He was ten feet away now. He raised the Browning,

clasping it in both hands. The rain lashed into his face. He ignored it. He stepped through the gate and onto the property beyond. It was a large, sprawling house. The lights were off, and there were no other signs that it was occupied.

The cab was in the same position as before. The headlamps were on, throwing pools of light against the wall of the house. Hicks moved closer. He could see the shape of a person in the driver's seat. The person was unmoving, slumped forward. The engine was running, a low hum that he could hear through the rain.

Five feet.

He came around the back of the cab. There was a hose attached to the exhaust. As he drew closer, he saw that it led around to the side of the car. He followed it, his gun ready, and saw that it trailed up the side of the chassis and was wedged into the driver's side window.

The body was propped against the wheel.

The window was fogged. He reached out a gloved hand and opened the door, careful not to dislodge the hose from the gap between the glass and the frame. The cabin was thick with acrid smoke, and it leaked out in lazy tendrils that were quickly smothered by the rain.

Edward Fabian was slumped forward, his sternum pressed against the wheel and his head lolling over the top of it. His face was angled to the door, and his eyes, open and unblinking, stared out at Hicks.

He depressed the pressel and spoke into the mic. "Hicks to Woodward."

"Go ahead, Hicks."

"He's dead."

"What do you mean?"

"Fabian's in his car. The engine is on. There's a hosepipe from the exhaust into the cabin. He's dead."

"Pull out, Hicks. Confirm."

"Confirmed. Pulling out."

He closed the door again and watched for a handful of seconds as the interior became clouded with fumes once more. He checked the windows of the house and confirmed, again, that there were no signs of occupation. He went to the gate and looked left and right. The road outside was empty. All he could hear was the sound of the raindrops as they exploded onto the pitted and potholed tarmac.

He wiped the water from his face again and set off, jogging back to the spot where Shepherd was waiting for him.

Part Two

A Lonely Death

Chapter Eighteen

THE RAIN stopped at dawn. Milton watched through the open hatch as the sun broke through the clouds. Light arrowed down onto the small park in the middle of the Square, droplets falling from sodden leaves and branches and dropping through the golden shafts.

Milton finished the shift and handed over to Cathy's son, a quiet and pleasant young man called Carl. It was a mile from Russell Square to Piccadilly Circus, and Milton was there at half past nine, thirty minutes early. The wide space around Eros was busy, even at this hour, with tourists sitting on the steps and others holding up their phones to take selfies with the statue and the kaleidoscopic billboards in the background. Milton walked on a little farther and found Savile Row. He ambled onwards until he reached the first of the suit-makers that had given the street its reputation. He looked in through the open doors to an oasis of beautifully minimal chic, expensive fabrics and a security guard with a Bluetooth headset nestled in his ear. Milton had worn suits like these, once, and had worn them in Monte Carlo and St Moritz and the Hamptons. It was a different world to the one he moved through now, and he found that he preferred his scuffed boots, dirty jeans and the white T-shirts he picked up in bundles of five for less than ten pounds in Primark.

He turned and returned to the Circus, where he scanned the crowd. Eddie wasn't there. He checked his watch. It was a minute after ten. He walked to the Criterion Theatre, leaned against the wall and took out a cigarette. A line of buses rumbled out of Regent Street and proceeded along Shaftesbury Avenue. Milton lit the cigarette and drew on it. A white flatbed truck pulled out into the steady flow of traffic. The tide of tourists thickened as more emerged from the underground, following a guide with a small Japanese flag hoisted atop a stick. Milton finished the cigarette, dropped it to the pavement and crushed it underfoot. He pushed himself away from the wall and looked left and right.

He checked his watch.

Twenty past.

Eddie was not here.

He looked for the journalist, searching for someone who might be waiting for a rendezvous. There were several candidates, but then this was a standard meeting place and Milton had nothing to go on save the reporter's gender. There was an older woman looking at her phone. A younger woman, early twenties, with her phone pressed to her ear. Three other single women, one sitting on the steps and the other two standing near to the theatre. Milton had no way to guess who it was who wanted to speak to Eddie. He considered whether he might approach them and ask, decided that was unlikely to be productive, and went back to waiting.

He gave it another ten minutes, until half past the hour, and then gave up. Eddie wasn't coming. He had lost his nerve. Milton had known that was a possibility. The man was frightened of the consequences of speaking out about what had happened to him, and it seemed that the thought of it had proven to be too much. That wasn't unreasonable. He'd been given a terrific fright. It was understandable that he would want to stay with his sister, away from the city. Milton was not about to criticise him for that.

There was a meeting of the fellowship tonight that Milton usually attended. Eddie often went to it, too. He wondered whether he would see him there and, if he did, what he would say.

Milton walked toward Regent Street. He would get the tube at Oxford Circus and head east. It would take him half an hour to get back to Bethnal Green. He was tired and ready for bed.

Chapter Nineteen

HICKS ARRIVED at the Cock of Tupsley at six the following evening. The Regiment was based at Credenhill, just outside the town, and it was always a standing joke that the three hundred men who formed its complement could easily be identified when they left camp for a drink or a little bit of R & R. Hicks looked around now and saw a couple of men at the bar who matched the profile of the typical SAS man: athletic rather than large, hair kept neat and tidy, wearing boots beneath well-pressed pairs of jeans. The two kept themselves to themselves, talking quietly and enjoying a couple of pints. If someone had asked them what they did for a living, they would have said that they were in the army. They would be charming and discreet and would go no further, but it would still be obvious to anyone with any experience.

He went through to the back and then climbed the stairs to the meeting room. The others were there.

The general was at the head of the table. "So," he said, "what do we know?"

"The police were called out by a local farmer," Woodward said. "He saw the cab with the engine running. They got there just after six. I spoke to my contact. They've put an old hand on it. They think it was suicide. They're not going to dig too hard."

"Who owns the house?"

"Yeah, I checked that. It's Fabian's sister. Lauren Fabian. Seems likely he was running there after Hicks warned him."

Higgins turned to Hicks. "Corporal?"

"It's possible. He would've been frightened. I was persuasive."

Higgins pursed his lips at that; an indication, perhaps,

that he was unconvinced. "What about the other car?"

"I got the plate."

"And?"

"I've requested details."

The general nodded. "Any other thoughts?"

"Whoever it was, they're clean. Very professional."

"How did they subdue him?"

"It wasn't obvious, sir."

Higgins waved his hand irritably. "Speculate."

Hicks had been thinking about it. "They could have tied him to the seat. A roll of duct tape, maybe. But there would have been a struggle. It would have been noisy. Maybe I would've heard, and I didn't."

"So they drugged him," Gillan said. "Chloroform."

"Chloroform is detectable in a post-mortem," Connolly said.

"Only if there's a lot of it," Hicks corrected.

"And only if they run the right tests," Gillan added. "This looks straightforward. Maybe they won't bother with toxicology."

The general finished his pint and replaced the glass on the table, running his fingers up and down it. He had surprisingly delicate hands for an old soldier, with slender fingers and nails that were so smooth that they almost looked polished.

"Yes," Higgins agreed. "Maybe. Whoever did this saved us the effort. But I want to know who it was. I don't like being in the dark like this." He turned back to Hicks. "Corporal, call me when you know who owns the car. And keep an eye on the rest of his family. Find out what you can about the sister." He pointed three times, including Hicks, Connolly and Woodward in the gesture. "Find out when the funeral is. The three of you go, keep an eye on it, see if anything comes up."

"What about the bloke he met in Russell Square?" Shepherd said.

"What about him?"

"Hicks thought he recognised him. Tell him, Hicks."

The general looked at him. "Corporal?"

"I thought I did," Hicks said, with an irritated sideways glance at Shepherd. "But I don't think I do. Thought it was someone I knew from the army. It was a mistake."

"You're sure about that?"

"Yes, sir."

"Have a look at him, too. Find out what you can. Fabian goes to see him, the next thing he does is drive out to his sister's and gets topped. I need more information. I don't like being blindsided like this. We should have been on top of Fabian and we weren't. That can't happen again."

The men nodded to acknowledge the old man's order. They spoke about business for another five minutes, but the main purpose of the meeting had been concluded. They finished their drinks, collected their coats and left.

#

IT WAS late when Hicks finally got behind the wheel of his car for the long three-hour drive back to Cambridge. He followed the M5 to Birmingham and then took the M6 and A14 until the lights of the city appeared out of the darkness. It was two in the morning when he parked the Range Rover in the garage. He lowered the door and took a moment to look at his modest house and the small garden that spread out around it. He looked up at the window to his bedroom and thought of his wife. He thought of the cancer and the money he needed to find.

He was confused. His thoughts were a riot, and he couldn't control them.

Would he have killed Fabian?

Would he have gone through with it?

He couldn't say.

What about Milton? What would he do if the general told him that Milton was a loose end who needed to be cut? What would he do if the general told him that offing him was his responsibility?

What would he do then?

Kill him?

A wave of dizziness washed over him and he put out his hand to steady himself against the wall of the garage. He felt as if he was caught in a vice: on one side was Rachel, the cancer, and the thought of an impossible life without her; on the other side was the general and the rest of the unit. He was trapped in the middle, squeezed tighter and tighter.

He thought of Fabian slumped against the wheel of his cab, and then to the other things that he and the rest of the men had done. He felt shame and then, as he thought of the general, there was anger with himself. He had allowed his desperation to lead him to the old man, to accept his offer of a place in the unit and all of the consequences that came with it. There was no way to leave the Feather Men once you were inside. It was a lifetime commitment.

And because of that, ultimately, all he felt was fear.

Chapter Twenty

THAT NIGHT'S MEETING was at St Giles in the Fields. The church was on the fringes of Covent Garden and was a large, grand place. Milton was interested in history and had researched the building after his first visit there. It had been the last church on the route between Newgate Prison and the gallows at Tyburn, and the churchwardens had made it a custom to pay for condemned men to have a drink at the next-door pub, the Angel, before they went to be hanged. Milton found that wryly amusing.

The meeting was held in the vestry house behind the church, and as Milton stepped off the busy street and into the church garden, he felt the usual peacefulness descend. He stopped outside the vestry room for a cup of coffee and a biscuit, nodding a hello to the woman who had held the role ever since he had started to attend here.

"Hello, John," she said. "How are you?"

"Doing well."

"Coffee with one sugar?"

"You remembered."

"Do this as long as I have, you remember everyone."

Milton thanked her, waited for her to make his coffee and took the mug, together with a chocolate digestive biscuit, into the vestry room. It was bright and airy, with large windows that reached from the ceiling all the way down to panelled wainscoting. Engraved boards recorded the names and dates of service of all the vicars who had worked in the church. A cast-iron chandelier was suspended above a large oval table with twelve chairs. There were more chairs around the edge of the room and a fireplace with a large mirror fixed above the mantelpiece. The walls had not been painted for years and there were chips in the woodwork. It would have been a grand room, once, but now it had been allowed to become shabby. But Milton liked it. It was full of character, and its decrepitude reminded him of all the thousands of men and women who must have sat in this room over the course of the decades. Today, the room had been decked out with AA posters and the long scroll that held the twelve steps. A small table held a supply of pamphlets and several brand-new editions of the Big Book, the bible that set out the creed of the organisation's founder, Bill Wilson.

Milton was one of the first inside and, instead of taking one of the chairs at the table, he sat in the corner at the back of the room. The idea of sitting where everyone could see him, his back to at least half of the room, was one he found profoundly unsettling. His position also allowed him to watch the others as they filed inside. It was a busy meeting, and the chairs around the table and then the others all around it were quickly taken.

Milton watched the doorway for Eddie, but he didn't come through. He had been to the last three or four meetings that Milton had attended here, but his absence today wasn't surprising. Milton wondered if he might have been embarrassed to have stood him up, or perhaps he was regretting his candour when he came to see him in the shelter. Or perhaps he had fallen off the wagon after all.

The secretary was a white-haired old lady who, Milton had heard, had once been something of a leading light in Tin Pan Alley, the street of musical shops that was close by the church. She sat down in the last remaining chair at the table and banged a small gavel.

"Good evening, ladies and gentlemen," she began. "This is the regular meeting of the St Giles in the Fields group of Alcoholics Anonymous. My name is Edith and I am an alcoholic."

"Hello, Edith," they resounded.

"Let us open the meeting with a moment of silence followed by the Serenity Prayer."

There was a pause as the attendees closed their eyes and

reflected. Milton thought of Eddie again. He had skipped the meeting because he was ashamed. He must have known that Milton would be here tonight; he had chosen not to attend to spare himself the humiliation. Milton found himself hoping that he had found another meeting. He had had the look of someone who needed one very badly.

Edith spoke again, her words echoed by the others in the room. "God, grant me the serenity to accept the things I cannot change, courage to change the things I can, and wisdom to know the difference."

Milton closed his eyes. There was nothing he could do about Eddie now. There was another meeting tomorrow; perhaps he would see him then. For now, though, he would listen to the shares of the men and women who were here with him, and try to find the meditative peace that always helped him to calm his mind.

"Amen," he intoned.

Chapter Twenty-One

THE POSTMAN was waiting outside the door to Milton's flat as he returned from his run the following morning.

"Special delivery," the man said. "John Smith?"

"That's me," he said, signing the docket and taking the package.

He went into the kitchen, took a knife and sliced through the brown paper. Inside was a cardboard box that contained the two smaller boxes that he had purchased from a private seller on eBay. The first contained what looked like the kind of passive infrared sensor that was fitted to the wall to detect motion for an alarm system. But this wasn't a sensor; instead, it was a disguised camera that could record video or broadcast it via Wi-Fi. He had seen the sensors in the flat next door while the door had been left open and noticed that they were identical to the ones in his flat. The council, who had owned the building until relatively recently, must have fitted the same alarms to all of the properties. Milton took the fake sensor and compared it to the one in his hall. It wasn't identical, but one bland white box was much the same as another, and there was enough of a resemblance that the fake would pass muster unless someone knew to look.

Milton went back to the kitchen and opened the second box. It contained a miniature microphone hidden within the fascia of a functional double wall socket.

Milton took two paperclips. He unfolded them and straightened the first all the way out, apart from a tiny upward kink at the tip. The first clip would be his pick. He removed both bends in the second clip until he had two straight wires with a curve at the end. He pressed the curved end down until he had a ninety degree bend that was about a centimetre long. This clip would be his tension wrench.

He took the camera, microphone, paperclips and a screwdriver, and went out into the vestibule. Ahmed's family had gone out half an hour earlier; Milton had heard the door shut, and had watched through the window to be certain. Both parents were at work and the children were at school. It was unlikely that he would be disturbed.

The door was secured by the same flimsy lock that was fitted to his door. He checked to ensure that he was undisturbed, inserted the wrench into the lock and then applied pressure, turning it in the direction that the lock turned. He inserted the pick into the lock and raked it, applying upwards pressure and setting the pins. There were five of them; he set them all and then carefully turned the handle. The door opened.

Milton went inside and closed the door behind him.

The flat was laid out identically to his, exactly as he had expected. He saw boxes of children's toys, shelves stuffed with children's books, a scrupulously clean and tidy kitchen. But Milton had no interest in looking around; he wanted to be in and out as quickly as possible.

There were motion sensors in each room, but the one in the hallway overlooked the doorways to the sitting room and bedrooms; it was the one that would most likely offer the widest coverage. Milton took his screwdriver and removed the little white box. He switched on the camera. It was activated by sound or motion, and had a battery that would last for a week; Milton would break in again to change it if nothing had happened by the time it was exhausted. He peeled off the adhesive strips on the rear of the fake and placed it carefully where the sensor had been, and then stepped back and checked that it was unobtrusive. It was.

He went into the sitting room. There was a mess of wires behind the television, with two adaptors connecting the various appliances to the mains. Milton disconnected them all and unscrewed the fascia. He took the replacement, wired it back in, and screwed it to the wall. It was an excellent fake, and, especially after he had reconnected the appliances, completely indistinguishable from the socket he had removed. The bug was mains powered and had its own SIM card; it worked just like a mobile phone, but without a screen or keypad.

It had taken Milton five minutes to break in and install the bugs. He checked that he was leaving with everything that he had brought into the flat, opened the door, and left. He went to his own flat, took out his laptop and ensured that he was receiving both sound and vision. He was. Satisfied, he switched the laptop off. He had no interest in spying on the family. He would only activate the bugs when he needed them.

#

THAT NIGHT'S MEETING was at St Mary Abchurch. Milton had had a terrible time finding it on the occasion of his first visit; it was hidden between Lombard Street and Cannon Street, in the middle of London's financial district. Both of those roads were busy thoroughfares, thronged with traffic and workers leaving their offices at the end of busy days, but as he turned south onto Sherborne Lane, the noise became more of a background hum. He felt the usual sense of tranquillity as he put the city behind him. There was a large pub called The Vintry at the end of the lane, and the church was to the left of that. The building was anonymous from this angle, a heavy red brick construction with stone dressings that, together with the office building on the right, provided the broad shoulders through which the narrow alleyway passed. Milton looked up at the four-storey tower, the leaded spire scraping the slate grey skies. A line of motorcycles was parked at the end of the alley, and the wide, studded oak door was open to allow access to the stone lobby and the church beyond.

The teas and coffees were served in the lobby, and smokers congregated outside to enjoy a cigarette before the meeting started. Milton took out his own packet, put one to his mouth and lit it. The secretary came into the lobby and announced that the meeting was about to start. Milton looked at his watch: seven. He finished the cigarette and dropped it to the ground. Rain started to fall, a light drizzle at first, but with the promise of something more. Milton went inside and the door was closed.

They had to pass through the main body of the church to get to the meeting room. It was an impressive sight, much grander than Milton would have expected having seen only the exterior of the building. The ceiling took the form of a large dome pierced by four windows. The interior of the dome was decorated with a painted choir of angels and cherubs surrounding a golden glow in the centre of which was the name of God in Hebrew characters. The church was cool and dark, and echoing acoustics had the effect of reducing conversations to reverent whispers.

The meeting room, on the other hand, was brightly lit and lively, with open three-bar fires providing the warmth. The others had taken their positions. Milton found an empty seat at the back of the room and sat down.

The secretary, a rotund American called Harry whom Milton found a little odd, was behind the table at the front alongside the man who had been asked to share his story.

Harry cleared his throat. "Good evening, everyone. This is the regular meeting of the St Mary Abchurch group of Alcoholics Anonymous. My name is Harry and I am an alcoholic."

"Hello, Harry."

"Thank you for coming on this damp and cold evening. First of all, I have some very sad news. I know some of you have heard already, but Eddie, a good friend of many of us and an occasional visitor to this meeting, passed away yesterday." The words cut through Milton's reverie and he sat up straight. "I don't want to speculate when the details are still unclear, but, from what I understand, he took his own life. It is obviously a terrible, tragic loss that is difficult to understand. Those of us who knew Eddie also knew that he had been struggling with his sobriety lately, but that as recently as the last meeting here, just two days ago, he shared that he felt he was close to a breakthrough. I'll say no more about it now, save that we should take this as a reminder that our disease can strike unpredictably and that it is something we must always be vigilant against. And it is something we should always look for in our fellow alcoholics. If we feel that someone is struggling, then it is our duty to reach out a helping hand. I don't know if Eddie asked for help. He was a private man; I suspect he kept his problems to himself. But I'm sure he would be the first to say that we shouldn't be afraid to ask for a helping hand. Let's just have a moment of quiet to think of him before the Serenity Prayer."

The room fell silent. Milton stared dead ahead, unable to concentrate. His mind was spinning. Dead? He immediately flashed back to the conversation that they had had in the shelter. Eddie had reached out for help. He had reached out to him. Why, then, after they had agreed on a way forward, had he done something as stupid—something as *final*—as this? He reached back, trying to remember the way that he had looked and the words that he had used. Had he been suicidal? Milton didn't think so. He was going to see his sister. He looked frightened, but not resigned. There was a world of difference.

The meeting continued. The share was from a man who said that he worked in the film industry, but Milton didn't hear a word of it. He thought about Eddie and what he had said to him and what could possibly have happened between him leaving the shelter and what had come next.

#

MILTON WOULD normally have left the meeting as soon as it was finished. He had to get to the shelter to relieve Cathy for the night, and it was a reasonable walk from here.

But he waited in the church lobby as the others filed out. Harry was still in the meeting room, tidying away the posters and rolling up the scroll so that it could be slipped back into its cardboard case.

Milton cleared his throat. "Could I have a word?"

Harry looked up. "Hello, John. What's on your mind?"

"It's Eddie."

"Awful," Harry said. "It's horrible."

"You said you didn't know whether he asked for help."

"That's right."

"He did. He came to see me."

"Really?"

"The same night."

"And?"

"And he didn't seem suicidal. I wondered if you knew anything else?"

Harry laid a hand on Milton's arm. "If you stay in these rooms as long as I have, you'll see this again. I know that's no consolation. You know what we say about our disease: it is cunning, baffling and powerful. Eddie wouldn't be the first to hide how he was really feeling, and he won't be the last."

"I'm sure you're right," Milton said quietly, his mind starting to turn over again.

Harry continued, but Milton didn't hear him.

"John," he repeated.

"Sorry."

"You know you'll have to go to the police."

"What?" Milton said vaguely.

"The police. Eddie came to see you. You'll have to tell them about what Eddie said to you."

Milton hadn't thought of that. "Yes," he said. "You're right."

"They'll have questions for you."

"Do you know where he was found?"

"In his taxi. He'd driven out into the countryside. I think it was near Oxford. Littleton? Littleworth? I can't remember."

"Do you know how?"

"They're saying he gassed himself in his car."

They continued for a moment or two longer, the usual platitudes that Milton was able to recite without really concentrating on what was being said.

"I better be going," he said at last.

"You mustn't blame yourself. It's not your fault."

Milton thanked him, but he wasn't sure whether he agreed with him.

#

IT WAS A FORTY-MINUTE walk from the Bank of England to Russell Square. The rain was coming down more heavily now, and Milton would usually have taken a bus or the tube to Oxford Circus. He waited at the entrance to the underground for a moment, watching the men and women waiting patiently to file down the stairs into the steamy interior, and decided against it. He wanted to clear his head, and it would be easier to do that with a little exercise.

He set off to the east, passing St Paul's Cathedral and following Newgate Street until it ran into Holborn. The traffic passed by, headlights reaching out into the gloom, red taillights refracting against the wet asphalt. The rain fell more heavily now, soaking his hair and running down into his eyes and mouth. He wiped it away, pulled up his collar and kept going.

He couldn't stop thinking about Eddie. The more he thought about it, the less he could accept that he had killed himself. It was true what Harry had said: alcoholism was a cunning disease, and alcoholics made for skilful dissemblers. But Milton was a good judge of character. He had been in situations where he had needed to read people, often instantly, and he always backed his intuition. Nothing about their meeting had given him anything to think that the man might not have been truthful with him or that he was hiding his real feelings. The idea that he had killed himself just felt wrong.

He turned onto Southampton Row and headed north. It was another half a mile and, by the time he reached the shelter, he was wet through. There were a couple of cabs parked outside and a third just pulling away. The driver, an Arsenal fan called Bob, sounded the horn as he saw Milton jog across the road and Milton raised his hand in greeting. He opened the door and stepped inside. Two cabbies were sitting on either side of the shelter, both of them working through bacon sandwiches and mugs of tea. The stove was lit and pumping heat around the small room. It was warm, almost stifling, and Milton was glad of it as he took off his coat and hung it on one of the hooks.

"Look at the state of you," Cathy said. "You're soaked through."

"I'll dry soon enough," he said.

She gave him a dishcloth and he used it to scrub his scalp until his hair was dry.

"Are you all right, love?"

"I'm fine," he said.

"You look preoccupied."

"There's a driver comes in here," he said. "His name's Eddie. Do you know him?"

"I can think of a couple," she said.

One of the other men looked up. "You mean Eddie Fabian?"

"I don't know his second name."

"The bloke who topped himself?"

"Yes," Milton replied. "Do you know him?"

"Well enough to pass the time of day with. He was a quiet bloke most of the time. Kept himself to himself. Terrible what happened, though."

"What did you hear?"

"I was speaking to a couple of the other blokes this afternoon. They said they found him in his cab out in the countryside. Parked up, put a hose on his exhaust and gassed himself. Bloody awful."

Milton went through into the kitchen. There was barely enough space for him and Cathy.

"Did you know him?" she asked quietly.

"Not really," Milton said. He wasn't about to tell her about AA. She seemed as if she was a broad-minded woman, but you never really knew, and Milton did not want to risk losing his job so soon after he had started it. AA was anonymous. And there was a duty of confidence, too. It was not his place to tell anyone else about Eddie's problems.

"I've got to get going, love," she said. "Off to the pictures tonight. It's our anniversary. The old man will kill me if I'm late."

He waited until she had left and then brought the cabbie who knew Eddie another cup of tea.

"Do you know where they found the cab?" Milton asked him.

"If you said the name, I might," the man said, screwing up his face as he tried to recall it. "It was on the news."

"Littleworth?"

"Could be that. Rings a bell."

Milton thanked him.

The shelter emptied out as the night went on, and Milton found that he had a little time to himself. He took out his phone, plugged it in to charge, and opened the map application. He entered Littleworth into the search bar and watched as the screen scrolled to the left until the sprawl of Oxford filled most of the screen. The location marker was planted between the villages of Horspath and Wheatley, the terrain around Littleworth marked out as farmland and the village itself not much more than a collection of houses gathered around a tangle of streets. There was nothing there that looked remarkable, no reason apparent why Eddie would have chosen it as the location to kill himself save that his sister lived there.

That was worth investigating, Milton thought. The sister. What did she know?

He would finish his shift, get a little sleep, and then pay her a visit.

Chapter Twenty-Two

MILTON HAD bought a car a few weeks earlier. It was an old Volkswagen Polo that he had found on AutoTrader.com. It was ten years old with ninety thousand miles on the clock and he had paid five hundred pounds for it. It was scruffy and scuffed, there was a dent in the driver's door and the windscreen bore a crack that meant it would fail its next MOT, but Milton was happy enough with it. It was reasonably clean and the engine was in decent condition. Milton wasn't an extravagant man, and, even if he had more money, he would not have been tempted to exchange it for something flashy. No-one was going to notice the car, and anonymity was important to him. Ostentation went against habits that had been ingrained over the course of the last fifteen years.

It was fifty miles from London to Littleworth. Milton followed the M40 north-west, driving under the cowl of a slate grey sky that promised more rain. He passed Beaconsfield and High Wycombe, his phone directing him to Wheatley services. He turned off and followed London Road as it tracked the motorway, passing through Wheatley until he reached the turning for Old Road. It was a narrow one-lane road, little more than a track. There was a collection of farm buildings just before the turning, and Milton had to slow to let a large tractor exit. He drove west, passing a large pink house hemmed in by a high hedge, and kept going. The landscape quickly became bleak and exposed. A telegraph wire ran along the left of the road and pools of standing water had gathered from the recent storms. He passed under the wires suspended between tall electricity pylons and continued on. The fields to his left were planted with rape. The view to the right was obscured by a hawthorn hedge.

Eventually, he came to another house. He slowed and stopped, took out his phone, and looked again at the photograph on the local BBC News report for the suicide. He was in the right place. He was almost at the end of the lane, so he continued on until he reached the junction with the Oxford bypass to make sure that there was nothing else that might be of interest. He did not find anything, so he turned the car and drove back to the turning. He stopped twenty feet away, pulled to the side and got out of the car. Rain started to fall almost at once. He drew his coat around him and approached the house.

It was unremarkable. A short drive led from the lane for six feet until it terminated in a cast-iron gate. The pillars were surmounted by decorative lions, and beyond the gate was a parking area and then the house itself. Milton took out his phone once more, wiped the rain from the screen and looked at the photograph again. The taxi had been parked off the road, inside the property, the gates open.

Milton put the phone away and looked around. It was quiet and still, with almost no noise save for the rain drumming on the roof of the parked car and the mournful cawing of a crow as it flapped overhead.

The gates were closed now. An intercom was set into the right-hand pillar. Milton pressed the button to speak. He heard the buzz as the intercom announced his presence to the house, but there was no response. He waited for a moment and then pressed the button again. Still nothing.

Milton stepped into the middle of the drive and peered through the gates. The house was a large bungalow, constructed with two wings that sprouted from a central hub. The curtains had not been drawn, but Milton could see no signs of occupation. He pushed the gates, but they were sturdy and did not give. He looked up: the gate was six feet high, and he could have scaled it easily, and probably without being seen, but he didn't think that he would find anything of interest. The house looked empty; most likely it was.

He wanted to speak to Eddie's sister, but it wouldn't be today.

He drew his coat around him and hurried through the rain back to his car.

#

THAMES VALLEY POLICE had responsibility for Littleworth. They were based in Oxford, just seven miles to the west. Milton followed the bypass and arrived at the constabulary headquarters thirty minutes later. The building was on St Aldate's, opposite the Crown Court, and Milton parked his car in the car park. It was a beautiful Georgian building made from warm limestone, three storeys tall and with plentiful wide, generous windows. Milton went to the entrance and made his way inside.

"Hello, sir," said the clerk behind the desk.

"There was a death," he said. "At Littleworth. A cabbie killed himself in his car."

The woman nodded her recognition. "That's right. How can I help you, love?"

"I've got some information that might be useful. I was hoping I could speak to the investigating officer."

"Let me see who's dealing with that." The woman turned to her computer and brought up the information she needed. "You need Detective Inspector Bruce. Let me see if he's around. What's your name?"

"Smith."

"Take a seat, love."

There was a row of plastic chairs lined up against the wall, and Milton did as he was told. He watched the woman speaking on the telephone and noticed her eyes as they glanced up from the screen to take him in. He looked away. He wasn't fond of police stations. They had the same smell the world over: disinfectant and sweat. The walls were painted green, the same shade that you always seemed to find in municipal buildings, and a cork board had been festooned with leaflets on crime prevention and posters of men and women wanted for questioning. There were two other people waiting. One, an older man, was anxiously massaging his hands. The other, a woman—the man's wife, perhaps—was staring at the posters on the wall with an expression of quiet anger fixed to her face.

Milton looked at his watch. Ten minutes had passed. He could have telephoned, but he knew that he would be able to derive more information on the investigation if he spoke to the officer responsible for it in person.

A young boy was led into the waiting area by a uniformed officer. The man and woman stood. The man looked relieved. The woman went over to the boy, who couldn't have been much older than twelve, and grabbed him around the bicep.

"Ow," he complained, "that hurts."

"We haven't even started yet," she said in a voice that was loud enough for Milton, the officer and the receptionist to hear.

The woman hauled the boy to the exit. The man apologised, thanked the officer, and followed in his wife's wake.

"Mr. Smith?"

Milton looked up. The man who had addressed him was older, mid-fifties, and wearing a cheap suit that had started to shine a little at the shoulders, elbows and knees. His face was wrinkled, his teeth had been yellowed by nicotine, and his hair, or what was left of it, had been swept across his balding scalp.

"Sir? I'm Detective Inspector Bruce."

Milton stood. "Hello, Detective Inspector. Thanks for seeing me."

"You have information on the suicide out at Littleworth?"

"I might. Maybe."

"Well, we can certainly have a chat about it. Would you come this way, please?"

Bruce led Milton along a corridor. There were two doors on either side; Milton guessed that they were interview rooms. Bruce tried one, saw that it was occupied and apologised to the people inside, tried a second and held the door open so that Milton could go through. It was a small room with a table and four chairs. The table was too small for all of the chairs to fit around it, so two of them were angled toward it; Bruce folded them up and put them to one side. There was a digital recorder on the table. The single window, which was large, was covered by a plastic blind that absorbed the dull sunlight from outside.

"Take a seat, please, Mr. Smith."

Milton sat in the seat farthest from the door with his back to the wall. He liked to be able to see all of the room. It was force of habit; he didn't even realise that he had done it.

Bruce sat down in the other chair and smiled at Milton. The policeman's face was marked by a scattering of old acne scars from his youth, and his eyes glittered with a shrewdness that put Milton on edge.

"Are you the investigating officer?"

"I am."

"CID are handling it?"

"That's right. Why is that surprising?"

"Is there anything suspicious about it?"

Bruce shook his head. "No, Mr. Smith, not really."

"And you're a detective inspector?"

"Yes. What's your point?"

"I've never heard of a D.I. being put on a suicide."

"Are you an expert on police matters, Mr Smith?"

"Wouldn't it normally be a detective constable?"

Bruce noticed that Milton was the one who was asking questions and shook his head, moving the conversation back in his direction. "Look, I can't say too much, Mr. Smith. The investigation is still ongoing."

"But?"

"Why don't you tell me what you came here to say?"

Milton nodded. "It's Eddie Fabian, isn't it? The dead man?"

"Yes, sir. Did you know him?"

"A little."

"Can I ask how?"

Milton paused. He was reluctant to say, but he knew that he would have to, eventually. "We both have—had—a problem with alcohol. I met him at an Alcoholics Anonymous meeting that I go to."

"I see. Did you know him well?"

"Not very. But I did see him on the evening he died. I think it's possible that I might have been one of the last people to see him alive."

"Where was this?"

Milton explained about the shelter and how Eddie had come in search of a conversation.

"And how was he?"

"Agitated. Something was on his mind."

"Did he say what it was?"

Milton would never have shared the contents of their conversation if Eddie had still been alive, but, now that he wasn't, it was better that he speak up. Milton related the story that Eddie had told him. He told him about the abuse and how he had come face to face with one of the men who had abused him. He said that Eddie had decided to speak to a journalist in an attempt to bring his abuser to justice, and that a man had broken into his house and warned him against it. Milton explained that he had agreed to meet him the following morning to help him go through with it. "And he never showed up," he finished. "I found out what happened to him afterwards. That's why I'm here."

"And you say he was attacked?"

"That's what he told me."

"Any idea who it was?"

"He didn't say."

Bruce took notes. "And he didn't speak to the police about it?"

"No. He said he'd never had much luck with the police."

"So?"

"He said he was going to go and stay with his sister. That's her house, isn't it? The place he was found?"

"Yes. But she wasn't there last night."

"So why would he come out here if she wasn't here?"

"I don't know. Maybe he had a key." Bruce looked at his notebook. "What time did you see him?"

"A little after midnight," Milton said. "When did you find him?"

"We were notified in the morning. I was there just after six. The local farmer found him. He saw Mr. Fabian's cab with the engine running. He saw the hose. He looked inside, saw Mr. Fabian, and called us. I went down with my duty sergeant."

"And you're happy it wasn't suspicious?"

The detective looked at him curiously. "Why would you say that, Mr. Smith?"

"I find it quite difficult to believe that he would have killed himself. I don't think he was suicidal when he left me."

"You said yourself that you didn't know him that well."

"Not particularly."

"Then I'm afraid I would say, with respect, that that's not an assessment that you're qualified to make. I've seen more than my fair share of suicides. Sometimes, you ask around and people aren't surprised. The person's been depressed. Something has happened to them that gives them a reason to do away with themselves. They've lost their job, their wife has left them, or their husband has shacked up with someone else. Normal things. Other times—and it's more often than you might think—it comes completely out of the blue. Maybe this is one of those times."

Milton let that go. Bruce was right. It *was* sometimes difficult to tell. Milton had seen suicides before, too. A soldier he had been friendly with had topped himself after it had become apparent that he was not going to pass selection for the SAS. Rather than return to his own regiment, he had taken himself off into the woods outside Hereford, tossed a rope over the low-hanging branch of an old oak, and strung himself up. There had been others, too, that Milton had made to look like suicides. He had sometimes stayed in situ long enough to watch the aftermath, to make sure that nothing was amiss, and he had seen the reactions of friends and relatives. Some were shocked. Others were resigned, as if the death had been expected.

But Eddie was different. There was something about his death that Milton couldn't square.

"You said it yourself. He was dealing with a difficult situation. He said he had been abused. Maybe that was why he had to drink. Maybe he couldn't handle it any more."

"Did you take photographs of the scene?"

"We did."

"Can I—"

"No. And there's nothing to see, really. There was nothing suspicious there at all."

"Just a quick look?"

Bruce shook his head firmly. "No, Mr. Smith. That's not appropriate." He stopped, regarding him for a moment. "What did you say you did again?"

"I didn't say. I'm a cook."

"I think, Mr. Smith, that it would be better if you stuck to cooking and left this to the police. If there was anything out of the ordinary, we would have seen it. Really."

Bruce closed his notebook and pushed his chair away from the table.

"Hold on a minute," Milton said.

"Mr Smith?"

"Are you going to look into what he told me?"

"About the man he said he had in his cab? Did he tell you his name?"

"Leo Isaacs."

"I can ask around."

"Ask his family."

"Yes," he said. "I will do that. But don't expect anything to come out of it. I spoke to them yesterday. None of them mentioned anything like that."

Bruce stood, but Milton stayed where he was. He thought of the Maserati and the Range Rover with the blacked-out windows. He had memorised the registration details of the second car. Milton could give that to Bruce, but what would he say? That he'd seen two vehicles pull out and follow Eddie's cab? It might have been late, but it was Russell Square. It was a busy area. There was nothing unusual about any of it. Were they even following? Most people wouldn't have given it a second thought, but then, he reminded himself, most people did not have his training or his instincts. He knew that there was something odd about what he had seen, but he knew, too, that he wouldn't be able to persuade Bruce. It would be better if he looked into it himself.

Milton stood, too. "You're right," he said. "If there's anything I can help you with, just let me know."

Bruce collected his notebook and opened it again. "Do you have a number I could contact you on?"

Milton recited his phone number and Bruce wrote it down. He closed the notebook again, slipped it into the inside pocket of his jacket and led the way back outside.

The waiting area was empty.

"Thanks for coming in, Mr. Smith."

"Not a problem."

"Did you come up from London?"

"I did. I thought it would be better than calling you."

"Well, I appreciate it. It's an awful situation. It's good of you to put yourself to the trouble."

"Do you know when the funeral is?"

"There'll be a forensic post mortem to determine the cause of death, and then his body will be released to the family. It'll probably be three or four days."

Bruce put out his hand and Milton took it. Milton knew, without question, what would happen now. Eddie's death would be classed as a suicide. There would be no follow-up work and no investigation. Milton, by coming here, had inadvertently made that more likely. He had given Eddie a motive to do what he had done. Would Bruce even ask Eddie's family about what Eddie had told Milton? Probably not. Bruce wouldn't want to upset them.

No.

This was a straightforward case of someone who was clearly upset with life—upset enough to have a problem with drink—deciding enough was enough and topping himself.

It would be case closed as far as the police were concerned.

Milton wasn't ready to accept that conclusion just yet. There was digging to be done.

Chapter Twenty-Three

MILTON DROVE BACK TO LONDON. He worked as usual that night and the nights that followed, asking the drivers who came into the shelter whether they knew the details of Eddie's funeral. Milton quickly got the impression that he had not been a particularly well-known driver, for none of the men he asked were familiar with him. He persevered, though, and, as the clock ticked over to three in the morning on the fourth subsequent night, he finally got a lead. A driver who usually came in for a cup of tea and a bacon sandwich said that he knew Eddie and that his family was based near Withington in the Cotswolds.

"You know about the Fabians?" the man asked.

"Not a thing."

The man chuckled. "Not the sort of people you'd want to get on the wrong side of."

"What do you mean?"

"They ain't straight, John. They get up to all sorts."

"Criminals?"

"They used to run the underworld. This was years ago, right after the war. They moved out when the Eastern Europeans and the Turks started throwing their weight around. They took all their money and went out to where they are now. The family has a place there. Big old country house, loads of land. The old man, Eddie's dad, he's still a serious player. You want to take some of the rumours with a pinch of salt, but I've heard all sorts of things about him over the years. They say he bankrolls big jobs. Puts teams together. There was gossip that he was involved in the Brinks job. Others, too. Like I say, serious."

"I had no idea," Milton said.

"There was one situation—I'm guessing this is ten years ago now—the police had him under surveillance. They had a man in the grounds outside his house. Fabian shot him. He went to trial and said it was self-defence. He got off, too."

"I didn't know," Milton admitted.

"Knew Eddie well, did you?"

Milton shrugged. "Not really. I thought he was a nice guy. I'd like to pay my respects, though. Do you know anything about the funeral?"

"No," the man said. "You'll have to ask around."

#

THE SHIFT was straightforward, and Milton was home in good time. He awoke at eleven, got out of bed, changed into his running gear, and went out for a five-mile jog. He returned to the flat, showered and dressed in clean clothes, and then took out the old MacBook he had picked up for next to nothing on eBay. It took an age to boot up, so he made himself a cup of tea and a slice of toast while he waited. He took his phone, opened Spotify, connected it to his Bluetooth speaker and then selected the playlist where he had stacked his favourite tunes from the Manchester musicians he preferred. He skipped through to Morrissey's "Everyday is like Sunday" and went back to the computer.

It didn't take him very long to find the information that he wanted. Kent Online had an announcements section, and it only took a little browsing to find the notice.

Edward Alan "Eddie" Fabian—much loved by all his family and friends. xXx

The announcement continued with the date and location of the funeral service, a request for no flowers, and the details of the undertaker. He checked the date, and then double-checked it.

The funeral was today.

He hurried through into his bedroom and opened the door to the wardrobe and his rather meagre collection of clothes. He had one suit, an old second-hand two-piece that he had bought in a charity shop for thirty pounds. He quickly ironed his only white shirt, polished his shoes, and dressed. He looked in the mirror. Not so long ago, his suit would have been bespoke from one of the finest tailors in London and presented to him with very little change from two thousand pounds. It was amusing to him how his situation had altered since he had stopped working for the government. It did not concern him—he had never judged himself by how wealthy he was, and those clothes had been no more than disguises to enable him to draw closer to his prey—and as he regarded himself he thought that he would just about pass muster. It would do.

#

THE FUNERAL was being held at St Michael and All Angels at Withington. The Cotswolds were ninety miles away. Milton got into his car and drove out of London, headed to the north-west. It was a straight run on the M40, passing through High Wycombe and Stokenchurch. The traffic was heavy, and there were several spots where they crawled at twenty or thirty miles an hour as first an accident and then road works blocked the way ahead. He thought that he was going to be too late, but the traffic cleared as he turned onto the A40 outside Oxford, and he was able to make good time. The rain fell heavily, a slick that seemed to perpetually blur his view out of the windscreen, but as he drove deeper into the Cotswolds it seemed to lighten a little and he was able to look out and appreciate the landscape around him. The area was famous for the golden-coloured stone that was quarried here and used to build the picture-perfect villages and the dry stone walling that demarked the rolling grass fields. It was beautiful.

He passed through Compton Abdale, following the single-lane road until he reached Withington. The landscape of the village and the seat of most of its settlement was a broad valley running from north to south. The village straddled either side of the River Coln, with an attractive pub residing on the east bank and climbing terrain on the west bank that led up to a knot of trees.

Milton drove through it until he reached the church. St Michaels was a large and imposing Norman building with a nave, chancel and tower. The original design had been enlarged with a south porch, a south transept chapel and a large clerestory. A school was adjacent to the church, and its playground had been opened up so that mourners could park their cars there. Milton turned off the road and found a space and then, with a glance at his watch, stepped out and jogged across the puddled road. There was an unpaved turning that ran around the boundary of the graveyard, and a glistening hearse was waiting there, a coffin being attended to through the opened back door. There were black BMWs and Mercedes there, too, the chief mourners waiting inside the vehicles.

He was just in time.

Other people were gathered at the porch, some sheltering beneath umbrellas, all of them aiming wary glances at the glowering sky as they waited to file inside. Milton joined the back of the queue. A boom of thunder rumbled overhead as he stepped through the doors.

Chapter Twenty-Four

THE CHURCH was full. Milton was only able to find a space on the end of a pew at the back next to a family with two young children who were evidently going to struggle to sit still for the duration of the service. There was an order of ceremony on the seat with a picture of Eddie on the front cover. He flipped through it, noting the hymns and that Eddie's brothers would be making speeches. His father would be delivering the reading.

He looked around. All the light came from the clerestory windows; the original Norman window openings were blocked up, which made the interior feel rather gloomy. To the west of the south door, through which he had entered, there was a curtained area. There were memorials and monuments on the walls, a font that looked several hundred years old, and a simple wooden pulpit that stood in contrast to the ornate decoration.

"Blackbird" by the Beatles started to play. The people near the south door stood, everyone else following their example. The chief mourners came first: a woman in an expensive black dress, a handkerchief clutched in her hand. There was a man with jet black hair and a craggy face striated by deep wrinkles that made him look older than Milton suspected he was. Two younger women came next, one barely more than a girl and the other in her twenties, both wearing similarly expensive black dresses. The coffin came into the church, borne on the shoulders of six solemn-faced pallbearers. The two men at the front were obviously related to each other. Two older men followed, one of them particularly large and powerful. The men at the back were younger, one of them still in his teens. They brought the coffin to the central aisle and then proceeded to the front of the church, where they carefully laid it to rest on the catafalque.

The vicar, a plump and homely-looking woman, took her place in the pulpit.

"For I am convinced that neither death nor life, neither angels nor demons, neither the present nor the future, nor any powers, neither height nor depth, nor anything else in all creation, will be able to separate us from the love of God that is in Christ Jesus our Lord," she intoned as the congregation settled in.

Milton had been around death all his life, but had only been to two funerals. His parents', after the car crash that had killed them, and a Regiment service in Hereford after one of the men who had undertaken Selection with him had died during the forced march on the Brecon Beacons.

"Death is not an easy thing to accept," the vicar continued. "Nature has its seasons, but death can come to anyone, at any time, in any place. Truly we know not what a day may bring forth."

Milton shuffled a little uncomfortably. It felt as if she was speaking to him.

The two men from the front of the coffin stood next, each of them telling a story about Eddie. They were his brothers, introduced by the vicar as Spencer and Marcus. They bore no resemblance to Eddie, and Milton remembered that Eddie had told him that he had been adopted. The two spoke with an East London accent, and they were eloquent and generous, recounting their memories of their adopted brother. The woman at the front sobbed loudly as Spencer told the story of when Eddie had fallen from the boughs of one of the big oaks in the grounds of the estate, refusing to go to hospital so he didn't miss a long-scheduled trip to watch Chelsea at Stamford Bridge. Marcus took Eddie's green and yellow Hackney carriage licence badge and laid it next to the coffin. His story was how Eddie had declined the offer of a position in the family business, choosing instead to be a taxi driver. There were some knowing laughs at Eddie's stubbornness. Looks were exchanged, too, and Milton could see that they were because of the unsaid nature of what the "family business" was. It was obvious that most people in the church knew, and from the reaction to the comment he guessed that, whatever it was, it wasn't legitimate. He remembered what the cabbie had told him in the shelter.

Finally, the vicar called upon Francis Fabian to say a few words about his adopted son. The man with the black hair and the craggy face stepped up and spoke movingly of how they had come to adopt Eddie and how they had always treated him as if he was their own. The woman, who Milton guessed was his wife, sobbed again as he recounted Eddie's introduction to the family. He spoke of the boy's difficult start to life, going no further than that. He spoke eloquently, just as his sons had before him, but there was an edge to his words that was impossible to mistake. Milton was an excellent judge of people, and his initial impressions of Frankie Fabian were clear: he was a hard man, intelligent, and not to be underestimated. He would remember that.

The vicar finished the service with a psalm and then a short reading from the Bible, and then led the congregation in a prayer. She commended Eddie to God's love and mercy.

The children next to Milton had been well behaved throughout the service, but now, as the pallbearers readied themselves to take the coffin once again, they started to fidget impatiently. The child immediately adjacent to Milton, a young boy of five or six, started to kick his feet against the pew in front of them. The mother, fraught with irritation, told him sternly to stop. Milton looked over at her and gave her what he hoped was an understanding smile.

The coffin went by, followed by the mourners, umbrellas unfurling as they stepped out into the rain again.

#

EDDIE'S COFFIN was loaded back into the hearse and driven away to the crematorium. The chief mourners got into their cars and followed the procession. The others gathered around outside, cowering beneath umbrellas and inside the shelter of the porch. The vicar was sharing consoling words with the mourners, and Milton nodded solemnly to her. He glanced around and saw, to his surprise, the detective inspector whom he had met at the station yesterday. He remembered the man's name: Bruce. The policeman saw Milton, too, and made his way over to him.

"Mr. Smith."

"Detective Inspector Bruce," Milton said. "I'm surprised to see you here."

"I thought it was the right thing to do."

Milton gave a discreet nod in the direction of the women in the black dresses who were waiting to get into their cars so that they could follow the hearse. "Eddie's mother?"

"That's right."

"And his sisters?"

"That's right."

Milton thought of what Bruce had told him yesterday, that the sister had been away from home when Eddie killed himself in her driveway. "What was the name of the sister Eddie went to see?"

"It's Lauren, Mr. Smith."

"Have you spoken to her yet?"

The man bristled. "I told you, I can't talk to you about the investigation."

"So there is one? An investigation?"

Bruce smiled indulgently. "It was good to see you again, Mr. Smith."

The policeman walked away. Milton crossed the gravel path to a spot beneath the boughs of a broad alder that offered some respite from the rain, and took out his cigarettes. He was observing the mourners when his attention was drawn to a large car that had parked at the corner of the unpaved track and the road that ran through the centre of the village.

It was a Range Rover, new, a splatter of mud across the

wing. Expensive. Darkened privacy windows.

Milton stubbed out his cigarette against the edge of a gravestone, dropped it into a rubbish bin, and made his way to the fringe of beech trees that marked the edge of the graveyard. He passed through the open gate and by the parish noticeboard, making no show of looking at the vehicle, just ambling along and pretending to look at something distracting on his phone. He opened the camera application, switched to video and set it to record. There was a row of cars parked nose first between him and the Range Rover: a red Audi, a blue VW Golf, a grey Mini Clubman. He aimed the phone down low, using the parked cars as cover so that he could approach as discreetly as possible. He walked by the Range Rover, filmed the registration details, and then walked up to the driver's door. He rapped his knuckle on the window.

The glass slid down.

"What?"

There were two men inside. The driver was of medium build, with short hair and stubble across his cheeks and chin. The passenger had longer hair and a distinctive scar across his forehead. The driver was wearing a black bomber jacket and the passenger a faded denim jacket.

"Sorry for bothering you," Milton said.

The driver shuffled around so that he could look right out of the window. "What do you want?"

"Smile for the camera, please."

Milton brought the phone up and aimed it into the car.

The driver frowned as Milton filmed him. He should have been angry, or at least surprised, but, instead, he bore an expression that mixed confusion and wariness. The passenger was angry, already reaching down to release his seat belt. Milton made his way to the front of the car. He aimed the camera so that he could be sure that he had recorded the registration plate, and then kept filming as he stepped back onto the pavement. The passenger stepped out, and Milton aimed the phone and took a few seconds' worth of footage of him. The man started forward and then, turning to look at the crowd of mourners—some of whom were looking their way—he stopped. Milton walked back to the cemetery, rejoining the clutch of people who were waiting for the family to leave the church. He didn't feel particularly threatened. There were too many people here for them to try anything foolish.

He heard the grumble of a powerful engine and, as he turned back, the Range Rover jerked forward into the empty road and accelerated away. The driver's window was open and the man turned to him as the car went by. Milton didn't get a very good look at him, but he felt a flicker of something—unease? surprise? recognition?—before the vehicle raced by him and disappeared around the corner.

Chapter Twenty-Five

MILTON FOLLOWED the procession of cars as the mourners transferred to the Fabian estate for the wake. Halewell Close was to the north of the village, along a narrow lane that doubled back after a sharp right-hand turn. Milton drove over a cattle grid, the Volkswagen's suspension juddering ominously, passing onto a private driveway that was demarked by two stone pillars that were topped by impressive electric lanterns. An engraving on one of the pillars revealed the name of the property beyond. The drive was long, perhaps a mile, and marked by regularly spaced yew trees on the right and left. Milton bore right around a shallow turn and the headlights cast out into the gloom across a wide lake, the water sparkling. The road swung back around to the left and the rough tarmac surface was replaced with gravel. It opened out as it approached a hill and then, as he crested the brow, the house below was revealed.

The building was old and had clearly been rebuilt and added to over the years. It was set into its own private valley, amongst a sprawling beech wood, and was huge. It was built from stone, with parts that were two storeys tall and others that were three. Milton took it in: he picked out the three granges, set into the shape of a U, the steep slate roofs and the stone walls the colour of mustard. The granges surrounded a courtyard. The west grange was the largest, comprising four bays; the other granges looked as if they had been added over the years. Lights blazed in leaded windows all the way across the house, casting a lattice of gold across the wide lawns. A new addition, with broad glass windows, was topped with thatch. A row of converted stables was on the far side of a wide parking area, and at the end of the lawn were a swimming pool and summer house.

The place was impressive.

Milton drove across a small bridge that spanned a stream. Wrought-iron lamp posts were set on either side of the final length of the drive, ready to cast their light across neatly terraced private gardens and the southern shore of the lake; there was a boathouse built next to a wooden jetty beside which a tethered rowing boat bobbed on the gentle swells.

Milton parked his battered old car in an empty space next to the stable block and got out. He lit a cigarette and observed the building in more detail. He saw an array of CCTV cameras, enough to offer a view of most of the property. He had noticed others along the drive, too. The gates were substantial, and Milton had noticed that he had driven over two pressure sensors once he had passed into the grounds of the house. Security was clearly something that Frankie Fabian took very seriously.

Milton dropped the cigarette and ground it beneath the toe of his shoe. Two carloads of mourners were headed toward the house, and Milton tagged on at the back.

#

TEA AND COFFEE were being served in the drawing room. Milton looked around, impressed once again at his surroundings. The place was grand, yet, as Milton looked a little closer, he could see that it was in need of maintenance. Skirting boards were loose, paint was in need of refreshing, woodwork needed polishing, and a couple of the sash windows were jammed open and closed off with plastic sheeting. In better times it would have been as impressive as the little châteaux that he had visited while he was surveiling a Saudi arms dealer in the south of France. But those days, Milton saw, were gone.

Milton took a coffee and a biscuit to the edge of the room and watched the other mourners. Small groups formed and he caught fragments of their conversation. Six middle-aged women shook their heads at the tragic waste of life and expressed sympathy for the family, particularly Eddie's mother, who, it was said, was taking things very hard. A group of hard-looking men, ill-suited to the delicate china coffee cups from which they were drinking, expressed similar sentiments, shaking their heads as they wondered at the surprise that they had felt when they heard the news.

Milton went in search of the bathroom, taking the opportunity to scout out the rest of the downstairs. There was a long corridor and from it were open doors that led to the dining room, a room that looked like a study or a library and a new kitchen that had been added to the existing property as an extension. He found the bathroom and then went back to the refreshments table for another coffee, taking a moment to look around the room. He searched for Eddie's sister, Lauren, and, after a moment, he found her. She was not a very attractive woman, with a masculine face that borrowed a little too liberally from her father at the expense of the softer lines of her mother. She was talking to a group of women, their laughter a little too easy for the occasion. Milton did not form the best impression of her.

#

MILTON WENT OUTSIDE and crossed to the opening of the large tent that had been pitched on the lawn. It had been set aside for smokers, although he was the only one there. He took out his packet of cigarettes and his lighter. One of the women from the drawing room followed him. She paused in the porch, glanced up with grim consternation at the sky and then hurried across to the tent.

Milton tapped a cigarette out of the packet when she walked over to him.

"Could I grab one of those?"

"Sure," he said, giving her the one that he had taken out and taking out a second.

She put it to her lips. He thumbed flame from the lighter

and she leaned in so that he could light it. He caught the smell of her perfume: something that reminded him of citrus.

Milton lit his own cigarette and inhaled. The rain came down harder, pattering against the canvas and leaving a fine spray as it rebounded against the ground.

"Great weather."

"Isn't it."

"Seems right for a funeral."

"Yes." He looked at her. He guessed that she was in her early thirties. She was wearing a simple black dress and he noticed that a silver crucifix shone against her pale skin. He recognised her immediately. She had been at Piccadilly Circus on the morning that he had arranged to meet Eddie.

"I'm Olivia," she said. "Olivia Dewey."

Milton pretended that he didn't recognise her. "John Smith."

"Did you know Eddie?" she asked him.

Milton shrugged. "A little. You?"

"Same. A little. Awful, isn't it?"

Milton nodded and drew on his cigarette. He had the feeling that he was being appraised.

She waved her arm in a gesture that encompassed the big house and the grounds. "This place is impressive."

"It is."

"Do you know the family history?"

"Only what I've heard. Not much."

"This house goes back years, obviously. It was bought by the Costello family originally. They were a big criminal family, but this is sixty years ago. They were into everything: protection rackets, they ran racing before the war, prostitution—you name it, they were into it. You can get a different story about what happened next depending on who you ask, but the story I heard is that the family was taken over by this guy no one had ever heard of before. He just came out of nowhere. His name was Edward Fabian, too—Eddie's grandfather by adoption. He ran the London underworld for years; then he handed the business down to his son, Frankie. You know him?"

"Gave the reading at the funeral."

Olivia nodded across the garden. Frankie Fabian was standing in the shelter of the boathouse that was down the sloped lawn at the edge of the lake. His black suit was impeccable and the whiteness of the shirt almost glowed beneath it. He had stepped outside to make a phone call.

"The apple didn't fall far from the tree with Frankie. They say he's a genius. From what I've heard, he's been involved in all the big heists of the last twenty years. Brinks Mat, the Knightsbridge Security Deposit job, all the big ones. The police have never been able to get close to him. He's very careful, stays well away from the action, but he's not someone that I'd want to get on the wrong side of. They say he's ruthless, too, the people I spoke to. They say he'll do anything to protect his family."

"But he couldn't help Eddie."

"You know Eddie was adopted?"

"I do." He finished his cigarette, saw that she had finished hers, too, and offered her another. She took it. "How do you know so much?" he asked.

She dipped her head again to light the new cigarette. "I've taken a professional interest in the family."

"What does that mean?" Milton asked. "You're police?"

She laughed. "Hardly."

"What then?"

"Journalist."

Milton pretended to be surprised.

"I recognised you straight away at the funeral," she said. "Eddie was supposed to meet me at Piccadilly Circus the morning after he died. You were there too. I saw you. Waiting for him. I've got a great memory for faces."

"I was," Milton said, feigning surprise.

She looked him right in the eye and then spoke with certainty. "I don't think he killed himself, Mr. Smith."

Milton didn't reply, and he tried not to react. He wanted

to assess her more carefully before he voiced anything about his own suspicions.

She was watching him shrewdly. "Can I ask you a question?"

"Of course."

"What happened outside the church? The men in the Range Rover—why did you go over to them?"

"They were parked in front of my car. I wanted them to move out of the way."

She looked disappointed. "Come on, John. Don't give me that. I'm not an idiot. Who were they?"

"I have no idea. I was just asking them to move."

She finished the second cigarette, dropped it onto the gravel and ground it underfoot.

"Nice to have met you," Milton said.

He started to head back to the house but she reached over and took his arm. "What are you doing now?"

"I was about to go."

"Can I buy you a coffee? I'd like to have a talk with you."

Chapter Twenty-Six

OLIVIA DEWEY drove an old and slightly battered Audi TT. Milton let her pull out of the row of cars that had been parked on the lawn and followed her down the long drive, over the hill and then through the wood to the main road. She bumped over the cattle grid, turned sharply to the right and took the narrow country lane to Withington. There was a pub in the middle of the village, a large sign fixed to the wall announcing it as The King's Head. She indicated and turned off, reversing into a slot in the almost empty car park. Milton slotted the Volkswagen next to hers and got out.

"This okay?" she asked as they walked to the door together.

"Fine."

Milton held the door for her and then followed her inside. It was a small pub, very quaint, with a low ceiling, exposed oak beams and horse brasses on the walls.

"What are you having?" she asked him. "My round."

"An orange juice."

"Don't want anything stronger?"

Milton shook his head. "No, thanks. A little early for me."

Milton took a table by the window and waited as she ordered a gin and tonic for herself, the orange juice for him, and a packet of cheese and onion crisps for them both. She brought the glasses and the crisps over, deposited them on the table and sat down.

She took a card from her purse and slid it across the table.

"Olivia Dewey," Milton said, reading it. "Freelance journalist."

"Used to work on the nationals, got sacked, now I work

for myself. I live in east London, I'm not married, I drink too much, I don't suffer fools gladly. That's me. Anything else you'd like to know?"

He smiled, amused at her candour. "No, I think that's all I need to know."

"And you?"

"Like I said. John Smith. I'm a cook. I live on my own. I like The Smiths, The Stone Roses and the Happy Mondays."

"John Smith. *Really*?"

"Yes, really."

"Where are you a cook?"

"I work nights at the cabmen's shelter in Russell Square."

Her face lit up. "Those green sheds? I've seen them before. They're actually open?"

"They are."

"That's where you met Eddie?"

He had no interest in telling a journalist that they had met at an AA meeting, so he took the opening that she provided. "Yes," he said. "He came in for meals every now and again. We got talking. He's a nice guy."

"He was," she corrected.

"Was, yes." Milton acknowledged that with a nod. "He said he'd spoken to a journalist."

"He called me out of the blue a while ago."

"And said what?"

"He'd read one of my stories. He said he had some information for me."

"What story?"

She sipped her gin. The ice cubes jangled against the glass. "You follow the news at all, John?"

"Not if I can help it."

"This was a while ago. There was a Tory MP who was arrested for outraging public decency on Hampstead Heath."

"Don't recall it," he said.

"Open-and-shut case. They had witnesses who were ready to testify that they'd seen this man having sex with another man, what happened, everything. Then, the day of the trial, the case collapses. The witness spontaneously changes his mind. Doesn't remember being there, doesn't recognise the man, doesn't know anything at all. I covered it for the *Sun*. I got friendly with the detective who was running the case. But as soon as the case collapsed, he stopped returning my calls. Wouldn't speak to me. I didn't give up. Found him in a pub one night, drinking on his own, and I asked him what was going on. He told me to stop pestering him, said he wouldn't speak to me and, when I kept at him, he got up and left. Two days after that, he killed himself. Threw himself off a multi-storey car park. And it wasn't as if he had any reason to do it. He'd just had twins. Whole life to look forward to."

"And you kept looking into it?"

"I was pretty green then, but even I could tell that there was a reason for what had happened. The case just dropped out of the papers. No one would cover it—everyone was afraid of getting sued. My editor knew I was still keen, told me to drop it. I said I would, but I didn't. I kept at it. I tried to find the witness, but he disappeared. Just vanished. And then I found him six months later. He'd died of a heart attack. It was a strange one: everyone said how fit he was, running marathons, keeping himself in shape, still young, too. But whatever. Shit happens, right? That's what I said. Shit happens." She said it with a sarcastic twist of her mouth.

"Shit happens," Milton agreed.

"In the end, I ran out of fresh places to look. I had a million questions, but no one I could ask. So I mothballed it, found another story and got on with my life."

Milton watched her as she spoke. She was animated, nervous, and she punctuated her sentences with little stabs of her fingers. He thought he could see fear in her, but she was hiding it behind an irrepressible energy.

"So time passed without me really thinking about it. I got the sack from the paper and started writing for websites. And then someone emailed me. Out of the blue. Anonymous address. He said I could call him David although that wasn't his real name. He said he'd read my old stuff, that he had a lot of information about the case and would I be interested? I said yes, of course I would, I'd look at anything he had. I got another email the next day. It was long, stream of consciousness stuff. It said that there was a flat in Watson Square in Pimlico and that thirty years ago, in the eighties, it was used as a brothel by some very high-end people. This place is a mile from Westminster. I went and had a look. Big place. Expensive. I went through the Land Registry details. More than a hundred MPs have apartments there. A dozen Lords. It's got an amazing history. Oswald Mosley was arrested there in the thirties. Princess Anne lived there. Churchill's daughter was evicted after throwing gin bottles out the window. You wouldn't believe some of the stories."

"And this particular story?"

"David said there were parties there every week, and the guests were politicians, civil servants, military, senior government types. And they had young kids there. Girls and boys. David said that he had been taken there several times over the course of a couple of years. He was in a boys' home in Jersey. He said that they were very organised, that they sent boys over on the ferry and then had minibuses pick them up from the port to drive them to the parties, then they drove them back again. He went into a lot of detail. Very credible detail. He said that they were made to drink whiskey until they were drunk, they were forced to dress up in women's lingerie, and then they were raped."

"I don't understand—why did he email you?"

"Because he'd read my old stories. He said the defendant in the case that got dropped, the man on Hampstead Heath—David said that he was one of the men who raped him at Watson Square."

Milton nodded, suddenly getting the distinct feeling that he was standing on the edge of a precipice and, if he wanted to step back, he should do it now. The more he found out, the harder that was going to be.

But he didn't want to step back.

"And then?" he said.

"And then nothing. I thought this guy, whoever he was, he must have lost his bottle, but then I got another email. More detail. Some of what he told me was sickening. He said he was raped over a bathtub while his head was held under the water. Another time he said he was ordered to punch another boy in the face, but he refused. He got a beating for that. He said that one of the men at the parties had medical training—they called him the Doctor—and he would treat the boys after they had been roughed up. He sent another email the next day and said that he knew of at least two boys who had been killed there."

Milton said nothing.

"You can imagine how I'm feeling now. The Hampstead Heath story was big enough, but this had the potential to be enormous. I told him I was treating his claims very seriously and that if he wanted to take it to the next step, we had to meet. I didn't think he'd follow through with it, but he did. He told me to name the place. I said I'd be under Waterloo Bridge last Saturday at five and he turned up."

"And this was Eddie."

"Yes. Eddie. We were there for three hours. I went through the story again, point by point, and he backed everything up. *Everything.* He was completely credible. I don't have any doubt in my mind that what he told me was true. The only thing he wouldn't do was go on the record. He said he had to think about that. I said he could have as long as he wanted, but that I thought his story needed to be told because these men need to be punished. And then he called me two days before he died. He said he'd do it, that he'd go through the story all again, and I could film him. We agreed to meet. Piccadilly Circus. I arranged for a cameraman to come, too, booked a hotel room where we could film it, but Eddie never turned up. And then I found out why. Gassed himself in his cab. Hours before he was going to give me the story. What are the odds of that?"

"You think that's suspicious."

"What do you think?"

"I think there are some questions that need to be answered."

She laughed. "He was killed, John. I've got no doubt about it."

"By who?"

"Someone who doesn't want the story to come out."

"The MP?"

"Maybe."

"His name is Leo Isaacs, isn't it?" Milton said.

"Yes. Did Eddie mention him to you?"

Milton nodded. "He told me a little. Not as much as he told you. How confident are you that this stacks up?"

"Very confident."

"Can you prove any of it?"

She shook her head. "That's the problem. All I've been able to find out are rumours and innuendo. Enough for me to print that *something* was going on there, but not enough to name names. A story like this, John, as big as this could be, you have to be watertight. The website I write for loves this kind of shit, but the editor won't run anything unless he's sure it stacks up—the risks of getting sued are too big."

"So what's next?"

"There is no next," she said. "Back to square one."

#

THEY STEPPED out into the car park together.

"There was one other thing," Milton said.

"What's that?"

"When Eddie came to see me, there was something else on his mind. Something about his family."

Milton saw a flicker of recognition pass across her face.

"Did he say what it was?" she asked with a caution that was a little too obvious.

Milton cast his mind back and tried to remember what Eddie had told him. "He said he had problems with them. Do you know what he meant?"

No," she said. But she took a moment too long to answer, and her eyes darted away from his face as she spoke.

"Olivia," Milton said, "what was it? What did he mean?"

"I don't know."

Milton knew that she was lying.

They shook hands, and she told him that he should contact her if he found out anything that might be of interest. Milton said that he would, although he didn't anticipate seeing her again. As he slipped into his car, he reached into his pocket and ran his finger along the edge of her card. No, he didn't think that he would see her again, but he would keep the card for now. He had no way of predicting how this was going to turn out, and maybe he would need an ally. He pushed it back into his pocket.

He put the key in the ignition and twisted it, realising that he had already started to plot his next move. He had allowed her to walk him up to the edge and her story had tipped him over. Something had happened to Eddie. Had he killed himself? Maybe. But Milton didn't think so. He wasn't a betting man—compulsive behaviours were unhealthy for a man with his weaknesses—but if he had been, he would have staked a generous amount that there was more to what had happened than the sad, pathetic ending of a life.

Eddie had come to him for his help.

Milton was going to find out what had happened to him.

Chapter Twenty-Seven

ALEX HICKS was parked up in Russell Square, watching the comings and goings around the taximan's shelter. He had taken the family car. He knew that John Milton had seen his Range Rover and he didn't want to draw attention to himself. The Ford Mondeo was aging. It had a dented bumper after a driver who had been looking at his phone had rear-ended his wife as she was driving home from the supermarket. It hadn't been washed for weeks, and the inside was littered with the bright plastic toys that occasionally distracted his boys enough to keep them occupied during the journeys to and from the nursery. Hicks was parked between two similar cars, close enough to the shelter that he could observe it, but not so close that it would be obvious that he was watching it. Hicks knew enough about John Milton to know that he had to be very, very careful.

In truth, he wasn't sure why he was here. The general certainly hadn't sent him. He still hadn't decided one way or another what he was going to do. But he had been unable to sleep following the night that had led to the death of Eddie Fabian, and he knew that it was his guilt and shame that had been keeping him awake. He knew that he had to do something to pull himself out of the mess that he had engineered for himself. The motives for his involvement with the general were irrelevant. The cancer was a useful excuse for the abandonment of his morals, but the planned murder of Eddie Fabian had been the moment that he had known that it would never be enough. The fact that Fabian had been killed by someone else did not absolve him of his shame. The fact remained: they would have killed him. He had been given the order, and he would have been expected to pull the trigger.

Hicks was there for an hour before he saw Milton. Black cabs came and went, the brightness of the shelter's interior briefly visible in the gloom of the square as the door opened and closed. It was cold and wet, and the drivers hurried inside and back to their vehicles, with newspapers serving as makeshift umbrellas to shelter them from the rain. Hicks watched as Milton arrived. He approached on the other side of the square, stepping out between two parked cars and crossing the road. He didn't hurry; he seemed oblivious to the rain. Hicks was too far away to get a good look at him, and he was silhouetted by the light that fell down from a streetlamp, but he knew from his bearing and his posture that it was the same man that he had seen the last time he was here, and at the church. The man he had recognised from years before.

John Milton.

Number One.

He waited longer. A woman, who he guessed must have been working the earlier shift, eventually left and stepped into a car that had arrived to collect her. There were three cabs parked alongside the shelter, and Hicks waited for another ten minutes until all three of them had been driven away.

He got out of the car, shut and locked the door, and jogged across the street.

#

MILTON TOOK the opportunity to clear away the dirty plates and mugs and wipe the tables down. He was tired, and there were hours to go before he would be finished for the night. He listened to the news on Radio 4 and was thinking about changing the channel to 6 Music when the door opened and someone came inside.

Milton was halfway to the kitchen and laden down. "Just a minute."

"Milton?"

The man said it and stopped. Milton paused, frowning. He hadn't used his real name for anything ever since he had returned to London. He put the plates in the sink and turned. It was the man he had seen at the funeral. One of the two men who had been watching from the Range Rover.

Milton put the plates on the counter. There was a knife on the chopping board. Milton rested his fingertips against the handle. "Who are you?"

"Hicks."

Milton paused.

"Alex Hicks. I was in the Regiment. Do you remember, sir?"

Milton felt a coldness, a prickling on the back of his neck. The name was familiar. And he had known that he had recognised the man.

"They recruited me to Group Fifteen, sir. Three years ago. You were Number One. You tested me."

"I tested a lot of people."

"You said I wasn't suitable. They sent me back to the army."

Milton had been drinking heavily then. He had held it together during operations, but he had cut loose between them, and his recollections of those years were cloudy and marked with regular blackouts. But he *did* remember Hicks. The soldier had been young and keen, but there had been a streak of empathy that ran right through the middle of him. He was a superb soldier—anyone who was recruited to the Group was the best of the best—but there was a fundamental quality of decency that Milton had detected immediately. It was that which had disqualified him. It might have been possible to scrub it out of him, to turn him into the next cold-hearted assassin to serve in the Group. But perhaps the quality would prove to be stubborn and difficult to remove, and perhaps it would lead to a moment of hesitation when delay might mean death. Those were good reasons for rejection, certainly, but Milton remembered something else about his reaction, too. There was something in Hicks that he had once thought that he himself had possessed: decency. Milton had been reluctant to try to scrub that virtue away, and he had sent Hicks back to the Regiment rather than try.

"I don't do that any more," Milton said.

Hicks glanced around the shelter. "I can see that."

"It was a long time ago."

"It was, sir."

"Don't call me that."

"Call you what?"

"Sir. Don't call me sir. This isn't the army. And," he repeated, "*I don't do that any more.*"

"Sorry. Old habits."

Milton watched him warily, picking up another dirty plate from the table. "What do you want?"

"It's about Eddie Fabian."

Milton looked at Hicks and saw that he was nervous. Milton left his fingers on the handle of the knife, his index finger tracing across the raised rivets. "What about him?"

"I saw you. With Eddie, in here. The night he died. I want to talk to you about it."

Milton left the knife on the chopping board. He went to the door and locked it, flipping over the OPEN sign so that it now read CLOSED.

"Sit down," Milton said, indicating one of the empty benches.

Hicks did as he was told; Milton stayed on his feet.

"Have you been watching me?" Milton asked.

"Just tonight."

"Why are you here?"

Hicks shook his head. "Because of what happened to Eddie. He didn't top himself. None of what they're saying about it is true."

"So you better tell me."

Hicks put his hands in the middle of the table and started to clasp and unclasp them. Milton didn't think he was aware that he was doing it; he was so nervous that he was unaware of the impression he was making.

"How much did Eddie tell you?" Hicks asked.

"About?"

"The things that happened to him when he was a boy."

"Enough. Is it true?"

Hicks nodded. "Yes."

"How do you know that?"

"He told you about Leo Isaacs? The MP?"

"He mentioned him."

"There was a story a while ago. He got into trouble with another man on Hampstead Heath."

"I know," Milton said. "I read about it. The case collapsed. The witness changed his story."

"That's right," Hicks said. "Right before the trial. Why would someone do something like that?"

"Nerves?"

Hicks shook his head. "No, not that. Why would the witness end up dead not six months after the trial collapsed? He was fit and well and he just dropped dead. Funny, right?"

"You're going to tell me what happened?"

"Leo Isaacs has been *protected*. The court case wasn't even the worst thing that was suppressed. What Isaacs did with Eddie and the other boys, all the other men who were implicated, they've all been protected. Rape. Abuse. Murder. Those men have been looked after."

"By who?"

Hicks didn't answer. Instead, he stared down at the table and clasped his hands so tight that they went white.

"Hicks?"

"This isn't easy. He's… the man doing it… he's frightening, Milton. I don't care about myself, but I have kids. Two boys. My wife is sick. They need me. If he knew I was here—if he knew that I was going to grass him up—he'd kill them, kill my wife, and he'd make me watch him do it. I'm not kidding. He's bad news."

"Who, Hicks? Who is?"

Hicks swallowed, his grimace suggesting that his throat was dry. Milton got up and fetched him a glass of water from the kitchen. He was finding the whole experience unsettling. Hicks might have been bounced out of the Group, but he had been nominated for selection. That meant that he was a hard man, a special forces soldier who would have killed before, and probably more than once. Yet here he was, sitting before him with the blood leeched out of his face, a nervous wreck.

Hicks took a drink and, when he rested the glass on the table, it rattled. His hand was shaking.

"Who is it, Hicks?"

"General Higgins. Richard Higgins. You know him?"

"Yes," Milton said. "He was Director when I was in the Regiment."

Milton had only been a trooper then, and so his experience of Higgins was negligible, but he remembered him. He had a reputation for brilliance, together with an irascible temper that had made him feared as much as respected among the men.

"Higgins has been blackmailing Isaacs and the others for twenty years. He calls it protection, of course, or 'reputation management' when he's had a drink and he thinks he's funny. They pay him every month and he makes sure that the stories stay buried. It's ridiculous. They think he's got their best interests at heart. Most of the time, they're paying him to keep quiet about what he knows. To sit on the evidence. It's extortion."

"What does he have on them?"

"Proof that what Eddie Fabian said is true. Photos."

"Have you seen them?"

"No," Hicks admitted. "But I know he has it. His brother was senior in the Metropolitan Police. Diplomatic protection squad. The men at those parties, they were as discreet as you would expect them to be, but it's difficult to hide secrets from the man who's been assigned to protect you. They must have found out about the apartment. The men who used it must have thought that it was secret; if they'd changed their location, maybe none of this would ever have come out. But they didn't, and they put themselves into a bad place. I don't know how long it went on for, but they've got cast-iron proof. There were men from the military, the civil service, the government, the police—everywhere. Very senior. If this came out, it would cause enormous damage."

"Where are the photos?"

"Hatton Garden."

"What—a vault?"

"Safe deposit box."

Milton nodded. "And Higgins knew that Eddie was going to accuse Isaacs?"

"Of course he did," Hicks said. "Higgins knows *everything*. Fabian ambushed Isaacs and Isaacs told Higgins."

"Yes," Milton said. "Eddie told me."

"And Isaacs went straight to Higgins. The slightest suggestion that his story is coming out, he's all over the place, on the phone, telling Higgins what he has to do. Of course, from Higgins's perspective, Isaacs and the others need to be looked after. The last thing he wants is for the story to break. If that happens, they go to prison, he loses all his leverage, they stop paying him. Maybe *he* goes to prison for suppressing the evidence. So when Isaacs called about Eddie, Higgins took it very seriously."

Milton pulled up one of the spare chairs and sat down. "Go on."

"We put observation in right away. Fabian was followed. The night he died, we broke into his house."

"We?"

"Me. I did. Higgins ordered me to do it." He shuffled on the bench. "I tried to warn Eddie off. Told him what he was doing was dangerous, he needed to leave it, but it didn't work. He went straight out, stopped and bought a bottle of booze, and then came here to see you."

"You followed him?"

"Me and the others."

"Two cars."

"You saw?"

Milton nodded. "A Range Rover and a Maserati. You pulled out just after he left."

"I was in the Range Rover. That's mine. Higgins had decided to get rid of him. He wanted us to do it here." Hicks gestured around the inside of the shelter. "You too. It was quiet, late at night. You wouldn't have seen us coming. But you were lucky. We were out of the car and on the way over here when Eddie left. Higgins called it off."

"And then you killed him afterwards."

Hicks shook his head and there was certainty in his voice. "No," he said. "We didn't. We followed him all the way to Littleworth. Just outside it. We had no idea what he was doing. He drove out of London and headed west. He kept going. Higgins wanted to stop him, wait for him to be somewhere quiet then pull him over and top him, but I put him off. I said it was too public, we would be seen, whatever I could think of." He was trying hard to absolve himself, Milton could see. He didn't want Milton's judgment, but it was too late for that. "He stayed on the motorway and didn't give us the chance. But then he did turn off. He drove into the middle of nowhere—we had no clue what he was doing—then he pulled into the driveway of a house. We went past. There was another car there. We drove by. Eddie was out of the car, waiting for another man."

"You see who it was?"

"No. Too dark."

"And then?"

"So we kept driving. I parked and got out once it was safe. Came back on foot. The other car came by first, a Jeep, and then I got to the house. The gates were open. Eddie was dead inside the cab. The engine was still running."

Hicks shuffled uncomfortably.

"You must have more to go on than that," Milton said.

"I do. I got the registration."

"And?"

Hicks looked up. "That's the thing. I ran the registration with the DVLA. It's Frankie Fabian's car."

Milton frowned. "What?"

"His father."

"I know who he is," Milton said curtly. "Was it him you saw?"

"I told you, I don't know. It was too dark."

"Why would his father have been there?"

"You tell me."

Milton remembered what Eddie had told him: that he was having problems with his family. But he had gone to his sister's house to get out of the way after Hicks had threatened him. He must have felt safe there. But then this had happened.

Hicks looked spent. He stared down at his hands. Milton felt a blast of annoyance; Hicks had no right to feel sorry for himself.

"Look at me, Hicks. Why did you come here? Why are you telling me this?"

"Because I need help. I've got to get out."

"So go to the police. Tell them what you told me."

"Are you mad? You think that'll do me any good?" He shook his head with sudden vigour. "Higgins would kill me. I should never have gotten involved with him."

"So why did you?"

"Because I need money. I need a lot, and I need it quickly. He runs a unit of men. All ex-Regiment. He turns over criminals, mostly, takes their money. The way he sold it to me, there was no harm in it. They were bad men. They deserved what they got. 'A moral equivalence,' that's what he said. I did one job with them before this. There was a drug dealer. Turkish, a murdering scumbag. We hit him and his men. Took them out, took their money. But Eddie was different. He was nothing like that. He didn't deserve what happened to him."

Milton's anger flickered. He got up and pointed to the door. "Just go, Hicks. I can't help you."

"Milton—"

"Get out."

Hicks spoke hurriedly. "The money isn't for me."

"No? I've heard that before."

Hicks spoke quickly. "My wife has cancer. She needs treatment that we can't get here, and if I can't get the funds together, she'll die. My kids lose their mum. Milton, please. I don't have anywhere else to turn."

Milton paused.

Hicks pressed on, the desperation evident in his voice. "I was in personal protection before. It pays well, but not well enough. Higgins made me an offer. Enough money to take her to America for treatment. It's our only hope. I didn't have any other choice. I wouldn't have accepted the offer if I'd known what they were doing—I know it's wrong, and I'm trying to do the right thing so I can fix it."

Milton considered. His impulse was to send Hicks on his way, but he didn't. He paused.

"Please, Milton. I need to get away from Higgins."

"So leave."

"Come on, it doesn't work like that. I know too much. I can't just leave. The only way I get out in one piece is if someone brings him down."

"Meaning?"

"What do you think? There's only one way. Higgins has got to go."

"And that's why you're here? I told you—I don't do that any more."

"But you don't forget, do you? How many people have you killed?"

"Too many."

"So one more makes no difference. Just help me."

Milton turned his back on him and went to the kitchen.

Hicks got up and followed him. "And there's going to be a lot of money. All I want is enough for my wife. You can have the rest."

Milton shook his head with irritation and then gestured around. "Do you really think I'm motivated by money? Would I be cleaning dishes if I was? I don't care about any of that."

Hicks didn't give up. "What, then? What *do* you care about? There must be something."

Milton held his tongue and considered that for a moment.

"There is one thing," he said.

"What?"

"Justice for Eddie Fabian. You think you can help me with that?"

Chapter Twenty-Eight

HICKS GAVE MILTON his telephone number and asked him to call when he had had the chance to consider a strategy that might succeed. He left soon afterward. Milton watched him go. He saw how nervous Hicks was as he hurried across the street to his car.

The rest of the shift was quiet, with just a handful of drivers, and he used the time to think about what he should do. They had spoken for a little longer. Milton wanted as much information as he could get. It was not going to be easy to work out the best way to proceed.

He felt no loyalty to Hicks. He certainly wasn't responsible for him. He had sympathy for his plight—if what he had said was true, of course—but his solution for finding the money to pay for his wife's treatment was not one that Milton would have chosen. Apart from the difficulty that Milton knew he would face in squaring the morals of any enterprise like the one that Hicks had described, there was the simple matter of Hicks's naivety. Had he not considered the possibility that he might be asked to do something that he found objectionable? It wasn't like Robin Hood, some romantic ideal that would mean that no one who didn't deserve to be punished would be made to suffer. Life wasn't like that. Life was not black and white: it was a spectrum of greys, infinite in variety, some darker than others. Milton knew that better than most. He had lived his life within that spectrum, and, eventually, it had become more than he could stomach.

The first option that he considered was the moral one: he would go back to Detective Inspector Bruce and tell him what he had learned. He could tell Bruce about Hicks and what he had said he had witnessed at Lauren Fabian's house. He would stand aside and leave it to the authorities.

He had almost persuaded himself that that was what he needed to do when another thought changed his mind. He realised what it was: he didn't believe that the policeman would follow up on the information in a way that might produce results. He had been dismissive and unhelpful and hadn't given Milton any confidence that he would treat any further information that he brought him in a different way. And, after all, maybe that would have been right. What did Milton really have? A story from Hicks that he would undoubtedly deny if Bruce was ever to interview him about it. And, above that, there was the danger that involving the police would bring. If what Hicks had said about Higgins was true, then making him the subject of a police enquiry would not be good for his prospects.

No. Milton postponed that idea. He would have to do it eventually, but not yet.

The second option was more straightforward. He could help Hicks take Higgins out. Hicks could lead the general into a trap, and Milton could close it, but while that might alleviate Hicks's problems, it wouldn't mean anything to Milton. It would bring him to Higgins's level, too, and Milton was trying to be better than that.

Milton wanted the evidence that would prove that what Eddie had been planning to say was true. He would give it to Olivia and then he would let her publish it.

Hicks wanted Milton's help?

Giving Eddie a voice would be Milton's price.

#

IT WAS FOUR in the morning when Milton called Hicks. He heard the sound of driving when Hicks picked up. Milton knew that Hicks had no room for negotiation if he wanted his help, and, after Milton set out what he was proposing to do, Hicks had quickly agreed to his terms. They had spoken for another thirty minutes about the best way to achieve their goals. Milton had identified one strategy, but it was audacious and he needed more information to assess whether or not it was possible. Hicks said that he would make enquiries and, after a few more preliminaries were taken care of, Milton had ended the call.

The shelter was quiet and Milton sat down at the table, a mug of tea before him as he rolled an unlit cigarette between his fingers. The evening's conversation had confused things. He had doubted that Eddie had taken his own life, but the mounting evidence that his suspicions were correct had brought more questions than it answered. Who had Eddie met on the night that he died? How was his family involved? Hicks said that he didn't know who it was, and Milton believed him.

Whoever they were, they had murdered Eddie. That meant that Milton needed to know their identity, too.

Chapter Twenty-Nine

MILTON WOKE up the following day and researched General Richard Higgins. He could remember a handful of encounters with him—he remembered his reputation for cantankerousness in particular—but he wanted to fill in the detail.

It was simple enough to find out all he needed from a few Google searches. Higgins had been commissioned into the Scots Guards at the start of the 1970s. It was a challenging time to be a British soldier, and he had completed several tours in Northern Ireland. By all accounts, Higgins had served with distinction. He completed selection in 1975 and was transferred into 22 SAS where he was eventually made commanding officer of the Regiment. His career after that was similarly illustrious: he held the command of the Airborne Brigade for four years and was then appointed Director Special Forces. There were further promotions, reaching major general before he became General Officer Commanding 4th Division before he retired. It was a glowing resumé. Milton couldn't imagine why he would blot his copybook as spectacularly as Hicks had suggested. But then, Milton knew, greed could be a powerful motivator.

Milton called Hicks. The two of them spoke briefly, and Hicks gave him two addresses: the address of the vault in Hatton Garden and the address of Eddie Fabian's house.

Milton decided to visit the vault first. It was a twenty-minute drive from Bethnal Green, and it was early evening and dark outside when he arrived. The streets were quiet, the shops were being shuttered, and the men and women who worked here were going home. Milton drove slowly past the address, looking at the big double doors and the low-key signage that announced the business that was transacted behind them. He thought of the vault, almost certainly in the basement, possibly beneath the road itself. He drove around the block, checking out all of the buildings that comprised it and looking for any obvious means of access. There were none. That was not surprising, but he felt better prepared for seeing the premises himself. He had known that he would need help if he was going to get inside, and this was the confirmation.

He drove out to Leytonstone next. It was half past eight. He didn't have very long before he needed to think about going to the shelter, but he wouldn't tarry any longer than was necessary. Milton waited in his car for ten minutes and observed the street. It was quiet, residential, with little passing traffic. The other houses on the terrace displayed signs of life, with lit windows and the flicker of televisions, but Eddie's was dark. Milton wondered whether anyone had been here since Eddie's death. Would the police have visited? Would his family? There was no way of knowing.

Milton collected a small bag from the passenger seat, got out of the car and walked slowly to the house. He walked onward for a few paces, confirmed that the street was quiet, and then turned back. He followed the pavement to the end of the road. He turned right and carried on until he reached the narrow alleyway that ran behind the terrace, offering access to the back gardens of the terrace that was adjacent to the one that included Eddie's house. The alleyway was dirty, with dustbins left outside back gates and black bin liners torn open by hungry rats looking for food. Milton picked his way along it until he reached the gate that he guessed would open out into the back garden of Eddie's house.

Milton took out a pair of latex gloves from his bag and put them on. He tried the handle. It was unlocked. He pushed the gate open and slipped inside.

The garden was small. There was a muddy square that might once have been a lawn, but there was very little grass there now. There was a bicycle propped up against the fence. Cardboard packaging had been left to the elements until it had shrivelled in the rain. Each house in the terrace had an extension to the rear, probably for the kitchen and bathroom. Milton crept forward, staying in the shadows, aware that the windows of the houses on either side were lit, and he could hear the sounds of conversation and activity from both.

Milton reached the extension and looked in through the window. It was the kitchen, the wan light illuminating it just enough to see that it was tidy. There was a door. It was locked, but Milton could see that the key had been left in the keyhole on the other side. He took a breath, reached down for a short length of pipe that had been discarded in the garden, and then, with a brisk jab, used it to smash through the pane of glass. He paused, listening hard, but he heard nothing that suggested that the sound had drawn attention. He reached his arm through the broken window, opened the door from the inside and went through.

He took out a pencil flashlight from his bag and switched it on. He worked quickly, going from room to room. The place had been given a thorough clean. The kitchen was spotless, the surfaces wiped down and the cupboards emptied of their contents and cleaned. The front room had no furniture, and there were holes in the wall where picture hooks might once have been.

He climbed the stairs. Both bedrooms were empty. The beds had been removed, with just the ghostly indentations in the carpet standing as evidence that they had ever been there. Milton stood in the larger bedroom and thought that this was where Hicks had threatened Eddie on the night that he had died.

He went into the bathroom. It, too, had been given a professional clean.

It was clear to him that someone—the family, most likely—had paid for the house to be cleared and then professionally cleaned. Perhaps the house would be sold or offered for rent. And perhaps they wanted to be sure that there was nothing left here that might prove to be a problem for them in the future.

He was about to leave when something caught his eye. He went over to the toilet. The cistern lid was not quite flush with the cistern. He lifted it up, set it down and peered inside. There was a plastic bag floating in the water. Milton reached down and fished it out. The bag was made from PVC and was sealed at the top with a zip. It looked like the kind of bag that a hiker might use to keep maps and other documents dry. Milton checked that the cistern was empty of anything else that might have been hidden there, replaced the lid, and took the bag back downstairs and into the kitchen. He unzipped it and withdrew an A4 scrapbook that fitted snugly within. He aimed his flashlight at it and started to flip through the pages.

He had expected to see something about the abuse, but that wasn't what he found. Instead, he found pages of newsprint that had been neatly clipped out and pasted to the coarse pages of the book. He had no interest in staying in the house any longer than was absolutely necessary, but he found himself unable to resist a glimpse through the pages.

The extracts were from ten years ago and they all reported on the same event. There had been an armed robbery in Headington, Oxford. Several thousand pounds had been stolen from an armoured car as the guards were collecting the takings from a local betting shop. One of the guards had resisted and, during a struggle that had been observed by several witnesses, he had been shot in the chest by one of the criminals. The guard had died from his injuries on the side of the road. The reports said that he was a local man and that he had left a young family. Milton flipped the pages. There was more on the robbery and then a page that contained a letter from the widow of the dead guard. It spoke of how the family had been torn apart and ended with an appeal for information that would bring the killer to justice. Someone had underlined the final sentence in blue ink and inscribed an asterisk in the margin.

Milton got to the final page, and a piece of paper dropped out onto the counter.

He opened it and read.

My name is Alan Edward Fabian. This statement regards the murder of Toby Masters. The time of the murder was Saturday morning, December 17, 2005. The place was outside Stan James, Bookmakers, Headington, Oxford.

Milton read on.

It was a confession.

He read through it quickly. Eddie wrote that he had been there, that he had been driving the getaway car. He said that his brother, Spencer, had killed the guard. He said that not a day went by when he didn't think about what had happened that morning, how they had ruined a family, turned a wife into a widow and stolen a father from two small children. He wrote of how that morning had haunted him ever since, and how he wanted to do whatever he could to make it right.

Milton folded the page and slid it back inside the book.

He had a much better idea about what might have happened to Eddie now.

He closed the book, dropped it into his bag and made his way to the rear door. He opened it and peered outside. The garden was empty and there was no sound from the alley. He pushed the door open, slipped outside, closed the door and then hurried through the garden, passing through the gate and into the alleyway. He peeled off his gloves and put them into the bag to be disposed of later. And then, without a backward glance, he straightened his shoulders and walked at a brisk pace in the direction of his car.

Chapter Thirty

MILTON WAS DISTRACTED at the shelter that night. It was busy, but not so busy that there was no opportunity to take out the book that he had taken from Eddie's flat. He read through it, reading all of the newspaper articles, noting where the pages had been annotated and, assuming Eddie was responsible for the underlinings and the highlighting, he tried to imagine what those marks meant.

He returned home and allowed himself four hours of sleep. It seemed as if his alarm beeped as soon as he had put his head down; he got out of bed, showered and changed into fresh clothes. He went to the local newsagents and paid 20p to photocopy Eddie Fabian's confession. Then, he got into his car and drove west. The traffic was light and he arrived back in Withington after two hours. The clock on the church tower showed a little after two in the afternoon as he drove by, passing through the village until he reached the turning for Halewell Close.

He parked the car in the wide gravelled turning circle. There were three vehicles already parked there: two white vans and a BMW. Milton waited for a moment, studying the house. The front door was open and a pair of men were ferrying catering equipment from the interior to the open doors of one of the vans. The tent on the lawn was in the process of being taken down, the canvas folded and folded again until it was compact enough to be fitted into the back of the second van. Milton opened the door to his car and was stepping out when he saw two men emerge from the open doorway of the house.

The first was Frankie Fabian, smoking a cigarette. The second, turning to shake Fabian's hand, was Detective Inspector Bruce.

Milton shut the door and set out across the gravel. Bruce

turned, saw Milton approach, said something to Fabian and then came across to meet him.

"Mr. Smith."

"Hello, Detective."

"What are you doing here, sir?"

"I didn't get the chance to speak to Mr. Fabian before. I'd like to pass on my condolences."

"Really? That's why you're here?"

"Yes. Is that a problem, Detective?"

"No, Mr. Smith. Not at all. But I'd just like you to remember that the family has had a bereavement. They might prefer a little privacy. I'm sure you have the best intentions in mind, but I wouldn't want to hear that they've been harassed."

"That's certainly not my intention, Detective. I just want to say how sorry I am."

Bruce looked at him dubiously. "Make sure that's all it is, Mr. Smith. I'll be seeing you around."

The detective gave Milton a nod, his face impassive, and made his way over to the BMW. Milton stood for a moment, waiting for him to reach his car. The policeman turned to look back at him, and Milton acknowledged him with a final dip of his head. Bruce opened the car and got inside.

What was that? Had he just been given a warning?

Milton waited until the policeman had started the engine and then crossed the rest of the parking area to where Frankie Fabian was waiting for him.

"Good afternoon, Mr. Fabian," Milton said.

The older man regarded him with suspicion. "Do I know you?"

"No. We haven't met. I'm a friend of Eddie. I came to the funeral."

"Really? I don't remember you."

"I'm not surprised. There were a lot of people here."

"Yes," Fabian said disinterestedly.

"Eddie was popular."

"Not really," Fabian said. He drew on his cigarette and didn't elaborate; Milton waited for him to speak again. "What's your name?"

"John Smith."

"So what do you want, Smith?"

"There's something I need to talk to you about."

"I'm busy, and I don't know you. I don't really have time. Sorry. Best you go."

Bruce's BMW crunched over the gravel as he turned it around. The car drew alongside and the window slid down.

Bruce leant across the cabin and called out, "Everything all right, Mr. Fabian?"

"Fine. Mr. Smith is about to leave."

Milton managed to suppress his impatience. He turned back to Fabian and, making sure that Bruce couldn't see or hear him speak, said, "It's about Eddie."

Fabian shook his head. "I've got nothing to say about that. I'm not interested."

Milton spoke firmly. "I need to talk to you about him. Eddie didn't kill himself."

Fabian inhaled, his eyes fixed on Milton's face, and then blew smoke. "What did you say?"

"He was murdered."

Bruce called out again, "On your way, Mr. Smith. You've said your piece."

Frankie Fabian looked at Milton, then looked past him to Bruce. "It's all right," he called back to the policeman. "Thanks, Detective."

Bruce wound the window up, put the car into gear and drove away.

"What did you say?" Fabian said again.

"Should we go inside?" Milton suggested.

#

FABIAN TOOK MILTON into the house and led the way to a smaller reception room than the one that had accommodated the wake. It was opulent: an impressive inglenook fireplace, wooden panelling on the walls, and furniture that looked old and expensive. There was a red leather Chesterfield sofa, and Fabian sat down in the middle of it. He waved a hand to indicate that Milton should sit in the nearest armchair to him.

"You know who I am, Mr. Smith?"

"Yes," Milton said. "I do."

"So you know I'm not the kind of man you want to annoy."

"Yes, I know that."

"I just want it to be clear between us. I wouldn't want to get off on the wrong foot." He folded his legs, revealing an inch of scarlet sock and a well-polished black brogue. "Now, then. Eddie. What did you mean?"

Milton nodded. He had rehearsed what he wanted to say as he had driven to Withington, and he was sure that he had it all down. But he knew that his success or failure depended more upon the impression that he conveyed than the content of his words. It was important that he come across as confident, even cocksure, with the kind of arrogance that would suggest that this wasn't the first time that he had tried to pull a stunt like this.

"I met Eddie at an AA meeting. Don't get the wrong idea—I've never had any time for any of that. It's a lot of religious nonsense, if you ask me. There's nothing wrong with a drink. If you find you're drinking too much, then you stop. Simple as that. All this happy-clappy kumbaya nonsense is a waste of time."

"But you went anyway."

"You could say it's my workplace."

"Meaning?"

"You'd be surprised the things you can learn in those meetings. All that honesty, people telling strangers their deepest secrets. It's tough to find a better place to get leads if you're into the kind of business that I'm into."

"And what kind of business is that?"

"The buying and selling of information."

"Blackmail?"

"If you like." Milton didn't bother to varnish his words for Fabian's benefit. He just needed him to believe his story. "That's what I do. I find people with interesting stories to tell, then I make a little money from them. Meetings like that are perfect. Alcoholics, gamblers, sex, drugs. I'll be honest with you, most of the time the opportunities are low rent. An alcoholic tells me he cheated on his wife. Maybe a woman tells me she stole the money for her next fix from her boss. You can use that information and turn a profit. Sometimes you'll get a high roller you can string along for a bigger payday. But mostly it's just people like Eddie."

"So, let me get this straight. You're a fucking cockroach?"

Milton ignored that, the audacity of the insult coming from a man like Frankie Fabian, and concentrated on laying the rest of his bait. "I go from city to city, meeting to meeting. I can't stay in one place for too long, obviously. People talk and then I have to move on. I came down to London a month ago. I found Eddie straight away, the very first meeting I went to. I could see he had a lot going on. Lots of troubles. Lots of potential. I made an effort to get to know him. He was vague about his family history, about you, but he told me enough so I could join the dots. I did my research. Learned all about you and what you do. The more I learned, the more I could see Eddie could be a really big score, so I pushed the boat out with him. I let him think we were best mates. I listened to him whinge and moan for fucking hours, Mr. Fabian; you wouldn't believe it. I thought I was going to drown in all his self-pity, but it was worth the pain in the end. More than worth it. He needed a sponsor, I offered, and he said yes. And then he told me why he had a problem with drink. *Specifically*. It was the guilt he carried around with him. The guilt—that was the reason."

Fabian looked at him cautiously. "Yeah? What did he

have to be guilty about?"

"Tell me when you want me to stop. I know the whole story. He told me that he was involved in an armoured car job ten years ago. Him and your two boys. He said a guard was shot. I looked into it. He didn't give me much to go on, but I found all the old newspaper reports. It was a big thing at the time, wasn't it? Big case. Police never got to the bottom of it."

Fabian didn't reply, but his eyes sparkled with fresh malice.

"I can see it's not something that bothers you. Doesn't bother your conscience the same way that it bothered him. I can see why: it was a long time ago. The guard probably got what was coming to him. Right? But, thing is, Eddie never got over it. He made it very clear to me: he always blamed himself for what happened. He's had it on his conscience for years. That's one of the things about going to AA. One of the things they make you do is to come clean about all the things that you did. That's what you do when you get to the ninth step. You have to unburden yourself, they say. You do that and you get rid of the reason why you've been drinking. All Eddie wanted was to go to the police and confess what happened."

"This is bollocks," Fabian protested. He said it angrily, but Milton could see it was bluster. There was no conviction in it.

Milton went on. "Did you know he'd written it all down? A confession. I think you suspected it, didn't you? He showed it to me. He didn't care. He was ready to go and give it to the police, but I would never have let him go through with that. He comes clean and the damage is done. There's nothing in it for me then. Because I knew that *you'd* care. I knew that you'd care a lot." Fabian rose up out of his chair, his fist clenched, and Milton raised his hand. "Don't," he said. "It's in everyone's interests that we keep it civil."

"You're full of it," Fabian said.

"No. I'm not."

Fabian glared at him, still standing, his hands braced on the table. "Prove it."

Milton felt his gut tighten up. This was the gamble.

Milton took out the confession that he had found in Eddie's house and handed it across. "This is a copy. The original is safe and sound. Read it."

Fabian looked at the first few paragraphs, his cheeks blooming with blood. He pushed the letter back across the table. "Where did you get this?"

"Eddie's house. I had a look around last night."

Fabian responded a little too hastily. "No, you didn't. There was nothing there."

"You'd cleaned the place up pretty well, but you didn't look hard enough. It was hidden in the cistern. There was more, too. A scrapbook with articles about the heist. Eddie had annotated them. Useful background, not that I needed it." Milton tapped a finger against the letter. "He's very clear what happened."

The conversation was going about as well as Milton could have hoped. It appeared that Fabian believed him or, at least, was not ready to call his bluff. He had included all of the information that he wanted to use. There was no point in mentioning anything about Leo Isaacs and the abuse. Suggesting that there was a noble intention to his intervention did not serve Milton's narrative. He had considered it and concluded that he stood a better chance of getting what he wanted by painting himself in the worst possible light.

Fabian's mood darkened. "I ought to have you shot," he said. "No one puts the black on me."

"Let's try to forget about the preliminaries, shall we? You wouldn't be talking to me if I didn't have a little leverage. I know you're not used to people you don't know talking to you like this, but try to put it to one side. Just listen. I have a proposal. A mutually beneficial arrangement. Let's concentrate on that."

"What do you want?"

"Your help, actually. You help me with something that I need, and the confession is yours. You can burn it, do whatever you want with it."

"And if I don't?"

"Then I'll send it to the newspapers and then I'll disappear."

"Go on, then. I'll humour you. What help?"

"I know what you do for a living. Safe deposit boxes and so on."

Fabian regarded him quizzically, and Milton could see that he was making a decision. "Fine. Go on."

"You have a specific set of skills. I'd like to take advantage of them."

"You want to break into somewhere."

"I do. The London Vault."

"In Hatton Garden?" Fabian chuckled and shook his head. "That's a tough nut to crack."

"Maybe. But that's my price. If you want this to go away, you need to get me in there."

"What for?"

"That doesn't matter."

"It'd be difficult."

"But not impossible?"

"Nothing's impossible." Fabian regarded him with sly aggression. "What do you get out of this? Really? What do you want? Diamonds?"

Milton gave a little shrug. "I'm used to making small scores here and there. There's only so much you can get a cheating husband to pay. This, though—it's something else. You know that. It could be the score that means I don't have to work ever again. You know better than I do. A place like that—it's millions, right?"

Fabian was tracing his finger across the photocopy of Eddie's confession. He was considering his response.

Milton tried to nudge him in the right direction. "Can I make a suggestion? Don't look at this and call it blackmail. You need to think of it as a business proposition. It's not what *I* get out of it. It's what we *all* get out of it. You get the confession. But we'll be in a vault, Mr. Fabian. I can only imagine what else is down there. You're not going to leave without opening a few other boxes, are you?"

Chapter Thirty-One

MILTON WAITED A WEEK without hearing from Fabian. He thought he might have to wait three days, maybe four. But a week? It felt bad. He went over their meeting again and again, trying to diagnose the moment when Fabian must have decided not to consider his proposal. There must have been a point when he had lost him. Maybe he didn't accord Milton with enough credibility to take his suggestion seriously. Maybe he was going to call his bluff.

Hicks had called him the day after he had returned from Withington to ask, again, for his help. Milton told him that he was still investigating his options and that he would get back to him when he was ready. Hicks sounded desperate, almost pleading for movement, but Milton reminded himself that Hicks wasn't his fault or his responsibility. He would help him, if he could, but only if that meant that he was able to do what he wanted to do for Eddie.

And, to do that, he needed Frankie Fabian's help.

By day eight, he had started to doubt that the plan would work. Fabian had seen through his ruse. The proposal was too difficult to pull off, or the risks outweighed the threat that Milton had presented. There was the possibility, of course, that Fabian would decide to follow a different course. Milton knew that he had put himself in danger by threatening him that way, and had stepped up his own security accordingly. He was cautious by nature, but he had examined his routines and eliminated all of the small bad habits that he had allowed himself to fall into. He took a different route to work every day. He stopped going to his usual meetings, travelling to alternatives in the West End instead. He had parked his car in a long-stay car park and taken public transport instead. He had been very aware of counter-surveillance when he had travelled back from

Withington to London on the day of their meeting, and he was sure that he had not been followed. The only link between him and Fabian was Eddie, but now that Eddie was dead, he couldn't think of any other way in which he might betray himself. But that didn't mean that he was prepared to take any chances by being slapdash with his behaviour. He took a small kitchen knife from the shelter, sharpened it until the edge was as keen as he could make it, wrapped it in a dishcloth, and kept it in his pocket.

#

HE WAS in the shelter one evening when his phone finally rang with a number that he did not recognise. He served his only customer with a plate of beans on toast and a tea, took the phone outside, and shut the door behind him. It was a cold night, the damp seeping into his clothes and chilling his skin. He took out his phone and accepted the call.

"Mr. Smith?"

"Speaking."

"Be at Bethnal Green station at midnight."

Milton tried to respond, but there was no reply. The line was dead.

#

MILTON CLOSED UP at eleven. The drivers would be annoyed, but he had no other choice. He took the Central Line from Oxford Circus to Bethnal Green and emerged at midnight, just as the guard rattled the station's iron cage door closed behind him.

Milton sheltered from the rain in the doorway of a betting shop and waited, staring into the night and smoking cigarettes. He had no idea how the next few hours would play out. He hadn't recognised the voice of the man who had called him, but he assumed that he was connected to Fabian. He must have considered his offer, and now he was going to deliver his verdict. Milton hoped that it would be the answer that he needed. If it was something else, he was going to have to come up with another angle. And that, of course, ignored the very real possibility that Frankie Fabian might not give him the chance to pivot and try something else. Milton had read as much as he could find about the head of the Fabian family. There was a lot of conflicting information about him, but one thing was constant: he was unpredictable. There was no way to foresee how the meeting Milton assumed he was about to have was going to play out. He would have to adapt to whatever came his way.

Milton looked out over the crossroads where Bethnal Green Road met Cambridge Heath Road. There was a church, St John on Bethnal Green, where Milton had attended meetings of the fellowship when he had first tried to leave Group Fifteen behind him. It was a dark, ugly building, reaching up to a dome with a golden cross atop it, fenced in from the street by iron railings. There was a park on the opposite side of the road to the church, and, opposite Milton, the landlord of the Salmon and Ball was just ejecting the last stragglers from the pub. There was a small concourse of shops, including a unisex hair salon and an off-licence. There were a few pedestrians passing by, and the queues of traffic that formed at the junction quickly dispersed once the lights turned green. A group of youngsters, wearing puffer jackets with the hoods pulled up, loitered in the park. Milton could see the red tips of the joints as they toked on them, passing them around.

He finished his second cigarette and was about to light a third when his phone rang.

Milton put the phone to his ear. "Yes?" he said.

"Where are you?"

"I'm here."

Milton looked left and right and saw a parked Audi flash its lights.

"I see you," Milton said.

"Hurry up."

He put the cigarette back in the packet, crossed the road and got into the car. There were two men inside. He recognised them from the funeral. Marcus and Spencer Fabian, Eddie's brothers. Marcus was driving. Spencer was sitting in the back. Neither looked pleased to see him.

"Hello," Milton said.

Spencer looked across the cabin at him. "We're going for a drive."

"Where to?"

"Maybe somewhere quiet where we can have a proper chat about what a great idea it is to try to blackmail our father."

Milton didn't respond.

"Just shut up," Marcus said from the front of the car. "You'll find out where we're going when we get there."

The car pulled away from the kerb and into the flow of traffic. Milton was acutely aware that he was barely armed, outnumbered, and being taken somewhere he didn't know.

Chapter Thirty-Two

THEY DROVE OUT to an industrial estate in Hounslow, beneath the flight path of Heathrow airport. Big jumbos roared overhead at regular intervals and, as Milton turned to watch the latest make its descent, he saw the lights of another four planes stacked up in the darkness behind it.

Marcus parked the Audi, killed the engine and got out. His brother followed him and Milton did the same. He looked around. There was a line of warehouses in the park, facing onto a narrow parking lot and hemmed in on all sides by a steep wire mesh fence. It was late, and the car park was empty save for their car and three others.

Spencer and Marcus didn't speak. Instead, they set off for the building that bore the sign HAMPTON PARK GARDEN FURNITURE. Milton trailed behind them. There was a large roller door at the front of the building, but it was closed. There was a secondary way inside through a door to the right of the building. It opened into a reception area that was furnished with a shabby collection of plastic tables and chairs, the tables bearing local free sheets that were several weeks out of date. There was a plain wooden door at the other end of the room, and Marcus held it open for Milton and then his brother to pass through. He followed them, closing the door behind him. Milton heard a key turning in the lock, but he didn't look around. He kept walking. If they were going to rough him up, or worse, there wouldn't be very much that he could do.

The warehouse was a large, dark space. Most of it was divided into a series of aisles by large storage racks, but there was an area in the middle of the room where a table and chairs had been arranged. A strip light was suspended high above the table, casting it in a harsh glow. Frankie Fabian was sitting at the table with a man that Milton didn't recognise. There was a woman there, too, but her face was turned away from him.

"Mr. Smith."

"Mr. Fabian."

The woman turned at his approach and Milton recognised her from the funeral. It was Lauren Fabian, Eddie's adopted sister. It had been to her that Eddie had turned after Hicks had threatened him. He had been found dead on her driveway.

Milton nodded to her and to the other man. They both glared at him with sullen hostility, but they did not speak. The other man looked comfortable and sat at the table in a relaxed and easy-going fashion. Milton assumed that he knew the family. It seemed likely that he was in their employ. Perhaps, he wondered, he worked with them on jobs like the one that Milton had proposed.

"You're Lauren," Milton said, indicating the woman. He gestured to the man. "But I don't know you."

"Vladimir," the man said.

Milton nodded to him. He was dressed in expensive jeans and a neatly pressed shirt. He looked extremely professional.

Frankie Fabian got up. "Mr. Smith," he said, "I've thought about what you said. You've left me with two choices. I could put a bullet in your head and call your bluff. No one knows where you are. We could do that and make your body disappear. I have to tell you, it's tempting."

"I was hoping you might prefer the other option."

"Doing what you suggested? Yes, that's the other choice. I gave it some thought, as I say. My boys here, and Lauren, they were all for option number one. They were persuasive, too. Apart from the fact that you disrespected me in my own house—you *threatened* me in my own house—what you proposed is not an easy thing to accomplish. But I like a challenge, and the upside is tempting. So I've decided that I will humour you. We'll do it. Marcus, Spencer, Lauren and Vladimir will break into the vault with you. Whatever it is you want, they'll help you to get."

"You're not coming?" Milton said.

Fabian shook his head. "I'm a little old for something like that."

Milton shrugged, masking his disappointment. He was going to have to amend his plan a little.

"You said it's difficult?"

"Yes, it is. As it happens, I've looked at the vault before. Ten years ago. It wouldn't have been easy then, and they've added a better alarm system since. It's a challenge, but I think it can still be done."

He walked over to the wall. Milton noticed that a series of architect's plans had been attached to it. He got up, went over and looked more closely. There were seven large printouts fixed there with strips of tape. They had been placed in a horizontal arrangement. Each printout was a plan of a particular floor.

Fabian tapped a finger against the nearest one. "Here's the building. Six floors and the basement. That's where the vault is. Very secure. There are two entrances from street level. The front door and one to the side. Both will be difficult to force and, even if we did force them, there are security doors inside plus another door when you get to the stairs. We could cut through them, but it would be very noisy and very messy. Anyone passing by on the street would hear. Not a good plan."

"So how are we getting in?"

Fabian pointed to the plan on the far right of the line. "Top floor. There's a skylight with a cage. We take off the cage and then take out the skylight and drop in."

Milton looked over at the plan. "What's on the sixth floor?"

"Just an office," Marcus said. "Diamond trader. There won't be anyone there."

"Now," Fabian continued, "there's a lift for the building, but it doesn't go all the way down to the basement.

So we can't use it to get down there."

"Stairs?"

"Security doors on all floors. We could force them, but it would take time and it would be noisy."

"So?"

"So, what you'll do, you get inside, send the lift up to the sixth floor and stop it. Go down to the fifth floor and get into the shaft. Then you abseil all the way down to the basement."

"Then?"

"Once you're down there, you'll be out of the way. Underground, too. It won't matter if you make a lot of noise. There's a shutter and a barred door. You force the shutter and cut through the bars. Neither should give you much of a problem. Then you get to the vault. That's different. It's a serious door. Eighteen inches of steel. There's no point trying to force it. You'll drill through the wall."

"Just like that?"

"It won't be easy, but you'll have the equipment you'll need and the time to do it."

"What equipment?"

"Industrial drill, angle grinders, everything. It's all taken care of. You bring it with you to the job and leave it behind when you're done."

Vladimir had been quiet, but now he raised his hand and pointed at the plans. "This is not simple. It will take time." He spoke with a harsh Eastern European accent. Russian, perhaps, to match his name. Milton wondered who he could be. Someone they had brought in for the job, perhaps?

"But?" Fabian asked.

"I agree. It can be done."

"You're going to go in this weekend," Fabian said. "The building will be empty Saturday and Sunday."

Frankie Fabian stood away from the wall, folded his arms across his chest and looked at the five of them. "Any questions?"

"What about the alarm?" Milton asked.

"We'll disable that remotely."

"How?"

"Don't worry, Smith. It'll be disabled. Anything else?"

No one spoke.

"Smith? Anything else on your mind?"

"No," Milton said.

"Good. Get an early night tonight. You'll be working through the night tomorrow; you'll need to be fresh."

"What time do we meet?"

"Back here tomorrow at six. We'll start at seven."

#

MILTON WAITED for someone to indicate that he was to follow them so that he could be driven away again. Marcus and Spencer said nothing to him, and Milton soon got the impression that he was going to have to find his own way home. He was doing up his jacket when Frankie Fabian walked across to him.

"Don't mess up," Fabian said.

"I'll do what I'm told."

"You want to be in the vault yourself?"

"Yes," Milton said.

"Why? If it's money you want, why don't you just ask me for money? I have plenty."

"I doubt you have as much as is sitting in that vault."

"No, Smith, there's something else. There's something in the vault you want. More than the money. What is it?"

Milton concentrated on presenting as blank an expression as he could. "It doesn't really matter, does it? You know my price. I don't care what else you do when you're in there, what else you take. That's not important to me."

"You're very trusting. What's going to stop me having one of my boys put a bullet in your head?"

"Because that wouldn't be good for you."

"Really?"

"Yes, really. I have a backup. If I don't come out again, the confession is sent to the police."

Fabian allowed himself a thin, humourless chuckle. He put his arm around Milton's shoulders and started toward the door with him. "I can't decide whether you're a genius or a fool."

Milton allowed his arm to stay there for a moment and then stepped away from him. "We're about to find out," he said.

Fabian opened the door for him and Milton stepped outside into the night. The rain had started to fall again. Fabian closed the door without another word.

Milton shrugged.

Hounslow.

That was a good distance from his flat.

He agreed with Fabian on at least one thing: he needed to get a good night's sleep. He set off across the car park, passed through the gates and onto the quiet road beyond. He took out his phone and checked his location. The last train would have left the station an hour ago. He would have to try to find a taxi. He aimed for the main road and started to walk.

Chapter Thirty-Three

IT HAD TAKEN MILTON an hour to find a taxi driver who was willing to drive him across the city. He had returned to his flat at two and had gone straight to bed. His mind had been buzzing and it had taken him longer than he would have liked before he had been able to settle. Once he did, he had managed a solid seven hours' sleep. He woke at ten and considered whether he might be able to get another couple of hours in before he needed to rise. He decided against it. Seven hours would have to be enough. He had a lot of work to do today before the events of the evening could begin, and there was no time to waste.

Milton decided that he didn't have time for his morning run. He showered, dressed in his suit and prepared his usual smoothie. He called Cathy and said that he was sick. He hated lying to her, but there was nothing else for it. She asked how long he thought he would need to recover and he said he didn't know—maybe two or three nights. She told him not to worry and to call her when he was better. Milton ended the call feeling much worse than before he had spoken to her.

He took a screwdriver and used it to remove one of the floorboards beneath his bed. There was a small void beneath it, and Milton had used the space to store his go-bag. He took out his extensive selection of fake passports and chose one that he hadn't used for some time. He also had a fake electricity bill that listed his address as an apartment in Kensington. He put both items, plus two hundred pounds in cash, into his pocket, went outside, locked the door to his flat and made the short walk to a local hardware store. He purchased a bunch of ten double-loop cable ties and then stopped at the newsagents next door. He bought two copies of the *Mail* and a pack of A4 envelopes. Satisfied, he paid for the items and took a bus into the centre of the city.

#

MILTON GOT off the bus at Holborn and stopped in a branch of Phones 4U. He bought a pay-as-you-go handset with a cheap plan and then walked to Hatton Garden, heading north until he reached the entrance to the London Vault. There was a luggage store halfway along the road, and he stopped to buy a small leather satchel into which he placed the items that he had purchased.

He thanked the proprietor and went back outside again, continuing to the north until he passed the vault, then proceeded farther up the street. He checked that the premises were not being surveilled. He didn't know how thorough Fabian would be, and it wasn't impossible that he had stationed someone to keep an eye on the building. Milton observed the street. The pavement was busy with pedestrians. A man leaned against a metal bollard, gazing down the street as if waiting for someone—his fiancée, perhaps, for an appointment to look at rings in one of the jeweller's. An old woman stood beneath an awning that was stencilled with PARIS JEWELS, clutching a handbag. Two Hasidic Jews, dressed all in black with long grey beards, were conversing. Milton didn't recognise any of the people he could see, and none of them looked as if they were watching the building.

He walked on. The rain had held off, although the sky was the same dark grey as it had been for days. He passed a branch of Costa Coffee, the Ace of Diamonds store, and a branch of EAT. He turned into St Cross Street and then Leather Lane, the road that ran in parallel to Hatton Garden. He had scouted the block in his car, but he took more time about it this time. He fixed as much of it in his mind as he could.

He looped all the way around until he was outside the

building again, opened the main door and stepped inside. There was a corridor and, at the end, what looked like a reception area. Milton looked up. There was a smoke alarm fitted to the ceiling and a series of nozzles for a fire-suppression system. He went forward, following the corridor for three paces and then passing through a pair of impressive security doors that were held open on magnetic stays. They were stainless steel and perhaps two inches thick. Frankie Fabian had been right: he could see that when they were closed and locked they would present a serious impediment to forward progress. He continued for another eight paces and reached the reception area. There was a smart desk, a table and two comfortable chairs. There was another security door in the opposite wall, but this one was locked.

The clerk smiled at him as he approached the desk.

"Hello, sir. How can I help you?"

"I'd like to rent a safe deposit box."

"Certainly, sir. You're in the right place for that. Have you rented a box from us before?"

"I'm afraid not. I've never had one before, actually."

"It's very simple. It'll take twenty minutes. Would you like to do it now?"

"Yes, please." Milton nodded down to his bag. "I've actually got the items I'd like to store with me."

"In that case, let me get the paperwork sorted out for you."

It was indeed a simple process. The man, who introduced himself as Michael, took him through the procedure. Milton took out the passport and electricity bill and handed them to Michael to be scanned. There was a simple lease agreement to be filled out and the first month's key deposit to be paid. It was a hundred pounds; Milton paid it in cash.

"There, Mr. Knight," Michael said when they were done. "Simple. Would you like to come downstairs to the vault with me? I'll get you your box."

Michael took an RFID card and swiped it through a reader next to the security door. There was a buzzing noise as the locks opened, and the door clicked ajar. Michael pushed it back and led the way inside. The decor immediately became less opulent. The corridor walls were bare concrete and there was no decoration. Back here, Milton saw, it was all about security.

"It's very safe," Michael said as he turned a corner and descended a flight of stairs. "The only way in is through the front, and there are two security doors between there and the vault."

They reached the bottom of the stairs and a pair of elevator doors. "Does the lift come down here?" Milton asked.

The man shook his head. "No. It serves the rest of the building, but it stops on the ground floor." He turned and pointed out a metal roller door and then, beyond that, a barred security door. "These are closed at night. Anyone who tried to get in through here would have to go through the two doors upstairs, then the roller door, then this one. There's a state-of-the-art alarm, too, of course. I don't like to tempt fate, but we've been here since 1912 and we've never lost any of our clients' belongings to fire or theft. We're as confident as we can be that there's no way inside when we've got everything locked up tight."

"It's very impressive."

They reached the vault. The door was formidable: stainless steel and secured by two locks that were opened with dials. There was a viewing room at the end of the corridor, and Michael ushered Milton toward it. He knocked on the door to ensure that the room was empty and, when there was no response, unlocked the door with a key that was clipped to his belt.

"If you'd wait in here, please, Mr. Knight. I'll get your box for you. I'll just be a minute."

Milton went inside. It was a small room with a table and no other pieces of furniture. The man came back after a minute with a reasonably large metal box. It was around four inches by twelve inches by six inches and, judging by the noise that it made as it was set down on the inspection table, it was heavy.

"When you want to open your box, you just need to come in and visit us. We'll check you in upstairs and then bring you down here to a viewing room and bring you your box. It has two locks." He turned the box around so that Milton could see the fascia at the front. There were two keyholes. The man inserted a key into one and turned it. "This one is for us, but you need to unlock both to open the box, and you are the only person who has the other key." He laid a key on the table next to the box. "When you're ready, open the box and leave your belongings inside. When you're finished, just ring this bell and I'll come and get you."

"Thank you," Milton said.

Michael left the room, closed the door behind him and locked it.

Milton examined the box. A small plastic plaque above the twin keyholes denoted that it was box 221. He committed that to memory. He unlocked the box with the key that the clerk had left him and opened it. He removed the empty tray from the box. He reached into the satchel and took out the things that he had purchased. He took out the pay-as-you-go phone, switched it on, and checked that there was a signal. There was: three out of five bars. He had been unsure whether it would operate in the basement, and it was a relief to find that it did. He entered a number into the phone's memory and then switched it off again. He tore open the cellophane sheath that held the envelopes together and collected the two copies of the *Mail.* He tore the newspapers into ten separate sections, folded them and slid them into the envelopes. He put the cable ties into the envelopes at the bottom of the stack. Finally, he dropped the phone into another and made sure to leave that one on top of the others. He sealed them all, replaced the tray in the box, closed the box and turned the key in the lock.

There was a button on the wall next to the door; he pushed it, a bell sounded in the corridor outside, and Michael unlocked and opened the door.

"All done, Mr. Knight?"

"Yes, all done. Thank you very much."

Michael smiled his satisfaction and told Milton to wait as he went back into the vault to store the box. He collected him, led him past the locked vault door, back up the stairs and into the reception area again.

"Is there anything else you need to know?" he asked him.

"No," Milton replied. "That's all I need."

Chapter Thirty-Four

MILTON WENT home to change into dark clothes and then took the underground out to Hounslow and walked the rest of the way to the warehouse. The car park was quiet once again, and he recognised the Audi in which he had been collected the previous night. It was parked next to a white transit van. He could see a line of light shining through the narrow gap between the roller door and the concrete sill, and, when he tapped on the side door that they had used yesterday, he had to wait only a few moments until Spencer Fabian appeared to let him inside.

Milton followed him into the main room. Frankie Fabian wasn't here tonight. Marcus and his sister, Lauren, were sat at the same table as before, the remains of a Chinese takeaway set out on the table between them. Vladimir was studying the plans on the wall. Marcus and Lauren turned to him, expressions of distaste very evident on their faces. Vladimir was more circumspect.

"You ready?" Spencer said to him.

"Yes," Milton said.

Marcus stood. "Before we get going, I want to make one thing clear. You do exactly as you're told, all right?"

"I understand."

Marcus walked over to him. "Put your arms out," he said.

Milton did as he was told. He knew that they wouldn't trust him, and could hardly blame them for that. He had expected to be frisked, and Marcus was thorough about it as he started at his shoulders and worked all the way down to his ankles.

"He's clean," he reported to the others.

"Good," Spencer said. "Just so you know, Smith, I've got this." He opened his jacket to show a holstered pistol.

"If you do anything I don't like—and I mean anything—I won't have a problem popping you in the head. We're clear about how this is going to be happening?"

"Very clear," Milton said.

Milton wasn't surprised that they had a weapon. It was possible, maybe even likely, that Marcus was armed, too. Milton had assumed that would be the case.

Marcus turned to his brother, sister and Vladimir. "Ready?"

"Ready," Lauren said.

"Whenever you are," Vladimir said.

Spencer nodded.

"Let's go."

#

LAUREN TOOK the wheel of the transit van and drove them into London. The others were in the back and conversation was at a minimum. Milton could diagnose the reason for the silence. It was nervousness. Milton was anxious, too. If they were caught, he wouldn't be able to count upon his previous connections to extricate him from legal difficulties. He wouldn't be able to call Control and ask for assistance. Michael Pope, the new Control, would have no choice but to ignore him, regardless of their friendship. Milton would be treated as a criminal, just as the others would be treated as criminals, and his punishment would be identical to theirs.

Marcus reached into a bag and tossed each man a pair of new gloves, the tags still on, and a balaclava.

Milton gazed through the rain-slicked windscreen as they drove into the city. The roads were wet, with standing water pooling out of overflowing drains, and the wheels of the van cast spray across the pavements as they splashed through the puddles. They entered the Square Mile, the tall towers of the office blocks scraping into the angry clouds overhead, myriad squares of light in the windows from offices that were always left illuminated. It was Saturday, and the city emptied out over the weekend, a stark contrast to the teeming throng that populated it throughout the week. Now, though, the pavements were almost empty and the stores and restaurants and cafés that were open were doing a sluggish trade.

Milton's hands were in his lap and, as he turned his gaze down onto them, he saw that they were clenched into tight fists.

Chapter Thirty-Five

MILTON DIDN'T know how they intended to get onto the roof. He followed the others until they stopped outside the branch of Costa Coffee that was four doors to the north of the vault at number eighty-six. It was a modern concrete building with five floors, each floor equipped with six long, tinted windows. Milton looked up to the top storey. It angled away, with a TV aerial just visible above the edge of the camber.

"Gloves?" Marcus said.

Milton was already wearing the pair that he had been given in the van.

"Balaclavas."

Milton took the close-fitting knitted cap and pulled it over his head.

Marcus nodded to his brother that they were ready. Spencer took a key from his pocket and looked up and down Hatton Garden. It was quiet, with no traffic and no pedestrians. The late hour, twenty past nine, meant that passing traffic was also at a minimum. Milton looked back to the van. Lauren was staying with it to keep a watch on the street and to warn them if anything required them to take action. That was fine as far as Milton was concerned; one less person to worry about when they were in the vault.

Spencer stepped up to the door, inserted the key and opened it. Milton heard the warning bleep of the alarm, but Spencer went straight to it and input the code. The alarm fell silent. This part of the job, at least, had clearly been facilitated by an insider. Milton wondered what must have happened to make that possible. One of the Fabian family's connections had infiltrated this business, perhaps, or they had told an existing employee that they were going to hit the shop and offered a percentage of the takings in return for giving them easy access. It didn't matter. They were inside now.

Spencer went through the café to a door in the rear wall, opened it and started up the stairs beyond. The others followed, each carrying his assigned bag of equipment. Milton's bag contained a ten-pound industrial angle grinder, and the blunt edges dug into his spine as the bag bounced on his back. The others carried the rest of the equipment that they would need, including the component parts of a powerful core drill and a wide selection of tools.

The stairwell led all the way up the middle of the building to the roof. It took them a minute to make their way to the top. There was a door there. Spencer took out another key, unlocked it, and pushed it open. Milton waited his turn to go through. He stepped out, a damp breeze whipping around him as he turned and gazed out over the tops of the nearby buildings. He could see the crenelated towers of the Barbican, glowing yellow from the lights within. He could see the taller spire of the Shard, the tapered finger of Tower 42, and the spectral cranes that told of the city's renewed prosperity.

This particular rooftop was bare and empty. There was a rail to guard the drop from the edge, but, save the aerial on a raised bracket, there was nothing else of note.

"Come on," Marcus called out in a quiet, tight voice. "Move."

They hurried back to the south. The building immediately adjacent was another modern construction, this one in red brick rather than plain concrete. The end of the roof that they were on was demarked by a raised concrete lip, but it was no more than four feet high. Milton anchored his hands on the top and pushed himself up, his boots sliding against the face of the wall until they found enough traction for him to shove himself up and over the edge.

The next building was flush against its neighbour, with a narrow path formed by an unguarded drop to the left and a recessed seventh storey on the right. They hurried across it. The next building was the one that they wanted, the building with the vault in the basement. There was a U-shaped gap between the two buildings. Milton reached the edge and stood next to Spencer as they both looked down. It was a drop of eight or nine feet. If they descended into the drop, crossed to the facing wall and then started up again from there, there would be a climb of fourteen or fifteen feet to get to the roof of the next building, with nothing for their feet to purchase.

Spencer unslung his rucksack, reached inside and withdrew a rope with a small grapnel fixed to one end. He took a moment to aim and then, after composing himself, sent the grapnel up and over the gap. The metal implement clanged noisily and then the teeth scraped as he carefully drew it back. The teeth fastened against the lip of the adjacent roof, secure enough to withstand a firm jerk. Spencer tied the other end around the chimney stack behind them, grabbed the rope, and, after taking off his pack, he hauled himself across. Milton removed his own pack and followed. The rope was fibrous and rough, but his gloves were thick enough that he couldn't really feel it. He reached the other side of the narrow gap, swung his leg over the edge and rolled onto the roof.

Milton waited to help Marcus and then they both helped as Vladimir secured the packs to a second rope so that they could be hauled across. Vladimir came over last of all, and they assembled at the skylight.

"Ready?"

"What about the alarm?"

"It's down. We took it out half an hour ago. That okay with you?"

Milton was not in a position to question him, and so he gave a nod. The others did, too.

Marcus took a large pair of bolt cutters and fixed the jaws around the padlock that fastened the security grate over the skylight. He pushed the jaws together and the clasp of the padlock was sheared right through. It dropped onto the roof. The grate was on hinges. Marcus put the bolt cutters aside, crouched down, and lifted the grate up and pushed it away. The skylight was installed on top of a short curb that was attached to the roof trusses. The inside of the skylight was a box constructed of plywood sheathing which was attached to the inside of the curb at the top and the ceiling joists at the bottom. Spencer knelt next to his brother and used a drill to unscrew the unit, removing each long screw and then carefully lifting the unit away, revealing the bare trusses and the opening that looked down into the top-floor office.

Spencer nodded. “Do it.”

Marcus fed a line of rope through the loops of his kit bag and lowered it into the building. Milton took the other end of the rope and fastened it around a large brick chimney. He tugged on it to check that it was secure, and then gave Marcus the thumbs-up. Marcus grabbed the rope and slid down it, disappearing into the darkness below. A flashlight clicked on, the light shielded, the beam carefully directed around the room. Marcus unfastened the end from the bag and hissed that they could draw it back up again. Spencer secured the rope to the second bag, a black fabric sheath that contained the industrial drill that they were going to use when they got down to the vault. It was a heavy piece of equipment—Milton estimated thirty or forty kilograms—and they lowered it slowly until Marcus hissed up to them that he had it. Spencer slid down the rope, then Vladimir. Milton took one final look at the rooftops and chimneys of the buildings around him, crossed his fingers that he wasn’t about to do something inherently stupid, and came down last of all.

Chapter Thirty-Six

THE FIFTH AND SIXTH FLOORS of the building were open-plan offices occupied by a diamond-trading firm. There were twelve desks on the sixth floor, each with a chair behind it. Each desk had a screen and a keyboard, and then the usual tangle of junk—photographs, pen holders, stacks of paper—that the employee who sat at the desk had collected. Milton had studied the floor plan for the building and knew the rough layout: there was a small kitchen over there, on the north side of the building, male and female toilets next to that, and two screened-off offices where management would sit. They had no interest in this floor save for the opportunity it would afford them to descend into the building.

They paused to equip themselves from the bag that Vladimir was carrying. They each had a workman's belt with a selection of clips and hooks attached around the circumference. Milton put his on. He took a shielded flashlight from the bag and secured it to his belt, then collected a headband that was fitted with a lamp. He put it on his head, leaving the torch unlit. The lamps were unshielded, and they would only use them once they were in the lift shaft.

Marcus led the way, walking between the desks until he reached the lobby area. The others followed. There was a reception desk, an old sofa and a coffee table, and a sign on the wall that advertised the name of the business. Marcus summoned the lift while his brother located the breaker box. The lift arrived and Spencer shut off the power, stranding the elevator car at the top of the shaft.

Milton opened the door to the stairs and led the way down to the fifth floor. He emerged into the lobby and, shining his flashlight carefully, checked the rest of the floor.

It was similar to the one above it: desks, a break-out area, a separate conference room formed by glass partition walls. It was empty, too.

It would have been much easier if they could have taken the stairs to the first floor, but, as Fabian had noted, the way down was blocked with sturdy doors on every floor, and so they had decided that it would be quicker and simpler to use the shaft.

Marcus was already working on the elevator doors. There was a small hole in the metal, barely larger than a penny. Milton knew what it was. An elevator usually had two sets of doors. The first set was on each lobby and the second was in the car itself. Both opened to allow access to the interior. Marcus took out a small drop key, inserted it into the door, and turned it. The lobby doors parted, revealing the empty shaft below.

It was pitch black. Tripping the breakers on the sixth floor had also killed the power to the emergency lights in the shaft, leaving it just an inky black hole that swallowed their torch light before it had shone down more than six metres. Vladimir dropped his bag on the floor and Milton collected the harness, ropes and other abseiling equipment that had been stored inside. He used a double fisherman's knot to anchor the rope to the handle of a door, slipped into his harness and tested that everything was secure. He slid the empty bag beneath the ropes to protect them from friction against the sharp edge of the floor, reached up for the lamp fitted to his helmet, flicked it on and looked into the shaft. There were pipes and bundles of electrical cables, junction boxes and components that were necessary for the safe functioning of the lift.

He leaned back into his cradle and kicked out, letting out enough rope to descend two metres beneath the lip of the fifth-floor door. Most of the stress on the anchor was exerted during the first few metres of descent, so Milton lowered himself carefully. He looked down, shining his headlamp on the wall beneath him to identify any hazards, and then kicked again. It was dark and dusty and he suddenly felt very vulnerable. Each floor was around three metres from floor to ceiling, and then there was the basement. He was halfway between the fourth and fifth floors; that meant there was a void that was at least fifteen metres deep beneath him. If the Fabians decided that they had second thoughts and wanted to get rid of him, it would have been a simple thing to untie or sever the rope and leave him to plummet to the bottom. The impact would either kill him outright or break his legs; either way, he would be finished.

He drew a breath and kicked again.

His boots landed on the exterior doors of the fourth floor.

He kicked again and then again, and the doors to the third floor passed him by.

Milton fed the rope through the karabiner with an easy, practiced motion. It was a difficult descent through the murk. He was unable to see all the potential snags and hazards until it was almost too late, but he had managed more challenging abseils than this. He was a little out of breath by the time he reached the bottom, but that was it.

He looked straight up and flicked his headlamp on and off two times. He heard the sound of the next climber clipping himself to the rope, and then the sound of boots thudding against the wall as the man started down.

Milton unclipped himself, removed his harness and shone his torch back up to just above the external elevator door. There was a roller in the mechanism atop it, and the roller locked the door from the inside. Milton pushed it up. The external doors opened a couple of inches and Milton was able to force them apart a little more.

No light was admitted into the shaft through the forced doors; it was just as dark on the other side. Milton shone his headlamp inside and saw that there was a security door blocking the way out.

He heard boots thud against the surface of the lift shaft

as whoever had followed him down reached the bottom.

Milton turned, his headlamp picking out Marcus, and watched as he opened his bag to take out a battery-powered builder's work lamp. The battery pack had three hours of life, and they had several spares. Marcus set it down on the floor and switched it on. The shaft was illuminated with a flood of light bright enough to reach up to the second floor. The third man was negotiating the descent. It was Vladimir. He was struggling a little with his harness, and, as he finally reached the bottom, Milton helped to release him.

"First time I've done that," he said, his accent coming through a little more clearly now that he was out of breath.

"Get a move on," Marcus said.

Vladimir shrugged his rucksack off his back, opened it and took out a hydraulic jack. The security door just outside the lift operated as a roller, pulled down and locked into place by mechanisms that had been set into the floor. Vladimir took out a jemmy and, inserting the tip between the bottom of the roller door and the floor, struggled with the lever for a minute until he had bent the metal just enough that it was possible to slide the toe of the jack between it and the floor. The jack was an expensive piece of industrial equipment, rated with a maximum lifting capacity of over twenty-five tons and more than powerful enough to handle the task at hand. Milton stood back as Vladimir switched it on. The metal groaned as the toe was pushed up, the sill creaking and then buckling as it was bent up and out of shape. Vladimir switched the jack off, repositioned it under the newly opened space, and activated it again. The jack forced its way up to full extension, buckling the door until there was a gap beneath it that was more than large enough for a man to slide through.

There wasn't enough space for Spencer at the bottom of the shaft, and he was waiting above for the signal that it was clear to descend. Vladimir removed the jack from beneath the door and placed it out of the way. Marcus slid beneath the door first, reaching back in to take his bag from

Milton. Vladimir went through next. Milton gave a quick whistle to signal that Spencer could come down, and then followed the others beneath the door.

He looked. It was familiar to him from the day before when he had been shown down here by Michael. There was a small space of around three square metres before it was curtailed by a second security door, this one barred and more substantial than the one they had just forced. The walls were bare, save for a fire extinguisher that was fixed to a bracket and a noticeboard to which was pinned health and safety information. The light from the work lamp in the lift shaft passed through the opening beneath the buckled roller door, but it was dim and Marcus augmented it by taking out and lighting a second lamp.

Vladimir appraised the door. "That's not going to be a problem," he said.

Milton went up to the door and looked through the bars. The basement corridor extended for ten metres, with a large metal vault door on the right-hand side.

He heard Spencer as he descended the shaft and dropped down to the floor.

Milton turned back to the door. Vladimir took out the cordless angle grinder that Milton had been carrying, got down on the floor and set to work. Just like the jack, they had not skimped on the equipment. The grinder was a high-quality DeWalt unit, and the blade sliced through the bars without difficulty. The operation created much more noise than when they had forced the first door, but Milton was content that they were deep enough below street level for most, if not all, of it to be muffled. Vladimir cut through the first bar, sparks flying out, and then moved onto the second, third and fourth. It took twenty minutes to cut through all of them and, when he was done, he put the grinder aside and turned to Milton.

"You look like you can handle yourself. Give me a hand."

Milton made sure his gloves were on tight, wrapped

both hands around the first bar, and pulled. It was strong and difficult to bend, but as Vladimir joined in they were able to yank it back until it was pointing at a forty-degree angle to the others. They repeated the feat for the other bars. Milton was sweating when they were finished, but the fruits of their labour were obvious: the bars had been rearranged so that there was plenty of space for them to slide through.

Milton went first.

Chapter Thirty-Seven

THE DOOR BEYOND was a much more serious obstacle. The roller door and the barred security door had been simple enough to bypass, but the door to the vault was of another order entirely. Milton recalled it from his visit yesterday. It was a top-of-the-range Chubb vault door, eighteen inches thick, with two large wheels and armoured hinges. The steel cladding that protected the exposed sides of the door was a mould, with reinforced concrete poured directly into it. The door was square, easier to suspend than the iconic round doors in the images that banks used to use in order to demonstrate their security. It was secured with massive metal cylinders that protruded from the door into the surrounding frame. Holding those bolts in place was a combination lock. The lock had two dials that controlled two locking mechanisms. Both locks had to be dialled open at the same time for the door to be unlocked, and no single person had both combinations. Both key holders had to be in place before the door could be opened.

It was an impressive obstacle. Milton guessed that it would have been possible to remove the door or to cut through it, but it would have taken hours—or possibly days—and they would have had to bring in a lot more equipment than they could have comfortably carried.

The Fabians' plan was to go around it instead.

There was enough space for all of them in the corridor. Marcus, Spencer and Vladimir set up work lamps, laid their bags down and removed the equipment inside. They had a Hilti DD350 diamond core drilling system. The drill bit was a hollow tube, half as long as Milton's arm, with clusters of diamond teeth fixed to its circumference with a strong resin. The bit was slotted onto the drill and secured in place. There was a power point on the wall, and the drill was plugged in. They had two tripods with a guidance rail suspended between them, and these were set up so that the drill bit was pressed flush against the wall. Vladimir wound the ratchet to position the bit against the surface.

"Water," Vladimir said.

They had a portable two and half gallon water supply, and the unit was attached to the drill with an extension hose.

Vladimir switched on the power and looked to Marcus for final approval. When he received it, he squeezed the trigger and started to drill. The operation made much less noise than Milton had anticipated. The diamond teeth bit through the concrete easily, and the motor did not need to work particularly hard to punch it through. Vladimir worked carefully, drilling a few inches into the wall and then withdrawing again. The hollow bit was full with a cylindrical cross section of the wall, much as an apple corer would remove a plug of apple. He removed the concrete core, cleaned out the bit, and then cut ahead again. The water from the supply unit sprayed directly onto the drill bit, damping down the dust that would otherwise have been thrown up.

The first hole took twenty minutes, much less time than Milton had anticipated. The water pooled on the floor, a dirty slurry that washed over their shoes.

Vladimir moved the rig, positioned the bit against the wall next to the freshly excavated hole, and started again.

There was nothing for Milton to do except wait.

The operation took just over three hours to complete. The aperture, when it had finally been finished, was small. Milton guessed it was no more than fifty-five centimetres across and forty centimetres from top to bottom. The wall was fifty centimetres thick. It was little more than a slot.

Milton looked at the others.

"I'll go first," Marcus said.

He stepped up to the opening, put his head and shoulders inside—there was no obvious space on either side of him—and slithered ahead. "Push me," he called back, and his brother and Vladimir helped, raising his legs and impelling him forward until his hips were halfway into the breach. Milton heard him grunt with effort, wriggling up and down until he managed to slide forward enough so that his widest point was safely through the gap. He slid ahead, dropping down to bear his weight on his hands and then clambering on so that his legs were all the way through. It had taken a minute. Milton wondered whether he would manage the same feat and, if he became stuck, what they would do. He was bigger than Marcus. The prospect of negotiating the opening was not appealing.

Vladimir went through next. Milton and Spencer collected the bags with the rest of their equipment and passed them through the hole into the vault.

"Your turn," Spencer said to him.

Milton knelt down next to the hole. He looked through and saw row upon row of boxes arrayed across the wall opposite. The opening was just higher than his waist, and he extended his arms and pushed ahead, sliding his shoulders through and then allowing Spencer to lift his legs and push him. The sensation of being so constricted was exquisitely unpleasant, and he was very aware of the concrete pressing at him on all sides. He wriggled ahead, quite sure that his hips would jam between the walls. They did not. He angled his pelvis and shoved forward, first sliding the right side of his body ahead and then following with the left. Spencer gripped his ankles and shoved, and, suddenly, Milton was far enough through the opening to put his palms on the floor and bring his legs through, too.

"Fat bastard," Marcus said derisively.

Milton stayed on the cold concrete floor of the vault for a moment and gathered his breath. He was going to have to get out again, and without help. Spencer slithered through the hole, his brother tugging his arms to ease him into the vault.

"Good work," Marcus said, "but we're just getting started. These boxes are going to be tough to open. We need to push on."

"You want to tell us what we're looking for now?" Spencer said, looking at Milton.

"Photographs."

"A bit more specific?"

"No. If you find anything like that, show it to me. I'll tell you when we've found it."

Vladimir rapped his knuckle against the nearest box. "What about the other stuff?"

Marcus grinned. "Into the bags."

#

THEY HAD four cordless metal drills, four chisels and four short-handled sledgehammers. Marcus distributed them and then went to the back of the vault to organise the bags that they would use to remove their loot.

Milton took a position to the right of the vault. He made sure that he was facing the drawers numbered 200 through 250. He had no idea in which box the files had been stored—indeed, he had no proof that they were even here at all—but this was the side of the vault that he wanted to be near.

"Come on, ladies," Marcus called out. "What are we waiting for? Let's open them up!"

They all set to work.

Milton took the sledgehammer and slammed it into the row of drawers until two of the metal fasciae were weak enough to dislodge, offering easier access to the locks behind. He took a marker and inscribed three Xs on the lock: two were over each keyhole and the other was on the far left of the lock, next to the edge of the box door on the side opposite the hinge. He took the drill and drilled the two keyholes for an inch until the bit pierced the lock. He stopped, removed the drill and looked into the hole. He could see the locking mechanism. He drilled into the third X, pushing it all the way through until the bit was spinning without resistance. The lock bracer that was holding the door shut was broken, and, without it, the door swung open. He made a show of taking out the tray and examining the contents: a collection of old war medals.

The others had tried different tactics to open the drawers, but Milton's method was the fastest and he was the first to get at the contents inside. He removed the drawer from the cabinet.

The vault was soon filled with a cacophony of noise: the crash as sledgehammers were driven into the metal fasciae and then the screams of anguished metal as the drills were used to force the locks. There came an exuberant whoop as Marcus went through the contents of the first drawer that he had opened. He tossed the empty tray on the floor and held up a tiara. It was mounted in gold and set in silver, with rose-cut and pear-shaped stones.

"Look at this shit!" he gloated. "Look at it! This is going to be insane!"

"Into the bag."

Milton went back to his corner of the vault. He addressed the box with the stencilled 221 and crashed the sledgehammer against it until the protective cover fell away. He drilled into the box, popping the lock and opening the door. Everything was as he had left it, as he had known it would be: the ten envelopes, one atop the other. The two at the bottom were uneven with the shape of the cable ties, and he felt the bulk of the mobile phone in the envelope on the top. He made a show of opening the top envelope and glimpsing inside it. He found the phone, reached inside, switched it on and hid it in his palm.

"Anything?" Marcus said. Milton looked up; Marcus was watching him suspiciously.

"No," he said. "Just papers."

"What kind of papers?"

"Newspapers."

"Let me have a look."

Milton readied himself for action. The timing was

unwelcome. He would have preferred them to have found the evidence before he was forced to put his plan into effect, but there was nothing for it now. He primed himself. Spencer wasn't looking, and he was the one with the pistol. Milton had the phone in his right palm, shielding it from Marcus. He held up the envelope and waited for Marcus to draw closer. His muscles itched with adrenaline. He would disable Marcus as quickly as he could and try to get to Spencer before he could draw the gun…

"*Ty che, blyad?*"

It was Vladimir.

Marcus paused. "You what?"

Milton spoke enough Russian to understand that Vladimir had cursed in surprise.

Vladimir was proffering a velvet bag, the drawstring held open. Marcus turned to look, temporarily forgetting Milton. Vladimir told Marcus to hold out his hand and poured out the contents of the bag: twelve large diamonds tumbled out, their facets sparkling in the glow of the work lamps.

Marcus exhaled. "Holy shit…"

Milton moved quickly.

He pressed DIAL on the phone and slid it into the hip pocket of his trousers. By the time Marcus had finished replacing the jewels in the velvet bag and dropping that in with the rest of their loot, Milton had stood and moved to start work on the box that was beneath 221, quickly prising it open and withdrawing a stack of fifty-pound bank notes that were held together by ancient, crumbling elastic bands.

Marcus turned to him, a quizzical look on his face as if he was trying to remember what he had been about to say. He paused there, his mouth open, before he laughed, gave a happy "fuck it," took up his sledge and went back to the drawers.

Milton felt the shape of the phone pressing against his leg. He had the sudden, awful thought that the tightness of his trousers might lead to the phone's buttons being pressed against his hip. If that happened and the call was interrupted…

He put the concern out of his mind. Nothing could be done about that now. He had to hope that everything held together. He considered himself a skilled improviser, but, down here, with three men against him, at least one of whom was armed… there would only be so much that he could do.

He forced the fascia of the box away, picked up his drill and set about the locks.

Chapter Thirty-Eight

MILTON REGULARLY checked his watch. It took around fifteen minutes to open each box: ten minutes to pulverise the fascia until it could be pulled off, then another five to drill inside without damaging the contents of the tray. Milton had been approached by the others on five occasions with what might have been the photographs that he was looking for. He opened the envelopes and wallets and skimmed through the contents. There were photographs, some of people in compromising positions, a couple that he even thought he recognised, together with wills and deeds and other legal documents. But there were no pictures that resembled those that Hicks had described to him. Milton started to worry that they would not be here at all. What if Hicks had been wrong?

It quickly became unbearably hot. The vault was not ventilated, and they were working hard. Milton had started to sweat and had been the first to remove his shirt. Marcus had looked at the tattoo of an angel that Milton had across his back and had made the kind of juvenile comment that he had come to expect of him; but, ten minutes later, he grumbled that he was hot, too, and took off his own shirt. His skin was white and he was put together like a featherweight, muscles taut with the exertion of the work. Within ten minutes Spencer and Vladimir had followed their example, with Spencer taking his pistol out of the shoulder holster and shoving it into the waistband of his trousers.

Another half hour had passed when Milton saw in the corner of his eye that Spencer had stopped working. He had just opened a box and was rifling through the contents.

"Is this it?"

Milton rested the sledgehammer against the cabinet,

picked up his shirt and used it to wipe the sweat from his face.

Spencer came across to him with the box in his arms.

"Well?"

Milton took the tray and looked inside. It was one of the larger boxes, and it was full. The bottom two-thirds was taken up by neatly stacked courses of banknotes fastened together with paper straps. Sitting atop the money were two clear plastic documents folders. Milton set the box down and opened the first folder. It held a sheaf of photographic paper. Milton took the photographs out and looked through them. He recognised Leo Isaacs, much younger then, shirtless and with a look of wide-eyed pleasure on his face. There were other pictures of Isaacs, together with several other men, some of whom Milton thought that he recognised. There were boys, too, young boys. Many of them were naked. There were pictures of the men embracing them. Milton felt a knot of anger in his stomach as he worked through the pictures.

"Is that it? What you're looking for?"

Milton blinked twice, bringing his focus back, reminding himself where he was and how much danger he was in. He put the box on the floor and stood. "No," he said. "Keep looking."

Spencer exhaled impatiently. "Come on," he said. He turned and indicated the wall of boxes. "We're nearly halfway through them. What is it you're after?"

"Now," Milton said.

"What?"

"I mean I'll tell you when I see it," he said.

Milton took in the room. He did it nonchalantly, without taking his attention away from Spencer, but he positioned each man in relation to where he was standing: Spencer, right in front of him; Marcus, at the other side of the room; Vladimir, behind Spencer.

"You have some nerve," Spencer said. "You turn up, tell us what to do, talk to me like you're in charge? Well, you ain't in charge. This says I am." He drew the pistol and waved it in Milton's face like an amateur. "What do you think about that?"

"Now," Milton said.

Spencer looked at him, confused. "What?"

"I think you should just relax."

Spencer laughed. "You're unbelievable." He turned his head to his brother. "He's unbelievable."

"Just put the gun down," Milton said. "You're in charge. But just put it down, all right? Put it down *now.*" He laid extra emphasis on the last word, trying to find a difficult middle ground between urgency and conciliation. It was difficult not to sound like he was delivering an order, and that appeared to be the way that Spencer interpreted it.

"I've had enough of this."

He raised the pistol.

"Do him," Marcus suggested. "He's bluffing about Eddie. We'll take our chances."

#

ALEX HICKS pressed the Bluetooth headset to his ear and tried to make out the conversation.

"What?"

"... should relax."

Shit.

Hicks pulled the balaclava down over his face, collected the plastic bottle and the rag from the seat next to him, opened the door and stepped out of the car that he had stolen earlier. He hurried across the street to the large black doors that led to the ground-floor reception area of the vault. He saw the white Transit van with the woman inside it. He had been watching her all night, ever since the van had delivered Milton and the other men. She was keeping a watch. He had been careful, and he didn't think that she had seen him. He had to hope that she was unarmed, but there was not much to be done about that now.

Laughter.

"... *unbelieve...*"

"... *gun down.*"

There were ostentatious signs fixed on either side of the door that announced THE LONDON VAULT LIMITED. The door was significant, with golden figures that read 88–90 above it and a brass letterbox in the right-hand door, next to a polished door handle. He pushed the letterbox open, jammed the nozzle of the plastic bottle into the gap and squeezed. He had filled it with turpentine, and he squirted it inside until the bottle was almost empty. Then, he took the rag, emptied out the rest of the accelerant, stuffed it into the letterbox and lit it with his lighter. He pushed it all the way inside.

He held the letterbox open and glanced inside. It was dark for a moment until the turpentine caught fire. The interior of the hallway was revealed in the sudden glow from the flames, oranges and reds and yellows, and Alex felt the waft of heat on the flesh around his eyes and against his lips. Black smoke gushed up to the ceiling and started to leak out through the letterbox and the gap between the door and the doorstep.

An alarm shrieked out a warning.

#

MILTON STARED into the small black hole at the end of the pistol. Where was Hicks? Something had gone wrong, and now he was underground, looking into the business end of a Glock with no support and no plan B. Spencer straightened his arm, the gun held out in a confident grip. What was their plan? Shoot him, leave him in the vault for the police to clean up? There was no connection between him and them. He would be a useful diversion, a red herring that would lead them away from the Fabians. And, in the meantime, they would have made a tremendous score from the loot they had been able to filch from the vault.

It was not how Milton had envisaged the end of his life.

"Do him!" Marcus urged.

The vault was suddenly filled with an ear-splitting shriek. There was an alarm on the wall on Milton's side of the room, and it was deafening. A half second later, the sprinklers in the ceiling gushed into life and water spilled down onto them.

There was a moment of confusion, and that was all that Milton needed.

Spencer had turned a fraction to look up at the alarm. His attention was off Milton just for a moment. Milton punched hard into Spencer's stomach, hard enough to knock him back. Spencer stumbled, tripping over a drill and falling to the floor, the contents of a nearby drawer spilling over him.

Marcus went for the small pistol that he had kept hidden inside the pocket of his trousers. Milton had anticipated that he was armed, and had prioritised him for attention. Marcus's fingers struggled to get into the pocket. Milton's right hand went out to the handle of the sledgehammer propped against the wall next to him, already moving quickly enough to yank it off the ground and begin a long and powerful swing. He hopped forward as he swung it, closing the distance enough so that Marcus was within the radius of the sledge. The head smashed into the side of his body with terrific force. Marcus collapsed. Milton let go of the sledge, crouched down and took his pistol—a Beretta—from him. He was wheezing as he inhaled, and Milton guessed that he had broken his ribs. That would be painful.

Milton quickly examined the pistol. It was a Px4 Storm subcompact with a single-action trigger and an ambidextrous thumb safety. The pistol was perfect for concealed carry, weighing less than thirty ounces when it was unloaded. This one weighed more.

Milton turned back to Spencer. He was on his back and the impact of his landing had jarred the Glock from his hand. Milton knelt down, collected the gun, and used it instead of the Beretta. He tossed the smaller pistol out of the vault.

Vladimir regarded him warily.

Milton trained the pistol on him.

"You," he shouted to Vladimir. "Go and get box 221. It's on the floor. Over there, where I was standing."

Vladimir did as he was told, collecting the tray from the floor and bringing it open.

"What are you doing?" Spencer wheezed.

"Open the envelopes at the bottom," Milton ordered Vladimir. "Tip them out."

Vladimir looked to Marcus and Spencer. "I—"

"Don't look at them," Milton said. "They don't have the gun. I do. Get on with it."

The man did as he was told, opening the envelopes and upending them until the double-loop cable ties poured out.

"Hands behind your backs, gentlemen," Milton shouted, making himself heard over the sound of the alarm. "Vladimir is going to tie you up."

Vladimir was resigned. He started with Spencer, looping the ties around his wrists and fastening them tight. Marcus grunted from the pain in his ribs as his arms were drawn behind his back. Milton then indicated that Vladimir should lie on his stomach and told him to put his arms behind his back. He knelt down so that his knee was pressed into Vladimir's spine and fastened the ties around his wrists, pulling them until they bit into his flesh.

"Why are you doing this?" Marcus croaked. "What was in that fucking box?"

Milton knew that he shouldn't tarry, but he couldn't resist.

He leaned over and spoke into Marcus's face, loud enough for them all to hear. "The night you killed your brother, he was coming to see his sister because he was frightened. He was abused when he was a child. He wanted to tell that story, just like he wanted to confess to the robbery that he did with the two of you, and someone had threatened him. I know you killed him. And he was my friend."

"You're dead!" Spencer Fabian shouted out.

Milton told them to sit with their backs against the wall and then worked fast. The alarm was deafening and the water continued to pour down from the nozzles overhead. He collected the tray from Higgins's box and upended it into one of the empty bags. The bundles of money were sodden, but he scooped all of them out and dropped them into the bag. The clear plastic folders had protected the photographs from the water, and he pushed those inside, too.

"Smith!"

It was Spencer again.

Milton turned to the three of them trussed up and arranged against the wall, the water running around their bodies.

"Don't worry," Milton said. "You won't be waiting long."

"I mean it," Spencer shouted. "You're dead."

Milton collected the bag and pushed it through the hole in the wall. "You're not the first person to tell me that. One day it'll be true, but not today. Don't do anything silly. The police will be here soon. You can tell them what you've been up to."

Milton collected his shirt. It was soaked through, but he put it on anyway. He pulled on the balaclava, put his head and shoulders into the hole and slithered ahead. It was an uncomfortable sensation again, made worse by the thought of the three men behind him and the clamour that announced that the emergency services must be on their way, and he was grateful when he managed to force his way through and into the corridor beyond.

He slid beneath the two doors that they had forced and reached for the rope.

He put the bag over his shoulder and started to climb.

Chapter Thirty-Nine

THE WHITE TRANSIT van drove away before Hicks could confront the driver. The sound of the alarm from inside the vault was loud, and smoke belched out from the gap beneath the door and a letterbox that didn't close all the way. Hicks guessed that the driver had made the assessment that there was nothing to be done, so she had evacuated the area to save herself before the arrival of the authorities.

That moment was close at hand. As Hicks slid back into the stolen car and started the engine, he saw the flashing blue and red lights of a fire engine as it turned off Holborn and started north up Hatton Garden. Milton and Hicks had looked at the map of the area and added the locations of the nearest fire stations. It was one and a half miles to Soho, the location of the station they thought most likely to respond. With no traffic on the road and travelling under blue lights, they had estimated that the engines would take five minutes to arrive.

That was going to be cutting it very tight.

The truck killed its siren and pulled to a stop outside the vault.

"They're here, Milton," he said into the microphone of the headset. "You need to be out of there."

No response.

The fire-fighters spilled out of the engine and hurried to the door, the tendrils of smoke uncurling into the light from the streetlamps. One of the men tried the door; a second went back to the truck and returned with a sledgehammer.

Hicks couldn't wait any longer. He put the car into gear and pulled out, driving carefully so as to avoid drawing attention to himself. As he turned into St Cross Street, he saw another fire truck and a police car racing north along Hatton Garden.

"Milton," he said, "respond."

Still nothing.

"You've got to get out, Milton. Now. I'm going to wait on Kirby Street for as long as I can."

Nothing.

#

MILTON STARTED the climb back up to the fifth floor. Smoke was dribbling into the lift shaft from ventilation shafts and between the imperfect seal of the lobby doors on the first floor. The sound of the alarm was louder as he ascended past the ground floor. The smoke thickened and he was glad of the wool of the balaclava over his mouth. He moved slowly and purposefully, hauling the rope hand over hand. There were plenty of footholds on his ascent, but the muscles in his arms and shoulders were burning by the time he reached the open doors. He stepped out and pulled the rope up behind him. He didn't think that the men in the vault would be able to free themselves, but, in the event that they managed it, he wanted to make sure that they would find it as difficult as possible to follow him. He was confident that they would still be there when the authorities arrived and, as he rolled his shoulders to relieve the ache, he heard the sound of sirens from outside.

He needed to move faster.

Milton took the bag and ran to the sixth floor. He jogged through the office and pulled himself up the rope that they had used to enter the office. He braced himself on the lip of the opened skylight and pushed until he was out and on the roof, inhaling the cool air. He crept to the edge and looked down. Blue light flashed against the walls of the narrow canyon that was formed by the buildings on either side of the road. Fire-fighters were disembarking from two tenders, and, as he watched, a police car raced from the direction of Holborn. It screeched to a stop as another car pulled away from the kerb, rolled up to St Cross Street and turned to the east.

Hicks.

The street was too busy for Milton to exit through the coffee shop without drawing attention to himself. He had anticipated that.

Milton quickly undid the knot that had fastened the rope to the chimney, coiled it around his arm and, with the bag over his shoulder, ran across the rooftop to the west. The block was wide, around eighty metres from one edge to the other, and the heights of the rooftops varied from building to building. Milton clambered up some and slithered down others, leaping gaps and vaulting over obstructions, moving as quickly as he dared while still maintaining his footing. It took him three minutes to reach the opposite edge. He looked down on Leather Lane. It was empty. He knew that it wouldn't stay that way for long, especially when the men in the vault had been discovered, so he quickly looped the rope around an air-conditioning unit and tossed the rest over the side. The roof was around twelve metres above the street, and the rope was only six metres long.

He lowered himself over the edge, snagged the rope with both hands and then started to slither down it. He moved slowly, passing the rope from one hand to the other. The top two floors were empty offices, marked out by the estate agent's board that had been fixed to the building below him. The rope ran out when he was at the level of the second storey. He shrugged the straps of the bag off his shoulder and let them slide down his arm. The bag fell, landing with a muffled thump that would not be audible above the din of the engines and alarms from the other side of the building. He looked down. There was a narrow cornice above the fascia of the shop below; Milton could see from the protruding circular sign that it was a restaurant called Soya.

He rested his boots on the sill of the nearest window and, letting go of the rope, lowered himself so that he was in a squat. He turned, gripped the wet sill as best he could, and, moving slowly, he gradually let his arms bear his weight. When his arms were fully extended, he took one final look down and then, hoping for the best, he let go. Milton's descent was swift, but he was able to arrest it by grabbing his left hand onto the sign and his right onto the exposed edge of the cornice. His shoulders shrieked from the sudden exertion and the sign creaked as two of the screws that held it into place were torn out of the fascia.

Milton glanced down to the pavement, let go, and dropped the final two metres to the ground. He landed in a crouch, absorbing the impact easily, collected the bag and then set off at once. He headed north, passing the skeletal struts and corrugated sheets of a temporary market being built for Christmas, following Leather Lane to its junction with St Cross Street.

The alarms continued to wail behind him and, as he walked, he heard a crash and the sound of splintering wood. The fire brigade were breaking into the building.

#

HICKS HAD parked on Kirby Street, opposite the offices of a trendy creative design agency. He saw the figure as it turned right on St Cross Street. It was a man, medium height and build, a bag slung over his shoulder. He walked purposefully towards the car, approaching from the rear. Hicks tapped his foot on the brake two times, signalling with the lights, and then put the car into gear. The figure drew closer and passed through the downward cone of light thrown out by a streetlamp. It was Milton. He left the pavement and crossed into the street, opened the passenger door and got inside.

"What took you so long?" Milton said. "Any longer and I would've been shot."

"I didn't hear you," Hicks said. "Reception wasn't great."

"Never mind."

"You get it?" Hicks said.

Milton rested his hand on the bag on his lap. "I got it."

"The others?"

"Left them inside."

Hicks pulled out and drove south to Greville Street. "You get all of them?"

"Frankie Fabian wasn't there. Just his boys and a man he put on the team. His daughter was in the van. What happened to her?"

"She left when the fire engines came."

Milton nodded. "She's next. Her and her dad."

#

MILTON TOLD HICKS to drive them south, to Peckham Rye. He drove carefully, aware that to invite police attention now would be a very bad idea. Milton was silent, his face lost in concentration. He was soaked through, his shirt and trousers sodden from the extinguishers.

"What now?" Hicks said.

"After we're done, I need to look at what I've got. The photos. When that's done, I'm going to get them published. Higgins is going to find out what happened soon. Tomorrow, most likely. It'll be on the news. I don't want to hang on too long."

"And Higgins?"

"Relax, Hicks. I gave you my word. You helped me, I'll help you."

"You still want to play it like we said?"

"Yes."

"I don't suppose there's a different way?"

Milton looked across at him, but didn't speak.

"Never mind," Hicks said.

They turned onto Bellenden Road and Milton told him to slow the car. They passed beneath a railway bridge and Milton pointed to the left, into a narrow road that offered access to the railway arches. Businesses had been established in the arches: a garage that specialised in clutch and gearbox repairs, another that offered MOTs, a warehouse. The two arches farthest away from the road looked as if they were vacant, and Milton told Hicks to pull up alongside them. He stopped the car and killed the engine.

"Lovely place," he said, looking out just as a train rumbled over the bridge, squares of light from the brightly lit windows passing across the blue-painted wall to their right.

They both got out of the car. Milton walked to the door of the nearest unit. The arch had been bricked in, with a metal door set into the middle of the new wall. There was a manual combination lock on the door, and Hicks stood guard as Milton tapped in a code. The door unlocked and Milton pushed it open. He went inside first and Hicks followed.

It was dark. Hicks couldn't see anything, but he could hear the sound of a powerful industrial extractor fan. Milton muttered that he couldn't remember where the light switch was, and Hicks was about to offer to go and collect his flashlight from the boot of the car when two big strip lights flickered on above them. The room was filled with light.

Hicks looked around. Metal racking had been fitted along three walls of the space. The shelves were empty.

"What was this?

"It was the south London armoury for Group Fifteen. They cleared it out years ago, but the code still works."

"That was fortunate," Hicks said. "It's quiet here."

"It's best that no one sees us."

Hicks nodded. He wasn't looking forward to what he knew was coming next.

"Your family?" Milton asked.

"My wife's taken the kids to a friend's cottage. Cornwall. Wish I was there, too."

"You don't get to relax yet. We're only half done."

Hicks felt a twist of apprehension. "I know."

"You want a recap?"

"No," Hicks said. "I got it."

"You know what you've got to say to Higgins?"

"I'm fine, Milton. I've got it down."

"You've got to be convincing."

"I will be."

"If you're not—"

"I know, I know. I will be."

"We've got to make it *look* convincing, too."

"I'm not arguing. Let's get it over with."

Milton took off his jacket and hung it over the strut of one of the empty racks. He rolled up the sleeves of his wet shirt and balled his hands into fists. "Ready?"

"Do it."

Milton drew back his fist and struck Hicks square in the face. Milton's knuckles landed flush with Hicks's cheekbone and the starburst of pain that exploded was sudden and vicious. Hicks shook his head to try to clear it.

"Fuck," he said. "That smarts."

Milton opened and closed his fist. "Ready?" he said.

"Again."

Part Three

The Amends of Eddie Fabian

Chapter Forty

RICHARD HIGGINS had followed his usual routine that morning. He had risen at five thirty, gone for a run in the fields around his village, returned to shower and shave, and dressed in the clothes that he had prepared the night before.

Satisfied, he checked his appearance in the long free-standing mirror and went downstairs.

Higgins lived alone. He had never married and had never really been interested in the idea of it. He had always been a solitary person, from his youth throughout his career in the army and beyond, and he couldn't abide the thought of sharing his time with someone else. He supposed, when he was honest, that it was a selfish trait, but he didn't care. He was not prepared to sacrifice the life that he had built for himself in order to allow someone else the privilege of sharing it with him.

His cottage was quiet as he came downstairs. He switched on the breakfast news as he went through into the kitchen to fix his cereal. When he came back, the presenters had handed off to an outside broadcast that was filming on a street that he thought he recognised.

He turned up the volume.

He *did* recognise it. The reporter was standing in front of the doors to the London Vault. He had passed through those doors many times over the course of the last twenty years. He felt as if he was going to be sick.

The reporter spoke into the camera: "Hundreds of safe deposit boxes were emptied from the London Vault Safe Deposit company in London's jewellery district over the weekend in a dramatic heist. The thieves reportedly entered the company's premises through an elevator shaft in the building before using heavy cutting equipment to penetrate the vault. The robbers were also able to disarm the security system, allowing them to cut through the vault over the weekend undisturbed. An estimated two hundred safe deposit boxes were emptied during the robbery."

Higgins watched until the end of the report, then collected his phone from the charger and took it outside into the garden. It was a cold morning, dew clinging to the flowers and glistening on the lawn. He dialled Woodward.

"Have you seen the news?"

"I was just about to call you, sir," Woodward said.

"Do we know anything?"

"No. I've made a couple of calls, but the police are keeping this pretty close."

"Nothing?"

"No," Woodward said. "I'm trying to find out."

"Have you called the vault?"

"First thing I tried. No answer."

"No clue whether our boxes are affected?"

"None at all."

"Jesus," he said. "We need to go down there. Right now."

"You want me to drive you?"

"Yes. Get here as soon as you can."

#

WOODWARD LIVED nearby and he was at the general's cottage within half an hour. His Audi was a comfortable and expensive car and it ate up the miles as they headed southeast on the A40 toward Gloucester. Higgins glared out of the window, trying to work out what they needed to do.

Woodward glanced over at him. "So, what—we go and see the police?"

"What else can we do?"

"What are you going to say?"

"I don't know," Higgins admitted.

"You'll have to register as an owner of a box."

Higgins scowled at him. "How can I do that?"

"I don't understand—"

"Think," he snapped. "They're going to ask what I had in the box, aren't they? If it's been taken and they recover it, they'll need to know what I've lost so they can give it back to me. What am I going to say when they ask me that? 'I have some photographs of some very, very senior public figures doing things they ought not to have been doing.' How can I *possibly* say that? Or tell them about the money that I had there—how am I going to explain where I got it from?"

Woodward was quiet.

"We do need to talk to them," Higgins said. "Work out how much was taken. Maybe they didn't get all the boxes."

"They were saying two hundred. There must be twice that in the vault."

"There are five hundred," Higgins said.

"So maybe we're lucky. Better than fifty-fifty odds that we are."

Higgins grunted and stared out of the window at the bleak landscape that was rolling past the car. He had a very bad feeling about what they were going to find.

#

THE INVESTIGATION was headquartered at Holborn police station. It was chaotic. Reporters were setting up outside and broadcast vehicles crammed up against the kerb, and pedestrians were being forced out into the street to bypass the scrum. The atmosphere was fervid, with the more seasoned hacks comparing the raid to other, more famous heists and suggesting that this was a return to a more romantic kind of crime. A victimless heist, carried out with an audacity that some of the reporters were clearly a little breathless to recount.

Woodward and Higgins shoved through the middle of the pack. The reporters and their cameramen were ready with invective until they saw the expressions on the faces of the two men with the crew cuts and military bearing, and then they stood aside. The station was an ugly sixties construction with a flight of stone steps that led up from the street to the entrance. Higgins and Woodward ascended and went inside. Woodward went to speak to the officer at the front desk and, when he returned, explained that he had registered and that he had been told to take a seat. He led the way to a waiting area that was furnished with hard plastic chairs, garishly orange and sticky with the residue of discarded gum. Higgins sat down, feeling the ache in his muscles from his morning run, and watched Woodward as he stood in a corner and made a call on his phone.

Higgins struggled to maintain his composure. The delay was intolerable. He watched the plain-clothes detectives and uniformed officers as they hurried through the reception area, and none of them filled him with any confidence. He thought of his brother. Thomas had served in the Metropolitan Police, but that had been in a different time when officers were unconstrained by propriety and before the shackles of politically correct behaviour had been applied. The line between the police and the villains they pursued was blurred then, and the tactics that ambiguity allowed would have meant that there was a better chance that a crime like this would be solved. Now, though? When the police were staffed by fast-tracked university graduates with no experience and denied the tools that would have generated the quickest results? Higgins was not confident.

Woodward returned and took the seat next to Higgins. Woodward knew the general well enough to see that he was in a foul mood, so he sat quietly with his hands in his lap, fidgeting with his mobile phone. Higgins drummed his fingers against each other until he could bear the silence no more.

"Get the men together," he ordered.

"I just called them, sir. They're going to meet us tonight. Usual place."

Higgins nodded. He looked up at the busy scrum of people at the reception desk. Most of them wore anxious expressions, and several looked anguished. He guessed that some would have been the dealers who stored their diamonds in the vault. That was why the business had been started in Hatton Garden. The local businesses, many of them holding diamonds worth millions of pounds, needed somewhere that they could safely leave their stock. They needed somewhere that could offer them complete anonymity, a place where they wouldn't be asked questions, somewhere that could guarantee that their valuables would be secure. All of those qualities were, after all, what had persuaded Higgins that the vault was the perfect place to secure the evidence. All of those supposed benefits had been exposed now for what they really were: promises that could not be kept. The thought of it made Higgins sick.

He gazed at the chaos outside. "Could this be more than a coincidence?"

Woodward turned to him. "What do you mean, sir?"

"That our boxes were here?"

"I don't think so. It's a vault. It's been hit for the diamonds. No one knows about us. How could they?"

"Maybe." He paused, something nagging at the back of his mind. "Who knows that you've got a box there? Apart from me and you?"

"Shepherd. And I should never have told him."

Shepherd liked a drink, and his raucous behaviour during their regular dinners now became a portent for something more ominous.

Woodward saw the concern on Higgins's face. "He's a pain in the arse when he's drunk, but he's not a fool."

The general shook his head, not convinced, but let it pass. Woodward fell quiet; Higgins could see that there was something else on his mind. "What is it?" he asked.

"Probably nothing," Woodward replied.

"There's something."

"I can't get hold of Hicks."

"What do you mean?"

"He's not answering his phone."

Higgins frowned. Hicks was the newest member of the unit. The most vulnerable, perhaps. Perhaps it was just a coincidence that they couldn't find him the day after the general's safe deposit box was ransacked. Surely it was more likely that the robbery was opportunistic, as Woodward suggested, the chance to get at the jewels and other valuables that were stored in the vault. But Higgins was a careful man, and he did not like coincidences.

#

HIGGINS AND WOODWARD had to wait an hour before they were seen. They were called forward and directed to an interview room, where they were greeted by a young detective who ticked all of the boxes that Higgins had expected to have ticked: he was young and he looked hopelessly inexperienced.

"What's your name, sir?"

"Albert Lane. I had a box in the vault."

"I'm very sorry to hear that, sir."

"I want to know what's happened to it."

"Yes, sir, I'm sure you do. What number was it?"

"287."

The officer looked down at the sheet on the desk. His face fell. "I'm sorry, sir. That box was opened."

"Opened? What does that mean? Were the contents taken?"

"It's a mess down there, Mr. Lane. Some boxes were opened and the contents were left. Others were emptied. We're still working it out. Can you tell me what was in the box?"

"I'm afraid that's confidential."

"You'll need to tell us. We won't be able to return stolen property if we don't know who it belongs to."

"Yes, I appreciate that. But not until it's necessary."

"Fine." The officer laid his pen across his notebook.

Higgins struggled to remain calm. "Can you tell me what happened?"

"I'm afraid not. The investigation is ongoing."

"You must be able to tell me *something*."

The officer shook his head. "Just what has been released to the press. A number of men entered the vault last night. They went down the lift shaft, drilled through the wall and opened a number of the boxes."

"Do you know who it was?"

"I'm afraid I can't say any more than that."

"You have *no* idea?"

The officer stood. "We have your details, sir. We'll be in touch with everyone who had a box in the vault as soon as we have more information on what was and what was not taken. But you will need to tell us what was inside. We won't be able to return anything we recover without it."

Higgins felt himself tremble with rage, but he knew that ranting at this officer would serve him no purpose. The information he had received was almost worse than nothing—he knew now that his box had been opened, but not that its contents had been taken—and now he was being told that he would have to be patient before he was given anything even remotely useful. He knew he wouldn't be able to reclaim the evidence. If it had been taken, then perhaps it would be abandoned. Perhaps the thieves wouldn't recognise the significance of the photographs. But even if it was recovered, they would never be able to reclaim it.

But his money… The fruit of his labours since he had left the Regiment, his reward for the operations that, he would have argued, had made his country a safer place—that would all have been lost, too. Higgins looked at the officer, who gazed at him with what he probably thought was understanding and pity, and wanted to smash the man's face against the wall.

Woodward knew Higgins better than anyone, and he

must have seen the signs that usually preceded the eruption of his temper. He put a hand on the general's shoulder and, with a quiet, "Come on, sir," impelled him toward the door. Higgins shook his hand off angrily, but he knew his aide de camp was right. He followed him to the door and then out into the crazed bustle on the street outside.

"We need to go and see Isaacs," he said.

Chapter Forty-One

MILTON HAD taken a room in the Premier Inn near Waterloo station. He had no reason to fear that Frankie Fabian knew where he lived, but he was not in the business of taking risks, no matter how small they might be. The room was simple, adequately furnished and clean. There was a sink in the armoury and Milton had used it to wash the worst of the grime and muck from his face and the streaks of Hicks's blood from his knuckles. He didn't want to attract unnecessary attention to himself, but his shirt was still damp and he was still dirty.

He stripped in his room's small bathroom and looked at himself in the mirror. His skin was streaked with muck, and his clothes, when he ran his hand across them, left smudges of grime across his fingers. He went through into the bathroom and showered, looking down as the dirty water pooled around his feet and drained away. He scrubbed his skin until he was clean and then emptied the sachet of cheap complimentary shampoo into his hair and kneaded his scalp until the water ran clear. He took his clothes, washed and rinsed them in the shower, and then put them over the back of the heated towel rail so that they could dry.

He wrapped a towel around his waist, went through into the tiny bedroom, and switched on the twenty-four-hour news channel. The headlines were read out at the top of the hour and, toward the end, reference was made to a heist in the heart of London's diamond district. Milton waited until the newsreader had worked through the prior items until the image cut away to an outside broadcast. Milton took the remote and turned up the sound. The reporter was standing in front of the vault. The doors had been smashed open, and a uniformed policeman was standing guard outside them. The reporter suggested that a heist had taken place in the building overnight, and that goods with an unknown value had been taken. The rest of the information was sketchy, and, as the reporter handed back to the anchor, Milton concluded that there had been nothing to give him particular cause for concern. He had been careful.

Milton made himself busy. First, he took the bag and put it on the bed. The money was still inside, but he left it there and took out all of the photographs and spread them out on the bed. He examined them, one by one. He looked at Leo Isaacs, much younger then, but still recognisable as the man in the Internet news reports that Milton had seen while he was researching him. There was one photograph in particular that he found himself returning to: Isaacs was shirtless, a champagne flute in his right hand as his left arm was draped around the shoulders of a boy, also shirtless. Isaacs was looking right into the camera, obviously unaware that it was there. His eyes were wide, his golden hair was messy and ruffled, and his mouth was open to expose two rows of small, perfectly white teeth. The photograph had captured something in Isaac's eyes that Milton found disturbing. It was an excitement, a hunger, not yet sated.

The boy was unmistakeably Eddie Fabian.

Milton took out his smartphone and photographed the pictures so that he had backups, should he need them. He emailed them all to his Gmail account so that he had a fall-back should he lose his phone, and then, in an abundance of caution, copied them to his Dropbox. Finally, once he was satisfied with his work, he put the pictures back into the folder and slid them under the mattress of the bed.

He emailed Olivia with the suggestion that they meet that afternoon, and then he lay down on the bed. He closed his eyes and allowed himself a few hours of rest. He was asleep within moments.

Chapter Forty-Two

MILTON STOPPED at Waterloo Station and checked the bag with the money into a left-luggage locker, paying in advance for a week's rent. Then he went down into the underground and took the Bakerloo Line north to Piccadilly Circus. Milton made sure to arrive fifteen minutes early and spent the additional time walking to Savile Row and then looping back again so that he could satisfy himself that he had not been followed. He was happy that he had not.

He returned to the Circus with five minutes to spare and found a spot next to a branch of the Allied Irish Bank where he was able to watch the ever-shifting throng of people as they emerged from and disappeared into the various subways that led to the underground station below. Olivia emerged at a minute before the hour and made her way to the statue. She was dressed in denim jeans, a white shirt and a faded brown leather jacket. She looked anxious, looking left and right in an attempt to locate Milton. He was partially obscured by a telephone box, and she didn't see him. He watched the crowd. There were hundreds of people. It would be almost impossible for him to say whether she had been followed.

He crossed the road and made his way directly to her.

She was facing away as Milton reached her. He reached out and gently took her arm by the elbow.

"Shit," she said. "You startled me."

"This way," Milton said. He impelled her to follow him toward Leicester Square.

"What's going on?" she asked with a little concern.

"Just follow me."

Milton picked a way through the crowds of tourists into Leicester Square. It had just recently been renovated, and it looked nothing like the seedy, dirty confluence that Milton remembered. Lazy pigeons were gorging on spilt popcorn from the Vue and they fluttered up as Milton led the way north into Leicester Court, the alley that led between the cinema and the Hippodrome Casino. It was pedestrianized, much less busy than the Square itself, and Milton paused at the junction with Lisle Street and looked back. A man had also paused. The man reached into his pocket and withdrew his phone, putting it to his ear, but not before Milton locked eyes with him. The man spoke into the phone and took a quarter turn away, facing the casino, no longer looking at Milton or Olivia.

Milton felt uneasy. "Come on," he said.

"What?"

He didn't reply. Lisle Street became Chinatown to the left of them. Strings of red, white and green paper lanterns hung overhead. Milton took Olivia by the arm and hurried into the throng of people. They passed restaurants on both sides of the street—Kintaro, Imperial China, Hing Loon, Beijing Dumpling—all of them marked by the gaudy menus in the windows and the waiters who patrolled the doorways, eager to usher wavering patrons inside. Milton turned his head as they walked and glanced back toward the junction. He couldn't see the man, but that didn't mean anything. If he had been correct and the man had been following Olivia, there could be others.

"What are we doing?"

Milton hurried them onward.

"Where are we going?"

"I think you were followed," he said grimly. "We need to get away from here."

They passed Waxy's Little Sister, the pub hidden behind a row of scaffolding and protective sheeting, and reached the junction with Wardour Street. Milton looked north and saw a black cab heading toward them from Shaftesbury Avenue. He put out his arm and whistled. The cabbie indicated that he had seen him and pulled over. Milton opened the door, ushered Olivia inside, and sat down next to her.

"Where to, guv?" the cabbie asked.

"Liverpool Street," he said.

Milton looked out of the smeared window as they rolled ahead, passing the entrances to Chinatown and then Leicester Square. There were hundreds of people on the street. There was no way of knowing whether any of them were watching Olivia, but he had survived for as long as he had by trusting his instincts, and he knew that this was the right thing to do. He looked back as they rolled through an orange light and picked up speed onto Whitcomb Street. He was looking for other cabs that might have been stopped, or vehicles that might have run the light in an attempt to keep up with them. He saw nothing.

#

LIVERPOOL STREET station was to the east of the city, on the edge of the financial district.

"What's going on?" Olivia asked as they drove past Bloomsbury Square.

"You were followed."

"By whom?"

"I don't know that. But there was a man behind us and I didn't like the look of him."

"How can you be sure?"

"Just a gut feeling."

"You told me you were a cook, John."

"Yeah," Milton said. "I am. But I've done other things."

It took thirty minutes to get to Liverpool Street, and they made the rest of the journey in silence. Milton spent the time looking out of the windows, checking the cars behind them in the event that he saw something that gave him cause for suspicion. The roads were busy, as they always were, and the traffic behaved normally. None of the cars or motorbikes seemed particularly interested in them. They reached the Rotunda, the roundabout that accommodated the Museum of London at the Barbican.

Milton told the driver to go around it twice, and, as he stared back at the cars in their wake, none of them tried to follow their manoeuver. The busy nature of a city like London meant that you could never say for sure, but, as far as Milton was concerned, they were clean.

"John," Olivia said, "what the hell?"

"Just wait," he said. "I'll tell you everything."

Chapter Forty-Three

THERE WAS A BRANCH of Starbucks on the north side of the station and Milton led the way inside. He told Olivia to go and buy two coffees. She did, and Milton used the opportunity to find a table at the back of the room where he could sit and face the entrance. He watched carefully, satisfying himself once again that they had not been tailed.

Olivia returned with two coffees and set them down on the table. She sat down, pried the lid off her cup and poured in a sachet of brown sugar. "So?" she said after she had taken a sip.

Milton left his coffee untouched and looked straight at her. "I need you to be honest with me."

"What makes you think I haven't been honest before?"

"Come on," Milton said. "No more games. I know that Eddie told you things that you've kept from me. You have to be straight with me now. It's very important."

"About what?"

"There was more than just the abuse, wasn't there? Eddie told you about more than that."

She didn't answer.

"This is how it's going to be. I'm going to be straight with you and you're going to be straight with me. No secrets. Okay?"

She nodded a little dubiously. "Okay."

"Eddie was in Alcoholics Anonymous. I am, too. That's how we met. He was having trouble with the ninth step. You know what that is?"

His admission didn't fluster her. "No," she said.

He looked her in the eye. "Alcoholics agree that they have to make amends to the people that they've hurt." She shuffled in her chair a little. "Eddie was going to get justice for himself, for what happened to him when he was a boy.

But he wanted justice for someone else, too. Someone he thought that he had hurt. He wasn't a hypocrite. He wanted to make amends."

He reached into his bag and took out the scrapbook that he had taken from Eddie's flat. He laid his palm atop it and slid it across the table. Olivia took the book from him and flipped through the pages. She bit down on her bottom lip as she scanned the newspaper reports that Eddie had collected.

"He was involved in that robbery," Milton said. "A man was killed. Eddie's family was responsible. His brothers. Eddie had a lot of demons. He was going to unburden himself of everything. The things he'd done, and the things that were done to him. And that's the other reason he was speaking to you."

Olivia's bottom lip had whitened from the bite. "He made me promise not to say anything about that," she said.

"That doesn't really matter any more."

"No," she said after a pause. "I suppose it doesn't."

"What happened?"

"He was there. He was the driver. His brothers had guns. They ambushed the truck and took the money. There was a struggle. One of the guards rugby-tackled Spencer Fabian, and Fabian shot him. Eddie has been cut up about it for years. It's like you said. He said he blamed himself. You're right: he did. He wanted to make it right."

Milton exhaled. He understood everything now. The angles were all revealed, the connections that joined events, the motivations of the players. "Have you told anyone else that he was talking to you about it?"

Olivia paused, then looked away.

Milton's heart sank. "Who?"

"Frankie Fabian."

"What? When?"

"Two days ago. I went back to Halewell Close."

Milton had to stifle his groan.

"What?" she protested. "Eddie was dead. What was I

supposed to do? I wasn't getting anywhere. I met you, but you went quiet. I didn't think you were going to give me anything. The story was just going to die, and I wasn't going to let it."

"What did you say to him?"

"I told him that Eddie had spoken to me about being involved in a robbery. I asked him whether he had anything to say about it."

Milton closed his eyes. "And?"

"He said it was crazy. He said Eddie was unstable. Eddie had said all sorts of things like that in the past—you just had to look at what he'd done to himself to know that he wasn't rational. He said that what Eddie said couldn't be trusted. Frankie's a good actor, but I didn't believe him. I didn't press it too hard, either. He's frightening."

Milton put his elbow on the table and rested his forehead against his palm.

"What is it?" she asked.

He paused, wondering whether he could trust her with everything that he knew. She was a journalist; everything was subservient to the story. He decided that he would take the chance. He needed a second opinion. "A car registered to Eddie's father was seen next to his cab in the driveway of the house where he killed himself. I think Frankie was there."

"How on earth could you know that?"

Milton shook his head. "Someone saw it. I can't tell you who. But Eddie got himself into a real mess. He was murdered that night. It wasn't because of what he was going to say to you about Leo Isaacs. It was because he'd told his family that he was about to expose them."

The colour drained from her face. "They did it?"

"I know they did."

"Oh God."

"You have to be careful now, Olivia. Very careful. I'm serious."

"You thought I was being followed…?"

Milton nodded, his face severe. "You said Frankie was frightening. He's all that and worse. He killed his own son—he's not likely to have any compunction about going after anyone else who he thinks might threaten him. You *were* followed today. Maybe it was someone working for Fabian. Maybe it was someone to do with Isaacs. I can't say; it doesn't matter. Both are dangerous. You have to keep a low profile. You have to be careful."

She found a little indignation and scowled at him. "Don't patronise me, John. I know how to look after myself."

"You think you do, but if it's Fabian, he won't play by the rules. You know what happened to Eddie. You've given the man who killed him a reason to think Eddie told you everything. And you're a journalist. It won't be too hard for him to join the dots. He'll see you as a serious risk."

"I'm a big girl," she said.

"And if it's someone to do with Isaacs, it's worse."

"Do you know something that you're not telling me?"

He had promised transparency, but he was going to have to qualify that a little. He didn't want to tell her about Hicks and the soldiers—not yet, and probably not at all. "No," he lied. "But I am serious. You said it yourself: if this comes out—"

"*When* this comes out," she corrected.

"Fine. *When* this comes out, it'll be big. Don't underestimate what you're involved in."

"You think I don't know that?" she said. "That's why this story is so important. My career is stuck in a rut. I need something to get me back on track again. Leo Isaacs could be it. Frankie Fabian could be it, too. And nothing this good comes without risk. I'll take my chances."

Milton could see that it was going to be difficult to persuade her to stand down. He reminded himself that Olivia wasn't his responsibility. She had been involved right from the start, before he was, and, as she said, she was able to make her own decisions. He tried to persuade himself that he should take a step back, but he couldn't. He saw it as it was: she was standing on the edge, teetering there, with no idea of just how steep the drop might be.

"Just do me a favour," he said. "Lie low for a few days. Don't go home."

"So what do I do?"

"Check into a hotel. Get out of the city. Visit your relatives. Anything. All right?"

"The story needs to get out there."

"Both of them do. Isaacs and Fabian, and you can tell both stories. But wait."

"I don't know if I can."

"You can. I'll make it worth your while."

"How are you going to do that?"

Milton reached into his bag again and took out the document folders he had removed from the safe deposit box. He opened the top one, took out the photographs and handed them across the table to Olivia. She glanced left and right to make sure that they were not overlooked—the café was empty—and then shuffled through the glossy prints.

"These are what I think they are?"

Milton nodded.

"Where did you get them?"

"Doesn't matter. Would they be useful for your story?"

"Of course they would!"

"Useful enough to wait?"

She bit her lip. "How long?"

"Not long. I need a few more days."

"For what?"

"There are some things that I need to do."

She paused, then nodded. "Okay."

"You'll wait?"

"Yes."

He collected the photographs and put them back into the folder. "In that case, you can have them. I want them publicised. You can break the story."

She looked as if she was going to ask Milton to give her

the pictures now, but she did not. He put them back into his bag.

She sipped her coffee and put the cup back down onto the table. "These things you need to do? What are they?"

"People are going to pay for what happened to Eddie. His family, for one. Leo Isaacs. Writing your story will help make that happen. But there are others who won't be affected. I need to take care of them first."

Chapter Forty-Four

DETECTIVE CONSTABLE Christopher Banks was frustrated. His specialty was surveillance, including on foot and mobile, and he had been following the pretty female journalist for thirty-six hours without a problem. It was boring, but it was easy, too. There were two of them on the job: Banks and his colleague Vince Edwards. Banks had handed her off to Edwards at midnight and had grabbed six hours of sleep. Then they had switched again at midday, Edwards handing her off to Banks as she took the tube to Piccadilly.

Banks had watched as she had met the man next to the statue of Eros, and then tailed them both as they walked to Leicester Square. He had known, immediately, that the newcomer was cautious. He checked back frequently, clearly looking to see if they were being followed. That wouldn't have presented a problem as long as they stayed in places where there were plenty of people, but the man looked like he knew what he was doing. He had turned onto a quieter street and had stopped without warning and looked back. It was a classic anti-surveillance move, one that Banks had been taught himself at the College of Policing, but it had been deployed so skilfully and abruptly that there was no way for him to avoid being made. He had busied himself with his phone, but he knew it was pointless. The man had seen him, and there had been nothing for it other than to lay right back. If Edwards had been here, they could have swapped, but Edwards was at the hotel. Banks idled along Lisle Street, just close enough to observe as the man and the journalist got into a cab and disappeared to the south.

There was nothing else for it but to confess: he had lost them.

Banks had called Edwards and told him to meet him at Leicester Square. His partner, bleary-eyed from lack of sleep, arrived half an hour later.

"What happened?" Edwards asked.

"She met a man at Piccadilly. They came here, then turned up the passageway on the other side of the cinema and stopped. He was looking for a tail. He made me. Nothing I could do about it."

"Where are they now?"

Banks shrugged. "They took a taxi. They were going south, towards the river."

"Shit."

"Yeah," Banks said. "I know. Shit."

"Bruce is going to kill us."

Detective Inspector Charlie Bruce was their gaffer. He had given the two of them the assignment two days ago, told them to find the girl, learn whatever they could, and then keep a close eye on her. The duty logs would be amended so that it appeared that they were on legitimate police business in the capital. They had followed that procedure before, and there had never been an issue with it. Bruce had given them a grand each as down payments on the work that they would have to put in. They would make five hundred a day after that. Banks knew that the money came from Frankie Fabian, but he didn't care. It was more than he'd earn in a week otherwise, and he had bills to pay. He had expensive habits, too, and money like that didn't just fall into your lap. It required a little ethical flexibility, but that was fine. Banks could be flexible. He'd done worse for Bruce than just follow a woman around London for a few days. Edwards was the same.

"This guy she met," Edwards said. "You got any idea who he is?"

"No. But I got his picture."

He took out his phone and scrolled through the photos that he had taken that morning. There were several of the woman on the train, unaware that she was being photographed, and then more as she made her way through Piccadilly station. He had taken a handful as she had emerged at ground level, pretending to take a video of the tourists who had gathered around the statue, and then two photos as she had met the man. Banks had been ten metres away when he had taken them, and the first picture was spoiled by a pair of tourists who had paraded through his shot just as he had hit the button to take it. The second, though, was better. The man was in profile, turned very slightly in the direction of the camera, and when Banks tapped the screen to zoom in, his features became a little clearer and easier to identify.

He held the screen up so that Edwards could see it. "You recognise him?"

Edwards shook his head. "Never seen him before. But you'd better send that to Bruce and tell him what's happened."

Banks nodded his agreement. He tapped that he wanted to share the picture by email, added Bruce as the recipient, tapped out a quick message and pressed send.

Chapter Forty-Five

OLIVIA HAD waited on the concourse at Liverpool Street station and watched Smith as he disappeared into the underground. She had asked where he was going and what he planned to do, but he had told her that he couldn't say. He said again that she needed to stay out of the way for a few days until he contacted her again. He promised that he would give her everything she needed to write the kind of story that she had been dreaming of writing ever since Eddie Fabian had contacted her. The kind of story that would win awards. The kind of story that would make her career.

There was a Travelodge near to the station. She took the escalator to street level and took out her phone for directions. But then she stopped.

She had listened to everything that Smith had said. She knew that there was a lot that he hadn't told her. She knew that he was not who he said he was. She knew, for *damned* sure, that he wasn't just a cook. She started to doubt herself, and him.

She had known that Frankie Fabian was a dangerous man. It had been a risk to confront him, but she hadn't had a choice. She had been stymied. Eddie was dead, and all she had was innuendo, nothing that she could even think of running without censoring it so severely that the story wouldn't make sense. The story was as dead as its source. She had had no choice but to visit Fabian and try to shake things up.

As she stood on the street with city workers streaming by on both sides, she had a terrible sinking feeling. There were the doubts about Smith, but she put them aside. If he had been right and she *had* been followed to their rendezvous that afternoon, what was to prevent whoever it was who was interested in her from visiting her apartment? Smith had refused to tell her who it might be, save vague threats about Fabian and vaguer and more worrying threats about people who were interested in protecting Isaacs. If they were interested in her story, what would they do to get hold of her notes? She felt ill as the ramifications of that possibility became apparent. She had backed up the story to an external hard drive and a USB stick, but both of those redundancies, and her computer, were in the flat. If someone broke in and took them, she would lose everything from her meetings with Eddie. She would be back to square one.

She took out her phone and was about to call Smith. Her finger hovered over the button for a moment, but then she changed her mind and put the phone back into her bag. She realised that she didn't know him, either. He was lying to her about what he did for a living and evasive about plenty more besides. Who was he? Was Smith even his real name? She had doubted it at the start, and it seemed even more unlikely now. What was to say that he wasn't involved in some angle that she hadn't been able to divine? What if he wasn't what he appeared to be? What if, for all his good intentions, he was working against her?

No. She couldn't afford to take any more chances.

She turned around and hurried back to the station. She would take the Central Line to Mile End and then change onto the District Line there. It wasn't far. She would be back at her building in half an hour. She would collect her computer and pack a bag, and then she would find a hotel.

Chapter Forty-Six

"WAIT HERE."

Higgins stepped out of Woodward's car and crossed the dark street to Watson Square. He avoided the main entrance, keen that the concierge not see him, and went around to the side of the building and an auxiliary entrance that was used for goods and tradesmen. He'd seen it before, and using it made more sense than going through the main entrance. The door was open, and Higgins was able to access the service lift without anyone seeing him. He pressed the button for the seventh floor and waited patiently as the lift—scratched and utilitarian in contrast to the luxurious alternative used by the residents—made its ascent. The lift opened into a service area where laundry trolleys and maintenance equipment were stored.

Higgins opened the door to the corridor, looked outside, and then made his way to apartment number eleven. He didn't think that he had been seen. He knocked on the door. After a moment, it was opened. Leo Isaacs stood aside and let Higgins into the flat.

"Richard," he said as Higgins made his way past him, "what's the matter?"

"Thanks for seeing me," Higgins said. He didn't look at Isaacs; his attention was directed to the flat itself. He looked in the bedroom and then the bathroom and the lounge until he was satisfied that they were alone.

Higgins's behaviour made Isaacs concerned. "What is it? What was so important?"

Higgins opened the French doors and stepped out onto the narrow balcony. Insipid drizzle was falling, a fine mist that clung to the skin. Higgins looked out into the courtyard beyond. It was dark, and the lighting in the gardens below was not strong enough to illuminate this high up. The other windows that Higgins could see were closed, and there was no one else visible on any of the other balconies. He was satisfied that they were unobserved.

Isaacs followed him outside. "What are you doing? It's bloody freezing."

"I wanted to say that I was sorry, Leo."

"Sorry? For what?"

"Things have gotten out of hand."

"What has? I don't understand."

"The situation."

Isaacs's mouth fell open. "You said it would be handled."

"It was, but events have overtaken us. I can't guarantee that it won't come out."

"And the money I've been paying you?"

"It bought you peace of mind for thirty years. You got good value."

"So what do I do now? If this comes out, there'll be an investigation. A trial. There'll be..." He stopped mid-sentence, the full horror of his future revealed to him. "I'll be ruined." He looked down at the floor of the balcony and when he looked back up at Higgins there were tears in his eyes. "You have to help me."

"I'm sorry, Leo," Higgins said. "There's nothing more I can do."

"I paid you to look after me!"

"And I will."

Higgins reached out and took the man by the shoulders. They were both old, but the difference between them was stark. Higgins worked out every morning and kept himself in excellent shape. But age had stalked Isaacs and withered him. Higgins felt Isaacs's bones through the fabric of his shirt as he manoeuvred him through a quarter turn, pushing him until his back was pressed against the metal balustrade. Only then did he realise what Higgins intended, because it was only as the general reached down for the old man's belt that he started to struggle. Higgins pushed his left hand hard against Isaacs's sternum as he fastened his fingers around the belt and pulled up. The old man pivoted, the balustrade acting as a fulcrum, and Higgins gave a final heave and tipped him all the way over the edge. He looked down, watching as Isaacs somersaulted once and then twice, his body bouncing up as it crashed into the ornamental gardens twenty-five metres below. It came to rest on the lawn, one leg bent underneath the body at an obscene angle, the arms flung out wide.

Higgins went into the kitchen and collected a dishcloth. He used the cloth to cover his fingers as he opened the cupboard underneath the sink and collected the kitchen cleaner. He went back to the French door and cleaned the handle, removing any trace of his fingerprints, remembering to leave the doors open. He returned the cleaner to the cupboard and closed the door with his foot. Then, finally satisfied that he had left no trace, he opened the front door by pushing down on the handle with his elbow, went outside and let it swing closed behind him. He set off for the service lift.

Chapter Forty-Seven

DETECTIVE INSPECTOR BRUCE waited in the car outside the development. He had driven up from Oxford as soon as Banks had told him what had happened. The three of them had been taking turns: one of them would be here, the other would be at the tube station, and the third would be at the junction with Bow Road.

"Turning your way now," radioed Banks.

Bruce leaned forward and started the engine. He was driving a Ford Focus Estate, rented under a false name, and he had parked it on the other side of the road, twenty metres from the security lodge. It would have been impossible to get to the woman without being seen, but the positioning would limit their exposure as much as possible. Bruce was relaxed about it. It wouldn't take long to do what they needed to do.

"I see her," Edwards reported. "Get ready."

Bruce had been furious when Banks and Edwards had reported that they had lost Dewey, and his fury had curdled to confusion and fear when he had recognised John Smith in the photograph that Banks had emailed to him. Bruce had never seen Frankie Fabian as angry as he had been when he was summoned to the house two nights ago. He was incandescent. Bruce had listened, agog, as Fabian had explained what had happened to Marcus and Spencer. Fabian had described how he had been blackmailed by Smith on the day after Eddie's funeral. Smith had threatened to release a confession that Eddie had written, and that Smith had somehow acquired, that would implicate Frankie's boys in a heist that had taken place years earlier. Bruce and his men had been responsible for searching Eddie Fabian's house the day after they had killed him. They had found nothing, and neither had the moving company they had sent in the following day to empty the place out. Bruce had vouched for the fact that there was nothing incriminating at the property, and he had had no option but to stand there and take it as Fabian tore into him. He had suggested that Smith was bluffing, and that had just made things worse. He had kept his own counsel after that.

Once he had mastered his temper—and that was a temporary cessation, at best—Fabian had gone on to recount how he had been visited by Olivia Dewey. She had suggested to Fabian that she was a reporter, and Bruce's enquiries confirmed that that was true. She had confronted Fabian with the allegation that the family had been involved in the heist and that Eddie had been the source of her information. Fabian told Bruce, with barely concealed contempt, that she was giving him a chance to put his response to the allegations on the record.

The mention of the old case had perturbed Bruce. He remembered it very well. It had been his first encounter with the Fabian family and the first time that he had accepted their largesse in order to smooth away potential legal problems. He had been one of the CID officers who had been put onto the team to investigate the robbery and the murder that had followed it. He had been junior then, a freshly minted detective constable, and, in exchange for a considerable sum, he had fed Fabian enough information that it had been possible to shield Marcus, Spencer and Eddie from any serious threat. He had believed that the matter was at an end, but now this reporter was ready to stir that all up. Dewey's last question, before Fabian had escorted her to the door, was to seek his thoughts on whether his adopted son's suicide, in the driveway of his daughter's house, might be connected to the story that she and Eddie had been ready to publish together.

Frankie had ordered Bruce to watch Dewey. And then she had met John Smith, and her involvement in Fabian's troubles had deepened. Fabian had told Bruce to bring her to him. He knew, from experience, that the future did not bode well for her, but he did not concern himself with that. Fabian's money insulated him from the annoyances of a pricked conscience.

He glanced into the mirrors and saw the journalist walking north, on the same side of the road as him. Banks was behind her. Edwards was waiting against the wall of the development, before the guardhouse, and as she drew nearer, he pushed himself upright and made his way down the middle of the pavement in her direction. Bruce watched as her expression changed from one of pensive thought to alarm. The two detectives timed their approaches perfectly, with Banks placing his hand on her elbow just as Edwards took out his warrant card and held it up before her face, too quickly for her to note anything but the badge and the suggestion of authority. Edwards stepped to the side as Banks impelled her onward, his hand still around her elbow, Edwards taking her other arm as she came alongside. She didn't struggle. She didn't shout or scream. Bruce had used the same tactics before, whenever Fabian wanted someone removed from the street with the minimum of fuss and bother, and it had always worked this way.

Bruce watched as the two constables marched the woman up the street to the car. Banks was nearest to the Ford; he reached out and opened the door before hurrying around to the opposite side. Edwards placed his hand atop the woman's head and pushed down, forcing her into the cabin. Edwards got in next to her, pressing her into the middle of the three seats. Banks opened the roadside door and got in, the two men pinning her between them. They continued to play it official, Banks deflecting Dewey's complaint with a polite, "We just have some questions for you, ma'am," but Bruce could see that the penny had started to drop. He pulled away just as Dewey reached out for the door, Edwards catching her arm before her fingers could reach the handle and pushing it back down to her side.

"Help!" she yelled out. "Help me!"

There was no one near them to hear her. Bruce had the

can of technical-grade chloroform that they had previously used on Eddie Fabian on the front seat. He took it and the rag that was next to it and passed it back to Edwards. He unscrewed the top, saturated the rag with it, and then pressed it to Dewey's mouth and held it there. Her protests were muffled by the rag and then, quickly, they became mumbles and moans as the chemical took effect. Her eyes rolled back in their sockets, her head tipped back and she was quiet.

"All okay?" Bruce asked, glancing up into the mirror.

"She's out."

"Open a fucking window," he said. "We'll all pass out otherwise."

Edwards did as he was told. Bruce turned his attention back to the road and started the journey to the west.

Chapter Forty-Eight

ALEX HICKS parked the car next to the pub. It was quiet, with just a handful of other cars parked in the wide space. He pulled down the visor and flicked on the courtesy light that illuminated the vanity mirror. His face was blackened and bruised. There was a cut along the line of his cheekbone where Milton had struck him, dried blood already crusted over it. His right eye was closed from the swollen purple contusion that spread out from a point on his brow, three darker indentations betraying the impact of Milton's knuckles. He looked terrible. He looked as if he had been given a thorough beating, which was exactly what he wanted to look like. He knew that his future would depend upon his ability to present compelling physical evidence to corroborate the story that he and Milton had concocted.

But that didn't mean it didn't hurt like hell.

He pushed the visor back, took a deep breath to compose himself, unclipped the seat belt and stepped outside. He heard the sound of muffled music from the jukebox in the main room of the pub, the occasional muted snatch of conversation. He was committed now. If he wanted to extricate himself from the quagmire into which he had allowed himself to slip, he had to go through with the plan. There was no other way.

He opened the door to the function room and went inside. It was brightly lit, and he had to blink until his eyes adjusted from the murk outside. The men were arranged around the table, empty pint glasses set out before them. He saw Gillan, Connolly, Woodward and Shepherd.

They turned at his entrance. "Hicks." Woodward half stood. "What the fuck…?"

He didn't have to work particularly hard to sell the injuries. Milton had not held back. Hicks had stomached it, closed his eyes and absorbed the punishment. He had thought, as Milton worked him over, that perhaps this was penance for the things that he had done and the things that he had allowed to be done. Atonement for his greed. He could have no complaints.

"Where's the general?"

He limped across the room and slumped down into one of the empty chairs.

"What happened to you?"

"The general. Where is he?"

"What happened?"

"You said he was coming. I need to talk to him. Right now."

#

HICKS REMAINED at the table while they waited for Higgins to arrive. The others tried to get him to speak, to tell them what had happened, but he said that he was in pain and that he would rather wait.

He heard the sound of a car driving across the gravel after twenty minutes, its headlights shining through the uncovered windows. Connolly stood and crossed the room to look out the window. "He's here."

Hicks heard the sound of a car door slamming shut and then the crunch of footsteps. Higgins opened the door and came inside. He was wearing a tweed jacket and salmon pink cord trousers. He came inside and, as he registered the men, his gaze stopped on Hicks. The anger slipped away, to be replaced by confusion.

"What happened?"

"We've got trouble, sir," Hicks said.

"I already know that. Who did that to you?"

"His name is Milton."

"Who?"

"He's bad news, sir."

The old man paused, his brow wrinkling as he tried to

remember. "Milton. I know the name."

"He used to be in the Regiment. He told me to tell you. He said you'd remember him."

"*John* Milton?"

"Yes."

"I do remember. He was good. Very good. MI6 poached him. He went into intelligence."

"Yes, sir. The Firm. Group Fifteen. He was a headhunter, in the same unit they tabbed me for. He was the senior agent when I was being tested. It was him who bounced me out."

"*He* did this to you?"

"Yes, sir. This afternoon."

"Why?"

"It was Milton's car I saw when Eddie Fabian died. Milton killed him."

"What? How do you know that?"

"Because he told me."

Hicks said it and tried to make it sound plausible. There were so many ways that he could be tripped up, and he tried not to think about them. If he allowed even the smallest sliver of doubt to enter his thinking, he wouldn't be able to persuade Higgins that he was telling the truth.

Higgins sat. "This doesn't make any sense, Corporal."

"Milton saw me the night Fabian died. I didn't think he did—I was in a ditch—but he did. And then he saw my car. We'd parked it up the road."

"That's true," Shepherd said. "But we—"

"He's observant. He saw it. Took the plate and got my details. He's been following me ever since."

Higgins closed his eyes.

"He jumped me. Put my lights out. I woke up and he had a gun in my face. I would never have said anything if it was just me, but he knew about my family. He threatened them. My kids. He said he'd kill them all if I didn't tell him what he wanted to know. I know what Milton is capable of. He would have done it."

Higgins raised a hand. "Wait a minute. Go back. What did Fabian have to do with Milton?"

"Milton's freelancing. He's been working for Frankie Fabian."

Higgins scowled. "I don't understand. Why would Fabian have Milton kill his own son?"

Hicks closed his eyes, desperately trying to remember the exact way that he and Milton had put the explanation together. "Eddie was involved with the Fabian family business. Milton said there was a robbery, years ago, and this guard got shot. Eddie was there. He regretted what happened, and he couldn't keep it to himself any longer. Guilt. Eddie was going to grass them all up. But his old man found out."

Higgins was staring right at Hicks. "Okay. Let me get this straight. Milton is an assassin."

"Yes."

"And Frankie Fabian pays Milton to kill Eddie Fabian."

"Yes, sir. Milton drugged him, gassed him, made it look like he'd topped himself."

Higgins frowned. Hicks didn't know if he was making headway or not. "But then Milton went to the funeral. You saw him—you all did."

"Yes, sir," Shepherd said.

"Why would he go to the funeral?"

Hicks had anticipated that. "Because he'd been following me. He knew we were involved."

"He took our photos," Shepherd added.

"He wanted to know who we were," Hicks explained.

Higgins held up his hands to stall the others from speaking. "So, he gets your registration. He tracks you down. He follows you. He takes you out. And then?"

"He took me to an empty lock-up. I don't know where it was. He put me in the boot of the car when he let me out. He dumped me in the middle of nowhere."

"What did he want?"

"Everything."

"And?"

Hicks shrugged. He would not normally have wanted to rouse the old man's anger, but now it was the only thing he wanted. Anger might mean that he believed what Hicks was saying. "I told him nothing, not at first. He worked me over; I kept my mouth shut. All I gave him was the usual: name, rank, number. He kept working me over, I told him I didn't know what he was talking about, but he told me he knew I was lying. He had audio to prove it."

"What?"

"Milton bugged my car." Hicks reached into his pocket and took out the voice recorder that Milton had given him. It was a BlackRange unit, available on the Internet for a hundred pounds. It was the size of his index finger, was equipped with a strong magnet, and had a battery life of seven days. "It was underneath my seat," he explained, using the line that Milton had prepared for him. "I found it when I got back to the car."

Higgins put his head in his hands. "Jesus. How long had it been there?"

"He put it in sometime after the night we went after Fabian, I don't know when exactly, but he played a recording of me on the phone to Shepherd talking about Isaacs after you and I met him. We spoke about the photos."

He turned to Shepherd. "Did you?"

"We might have done. It's not impossible."

"Did you say where they were?"

"I think we did," Shepherd said quietly and then, with more heat, "but it wouldn't have mattered if this fucking amateur hadn't allowed his car to be bugged!"

The general's face had gradually turned a deep shade of mauve. His temper was never far from the surface, and it was close to overflowing now.

"So Milton knew about the vault?"

Hicks nodded.

"He did it?"

"He went back to Frankie Fabian and told him. Fabian

put a team together. But Milton was involved."

"*Fuck!*"

"Fabian has it all now. The evidence. He doesn't care about his son. Maybe he takes out the pictures with Eddie. Maybe he doesn't. He sees the bottom line: it's a chance to make a big score. Milton says he's going to blackmail Isaacs and the others."

"Good luck to him," Higgins said.

"What?"

"You see the news, Hicks?" Woodward said. "You can't blackmail a dead man."

Hicks understood what must have happened. The general was tidying up.

Higgins was still glaring at him. "What about the rest of the box?"

"Sir?"

"It wasn't just the evidence. I had assets there. Money. A lot of it."

Hicks nodded that he understood. Milton had explained that to him, too. There had been cash in Higgins's box. Milton had opened the bag and showed him.

Higgins was still talking, saying that Woodward had money in the vault, too, but Hicks had temporarily zoned out. He swallowed hard on a dry throat. This was it. He had baited the hook as best he could. Everything depended on the hope that he had done enough. He had to pray that Higgins would bite.

"Hicks," the general was saying. "*Hicks*, wake up."

"I'm sorry. I'm full of Brufen. I feel a bit light-headed."

"Why did Milton let you out?"

"He wants to talk to you. Fabian has everything in your box and all the other boxes they opened."

Higgins got up and paced the room. He turned back, his face dark with anger. "He wants to *talk*?"

"He has a business proposal for you."

"You're kidding? He stole from me; now he wants to talk business?"

"I—"

There was a glass on the table. Higgins swiped out with his arm, grabbed the glass and flung it against the wall. It shattered just behind Gillan. The big man flinched from the shock of it, the shards of glass falling down onto his shoulders.

Hicks recoiled. "He only cares about money. Fabian paid well. He said maybe you'll pay better. He said he'll help you get your property back in exchange for half of it. It's not just your property, though. It's half of everything they took. Milton says it's millions. He says you'll come out of this ahead."

"Anything else?" Higgins asked, not trying to hide his scorn and anger.

"He said you needed to remember him. What he's capable of doing. He said accept what's happened, that it was just business. If you're not interested, then he said you should let it go. If you don't, he'll come after you."

"He's warning *me* off? Who the fuck does he think he is? Who the fuck?" He turned back to them all, his clenched fists resting on the table. Hicks knew that this was it: this was the moment where the decision as to whether he lived or died was to be taken. Had he played the part well enough? He couldn't say.

Higgins was shrewd. He cleared his head, and, when he spoke again, there was more control in his voice. "Fine. I'll speak to him. Have a little chat, see what he has to say. Maybe he can help, maybe he can't. One way or another, I'm going to burn down Fabian's house and then, when I've got my money back, I'm going to find Milton and take my time finishing him off."

Chapter Forty-Nine

OLIVIA CAME AROUND as they dragged her out of the Ford. Her head pounded, as if she had been out drinking all day and now she was suffering with a brutal hangover. She had no strength in her legs, and she was too dazed to struggle as the men on either side of her carried her across a parking area and into a house that she thought she recognised. She let her head hang down, trying to suppress the bout of nausea that rose along her gullet, and failing. She threw up, hot vomit that spattered down onto the gravel that she was being carried across.

"Shit!" she heard one of the men protest.

"Not on my shoes!"

"Get her inside."

She heard the crunch of their footsteps and the scrape of her feet as they dug furrows through the stone chips. She felt sick again and started to heave, but there was nothing left to bring up. She spat, trying to get the taste out of her mouth, and blinked her eyes to try to clear away the wooziness.

She started to remember.

"No," she moaned, much too weak to do anything to disturb the men who were dragging her toward the house. "No. Let me go."

They carried her into a porch and then into a hall. The difference in temperature was stark, and it made her feel queasy once more. Another wave of lassitude swept over her, and she lacked the strength to even raise her head. She closed her eyes again.

"What've you done to her?" a third voice asked.

"Just knocked her out for the journey. Where do you want her?"

"Put her in the kitchen. Give her a glass of water."

She was carried through the house, aware of the sound of conversation around her, but unable to distinguish the words from the droning buzz. She felt something bump up against her legs and then something firm and flat onto which her weight was lowered. A hand on her shoulder held her upright. She heard the sound of running water and then tasted it on her lips. She sipped it, using it to wash away the taste of the vomit. It gave her a measure of strength, and she raised her head and opened her eyes.

She was in a big country kitchen. She saw a long wooden table, big enough for a dozen people, freestanding units, a large cast-iron range. There were four men in the room with her: one, to her right, was supporting her in the chair; another was to her left, the man who had badged her before she had been taken to the car; the third, the man who had driven the car, was older; the fourth, holding the glass to her lips, was Frankie Fabian.

"Hello," he said. "How are you feeling?"

"You… kidnapped me."

"I wanted to have a talk. Some things have happened that have caused me a bit of a problem. I think you can help me to understand them."

She turned her head to look at the driver of the car. "You… drugged… me."

"Sorry about that," the man said, chuckling as he turned away, and Olivia remembered where she had seen him before: it was the detective inspector to whom she had spoken in the aftermath of Eddie Fabian's death. His name was Bruce.

Olivia felt the fatigue returning, and her head fell forward, her chin resting on her chest. There was a gentle slapping on her cheek.

"Wake up, Olivia," Fabian said.

She felt water on her face. It was in her eyes, on her cheeks, in her nostrils and her mouth and her eyes. She shook her head and snorted, and blinked to clear her eyes. The sudden coldness shocked her back to awareness again.

"Wake up," Fabian was saying, his voice suddenly purposeful and stern. "I have some questions for you, and you are going to answer them." He slapped her again, harder this time, and she opened her eyes and looked up into his. His face was close to hers, inches away, close enough to see the hairs in his nostrils and smell the alcohol on his breath. His eyes were blank and pitiless. "Let's start with John Smith. Who is he, Olivia? Tell me everything."

The last dregs of the narcotic fugue were blown away, and Olivia started to feel afraid.

Chapter Fifty

MILTON LEARNED ABOUT the death of Leo Isaacs on the news. He was back at the hotel, waiting to hear from Hicks. The phone was charging on the table, and Milton had been casting glances at it in the hope that, maybe, it would make it ring a little quicker. It did not, of course, and, as the hours passed, he had started to worry that Hicks had not been as persuasive as he would have needed to be. If Higgins didn't believe him, his future prospects would not have been particularly bright. There was nothing that Milton could do to help him now. That would come later. For now, it was all on him.

He had switched on the television because he wanted a distraction. The hotel was budget, with a limited selection, and he had flicked through the end of a football highlights show before settling on the late news. He watched it distractedly, not really paying attention, until the newscaster mentioned Leo Isaacs's name. Milton sat bolt upright, reached for the remote and turned up the volume. The woman explained that Isaacs, who she said had been a prominent member of the government during the 1980s, had been found dead that evening. She reported that the man's body had been found in the gardens of the apartment block where he lived, the working hypothesis being that he had fallen over the edge of his balcony and plunged to his death. The police were investigating, but there were no current suggestions of foul play. It was, she said, looking like a tragic accident.

An accident? Milton shook his head. It wasn't an accident. Higgins was moving quickly to insulate himself.

He was considering how that might change the equation when the telephone rang.

"Hello?" he said.

"John," a voice replied. It wasn't Hicks. It was a woman. Her voice was cracked and hoarse. She sounded terrified.

Milton felt a moment of intense worry. He recognised the voice. "Olivia?"

"I'm in the shit, John."

"Where are you?"

She didn't answer.

"Where are you?"

Olivia still did not reply.

"Olivia?"

"She's with me."

It was Frankie Fabian.

Milton clenched his jaw and tightened his grip on the telephone, but he did not respond.

"Are you there?"

"I'm here," Milton said.

"You were with Miss Dewey yesterday. We picked her up after you left. I thought it would be helpful to have a discussion."

"About?"

"Well, you, for one. You are a very interesting man. And then there's the story she was thinking about writing. I say story—I should say stories, I suppose. The armed robbery and what happened to Eddie when he was a boy. She's explained what you really wanted in the vault."

"She has nothing to do with me. If you think you can get to me by threatening her, you're wasting your time. Do what you like. I don't care."

"Really? You're bluffing."

"Try me."

"Please, Mr. Smith, just stop. You *are* bluffing. You didn't go into the vault for money. I've spoken to my boys' brief. They said you left almost everything there. No diamonds. Some cash, but not as much as you could have had. So what you told me, all that nonsense about extorting Eddie, it was all a pack of lies. You went to get photographs of Eddie from the eighties, didn't you? I've been trying to work out why you would do something like that? Eddie is dead. You don't owe him anything. And what you did was very, very dangerous."

Milton knew he shouldn't rise to the bait, but he couldn't quench the upswell of anger. "Because Eddie deserves the chance for his stories to be told. Both of them."

Fabian chuckled. "See, I was right. You have a conscience, Mr. Smith. You have a bleeding heart. You don't want anything to happen to the girl. Stop pretending."

Milton clamped his teeth together until the pressure made his jaw ache.

"Mr. Smith?"

"What do you want?"

"A second chance. We got off on the wrong foot. I'd like to start again. Do you think we could do that?"

"What's the point?"

"Because there's a way out of this that would make everyone happy. I don't want the story about Eddie and my boys to be published. Olivia wants to get home to write the story about Eddie being abused. She should be able to do that. I'd like her to do that. I'd even be happy to help. And you, Mr. Smith, I think that should be enough for you, too. I won't lie—I'm angry about what you did. But the damage can be repaired. My boys are coming out tomorrow."

"What?"

"They're being bailed. One of the benefits of having a bit of cash behind you is that you can hire the absolute best. They're bang to rights, of course, no getting around the fact they were found in the vault, but there are ways we can manage the fallout. I'm telling you that because I don't want you to think I'm going to hold what happens to them over your head. I'm bigger than that."

"What are you suggesting?"

"Let's talk. Work it all out."

"Where?"

"Come to the house."

Milton laughed. "I don't think so."

"You don't trust me."

"Funnily enough, I don't."

"Fine. Somewhere public. Lots of people. There's a restaurant in Covent Garden. Rules. Do you know it?"

"I'll find it."

"Be there tomorrow night. I'll have a table booked for seven."

Chapter Fifty-One

A COLD WIND blew in off the Thames and its frequent gusts flung stinging drops of rain against the faces of the few commuters who hurried across the bridge on their way to work.

Milton was in the middle of the span, as he had said that he would be when General Higgins had called him on the number that Milton had given to Hicks. He had chosen this location for several reasons. First, and most important, was that it would be very difficult for him to be approached without being aware of it. There were only two ways to approach him—from the left and the right—and the bridge was three hundred and seventy metres wide. From his placement in the middle, anyone approaching would have to cover one hundred and eighty-five metres without being seen, and Milton trusted his instincts well enough to know that he would be able to detect a threat with enough time to formulate a response. Second, there was an easy escape, should he need it. He would vault the railing and trust that he was strong enough to withstand the treacherous currents in the river ten metres below.

He looked out over the rails toward the National Theatre and, beyond that, the dome of St Paul's and the skyscrapers of the city beyond. Most of the men and women whom Milton had known who had shared his line of work had at least a passing interest in the golden age of espionage between the end of the war and the fall of the Berlin Wall. Most knew, for example, that Georgi Markov had defected from Bulgaria and found a job in London with the BBC. The KGB, displeased with the trenchant views that Markov was now broadcasting, had determined to put an end to them—and him—in 1978. Milton could have pointed to the bus stop, the site of which was unchanged to the day, where Markov had been assassinated by a KGB agent. The man had been killed by a ricin pellet that had been injected into his thigh by a rigged umbrella. Milton knew the case well because Group Fifteen had kept a file on the assassination and had liquidated the main suspect in Copenhagen several years after the original hit. The files were easy to recall, and the possibility that he might face a similar fate to Markov and in a similar spot was not lost on him.

He saw Higgins approaching from the south side of the river. There were twenty-one people between Milton and the general, but he recognised him quickly from the description that Hicks had given him. He was walking purposefully, a black umbrella held aloft to provide some defence against the elements.

Milton waited against the rail as the other twenty people filed past. As he drew closer, Milton noticed more and more about the old soldier: the lines in his face, the way the rain had flattened his hair against his head, a robustness that belied his age.

Milton stepped out to meet him.

"Milton," Higgins said.

"General, shall we take a walk?"

They set off together, one next to the other. The commuters behind them and the men and women who drove by in taxis and on busses might have seen the two men and mistaken them for work colleagues chatting amiably as they walked to their office.

"Did we ever meet, soldier?"

"Not really, sir."

"But I do know you. Your reputation, I mean. What are you doing getting involved in something like this?"

"What do you mean?"

"Assassinations I can understand, especially with your experience. But theft? It doesn't match what I know of you."

"It doesn't sound as if you know me at all."

"Well, let me see. I might have been out of the game for a while, but I still have a few connections. I was able to pull your Regiment file overnight, just to fill in some blanks. I remember you went to the Firm after the Regiment. You were a headhunter?"

"I was."

Higgins nodded. "What happened? Why did you leave?"

"A civil servant's salary seemed a poor substitute for what I could make on the open market."

"Really?"

"I think you know, sir. You've done something similar."

They walked on for several steps without speaking.

Milton broke the silence. "You've been busy, General. You've started to clean up behind you."

"You mean Isaacs? Yes, of course. That's because of you, not that I'd expect you to care. You compromised everything. I didn't have a choice. Leo Isaacs was a weak man. I'm not talking about his perversions, although those were bad enough. He wouldn't have been the sort who would have been able to keep his mouth shut. It would have taken the police ten minutes to get the whole sorry story out of him. Best to make sure that didn't happen."

"The police think it was suicide?"

"Yes, that's very straightforward. He's been hounded by these unfortunate rumours for years. The pressure—I don't know, it must all have gotten too much for him."

"What about the others?"

"There was only one other. The rest died years ago. Isaacs and Harry Grainger were the only ones still alive."

"And Grainger?"

"The same, I'm afraid. Heart attack. He lived alone. His cleaner does his house every Friday. She'll find him then. Terrible shame."

They walked on.

Higgins glanced at him. "Hicks says you have a business proposal for me?"

"I do. What do you care about, General?"

"My money."

"I can get you a lot more than the money you lost."

"But you want half of it."

"I do."

"You think that's a little generous?"

Milton shrugged. "Half of what you could get is a lot more than what you had in that box. And you don't get anything without me."

"After you took it in the first place, Milton? You expect me to trust you?"

"Not really. But you'll have to get used to the idea."

A bus rumbled by in the outside lane, throwing a curtain of water over two tourists who were pausing to take a selfie with the Houses of Parliament in the background.

"If I said yes, what would it look like?"

Milton knew what he had to say. This was it: the sell. He would reinforce what Hicks had already said. "Frankie Fabian trusts me. He's seen what I can do and he wants me to work with him on a permanent basis. I've said I'd think about it. I could tell him I wanted to see him to talk about it. I could tell you when the sit-down might take place. It would probably be at his house. I could tell you what his security disposition is like. How many guards he has, what they carry, how they patrol. It's minimal. Nothing that would give you and your men any trouble."

"And?"

"You go at it. Send your men—all they need to do is create a distraction. I go in, too. If Fabian has the money there, I'll top him and bring it out. If he doesn't, if he has it somewhere else, I'm betting you know how to get what you need out of him. And if you don't, I do—but that would cost you another ten per cent."

"Don't worry, Milton, I won't need any help for that."

They were nearly at the end of the bridge now, the lights at the junction with the Strand glowing in the gloom.

"And if I said yes?" Higgins said.

"Then you wait for me to tell you when it's going down.

You do your part, I get your money, you give me half."

"And if I say no?"

"I know you're a dangerous man, Higgins. I know the men who work for you are dangerous, too. And I know that you're not the sort to let bygones be bygones. I don't know how it'll end up. But I like peace of mind. So, if you turn me down, one way it might end up is that I go after all of you. And you know enough about me to know that that's my special skill. I'll go after you one by one until I feel safe again. I wouldn't recommend calling my bluff, but that's for you to decide."

They reached a bus stop with a double-decker waiting to pull away.

"You've got my number," Milton said. "Call me. If I don't hear from you by this time tomorrow, I'll take it that you're not interested."

Milton didn't wait for Higgins to speak again. He hopped aboard the bus just before the doors hissed shut, pressed his prepaid card to the reader and then went to take a seat at the back. The bus edged away from the kerb before being caught in the traffic at the junction. Milton sat down and exhaled, the tension of what he had just done flowing out of him. He turned in his seat and looked back through the rear window. It was partially obscured by condensation, but there were patches that were clear and Milton could see Higgins standing on the pavement where Milton had left him, watching the bus as it rolled ahead, crossed the junction and carried him away.

Chapter Fifty-Two

MILTON STAYED in the Waterloo hotel room for most of the day. He watched the news, always nervous that details of the investigation into the robbery would be revealed. If the police announced that they had suspects under arrest after finding them in the vault, it would make his selling job on Higgins that much more difficult. There would be questions, then, that he would be unable to answer.

But the story passed down the running order with each successive bulletin. By five o'clock, it had been dropped altogether. There were no damaging revelations.

There was a branch of Ned's Noodles opposite the hotel, and Milton went down to it for his dinner. He ordered udon noodles with chicken and yakisoba sauce. He was sitting at a window seat, gazing out into the dreary evening, and he found himself thinking of Olivia. He wasn't responsible for her, and she was in the mess she was in because she had ignored his very clear advice. But that didn't mean he was able to abandon her. If she was still alive, it was only because Fabian thought that she might prove to be useful leverage against Milton. The moment that calculation changed, she would serve no further purpose, and Milton was in no doubt that Fabian was not the sort of man to just let her go. He had demonstrated how ruthless he was with Eddie. She was worth nothing to him by comparison.

He was collecting a pair of plastic chopsticks when his burner phone rang.

It could only really be one of two people: Fabian or Higgins.

"Hello?" Milton said.

"Milton?"

"Yes."

"It's Higgins."

Milton lodged his chopsticks in the mess of noodles and switched the phone to his right ear.

"And?"

"We're in."

"I'm glad to hear it."

"How do we proceed?"

"I'll need to make the arrangements."

"What does that mean?"

"I told you. I need to set up a meeting with Fabian."

"Where? His house?"

"Leave it to me. I'll call you tomorrow. Be ready to move. We won't have time to wait."

Chapter Fifty-Three

MILTON WENT STRAIGHT to Covent Garden. Rules was on Maiden Lane and was, according to the sign outside, the oldest restaurant in London. Milton glanced in through the window and saw Frankie Fabian sitting in a booth at the back of the room. He went to the door, pushed it open and went inside.

"Good evening, sir," the maître d' said.

"I'm here to see a gentleman. He's inside."

The woman smiled and gestured that he should go through into the dining room.

Milton did as she suggested. The room was old fashioned, with lots of wood and a gloomy, slightly stultifying atmosphere. It was quiet, too, with just a handful of diners, the only sounds the low murmur of conversation and the chink of cutlery ringing against china. Milton glanced back at Fabian's table. He was dining alone, a bowl of soup set out before him. Two large men were sat in the booth next to him, neither of them much interested in the meals before them. Milton could identify bodyguards when he saw them. They were muscle, there to make sure that the meeting passed off without incident. Milton felt comfortable enough. Nothing would go down in a public place like this.

Milton approached Fabian's booth and sat down opposite him.

"Mr. Smith." Fabian laid his spoon down and stared at Milton. His expression was eloquent, and Milton was left in no doubt as to what he would like to do to him if he was given the chance. "Thank you for seeing me."

"Shall we get something straight, right away?" Milton said. "You're wasting your time with the reporter. She doesn't mean anything to me."

Fabian smiled. "You would say that, but I don't believe you. Let's not start off on the wrong foot again. I'm going to send the young lady back to London. I want her to write the story."

"Which one?"

He smiled at that. "The one about Isaacs. I want that to be published. You might not believe me, but I loved Eddie. And those perverts deserve to be punished."

"And the other story? About the robbery?"

"That's what I'd like to talk to you about."

Milton shook his head. "I can't help you. I'm sorry if you came here on false pretences, but it's not up for discussion. Neither of them are. They both have to be written. It's what Eddie wanted."

"How do you know what he wanted?"

"Because he told me. He wanted to make things right. The things he'd done and the things that were done to him. He wanted to get justice and dispense justice. And I'm going to make sure that happens."

"Eddie's dead. Maybe you should think about what his father wants."

"I don't think you have a right to speak on his behalf."

"And I don't—"

Milton interrupted him. "Enough. Stop. I know what you did. I knew the first time we met. You murdered him."

Frankie Fabian was an excellent actor, his poker face honed through interviews with hostile police and during three criminal trials, but Milton's mild threat generated a flicker of discomfort that passed quickly across his face. "You know Eddie was adopted?"

"Yes. He told me."

"I didn't want him originally. Funny, the way things play out. It was my wife. She's a soft touch. Always has been, bless her. She wanted to adopt a child who needed a family. A hard-luck case. I couldn't care less about charity, but I let her do it. And that was Edward. He was a lovely boy. Sweet as you like. Had his problems, but he'd been moved around from pillar to post, so we put it down to that. Who wouldn't have had problems with that kind of history?"

Milton didn't react and waited until Fabian continued.

"Treated him like my own flesh and blood. Got him involved in the family business. But his problems got worse. He had no stomach for it. I tried, but it made no difference. I think I knew something had happened to him before we adopted him. Something in the homes. Something made him the way he was."

"The way he was?"

"My boys would say that he was a faggot, but I didn't care about that. My old man's father was gay. Built my family into what it is today. Couldn't give a shit. No, I mean it was the way he was wired. This guilt he had. The way he couldn't be happy with anything. The way he couldn't take the things I gave him and be grateful for them." Fabian shook his head sadly. "I don't care whether you believe me or not, but I loved him. Despite everything, all the trouble he gave us, I loved him."

"Even when he threatened to go to the police about the guard who got shot?"

"He said he couldn't stand the guilt about what happened." Frankie shook his head, and Milton thought he looked almost sad. "Couldn't stand the guilt. Ridiculous. He said it'd been eating him up. It's the most pathetic thing I ever heard. The bloke had it coming to him. You see a man waving a shotgun at you, what do you do? You do what you're told. He didn't, he was stupid, he got shot. End of story. But Eddie couldn't get over it. Just couldn't. He said it was his fault. Started drinking, said the only way he could live with himself was when he was too pissed to remember what had happened. I couldn't get it into his thick head that he was overreacting. And the drinking just made it worse."

"So you killed him."

He took his glass and sipped from it. "That's right," he said diffidently.

There was no sadness there, not now. The melancholy

had gone as soon as it had appeared. He glared at Milton. There was defiance and anger. It was what Milton had expected to see. It was what he had *needed* to see to decide, once and for all, that the course of action he had set in play was the right thing to do. Coming here had been a chance for Frankie Fabian to argue for his right to continue to draw breath. His arguments had been selfish. They had utterly failed. If he had known the danger he was in, perhaps he would have behaved differently.

Milton had heard all he needed to hear. "Thank you," he said, and started to rise.

Fabian carried on. "One thing about me you need to know. Family is the most important thing in my life."

Milton paused.

"I'd do anything for my boys. Anything. I gave Eddie a life he never would've had otherwise. Money. Lifestyle. Choices. He couldn't accept any of it. He was too fucked up. Too broken. They did that to him. Those men in the photographs. I tried and tried, but none of it did any good. And in the end I didn't have a choice."

Milton listened to it all—the attempt to justify what he had done—and fixed him throughout with a steely, icy gaze. He knew the effect that his cold and emotionless eyes could have on a person; he had seen it hundreds of times before.

Milton sat down again. "Does it feel better to get that off your chest?"

Fabian looked rattled at Milton's complete lack of a reaction. He glanced over at the muscle on the other table. The men started to rise.

"Do I look like a priest?" Milton asked. "Did you think I was here to take your confession?"

"What, then? Why are you here?"

"Because I wanted to tell you what's going to happen next. I'm not negotiating with you. I'm *telling* you. And I want you to know why."

He jutted out his chin a little. "And what's that?"

"I'm going to kill you, Frankie."

Milton watched his face, the infusion of blood in his cheeks, the way his brow lowered just a fraction, the stiffening of his jawline. Milton could see that his words had had the desired effect. Fabian's larynx jerked involuntarily and a tiny muscle in his cheek twitched once and then a second time. His hand scurried back across the table to the place setting and his fingers traced over the knife that had been left there. Fabian was a hard man, but he was worldly enough to know when he was looking into the eyes of a predator. Fabian was frightened.

"Do you think I'm afraid of you?" he said, regardless.

Milton kept staring. He had to be his most persuasive here; his plan depended upon Fabian taking him seriously. "You should be afraid. You asked what I used to do. I never did tell you. I was in the military, at first. The SAS. But then I was transferred into intelligence. I did wet work. You know what that is? I was the person who was sent to kill you when you became a threat to the government's interests."

Frankie responded with an unconvincing laugh. "Don't make me laugh. What are you trying to say? You were James fucking Bond?"

"I've killed more than a hundred and fifty people in my life. I scouted them, learned everything there is to know about them, and then, at a time of my choosing, I reached out and snuffed out their lives. That's what I'm going to do to you. I could've done it when we met, after the funeral, but I needed your help to get into the vault. I don't need your help any more, Frankie."

"You're full of it."

"You won't know when, you won't know how, and you won't see me coming. It might be quick or it might not. But I want you to know that I'm going to do it, and the reason I'm doing it is because you murdered Eddie. You killed your own son."

Milton stood. The two men at the adjacent table were on their feet, too, but Milton froze them to the spot with a glare. The promise of violence was written in his eyes.

"There's one other choice. One chance."

"To do what?"

"To bring this to an end without any more bloodshed. Your blood, Frankie. And your sons, your wife, and anyone else who stands between me and you. First, you let the girl go. She doesn't mean anything to me, but she needs to write the story about Leo Isaacs. And, second, you go to the police and confess to what you did. About how you killed Eddie, and about how your son murdered that guard. You've got one day. If you don't do it, I'm going to pay you a visit. And it won't be nearly as civilised as this."

Fabian stood, brushed his hands down his shirt and the front of his trousers, and collected his jacket from the back of the chair.

"You do that, Mr. Smith. You'd be welcome. I think you're bluffing, but maybe you're not. Maybe you're as stupid as you sound. I don't know. But you know where to find me. I'll be waiting for you."

Fabian took out his wallet, pulled out a fifty-pound note, and laid it on the table. He left without looking back. Milton turned to watch him as he went, saw him leave the restaurant and cross the street to his car. He waited until the taillights came on and the car drove away, and then, finally, he took out his phone. He dialled a number and waited for it to connect.

"It's me," he said.

"I'm here," replied Alex Hicks. "I've got him."

"Follow him."

Chapter Fifty-Four

MILTON WENT to a meeting that evening. He wanted an hour's worth of peace, a small interval where he could close his eyes and listen to the shares of the men and women who were just like him, with the same compulsions and problems, the same urge toward self-destruction. The meeting was in Fitzrovia, at the St Charles Borromeo Church on Ogle Street. He hadn't been to the church before; it was a Step & Tradition meeting, focusing on the twelve steps and the twelve traditions. The step that had been chosen for discussion was the third, requiring that alcoholics made a decision to turn their will and their lives over to the care of God as they understood Him. Milton sat at the back and listened. He didn't have the piety of others, and, although he did not believe in God, he tried to clear his mind in the hope that he might receive a sign that what he was about to do was right. He had orchestrated a course of events that had its own momentum now, and there could be no resiling from it, no stopping it from hurtling toward its inevitable conclusion. Milton had done it for Eddie, but he realised as he sat in his plastic chair that he hadn't considered whether this was what Eddie would have wanted. The realisation flooded him with uncertainty. He wondered whether—instead of the selflessness that he thought he had been striving for—his behaviour was, in fact, selfish. An attempt to seek redress for his own wrongs by arrogantly assuming that he was doing good.

He didn't get the peace of mind that he had hoped to find at the meeting. All he left with were more doubts.

#

THEY MET in a lay-by on the road just outside Oxford. It wasn't far from Littleworth, the village where Eddie had been murdered. Milton pulled off the road and parked his battered Volkswagen next to Alex Hicks's sleek Range Rover. He got out and hurried ahead, sliding into the passenger-side seat. It was dark, and rain was falling heavily onto the windscreen. The two men sat there for a moment, watching as it sluiced down the glass. The taillights of the cars passing by on the road became indistinct red swipes, blurred and smeared by the water. They were both wearing black. Milton was wearing a tactical shirt and matching trousers, and he had a balaclava and a pair of gloves in his bag back in the car. Hicks was dressed in similar fashion.

Milton broke the silence. "You ready?"

"I think so."

"You need to do better than that, Hicks."

"I'm ready."

"You get what I asked for?"

"There," Hicks said, jerking his head to indicate the leather satchel on the back seat. "It's all there."

Milton swivelled around and reached for the straps of the satchel. He hauled it into the front, unzipped it, and looked inside. There were three items: the first was a holstered Sig P226. It was a superb weapon, with a twenty round magazine capacity, double-action first round capability and class-leading accuracy and reliability. This one was chambered in 9mm. Milton had used the Sig on many occasions and was as comfortable with it as he could be.

"Is this yours?" Milton asked him.

"Yes. You don't need to worry. It's in good condition."

The second item was a pair of night-vision binoculars.

The last piece of equipment was a small box with a belt clip, a press-to-talk switch and a headset. It was a H4855 Personal Role Radio, the same model that the British army used.

"What channel will the men be on?"

"Two."

"And us?"

"Twelve. You used this before?"

"Of course." It was an excellent piece of kit. The inbuilt receiver enabled the radio to be keyed remotely with the press-to-talk switch fob. Milton would attach the radio and the pressel to his belt.

"Has Higgins bought the story?"

"I think so. He's on board, anyway."

"What's he planning?"

"A five-man fire team. All of us. He's not taking any chances."

"What about him?"

"He'll stay out of range."

"But he'll be there?"

"Yes."

"What does he want you to do?"

"Lay back and snipe. I've got my HK in the back."

Milton nodded. That was about as fortuitous an assignment as Hicks could have hoped for. It meant he would be able to stay out of the way. It was fortuitous for Milton, too. It was more than likely that he would need covering fire at some point, and Hicks would be able to provide it.

"Are you clear on what we need to do?"

Hicks nodded. "You're taking the biggest risk."

Milton shrugged that off. "If there's enough of a distraction, I'll be able to get in and get out. You don't need to worry about me. Just watch your back, that's all. If Higgins sees through the plan, he'll come for you."

"I know that."

"Your wife and kids?"

"They're still out of the way."

"Good."

Milton collected the leather satchel, opened the car door and stepped outside. Traffic sped by in both directions, and a large eighteen-wheeler rumbled past just a few feet from where he was standing. The air was damp, and the grim sky promised yet more rain.

Milton held the door open. “Good luck.”

“You too,” Hicks said. “And thank you. For helping. You didn’t have to.”

“I’m not doing it for you,” Milton said.

He closed the door and made his way back to his car. He opened the door and dropped down into the seat. He put the satchel on the passenger seat, the mouth of the bag falling open so that he could see the ominous blackness of the Sig inside.

Part Four

Halewell Close

Chapter Fifty-Five

MILTON HAD chosen a good spot from which to surveil the house and a wide portion of the southern grounds. The estate was surrounded by a dry stone wall, typical for the Cotswolds. He had driven to the main gate and then followed it around to the west and then the north, trailing the perimeter until he found a spot that he liked. He had parked out of sight at the side of a switchback lane and then prepared himself. He applied camo paint to his face, smearing it across every last inch of skin until only the whites of his eyes stood out when he checked his handiwork in the mirror. He pushed the in-ear plugs into place, pulled his balaclava over his head and settled it all the way down so that the skin around his neck and throat was covered, too. He put on the shoulder holster, jammed the Sig into place, and checked that he could easily withdraw it. He could.

He collected the small rucksack that was sitting on the seat next to him, stepped outside and went around to the boot of the car. He had stopped at a Shell garage on the drive west and bought the additional supplies that he thought he might need. He opened the plastic carrier bag and took out the two bottles of wine. He unscrewed the tops of each bottle and poured the wine out onto the verge. Then, he took out two bottles of motor oil and a jerry can that he had filled with petrol, filling each wine bottle half and half with each. He took a thick rag, used his knife to slice it in two, and used the halves to seal the mouths of the bottles, covering each with several layers of duct tape. He opened a packet of tampons, removed two, and taped them to the sides of the bottles.

Milton wrapped the Molotov cocktails with the remainder of the torn rag so that they didn't jangle against each other, and put them and the knife into the rucksack. He slung it across his back and crossed the road to the wall. It was eight feet tall. He pulled on his gloves and leaped, his boots jamming against the rough stones so that he could pull himself up. He clambered to the top, quickly checked the landscape beyond—there was nothing to concern him—and then dropped down onto the other side.

He lowered himself to his belly and surveilled. He was in an area with plenty of untamed vegetation. There was a narrow strip of cleared land between the wall and the trees that had been planted alongside it, and then beyond that was an expanse of overgrown grass and weeds that swayed sluggishly in the gentle night-time breeze. Milton crept between the trunks of two squat birch trees, then slithered forward through the grasses until he reached the point where they had been trimmed, allowing him a clear view of the estate and the house beyond.

He had given some thought to undertaking this operation himself, without help. He remembered much of the layout from before. It was his habit to pay close attention to his surroundings, and he recalled enough details from his visit here for the wake that a full reconnaissance had been unnecessary.

He took out the binoculars and used them to scan the grounds from the main gate, following the winding drive into the gentle hollow with the lake at the bottom and then to the house itself. He remembered that it had been equipped with an excellent security system, and he confirmed that now. The gates were substantial and observed by a CCTV rig. But that had been easily avoided; he had simply breached the perimeter over the wall and away from the cameras. But that would not be the end of the matter. Milton recalled seeing motion sensors and security lights as he had driven nearer to the house, and, although he could see nothing now from his distant vantage point, it was a reasonable supposition that the measures would be continued throughout the grounds. But he was confident that he could get to the house without gaining attention.

That, then, would leave the matter of getting inside.

It would be difficult, but Milton could do it. He had breached more impressive security than this.

He had considered his options, but he had elected to do things a different way. There were two parties deserving of punishment for what had happened to Eddie Fabian. On the one hand, there was Frankie Fabian, and, on the other, Richard Higgins. Fabian had killed his own son, but, had he waited for just a few hours, Higgins would have done it for him. That, in Milton's estimation, was enough to bring Higgins and the Feather Men within the ambit of his vengeance. Higgins had also been responsible for suppressing the stories that would have brought his hideous paymasters the public scrutiny their previous actions had deserved. There was a payment to be exacted for that, too. Milton could have gone after them both, one after another, but he liked the symmetry of setting them off against each other like this. The Feather Men were impressive: well armed and trained to the highest standards. Milton had needed Fabian to understand that he was in danger, and to bolster his security appropriately, for Higgins and the others would have overwhelmed him otherwise. Milton wanted there to be a stalemate, at least for a short while, because, in the chaos that would ensue, he would be afforded the opportunity to slip into the property and see that justice was done.

There was Olivia to think about, too. She had complicated matters.

He put the binoculars to his eyes and scanned down into the hollow. He saw the lake and the boathouse and the single guard who was smoking a cigarette while gazing out over the still waters. The man was leaning against the wooden balustrade that prevented a drop down into the water, and Milton could see the tip of his cigarette as it flared with each breath that he drew in. Milton thought he could make out a shotgun resting against the side of the building.

He scanned left, following the path through the gardens to the dark expanse of lawn, across the gravelled parking area and finally to the house itself. It was brightly lit from security lights that threw illumination up onto the walls and out over the parked cars and down to the lawns. The curtains in the windows had been drawn, the glow from the lights inside visible as a muted glow through the fabric and more brightly down the middle where they had not been properly pulled together. The kitchen's grand extension at the back of the house had been finished with a thatched roof, as Milton remembered. He angled the binoculars up a little and scanned across the first-floor windows: some were lit, their curtains drawn, too, while others were dark. Olivia was probably being held in one of the upstairs rooms; that would have been where Milton would have kept her.

He waited a little longer, studying the building, and was rewarded when he saw the front door open and two men step out. Each was armed with a shotgun.

Milton watched and waited as the men set off on a lazy patrol, one of them splitting off to descend the gentle slope of the lawn to the lakefront, where he joined the first man that Milton had seen.

Milton waited there for two hours. He was in position long enough to observe as an Audi Q7 travelled down the drive, delivering four men and then the driver. He watched as the front door of the house opened and a man stepped out to meet them. He pressed the glasses to his eyes and adjusted the focus, waiting until the image was crisp and sharp before he was sure that the newcomer was Spencer Fabian. The men spoke with Fabian for a moment before they were directed to an outbuilding that Milton remembered from before: some of the old barns had been converted into guest accommodation. That, then, was where the extra muscle was staying. Fabian stayed there to speak with one of them for an extra minute and then went back into the house.

Frankie Fabian had not been bluffing, then. His boys had been bailed. Milton had no idea how that had been managed, but it was bad luck for them. They would have been safer in custody.

Chapter Fifty-Six

ALEX HICKS was on his belly, pressed close to the muddy earth. He had his Heckler and Koch 416A5 laid out in front of him, its weight supported by the after-market bipod that was screwed into the housing just behind the bayonet lug. He had attached a flash hider to the muzzle; it would eliminate some of the visual evidence of his position, but not all of it. He had left his sub-compact variant at the lock-up where he kept his weapons and had selected the full-sized iteration of the weapon with the longer 19.9-inch barrel. It was more accurate at distance, especially with the PVS-14 night vision monocular sight that he had mounted to the rail. Hicks knew that he would be taking shots from range tonight.

The general had tasked all of the unit with the operation. Milton's intelligence to the general had been that the house would be guarded, and Higgins was not the sort of man to take chances. He had decided to send them all in. Gillan, Connolly, Woodward and Shepherd were in the broad grounds of the estate with him, each man scaling the wall at a separate point and advancing slowly and carefully. The house itself was not visible from the southern wall where Hicks and the others had breached it. They had proceeded to the north, passing from cover to cover, grateful for the areas on the other side of the driveway that were generous with trees and bushes. All five men were wearing black, and they had all daubed their faces with black camouflage paint. They approached in a line formation, fifty metres between each man. Hicks could just see the outline of Gillan to his left as he was similarly pressed to the ground. Connolly was to Hicks's right, but he was deep within a copse of fir and rendered invisible within the gloom. Woodward was beyond Connolly.

The general had stayed in his car, laid up in a quiet turning before the estate's main gate. Hicks heard his voice through his earpiece.

"*Report.*"

Connolly spoke. "*In position, sir.*"

"*Anything?*"

"*Affirmative. Multiple guards, sir. Two by the lake, two others just coming out of the cottage to the side of the house. We've seen another four on top of that.*"

"*Hold position.*"

Hicks found that he was holding his breath. He knew that he and Milton had been fortunate to be able to persuade the general to mount the operation. The story that they had constructed in Milton's hotel room was decent, but it wouldn't have stood any real investigation. Hicks had known that the general was motivated by greed, and it had been that upon which he had staked his hopes. They had presented the old man with an opportunity to recover the money that had been taken from him, and the chance to confiscate enough additional loot from the vault to make even that look like small change.

Woodward radioed: "*General?*"

"*I'm blind from here. Recommendation?*"

"*I can only see three men now. The fourth has gone around the back of the house and the others are inside. Hicks—can you take the two by the lake?*"

"Affirmative," Hicks replied.

"*I can get close enough to take the third out. Connolly and Gillan can attack the cottage. I say we go ahead, sir. We're here and we have surprise on our side.*"

There was another pause, marked by a crackle of static across the troop net.

"*What about Milton?*"

"*He knows what he's doing. We give him a distraction.*"

"*Afterwards?*"

"*You can leave that to me.*"

"*Copy that, sir.*"

"You're clear to proceed. In and out as quickly as you can. Higgins out."

Hicks felt a moment of relief, but it was quickly washed away by a surge of adrenaline as his body prepared itself for the concentrated burst of action that was about to be unleashed. There was fear, too, because the course he had chosen to take did not allow for the possibility of failure. If it went wrong, he was dooming himself and, more than that, he was dooming his family. It was only because he was so desperate to leave the Feather Men that he had even contemplated what Milton had suggested.

"You heard the man. Hicks, take out the guards by the lake. I'm going to go around it and get as close to the house as I can. Gillan—cut the telephone line."

"On it. Cutting in three, two, one. Line is down."

"Fire on my mark."

"Copy that."

"And don't fuck it up, Hicks."

I don't intend to, he thought.

Chapter Fifty-Seven

DETECTIVE CONSTABLES Banks and Edwards were leaning against the balustrade that protected against the short drop into the lake beyond. They had their elbows on the pitted, weather-beaten wood. It was a cool night and a bracing breeze curled small waves across the surface of the water. Banks looked up into the sky; the thick cloudbank that had been in place all day was unmoved by the wind. It smothered the light of the moon, but at least the rains were holding off.

Edwards took out his packet of cigarettes. "Smoke?"

Banks took one, took Edwards's lighter and lit it. He inhaled smoke and blew it out, watching as the breeze tore it to pieces. "What are we doing here?" he said.

"Tell me about it."

"The DI say anything to you?"

"About what?"

"About how long he expects us to freeze our arses off here?"

"Smith put the wind up Fabian. We'll be here all night."

"Can you believe his lads got bail? It's ridiculous."

"Money talks." Edwards shrugged. "And Fabian has a lot of it. Bruce said that he has a pet judge. There were all sort of restrictions on the bail—residence, passports surrendered, curfew."

"Doesn't matter how much money he's got. It won't be enough to get those two off the hook. They were caught in the vault, mate. Bail's one thing, but they're still going down. They've got to be looking at ten years for what they did."

Edwards shook his head. "You don't know?"

"What?"

"He's getting them out of the country. He's got a plane

coming to fly them out tomorrow afternoon, Bruce said. They'll be on the Costa del Sol working on their tans."

"Lucky bastards." Banks shivered. "I bet you anything you like it pisses down before we're done."

"I had a lovely plan to go and get smashed tonight. You know the girl behind the bar at The Cat and Mutton?"

"Piss off."

"Seriously. Been seeing her for the last couple of weeks."

"You dirty old man. She's half your age."

Edwards reached out, put his arm around Banks's shoulders and squeezed. "Jealousy's all right, mate. I'd be jealous, too."

#

MILTON TRAINED the binoculars on the house. He had done his research. The property had been in the Fabian family for decades, but it had come onto the market fifteen years ago. The reason for the attempted sale was unclear and it had been quickly removed, but not before Google had cached the sales page. The agents had prepared a plan of the property for prospective purchasers, and Milton had printed it, blown it up to A3 size, and then fixed it onto the wall of his hotel room. He had studied it and assessed the means of attack that would be most likely to yield results. There was a boot room at the back of the property that offered access to the kitchen extension and then the rest of the house.

He heard a voice over the radio.

"I can only see three men now. The fourth has gone around the back of the house. Hicks—can you take the two by the lake?"

Milton recognised Hicks's voice: *"Affirmative."*

"I can get close enough to take the third out. Connolly and Gillan can attack the cottage. I say we go ahead, sir. We're here and we have surprise on our side."

The conversation was hushed, tight with the

anticipation of imminent violence.

"What about Milton?"

"He knows what he's doing. We give him a distraction."

"Afterwards?"

"You can leave that to me."

"Copy that, sir."

"You're clear to proceed. In and out as quickly as you can. Higgins out."

Milton swung the glasses around and tried to spot the soldiers. There were plenty of places that they could hide, and he was unable to place them.

He heard the first man's voice again. "*You heard the man. Hicks, take out the guards by the lake. I'm going to go around it and get as close to the house as I can. Gillan—cut the telephone line.*"

"On it. Cutting in three, two, one. Line is down."

"Fire on my mark."

"Copy that."

"And don't fuck it up, Hicks."

Milton wriggled forward a little more. He held his breath. He waited in the cover of the undergrowth until he saw the first muzzle flash spit out against the darkness.

The first flash was two hundred metres to his five o'clock, a split four-way burst that was quickly followed by a single barked report. That was Hicks and his HK, Milton assessed; the gun was equipped with a muzzle suppressor. Milton scanned back to the lakefront and saw that one of the two men who had been smoking had fallen backwards, landing on his backside, his hands pressed to his chest.

The second and third shots followed quickly after. Milton watched as the second man by the lake dropped to his side, his legs twitching.

The fourth shot was aimed at the guard who had stayed by the house, and it was a more difficult shot, especially so given that the man had heard the first three cracks and perhaps seen his colleagues drop. The guard threw himself to one side, rolling until he was in the cover afforded by the parked Q7. The shot missed, ploughing into a window and detonating the glass with a crash and then the jingle of shattering fragments. An alarm sounded from inside and the security lights that Milton had noticed earlier flicked on, throwing out blinding sheets of light.

Milton pushed himself to his haunches and then crouched low, his muscles aching for action, the adrenaline pulsating through his veins. He needed to wait. Needed to assess.

"Two down."

"Eyes wide, boys. Advance."

Milton saw the suggestion of movement through the undergrowth. He knew where to look, and, even with that advantage, it was still difficult to be sure that his eyes were not deceiving him. The men were SAS veterans, honed by months of training and years of operational experience. This kind of assault, backed by the benefit of planning, would not faze them.

"Firing."

Milton saw the starburst and heard the angry chug as an automatic rifle fired. The shooter was a hundred metres to his four o'clock.

Now.

Milton set off quickly. He hugged the trees and moved with cautious speed. He hurried with his head down, careful where he placed his feet.

He heard the sound of automatic gunfire from behind him, and he quickened his pace. The terrain dipped down into the shallow depression and then climbed up again. When Milton crested the top and paused to take his bearings again, he was adjacent to the house, at the corner, with a view that allowed him to see around to the wide patio area, the outside kitchen to the rear and, closer to him, the screened-off area that he had noticed when he had visited the house for Eddie's wake. It was the location of the domestic oil tanks.

There was a man there, pressed against the wall, cradling a submachine gun.

Milton paused.

He watched as the man stayed down low and then sprinted ahead, scurrying into cover behind the Q7.

"Movement!"

"Behind the car."

There came another burst of automatic fire from the vicinity of the lake. Bullets thunked into the bodywork of the Audi and then the windows were blown out.

Milton ran. He stayed in cover for another twenty metres, stopped, satisfied himself that the way ahead was clear, and then broke cover and sprinted as hard as he could for the cover of the fuel tank. If he could get there and then around to the back, he would be sheltered from the firefight behind him.

"Movement! By the wall!"

Milton caught his breath. Shots cracked out and he flinched as he heard the rounds whistle overhead.

"Fuck! Missed."

"Stay on the car. Pin them down."

Milton reached the screened area and slid down into cover. A reed fence had been erected around the tank. The set-up had been installed in the centre of an excavation that had then been lined with concrete. Milton forced the reed screening aside and dropped down next to the tank. He shucked his small rucksack from his shoulders, opened it, and pulled out one of the wine bottles that he had prepared earlier. He shook the bottle to mix the oil and petrol, took out his lighter, and lit the fuse. He counted to three and then, popping up just as long as necessary, he tossed the bottle toward the house. It was ten metres from his position to the kitchen extension, but his throw was accurate. There was a brick chimney above the kitchen, protruding from the midst of the thatch, and the bottle struck it plumb in the middle. The glass smashed, spilling the fuel over the straw beneath. It lit at once, the orange-red flames spreading out across the roof.

He ran hard to the side of the house. The security lights

overhead blazed out into the grounds, creating an inky pool of darkness beneath them that he could melt into. There was a small wall that defined the perimeter of a kitchen garden, and he dropped behind it. He heard more shots from the front of the house, and then the sound of more glass being blown apart.

Milton heard a tense voice in his ear. *"You see that?"*

"Roof's on fire."

"Milton?"

"Concentrate. We need to get this done. It's taking too long."

Milton gritted his teeth. The fire had taken hold of the thatch and he could feel the heat pressing down from above him. The flames roared and patches of straw, lit up, fell down to the ground.

It was now or never. He ducked his head, took a breath, counted to three, and then stayed low as he made his way around to the rear of the house. He stopped at the edge of the house and then peered around the corner.

He looked for extra guards.

There was no one.

He recalled the plan of the building, saw the entrance to the boot room, took another breath and then ran for it.

Another round of shooting.

"There—by the house!"

"Get him?"

"Affirmative. He's down."

"Flanking now."

Milton reached the door. There was a glass panel that he could use to see inside. He peered in: the room beyond was empty, the glow of the fire lighting it brightly. He reached out a gloved hand and tried the handle. It was locked, but he could see the key was in the lock on the inside. There was no need to be delicate about how he proceeded. He took a step closer, clenched his fist, punched through the glass and then turned the key. He opened the door and slipped inside. The heat washed over him at once.

Chapter Fifty-Eight

FRANKIE FABIAN had gone upstairs to his bedroom. He had arranged for some of his best men to stay in the guest accommodation until he was able to leave the country tomorrow. He had a team he trusted; some of them were ex-soldiers and ex-police, all of them with experience in his line of work.

Frankie's wife and daughter were already on their way to Florida and his sons were leaving tomorrow by way of a private plane to avoid the legal proceedings that had been brought against them. Frankie was going, too, first class from Heathrow. He had not been in any doubt that Smith meant everything that he had said, and there was something about him—something cold and unmistakeably authentic—that had made it very clear that it would be foolish to underestimate him or to fail to take the necessary precautions. Fabian had brought in enough men to protect him and his boys. His packed suitcases had been moved down to the lobby. He was booked on a flight to Florida tomorrow, but it looked as if that might be unnecessary now.

Smith was here.

Spencer had a walkie-talkie pressed to his ear as he spoke to Bruce. The detective had brought two of his men and was waiting downstairs. Marcus was holding a shotgun. Smith had broken Marcus's ribs, and he grimaced in pain every time he stepped to the window to risk a glance outside. Both of his boys were nervous. Spencer was pale as he swore at Bruce. Marcus was drumming his fingertips against the barrel of the shotgun.

"Fuck!" Spencer said as he clipped the walkie-talkie to his belt.

"What?" Marcus said.

"Bruce tried to call for help. The phone's out and I can't get a signal."

"Out?"

"The line's been cut."

"I don't—"

Marcus stopped. They all noticed, with sudden shock, that the curtains were glowing bright orange.

"What's that?" Marcus said, forgetting where he was and reaching for the curtains.

Spencer grabbed his arm before he could move the curtains aside. "Don't."

"Well, what was it?"

"The kitchen," Spencer said. "He set the thatch on fire."

Marcus went back to the shotgun. "This is ridiculous. He can't be on his own."

"So who the fuck is helping him?" Frankie snapped.

"Doesn't matter, Dad. There are loads of us. You stay in here. We'll keep him outside."

"Why is he doing this?" Marcus said quietly, almost rhetorically.

Spencer took the walkie-talkie and put it to his ear again. "Bruce," he said. "Bruce—what's going on?"

All Frankie heard was the squelch of static.

Spencer swore.

"What is it?" Marcus asked.

"He's not replying."

"Go and check," Frankie said.

Spencer clipped the unit to his belt and collected his pistol from the table where he had left it. Frankie took his own pistol and checked, for the fifth time, that it had a round in the chamber ready to fire. Spencer held his pistol in his right hand and, carefully, reached out for the door handle with his left. He opened it, glanced outside and slipped into the corridor.

"Who *is* he?" Marcus said.

"He said he was a soldier."

"Why is he doing this? Why is he coming after us?"

"I told you," Frankie snapped. "It's Eddie. This is about him. It's about what we did."

"Eddie didn't have any friends. He didn't have any—"

All of the lights went out.

Marcus stopped mid-sentence.

The room was completely dark. Frankie couldn't see the end of his nose.

"Dad?"

"I'm here."

"Hold on." There came the sound of frantic fumbling. "I've got my phone."

Frankie reached for the wall, placed his palm against it and then backed away from the door. The darkness seemed to lengthen the time it took for Marcus to find his phone and, as he waited there, Frankie could hear the sound of automatic gunfire from the grounds outside. It came in concentrated bursts.

There was a flash of light as Marcus activated his torch app. The beam swung around the room, casting deep, eerie shadows against the wood-panelled walls. Marcus trained the beam on Frankie, so bright that he had to look away.

"Not in my *face*," Frankie said.

"He got to the fuse box."

Frankie tried to remain calm.

There was an almost immediate clatter of gunfire from outside the window.

Chapter Fifty-Nine

THE KITCHEN had quickly become an inferno. There was a gaping hole in the ceiling where the fire had consumed all of the thatch and then the boards beneath, and the flames had rushed inside in search of more fuel. The large range ran on oil, and as the fire swept over it there was an audible pop and then a sudden outrushing of flame as the oil was devoured. Milton was glad of the balaclava across his mouth as he hurried through the room, feeling the heat through the wool that was pressed against his skin. The fire alarms were screaming now and the flames were roaring with a ferocious hunger, the two combining to create a deafening cacophony through which it was almost impossible to hear the small-arms fire that continued outside. It meant that it was unnecessary for him to be careful about making too much sound, but he stayed low and proceeded carefully, aware that there were likely to be armed guards inside the house.

He found the junction box without too much difficulty. He had already located the cable that connected the house to the grid, and it was a simple enough matter to follow it as it traced a path between the join of the ceiling and the wall. The wire disappeared into the kitchen's large walk-in larder and terminated at the back of the larder in a junction box. It had a simple plastic hinged cover, and when Milton pushed the cover back, he saw all of the switches. The master switch was red and at the end of the line; Milton pulled it and all of the lights were immediately extinguished.

There was a door at the end of the kitchen, and Milton pressed himself against the wall to compose himself. The flames were close, the heat singeing his clothes. There was a tremendous crash as a fresh span of the ceiling, already weakened, was dislodged by the fire that had rushed across it. Flaming plasterboard slammed onto the floor.

Milton had to move. Fabian was in the house. Olivia might be. He wanted them both.

He took the Sig from its holster and glanced around the edge of the open doorway into the hall beyond.

He saw a man with his back to him who was toting a handgun. Milton drew a bead on him, stepped out of the doorway, braced his gun in a tight two-handed grip with his left hand canted toward the ground, and fired twice. It would have been impossible to miss from close range, but he put both shots into the man's torso to be sure. The man stumbled forward and then fell to his knees. Milton approached, his gun up, the fire roaring at his back. The man buckled, propping himself up with his right arm. He turned. Milton doubted that the fallen man would be able to recognise him, silhouetted as he was against the brightness of the conflagration, but Milton could see him.

It was the detective.

Bruce's pistol was in his right hand, pressed to the floor. He tried to pull his hand up to aim it, but the attempt merely overbalanced him and he collapsed onto his stomach. He dropped the pistol. Milton stepped up to him, kicked away the pistol, and rolled the older man onto his back. He lowered himself to a crouch and pressed the barrel of the Sig against Bruce's temple.

"Where's the girl?"

"What?"

"The journalist. She's here somewhere. Where?"

Bruce tried to speak, but, when he opened his mouth, his words were so quiet that they were inaudible amid the din.

"Say it again," Milton pressed, leaning down a little closer.

Bruce gasped, unable to speak. Instead, his eyes flicked up to the stairs and the first floor.

"She's up there?"

Bruce nodded.

"Fabian?"

Bruce's eyes flicked up to the stairs again.

Milton stood. The policeman was done for. Both shots had taken him in the gut, and he would bleed out unless he received treatment. There came another huge crash as a beam from the kitchen ceiling worked loose and slammed down onto the floor. Flames burst out, as if blown into the hall on a vicious wind, and the paint on the walls started to blister. The house was finished now. It was going to burn to the ground. Milton had neither the time nor the inclination to help the policeman, and neither was it his responsibility; the man had brought it upon himself. But he had given him a tiny amount of help, and he would recognise that.

He aimed down with the Sig and fired one more time. A mercy shot.

"Status?"

Milton recognised the voice of Richard Higgins across the troop net.

"Status?"

"*Milton was wrong.*" It was one of the unit. His voice was ragged; he sounded out of breath.

"What?"

"*He was either wrong or he was lying. It's a trap. Fabian was waiting for us.*"

"What's happening?"

"Gillan is hit."

"Can you exfil him?"

"Negative. He's dead."

"Pull back."

"Negative. I'm pinned down. There's too many of them."

Movement from the stairs. Someone was coming down. There was a door opposite him. Milton pushed it open and, his Sig raised before him, hurried inside.

Chapter Sixty

SPENCER FABIAN COUGHED. The kitchen was on fire, and clouds of smoke were billowing out into the rest of the house. The corridor was dark without the lights, but the fire was throwing out enough of an orange-red glow that he could see his way. He held the pistol up ahead of him, working to keep his hand from shaking, and made his way forward step by step. He reached the end of the corridor and turned to look into the kitchen. A wall of radiant heat slammed into him. The ceiling was burning and, as he watched, a huge chunk of singed and smoking plasterboard was dislodged. It crashed down to the tiled floor, landing across the body of a man who had been lying there. He glanced down and saw that it was Bruce. His shirt was red with blood and there was a neat hole in the centre of his forehead, right between the eyes.

Spencer looked up to the end of the corridor. A run of flames rushed ahead, pouring out of the kitchen as if they were alive. They spread out, quickly multiplying until they covered the walls and the ceiling and the furniture, and then they started to advance.

Spencer felt a twist in his gut, the sensation that he was not alone. He turned, the gun held up before him, but he never had the chance to use it. A dark shadow separated from the smoke and slammed into him. The impact was sudden, launching him against the wall, driving the breath from his lungs. He felt a strong hand grasp his right wrist and was helpless as his hand was pushed up and away, impotent as the pistol was prised out of his fingers. His assailant was behind him now. Whoever it was had one arm across his throat and the other clasped at a right angle to it, pressed up vertically against his head. Spencer felt the pressure increase and suddenly found that it was almost impossible to draw breath. He gasped, taking in as much smoke as air, but then the pressure was ratcheted up again and he couldn't breathe at all.

He felt his eyes bulging. He struggled, but the man behind him was much too strong. He tried to breathe, but he could not. Darkness gathered at the edges of his sight.

He felt something touch against his ear and then he heard a soft voice over the roar of the flames.

"This is for your brother."

#

HICKS HAD ADVANCED to an excellent vantage point. He was at the southern edge of the lake, with the wide expanse of the water ahead of him, which meant that he had nothing between him and the house. There was a muddy slope half a metre away, a sharp gradient that ran down to the water. The conflagration rendered his night-vision sight almost redundant. His main problem had been the glare from the security lights that blazed out over the water, but Milton had extinguished them when he cut the main power supply. Now, he had more than enough indirect light to pinpoint his targets and nothing to distract his aim.

"What's happening?"

"Gillan is hit."

Hicks had taken out three of Fabian's guards. He had been presented with several opportunities to take down other men, but he had passed up those shots. He didn't want to make things easy for Woodward and the others. He wanted them to struggle. Milton would be compromised if either the attackers or the defenders found success too soon. Deadlock was to be encouraged, so Hicks had waited and observed.

"Can you exfil him?"

"He's dead. Shot to the head."

"Negative. He's dead."

"Pull back."

"Negative. I'm pinned down. There's too many of them."

Hicks pressed the sight to his right eye and slipped his index finger through the trigger guard until it was against the trigger. He squeezed, just a little, feeling the tension in the mechanism.

Woodward's voice was fraught with tension. *"Hicks—do you copy?"*

"I see you."

Woodward was sheltering behind the wall of one of the cottages. The cottage was between him and the main house, the cover protecting him from the guards that were hunkered down behind the parked cars. Hicks placed Woodward squarely within the targeting reticule. He breathed in and out, nice and even, and then drew in a breath and held it.

He started to squeeze the trigger, slowly applying pressure and drawing it back.

#

THE FIRE had taken hold of the house with alarming speed. The heat blistered the paint on the corridor walls and, as Milton laid Spencer Fabian's body on the floor, small patches of flame bloomed ahead of him.

He stepped back into the hallway and heard the voice of one of Higgins's soldiers in his ear.

"Hicks—do you copy?"

Hicks responded, *"I see you."*

The other man's finger must have been on the switch to open the channel. Milton heard the single report of the sniper rifle, a groan of pain and then, as the finger came off the switch, the channel was closed.

"Woodward?" It was the general. *"Woodward, report."*

There was no answer.

"Hicks? What's happening?"

Hicks did not respond. Milton reached down to his belt and switched the dial to channel twelve.

"Hicks, it's me."

"*Where are you?*"

"Inside. Are you okay?"

"*I'm fine.*"

"How many left?"

"*Gillan and Woodward are down.*"

"Fabian's men?"

"*I can still see six. They're all in cover. I think there are others.*"

Milton heard a clatter of gunfire; it sounded close to Hicks.

"*Hicks?*"

"*I'm okay. They got Connolly. There's only Shepherd left.*"

"Pull back."

"*What about you?*"

"Don't worry about me," Milton said. "Go and get Higgins."

"*How are you going to get out?*"

"Leave that to me. Go."

"*Copy that. Good luck.*"

Chapter Sixty-One

MILTON CLIMBED the wide stairs to the first floor. There was one flight, then a half landing, then a second flight. He stayed low, beneath the level of the balustrade, and paused halfway to observe and listen. The fire was everywhere on the ground floor, with smoke pouring from all of the rooms. Milton had anticipated that it would be easy to set the kitchen thatch alight, but he was surprised by how quickly the blaze had spread. The noise was thunderous, punctuated every now and again with the popping of burst windows and the thudding impacts of beams and rafters that were sent crashing to the ground.

He edged around the corner formed by the banister and the balustrade, saw that the next landing was clear, and ascended the stairs quickly.

The landing was generous, with hallways leading into it from two directions.

He took the turning to the left.

There were doors off the corridor on both sides. He remembered the plan of the house. There was a large family bathroom off this corridor and four bedrooms.

Milton would have to clear the rooms one at a time until he found either Olivia or Fabian.

He moved quickly and carefully. He held the Sig with his right hand, pressed himself against the wall and reached for the door handle with his left. He turned the handle and pushed the door open. Nothing. He concentrated, listening for any sound from inside the room. Still nothing. He took his flashlight in his left hand, switched it on and held it against the Sig, and then stepped quickly out from behind the wall. With the gun and the torch aimed into the darkness, he swung the beam of light across the room beyond the door. He moved from left to right, his finger on the trigger and ready to fire.

The room was empty.

He went back to the corridor and tried the next door.

#

FRANKIE FABIAN HEARD yet more gunfire and then a tremendous crash as a part of the house collapsed. Both he and Marcus had taken a risk by going to the window a minute earlier, and they had seen the flames that reached up into the darkness, the fire gorging on the roof of the kitchen. The crash must have been the skeleton of the roof collapsing.

"We can't stay here," Frankie said. "We've got to get out."

"How? It's a war zone out there."

"There's the Land Rover out the back. We could drive to the north gate."

Frankie had been thinking about it. It was the only way out he had been able to come up with. The activity seemed to be centred on the front of the house. His guards were there, and they would make it difficult to get around to the back. It would be dangerous to go outside, but it might be more perilous to stay. They had an old Land Rover, battered but still reliable, parked in the barn at the rear of the house. If they could get to it, they could drive to the north gate, get through it and onto the road beyond. There was something to the idea. At least they would be doing something, anything, rather than waiting here for Milton and whoever it was outside to find them.

"All right," Marcus said. "Better than staying here. We get Spencer and go." He took his shotgun.

"Give that to me," Frankie said, exchanging his pistol for the long gun.

Marcus stood beside the door. Frankie stood before it, the shotgun pointed ahead as Marcus turned the handle and opened it.

"Clear," he said.

Marcus stepped out into the corridor, pausing to check to the left and right. He glanced back into the room. "Clear. Come on."

The sound of the conflagration was louder out here, and Fabian could feel the prickle of the smoke against the back of his throat.

"What about the girl?" Marcus said. "We can't leave her."

"No," Frankie agreed. Marcus was right. They couldn't. "We'll sort her first."

#

MILTON OPENED the fourth door.

He heard something and raised the Sig.

"Help."

The voice was low and quiet. Female.

"Olivia?"

"Help!"

"It's John Smith. Are you alone?"

"Yes. Please—help me."

Milton flicked the switch of the flashlight and the narrow beam played down onto the floor. He brought it up and aimed it in the direction of the voice. He saw Olivia Dewey. She was sitting on a four-poster bed, her hands behind her back. Milton crossed the room and put the flashlight on a bedside table so that the beam bloomed against the wall, leaving him enough light to address the length of rope that had been knotted around her wrists, the other end secured to one of the bed's columns.

He pulled the balaclava off his head so that she could see his face. "Hold on," he said.

He took the knife from his belt and sliced through the knot that held her wrists together. The knot came apart, Milton tugging at it until Olivia's hands were released.

"We need to get out of here," Milton said. "Do you understand?"

She stared up at him, her eyes blank. Her mouth opened and closed soundlessly. Milton diagnosed shock.

"Olivia," he said, "the house is on fire. We need to leave."

She nodded.

Milton told her to stay on the bed and, the Sig in his hand again, he went back to the door. He opened it a fraction and heard the sound of the blaze. He saw the angry colour of the fire from the end of the corridor, the fingers of smoke reaching up from below. The flames had spread with frightening speed. The house, with all the old wood, was one big tinderbox.

He thought about Frankie and gritted his teeth in frustration. He couldn't leave Olivia here and he couldn't take her with him. She would impede him, and it would be dangerous. And they didn't have time. The house was burning down. They needed to move fast.

"Come on," he said, pulling on his pack again. He reached out, took her hand, and drew her after him into the corridor.

Chapter Sixty-Two

HICKS WATCHED THE SHOT GO. Woodward had been fifty metres away from him, crouched in a static position and presenting himself in profile. He made for an easy target. The bullet took but a heartbeat to cross the distance that separated them, and Hicks watched as Woodward's head snapped to the side, bouncing back up from his left shoulder even as his body went limp and collapsed. Woodward lay flat, still and unmoving.

Hicks had his rifle in his right hand and pushed down with his left until he was on his knees. He thought he heard something and, turning in the direction of the sound, he saw a flash of motion as a dark shadow passed across the gathering flame and rushed at him. He was knocked onto his back, and as he twisted his head so that he could look up, he saw the grim flash of a blade as it was thrust toward his chest. He threw up his left hand and reached for the knife. His palm was cut open as the edge of the blade sliced into the flesh. Hicks blocked the pain and pushed, closing his hand around the wrist of the man who was now kneeling astride him, feeling the warmth of his own blood as he tried to secure his grip. Warm gobbets dropped onto his face, into his eyes, his mouth. The blood was slick, and he found it difficult to maintain a firm grip. The man atop him leaned forward to exert more pressure and, as he did, he revealed his face.

Higgins.

The general's mouth was twisted into a grimace of effort as he pressed down. The flames cast his features in a diabolical light, little pinpricks of fire that danced in his black eyes. Higgins had the benefit of leverage and Hicks's left was not his strongest hand. He dropped the rifle and tried to punch up at the general with his right. Higgins managed to get his knee across Hicks's right arm, pinning it, and then pressed down harder. The blade jerked lower and lower, the point wavering just inches from his face, switching in and out of focus as Hicks fought.

"I saw what you did," Higgins grunted.

Hicks tried to resist, but the general was strong for a man of his age. Hicks's strength was failing.

"*Traitor.* You betrayed the men."

The blade shot down and it was all Hicks could do to divert it from his neck. The point pierced his jacket and then his flesh, lancing down into the flesh of his left shoulder until it scraped off bone. The pain was severe, dimming his vision, but he fought it.

"You betrayed *me*."

Now they changed roles: Higgins tried to pull the knife out, and Hicks tried to hold it in place. Hicks's left hand remained locked around the general's wrist. Hicks pulled down, holding the knife there, biting down against the pain, his teeth chewing into his lip until he could taste fresh blood. Higgins jerked, trying to free the knife, the blade widening the incision as the two of them struggled. Hicks tried to free his right hand, but it was pinned firmly, and he couldn't manage it. Higgins changed tactics; he pressed down with his left hand while his right went to the shoulder holster where he wore his Browning.

Higgins pulled the pistol free. Hicks closed his eyes. There was nothing else that he could do.

The shot did not come. Instead, Hicks heard the sound of something crashing through undergrowth and then a loud curse. Higgins heard it too and pivoted to the right. There was a man there, a shotgun in his arms. Higgins swivelled his hips, brought the pistol up and around and fired at the newcomer.

Hicks couldn't see whether the general's shot had hit or missed, and he didn't have the luxury of time to check. The moment presented him with an opportunity. The general's weight had fallen back onto Hicks's knees and his right hand was suddenly free. Hicks sat up, the knife still in his left shoulder, clenched his right fist and put everything he had into a wild haymaker that caught the older man flush on his cheekbone.

Hicks tried to extricate himself from the tangle of legs and stand, but the struggle had brought him right up against the top of the gradient that sloped down to the lake. His boots slipped through the wet mud and he overbalanced, thudding down on his back and sliding down the slope. He tried to arrest his descent, but it was impossible. He shot off the edge and into the water. It was deep here, and he plunged all the way beneath the surface without any indication of where the bottom might be.

The water was ice cold, and it forced its way into his mouth and nostrils and stung his eyes. He put out his right arm and used it to slow his momentum until he was able to correct his positioning and kick away from the bank. His lungs burned, desperate for air, but he stayed beneath the water and kicked again and again. When he finally had no choice but to break the surface, he found himself in the middle of the lake, several metres from the slope. He searched for Higgins or the man who had disturbed them, but could see neither. He took a breath and sank beneath the surface again, kicking for the opposite bank to the one from which he had entered the water. He came up for a second time and realised that he couldn't hear gunfire. He stroked to the bank, gentler at this side of the lake, and clambered out, each jarring motion sending a spasm of pain through the stab wound in his shoulder. The shoreline was quiet, with no sign of movement, but Hicks hurried across the mud and through the straggled reeds until he was in the cover of a spray of ferns.

Hicks looked back at the house. The night sky was lit with flames that reached high above the structure of the building. The blaze was hopelessly out of control now; it would stop only once it had exhausted its fuel.

If Milton was still inside…

Hicks put the thought out of his head. He should have been dead, yet he had been given a reprieve. There was nothing he could do. His shoulder was badly injured and he was losing blood. He needed medical attention.

He had to get away, as far and as quickly as he could.

Chapter Sixty-Three

MILTON LED THE WAY. The smoke was pouring up from the ground floor now, a thick column that pooled against the ceiling and then dispersed into the two connecting corridors. The roar of the fire seemed to be growing louder, but Milton realised that something was absent: the staccato punctuation that had been supplied by the small-arms fire. The Feather Men had served their purpose and Hicks had done what he needed to do. Milton hoped that meant that the general was out of commission, too, but that wasn't his problem. Hicks was on his own with Higgins.

Milton had Olivia's hand in his left hand as he advanced down the corridor. The Sig was in his right hand.

"John," she said, tugging him to a halt.

Milton paused.

"I'm scared."

He had started to turn to face her when he glimpsed the dark shapes of two figures approaching from the corridor to his right. The men were facing him, one of them with a shotgun lowered and ready to fire. Light from one of the windows fell upon them: Frankie and Marcus Fabian.

Milton launched himself backwards as the boom rang out through the house. He felt the scrape of the shot as fragments ripped into his shirt and clawed across his skin. He landed on his shoulders and instinctively aimed the Sig with a double-handed grip. He returned fire back into the other opening.

He heard a shriek of pain. He had hit at least one of them.

He scrambled to his feet. Olivia was behind him, on the floor. He hauled her back, too.

"Smith!" came a voice.

"Olivia?" Milton said. "Are you hit?"

"No," she said. She scrabbled her feet beneath her and followed him back along the corridor.

Milton backed up, aiming back to the landing.

"Smith! I know it's you."

It was Frankie Fabian.

"You're not going anywhere, Smith."

They reached the door to the room where he had rescued Olivia. Milton pushed her back inside again, shrugged his pack from his back and unzipped it. He reached down for the second bottle. It was unbroken. He turned it upside down, holding onto the neck, and lit the tampon. The finger of flame cast an orange and yellow glow into the darkness.

He tossed the bottle back onto the landing. The glass shattered against the wooden floor, the fuel spilled out and the fuse lit it. There was a loud exhalation, audible even through all the noise, and fire ran in all directions.

There was another scream. More urgent this time. Sharpened with pain.

Milton shut the door. The new fire would buy some time, but if Fabian was out there with a shotgun, then the odds were against them. They would have to get out of the building another way.

#

FRANKIE FABIAN cracked open the shotgun, ejected the two spent casings from the chamber and thumbed two more cartridges inside. Marcus was on the floor, five feet behind him, cursing from the pain. One of the rounds Smith had fired had hit him in the thigh; his leg had gone from underneath him and he had dropped to the floor. Fabian didn't know whether he had hit Smith with the spread that he had triggered. It was dark and he couldn't be sure. He brought the barrel back up and snapped the shotgun shut.

"My leg!"

Fabian ignored his son. He pressed the butt of the shotgun into his shoulder and took a step toward the corridor that led from the landing to the bedrooms. The angle of the wall provided him with cover.

"Smith!" he called. "I know it's you."

He thought he heard the sound of a door opening.

"You're not going anywhere, Smith."

Fabian took another step ahead, coming up to the entrance of the corridor. He was sweating. The fire below them was shimmering in the air, but the perspiration was from fear as much as the heat. It was in his eyes, running down his spine, on his hands, his index finger sliding against the trigger.

He saw the pinprick of flame emerge from the dark mouth of the corridor. It was rotating, round and round, and he didn't know what it was until it passed through a shaft of dim light. Then he knew: it was a bottle. The flame was a fuse. It was a Molotov cocktail.

The bottle shattered. Fabian felt something wet splashing against his clothing, and, as he stumbled back to the stairs, he saw flame and heard the gasp of a sudden conflagration. He held out his arms and saw, to his horror, that the sleeves of his jacket were thick with oily flame. He dropped the shotgun, took off his jacket, staggered back to the stairs and overbalanced. His foot slipped off the tread and he fell back, crashing halfway and tumbling down to the half landing.

Fabian was dazed, but the shock jolted him quickly back to awareness. He scrambled away, putting the turn of the staircase between him and the top landing. A new fire had started up there, the heat from the flames above joining with that from those below, squeezing him like a vice.

He stood and put out his hand to steady himself against the balustrade; he quickly jerked it away, the wood so cooked that it burned to the touch.

"Marcus," he croaked. "*Marcus.*"

There was no reply.

He stumbled down the stairs.

Chapter Sixty-Four

MILTON DRAGGED a dresser across the room and jammed it against the door. He went to the window and carefully parted the curtains. He had memorised the layout of the building from the estate agent's plans, but the events of the last twenty minutes had him doubting himself. It was with relief, then, that he saw that he had been correct: the window faced toward the rear of the property. The area was lit up by the fire, orange light that stretched across the outside kitchen, a swimming pool, down a sloping meadow to a series of farm buildings and then, finally, a wood.

Milton unlatched the window and pushed the sash up. The wood was rotten, and it crumbled in his hands. He looked out again, glancing down. The window was three metres above the ground, but there was a drainpipe within reach to the right-hand side.

Milton opened the window all the way.

#

THE HEAT was unbearable on the ground floor. The smoke was dense and disorientating, and, for a moment, Frankie Fabian didn't think he would be able to find the boot room. He was light-headed, dizzy with the heat and the smoke that he had inhaled, and he reeled as he crossed the room to the door. The door was already open. The cool air was a balm on his face as he stumbled outside.

Fabian couldn't hear the gunfire that he had heard earlier, but the darkness was full of the roar of the flames as they continued to eat away at the house. He saw the barn, next to the outbuildings at the bottom of the meadow, a hundred yards from the house. If he could get there, he could use the Land Rover. There was a track that he would be able to follow to the north gate.

He checked left and right, then set off.

#

MILTON WENT down first; if Olivia slipped, he wanted to be below her so that he might break her fall. He sat on the windowsill, turned around and then reached out for the drainpipe. It was old and the fixings were corroded and weak, and, as Milton descended, the brackets that fastened it to the bricks snapped and the drainpipe tore away from the wall. Milton was halfway down as he started to fall back; he released his grip and fell the rest of the way. He looked back up and saw that the drainpipe had detached so that the portion nearest to the window was now at a forty-five-degree angle to the wall.

He looked over to the window. He saw Olivia there, her face white. "Jump," he said.

She clambered out of the window, her legs dangling over the sill.

"Smith," she called down, pointing behind him.

Milton turned. He saw the figure of a man hurrying through the meadow that led down to the outbuildings and the wooded area beyond. It was darker there, the light weaker, but he recognised Frankie Fabian.

Milton looked back up to her. "Come on," he said. "Jump!"

She paused there, daunted by the drop beneath her, until there came a tremendous impact from the direction of the kitchen. Another beam, Milton guessed, the roof coming down bit by bit. It was enough to focus Olivia's mind and, her eyes closed, she allowed herself to slip forward from the sill. She dropped quickly and Milton caught her, scooping one arm beneath her knees and the other around her back. He set her down and then set off with her into the meadow. There was no sign of anyone else. Fabian's men, if they were still alive, were around the other side of the building.

"Get into the woods," Milton said, pointing away from the outbuildings to the nearest fringe of vegetation. "Don't wait. There's a track that goes through the grounds to the north. I think there's a gate, but, if there isn't, just get over the wall."

"What about you?"

"I'll catch you up."

"Come with me now."

"Not yet," he said. "Please—go. I'll be as quick as I can."

#

MILTON DESCENDED the sloping meadow down to the outbuildings. There was a barn, a stable block and, beyond that, a fenced-off riding school. Trees fringed the paddock beyond the school, a line of ash and fir that were cast in golds and oranges by the fire that had taken hold of the house. Fabian had gone into the barn. It was a derelict building, with gaps in the roof where the clay tiles had been lost and a jagged crack across the facing wall.

Milton made his way ahead, the pistol in his hand. He was aware that he had only very limited tactical information as to the results of the gun battle that had taken place at the front of the house. He did not know, for example, how many of Fabian's men were still alive. He had to proceed carefully.

Milton reached the yard just as he heard the sound of a starter engine whining. The engine spluttered, whined again, spluttered and fell silent. Milton heard the sound of a man cursing.

The entrance to the barn would, at one time, have been fitted with two large double doors. It had one now, and that was hanging from a single hinge and was propped back against the wall. Milton edged forward. The barn looked as if it might have been a cattle shed, with brick cobbles on the floor and cattle mangers fitted along one of the walls. A

Land Rover was parked inside. It was old and beaten up, with mismatched bodywork and without its windshield.

Frankie Fabian was in the driver's seat, turning the engine over and trying to get it to start. The starter motor coughed and choked, but the engine did not start. Fabian cursed again.

"Frankie," Milton said.

Fabian looked up, his eyes wide and fearful.

"Hands," Milton said, gesturing with a flick of the gun. "And get out of the car."

Milton watched Fabian as he shifted his weight, his upper arm visible as he reached out for something—the shotgun, maybe—that Milton couldn't see.

"Don't," Milton said, holding the Sig out straight and nodding down at it.

Fabian ignored him, his hands remaining out of sight below the dash. "What are you doing this for?"

Milton put pressure on the trigger. "*Hands*, Frankie. Let me see them."

His hands stayed where they were. "Who *are* you?"

"You know why, and it doesn't matter who I am. Last chance, Frankie. Hands."

Milton didn't want him to raise his hands. Not really. He wasn't going to let him walk out of the barn. Perhaps Fabian could see that, too; he brought up his right hand in a flash of sudden motion. It held a pistol. Milton was at medium range, five metres away from his target, and the Sig was held in a steady and unwavering hand. Milton squeezed the trigger, and then, half a second later, he squeezed it again. Milton had aimed into Fabian's body, right down the centre line, in a neat square between the top of his sternum and the line of the dash. Both rounds found their mark. Fabian was punched back into his seat by the first shot, and then his arms flailed as the second round hit.

Milton approached, the Sig held out in front of him, still covering Fabian. He came around the side of the Land Rover and looked into the cabin through the open door.

The shotgun was wedged in the foot well, barrel down. The pistol was on the seat next to it. Fabian was still alive. He had dropped the weapon and now his hands were pressed to his chest in an attempt to staunch the blood that blossomed on his white shirt. It was futile. The crimson pumped through his fingers.

Milton eyed him, the discarded pistol and the shotgun. "I warned you," he said.

Fabian tried to speak. His mouth opened and closed, but all he could manage was a series of gasps. His lungs had been punctured by the two rounds. He couldn't hold in any breath. The air hissed out as if from pierced balloons.

Milton said, "I gave you a choice."

Fabian looked up as Milton took aim through the window. There was no hope in his eyes, no entreaty. Perhaps he saw something in Milton. A kindred spirit. A killer, like him.

Milton squeezed the trigger a third time. Fabian's head jerked to the left, and then his body fell limply sideways over the brake lever and across both seats.

Milton turned.

Olivia was in the doorway of the barn.

He didn't need to ask her how long she had been standing there. Her expression was answer enough.

"Let's go," he said.

Part Five

The Ninth Step

Chapter Sixty-Five

IT WAS A BRIGHTER DAY than it had been for what seemed like weeks, and Milton looked up at the rooftops and the blue sky beyond them as he walked to the bus stop. He decided, as he approached the stop on Redchurch Street, that he was being lazy. It was only twenty minutes from here and, with the weather much more pleasant than it had been for days, he decided that he would walk.

He followed the road and, as he turned onto Shoreditch High Street, he allowed his thoughts to drift. He had been thinking about the Ninth Step for several days. That stage of the program was always close to Milton's thoughts, but he had been thinking about it more than he usually did. He couldn't help but compare his own cursory attention to that requirement of the program against what Eddie had been prepared to risk in order to wipe his slate clean and fully embrace his sobriety. Milton knew that he would never have the courage to do the same thing himself, and the certainty of that had plunged him into a funk that had lasted for a week.

He kept going back to it: Eddie had been prepared to abandon his family to atone for the crime that had been committed ten years earlier. He must have known that would bring punishment upon himself, as well as the certainty of retribution for his brothers. Eddie had decided to take the step anyway, and his adopted family had killed him for it.

How could Milton follow that example? He could go to the police in a dozen countries around the world and hand himself in as the culprit of more than one hundred and fifty murders. Some of his crimes were so expert that the body had never been discovered. Homicides had been staged to look like suicides or deaths from natural causes, and crime had not been suspected at all. He could go to the local law enforcement and confess. Some would dismiss him as a crank. Others, perhaps, might look into his suggestions and, maybe, they would find that there was truth in his words. Perhaps they would take him seriously. Arrest him, even. None of it would matter. The British government would send out an emissary, one of Milton's successors in Group Fifteen or whatever agency had replaced it, and Milton would be silenced before he could bring any more damage down on the national interest. Milton knew that that was what would happen. It was as certain as night following day.

There were other alternatives. If he wanted to broadcast his message more widely, he could try to find a journalist who would be willing to run with the story. Someone like Olivia. The stories Milton could tell would win Pulitzers, but the journalist would not be alive long enough to collect them. Speaking to Olivia would be the same as putting a gun to her head and pulling the trigger. It would be a death sentence, and Milton already had too much blood on his hands.

It was a problem that Milton didn't know how to solve.

He had no sponsor to speak to, and he couldn't share his thoughts in a meeting, so he had taken to deciphering his confusion himself. He had stayed in his flat and studied his copy of the Big Book, the bible of the fellowship.

The Eighth Step.

Made a list of all persons we had harmed, and became willing to make amends to them all.

Milton drew up a list, at least of the victims that he could remember. He had ended up with two pieces of paper.

The Ninth Step.

Made direct amends to such people, wherever possible, except when to do so would injure them or others.

That was where his progress stopped. He could not make amends to those who were dead.

#

THE SIGNAGE above the shop read TATTOO over a line of stained-glass windows and the business name—PRICK TATTOO & PIERCING—was advertised with a neon sign that glowed out of the window. The man behind the desk was large, with a shaven head and piercings through his ears and the bridge of his nose. His name was Henry. He looked over at Milton as he came inside.

"Mr. Smith," he said, "right on time. Come through, please."

Milton followed Henry into a room at the back of the shop.

"Take off the shirt, please."

Milton started to unbutton.

"I can't remember," Henry said. "You had a tattoo before?"

Milton turned around to reveal the tattoo of the angel that stretched from shoulder to shoulder and all the way down to the small of his back.

"Very nice. Where'd you get that done?"

"Guatemala."

"How long did it take?"

"Can't remember," Milton admitted. "I was very drunk."

"Got to be four hours. Maybe five." Henry nodded in appreciation. "Good work. It's simple today, right? That's what you said?"

Milton reached into his pocket and took out the design that he had sketched out himself: the number nine, represented in Roman numerals.

"All right. Easy. Won't take long. Where'd you want it?"

Milton rested a finger on his left breast, above his heart. "Here."

Henry said that would be fine and invited Milton to sit. He disappeared into another room to prepare the transfer, leaving Milton to regard his reflection in the long mirror opposite the chair. He looked at the pattern of scars that criss-crossed his torso. He could remember receiving some of the injuries, but the memories of others had been obscured by the frequent blackouts during his drinking days.

Henry returned with the transfer. He took out a bottle of rubbing alcohol and poured out a measure into a cloth. He wiped the area Milton had selected and then took a disposable razor and shaved the hair away.

Henry pointed at the puckered scar that marked a stabbing in Milton's abdomen. "You've been in the wars."

Milton shrugged. "Been knocked around a bit."

"What do you do?"

"I was in the army."

"What about now?"

"This and that."

Henry took out a deodorant to moisten the skin. "You don't talk much. Want me to get on with it?"

"I'm sorry. I've got a lot on my mind."

"Not a problem. Just settle back."

Henry reached over and pressed play on an old-fashioned boom box, and Iron Maiden started up. He pressed the transfer over Milton's skin and held it there for a couple of minutes until the outline of the image had been etched onto his skin. He pulled on his latex gloves and prepared his ink caps, decanting ink from jugs into the small cups. He took sterilised needles from a sealed bag and prepared his Vaseline and ointments. He put the needle into the machine and started to follow the outline. It felt like a scratching as he traced out the numbers, the needle pecking in and out and in and out.

"How's that?"

"Fine," Milton said.

The first stage took ten minutes. Henry pulled away and nodded at the fresh tattoo on Milton's breast. Milton looked down at it. It was just the outline, but his work was excellent, the lines clean and neat. The flesh around the outline was inflamed from the needle, but that was of no consequence to Milton.

"Not too painful?"

"No."

"Another twenty minutes and we'll be done. It's going to look good. Do you mind me asking? What's it for? The nine, I mean."

"Something very important to me," Milton said.

Chapter Sixty-Six

THE STORY broke big, and seemed to get bigger every day. Olivia had crafted it with an expert hand, gradually drip-feeding the information and always ending with the promise of more. The first exposé was shocking, leading with one of the pictures of Leo Isaacs and the other men. The second day's story focused on Eddie Fabian, explaining how the tragic victim of the piece had been murdered by his own family after he had threatened to go public with what had happened during an armed heist in Oxford years earlier. Eddie was the ingredient that held everything together. Milton was pleased with the sympathetic way in which Olivia had told his story. He emerged as a noble, honest and worthy man. He emerged as a man Milton recognised.

Olivia had placed the story with one of the national tabloids, and, once the shock had subsided, all of the other newspapers ran with it. Milton lay on his bed, a copy of today's *Sun* held out before him. This was the third day of the story, and the focus was on the cover-up that had allowed the Westminster paedophiles to remain undetected and unpunished for so long. Olivia named Richard Higgins, and described how he had protected the conspirators for so long. The article finished with the suggestion that Higgins was on the run. Olivia had spoken to the senior detective who had been assigned the historic case; the woman suggested that the general was someone with whom the police would be very interested in speaking.

Milton took out his phone and fished out a crumpled business card from the pocket of his jeans.

He dialled.

"Hello?"

"Nice story."

"Smith? Is that you?"

"Yes. I'm reading it now. Is it getting the reaction you wanted?"

She laughed drily. "More. You just caught me, actually—I'm on TV tonight talking about it. There's a car outside now to take me to the studio."

"That's great. You sound happy."

"I am." She paused. "I… I just want to say thanks. For saving my arse. For everything. I wouldn't have been able to do this without you."

"Forget it. Someone had to tell the story. I'm glad you've done right by Eddie."

"You think so?"

"I do."

He could hear her hurrying about her apartment. "Could I buy you a drink?" she said. "To say thanks?"

"I don't think so."

"Why not?"

"I'm probably going to move on. I don't like to stay in one place for too long."

"So I won't see you again?"

"Probably not." There was a moment of silence, and then Milton heard a knocking on the door. He thought for a moment that it was his door, but, as he took the phone away from his ear and listened, he realised that it was the door to the next-door flat.

"John?"

"I have to go," he said. "Good luck, Olivia."

The knocking came again, louder and with each knock closer to the last one, angry and imperative.

He heard a man's voice, heavily accented. "Open door," it said. "Open door now."

Milton sat and swung around so that he could stand and then collected his laptop from the dresser. He booted it up, navigated to the camera app and switched the camera on. The screen was filled with a view of the hallway next door. The camera's fisheye lens distorted the proportions a little, but it offered a clear and unobstructed view of the room. The microphone in the sitting room was working, too, and, as he switched it on, he heard the sound of conversation from the hallway. He set both sound and vision to record, the equipment transmitting the data remotely so that he could store it on his hard drive. He only had to wait a moment before he saw the two men he had observed before, and he stood clenching and unclenching his fists as they bustled by the mother and father to make their way inside.

"Have you got it?" the large, fat man said.

"Most," the father said. He had a plastic carrier bag and he reached inside and withdrew a bundle of bank notes.

"I did not say I wanted most. I wanted all."

"It was the best I could do," the father protested. "I'll have the rest next week, I swear."

Milton stood and paced, his attention on the screen, but his thoughts concerned with what he would do if the collection turned nasty. The fat man took the bundle of money and riffled through it, held it up so that his partner could see it and then stuffed it into his jacket pocket. He turned to the father and, without warning, backhanded him across the face. The father staggered back, the back of his legs bumping into a low table and overbalancing him. He fell back, his arm reflexively raised in front of his face to ward off another blow.

Milton stopped as a fifth person came into the room. It was the boy, Ahmed. He went to his father and hugged him, putting himself in the way of the fat man and shielding his father from further violence.

Milton stopped pacing. He clenched his fists and left them closed, squeezing them into tight balls until his fingers ached. He closed his eyes and worked hard to control his breathing. All of his instincts told him to go and kick down the door to the opposite flat and punish the two goons.

"Ahmed," the boy's mother said.

He didn't respond, and he stayed where he was, a shield

to protect his father.

The rent collectors laughed uproariously.

"Your boy," the fat man said, "we say he has *yáytsa.* Balls, more than his father." The fat man turned to his partner and nodded to the door. "We go now, but we come back this time next week. We come for all of the money, plus interest. Understand?"

The two men walked out of sight of the camera. Milton navigated to the folder where he had recorded the data, quickly compressed it and emailed it to his Gmail account.

He heard the door slam shut and then the sound of raucous laughter from the vestibule outside his own front door.

He put on his jacket, collected two identical sports holdalls from the hall, went outside and locked the door to his flat. The door to the next-door flat was closed now, but Milton could hear the sound of sobbing from within. He didn't need any persuasion that what he was about to do was the right thing but, had he, the sound of their misery and desperation would have been more than enough. It lit the fuse of his anger, too, and he allowed that little flame to flicker and grow. That would be useful.

The men were walking out of the building, heading down to the BMW 5-Series that Milton had seen them arrive in before.

He followed.

Chapter Sixty-Seven

THE TWO MEN were very easy to trail. There was no reason for them to suspect that anyone would want to follow them. Milton had come across bullies like them on many previous occasions, and it wasn't difficult to guess how they would think. They would have been so used to the timid and fearful tenants whom they shook down day after day that the notion that someone might be prepared to resist them would never have crossed their minds. Their arrogance would be their downfall.

The men were evidently in the middle of their weekly collection round. Milton had followed the 5-Series for only a short distance when it pulled over and parked. Milton drove on, turning a corner and parking in a slot that allowed him to still see the car. Milton noticed another car—a Nissan Note—as it went by and slotted into another space fifty feet up the road. Both men got out and went into another similar block to the one where Milton lived. They were absent for five minutes and, when they returned, they were laughing and joking with each other. Milton watched them coolly, stroking his fingertips against the raised stitching of the faux leather that covered the steering wheel.

They stopped six more times, visiting similar properties in Bethnal Green and Hackney. Each time the men returned to the BMW with broad smiles and laughter, and each time Milton hated them just a little bit more.

The drizzle was falling a little more heavily now, persuading the pedestrians who were out to hurry to their destinations, some sheltering beneath umbrellas and others with their heads bent as they maintained a determined pace. Cars and busses passed on both sides of the road, each one sending up a cascade of spray as wheels rolled through the quickly gathering puddles that pooled around glutted drains. Milton glanced in the mirrors and noticed that the same Nissan Note that he had seen earlier was still behind him. He was being followed, too. He knew who it was, and he relaxed; it was under control.

The fact that the rent collectors stopped so many times in such a short space of time should have meant it was impossible for them to have been tracked by just one operative in a single car. Even the most rudimentary of anti-surveillance routines would have meant that they would have seen the battered old Volkswagen that stayed with them throughout the afternoon, following a hundred yards behind them, stopping just out of sight when they stopped, picking them up when they set off again. If they had been just a little more vigilant, then he would have had a devilishly difficult time remaining unobserved, but they were so wrapped up in the ease of each collection and the sense of power that they seemed to derive from each freshly beaten-down tenant that they paid little heed to their surroundings. Their arrogance made them lazy and overconfident, and it meant that Milton was able to stay behind them without being noticed. He remembered similar targets that he had followed in police states where the strength of the regime meant that the suggestion of hostile action was so preposterous as to be beyond consideration. Those men and women had been easy kills. It was the targets who were wary or fearful for their lives that made for the most difficult assignments. These two had more in common with the arrogant than the fearful.

Their journey finally brought them to Beckton. It was a grim, joyless area that had once been promised as a utopia, served by the futuristic Light Railway, but had since had its optimism ripped away. The locals who had been persuaded to leave the inner city now looked resentfully at the immigrants who poured in for the cheap housing that no one else wanted. Milton drove by pubs and cafés that were full of white faces, early drinkers staring balefully out into the street, many of them wearing England football shirts.

The two men drove south on the A117, turned off onto Alpine Way, and then took the first right onto Whitings Way. Milton checked behind him again, but couldn't see the Nissan. He put it out of mind.

The goons slowed at the entrance to a large retail park, waited for a man to push a large double pram across the road, and then drove through the open iron gates. There was a wide selection of stores inside the park, all of them housed in hangar-sized industrial units.

Milton parked the car. He opened the glove box, took out a mini-Maglite and put it into his pocket. He stepped outside and continued on foot. The car pulled into an empty space and he watched as the two men got out and made their way to the largest unit in the park. A colourful green and yellow sign announced it as Polanka Delikatsey. The two men went inside. Milton followed them.

It was large and spacious inside. While the business catered explicitly to Polish immigrants, it stocked brands from across Eastern Europe. Milton followed the two men along an aisle of Lithuanian pickles. He passed a table that had been decorated with a banner that seemed, to Milton's inexpert eye, to be encouraging votes in a referendum on some domestic Polish matter or another. Another table was stocked with anti-Putin pamphlets.

There was a flight of stairs at the end of the store that rose up to the first floor. Milton followed the men as they ascended. The stairs led to a confusing mishmash of stores and businesses. There was an art gallery, with ugly Russian paintings hung around the walls. There was a stall selling cheap phone cards for those who wanted to call home. An Internet café. A small bookshop stocked with Polish books.

The men walked to a plain door, knocked, and went inside. The door closed. Milton paused, attending to a lace that did not need to be tied, and then walked on, slowing as he approached the door. He examined it: plain, solid, expensive. There was a window next to the door, but the glass was smoked and he couldn't see inside. There was also an intercom next to the door. A notice below the intercom read Klub Orła Białego. A single line of English below that offered a translation: White Eagle Club.

Milton went back to the café. A group of middle-aged women were sitting at a table, gossiping as they enjoyed their teas. Another table was occupied by three young men in cheap tracksuits. He went to the desk and ordered a coffee. The owner was in her early thirties, trying to grasp the last of her looks with a blonde bleach job that had dried her hair out badly. She flirted with him, then tried to get him to buy a pastry. She spoke in Polish, and Milton—who did not speak it, nor wanted to reveal that he did not—answered with a shake of his head and refused to engage with her. She eventually got the message and went back to the crossword that she was doing.

Milton took a seat where he could watch the door and observed for ten minutes. There were no comings and goings, and the door remained closed. He took out his phone and opened his browser. He Googled the name of the club and found a series of pages in Polish. He couldn't read the text, but it was apparent that the door led to a bar and nightclub.

He weighed his options. He knew where the men were based now. He could return later, when he had been able to study the building a little more and perhaps get an idea of the business that ran the club. There might be a company there, and he would be able to search Companies House for details on it. He might be able to find plans for the building. And then he could break in and look around.

That would have been the most sensible, the most careful option.

But Milton had watched the two of them shake down seven different tenants this afternoon. He had watched as the fat man had struck Ahmed's father and threatened him with more. There was no point in trying to pretend that he wasn't angry. He wasn't reckless and would never have allowed his decisions to be sullied by anger, but there was a benefit to harnessing it and acting now, rather than later.

Chapter Sixty-Eight

MILTON WAITED another hour, just getting a feel for the place and watching the door. There were no other comings or goings.

He navigated to Gmail and checked that the video and audio from the bugs had uploaded successfully. The file was there, and he watched it through to ensure that it would underline the point that he was going to make.

Satisfied, he collected his bag from the floor, collected his leather jacket and walked to the door.

He looked back to the rest of the open floor. People were going about their business. No one was paying him any attention.

He pressed the intercom.

"No visitors."

The intercom crackled as it was shut off.

Milton pressed the buzzer again.

"I tell you! We are closed."

"I'm not going until you let me in."

"I send someone down, make you leave."

"Fine. I'll be right here. Send them down."

The intercom hissed again and fell silent.

Milton took the mini-Maglite from his pocket. He clenched his fist around it, feeling the cold, hard metal as it solidified the structure of his fingers. He hid his hand in the pocket of his jacket.

He pressed the buzzer and then held his thumb against it.

The intercom stayed silent. Milton waited for twenty seconds until the door opened.

It was the smaller of the two men whom Milton had been tailing all afternoon. He was a similar height and build to Milton. He had taken off his jacket and rolled up his shirt to reveal sleeves of tattoos on both arms. Milton could smell alcohol on his breath. Perhaps he had been celebrating a successful afternoon's work.

"I tell you. No visitors." The man looked at him as he spoke. There was a flicker of recognition. "Wait—I know you."

"My name's Smith."

"I see you before."

"You did. I live at Chertsey House. I've been following you all afternoon."

The man's mouth twisted into a grimace of irritation. Milton stepped forward, planting his right foot against the door. The man cursed in Russian and tried to close the door but could not. Milton had distracted him, and he didn't notice as Milton raised his fist, squeezed the flashlight even tighter into his palm, and drilled him with a stiff jab that landed square against his chin. The force of the blow, amplified by the flashlight and surprise, meant that the man was unconscious before he hit the floor. He toppled back, falling against the stairs, the back of his head bouncing against one of the treads.

Milton stepped inside, closed the door behind him, and climbed the stairs.

#

THE FAT MAN was eating a plate of kielbasa, cutting up the sausage and shovelling it into his mouth. He was sat behind a table, the edge pressed into his pendulous gut, so close that he was unable to stand quickly enough when he saw Milton approach him. There was a glass of vodka on the table and, next to that, a pistol. Milton recognised it as a Russian Makarov.

"Hello," Milton said.

"Where is Yuri?"

"Relax," Milton said, fighting the urge to take the man by the back of the head and drive his face into his dinner.

"He's fine. Just having a rest."

The man shuffled back in his chair, making enough space that he was able to stand. His fat hand pawed the Makarov. He stood and aimed it across the room.

"Put that down," Milton said wearily.

"You don't tell me what to do. Where is Yuri?"

"Who's in charge here?"

"Maybe me," the man said, stabbing the pistol forward in Milton's direction.

"No," Milton said, allowing a little more weariness to drip into his voice. "You and your friend are the muscle. You don't have the intelligence to run an operation like this. You want to know how I know?" He waited, but nothing passed across the man's face to disturb the blackened, piggish anger; Milton's sangfroid was confusing him. "I'll tell you how I know. I just knocked out your friend, saw he was carrying a weapon and I still came up here. If you were smart, you'd be asking yourself what would possess me to do a thing like that. Either I have a death wish—and I don't—or I have something to tell your boss, something I'm very confident indeed that he'll want to hear. But you didn't think about that, did you? You just pulled your gun. And that's how I know that you're just the monkey. I came here to talk to the organ grinder. So go and get him, please."

The man stood there, confused, and Milton could almost see the gears in his head as they started to turn. He wondered if he was going to have to goad him into action, but, after a long moment, the man told him to stay where he was and disappeared into the adjoining room.

Milton waited. He looked around. It was a pleasant room, furnished to a standard that was out of step with the supermarket below and the rest of the building. There were pictures on the walls in ostentatious gilded frames, a chandelier hung from the ceiling, the bar was crafted from polished oak, and the bottles behind it were lit. Milton went over to the bar. There was a bottle of Zubrowka Bison Grass vodka standing there. Milton picked it up and glanced at the label, then returned it.

Milton waited for another minute until the fat man returned with another man trailing behind him. The newcomer was wearing a grey suit, a shirt that he wore with the top two buttons undone, and heavy jewellery on his fingers and around his wrist and his neck.

"What is your name?"

"Smith. And you?"

"My name is Emil Zharkov. How can I help you, Mr. Smith?"

"You own a property in Bethnal Green. A flat in Chertsey House."

Zharkov looked to the fat man. "Dmitri?"

"There is a family there, Emil. This *mudak* lives next to them."

"And this *sooka* should be careful how he talks to me," Milton retorted, the imprecation delivered with a perfect accent.

The suggestion that Milton might understand their language evidently gave them pause for thought. The fat man, Dmitri, looked confused for a moment before he realised that he couldn't afford to lose face in front of his boss. He squared up to Milton and stepped forward until his face was six inches away. Milton stood his ground. He could smell the vodka and garlic on the man's breath and see a fragment of sausage caught between his teeth.

"Say that again," Dmitri said.

"Step back," Milton said instead.

"Or you will do what, *mudak*?"

The fat man raised both hands and pushed Milton on the shoulders. Milton took a step back so that he was closer to the bar and then, without giving him a second warning, backhanded him across the face. The fat man fell to the side, his nose streaming blood.

"I'd like to speak to you without being threatened," Milton said to Zharkov, not even out of breath. "Will that be possible, Emil?"

Milton knew that he had taken a risk, but he wanted to demonstrate that he was not to be taken lightly. Emil might be offended. He would probably feel threatened. But he hoped that he would take him seriously. The Russian paused, appraising Milton, considering how to respond, and then, after ten seconds, he responded with a friendly chuckle.

"You are an interesting man, Mr. Smith."

The fat man pushed himself to his hands and knees and raised his head; blood dripped out of both nostrils. "Emil! He hit me!"

"Shut up, Dmitri. Go and clean yourself up. I talk to Mr. Smith now. If I need you, I call you."

The fat man used the back of the chair to help him rise to his feet. He gave Milton a baleful stare, but he was not prepared to disobey his boss. He looked woozy, and as he relinquished his support, it looked for a moment as if he was going to fall; he managed to find his balance and slowly left the room.

"What do you do, Mr. Smith?"

"I work in a café."

"Really? You work in café yet you have the guts to come here, to my club, to beat two of my men in front of me, when you must know that I am dangerous man." By way of emphasis, he flicked back his jacket to reveal a shoulder holster with a pistol inside it. "You know these things, yet you still come here. No, Mr. Smith, you do not just work in café. Who are you really?"

"It doesn't really matter who I am. I'm here to make you an offer."

Emil sucked his teeth. "Very mysterious, Mr. Smith. But I admire your courage. Make me your offer. I will consider it."

"The couple in the flat next to mine can't afford to pay the rent that you are charging. Maybe they could when they moved in, but perhaps you have increased it?"

"It is free market, Mr. Smith. A man must make a living in this world."

"I understand that. I'm not telling you your business. You are obviously successful."

"Yes, Mr. Smith, I am. And you work in café." It was a gentle reminder of their respective stations, and Milton was not minded to question it. "What is your offer?"

"The flat in Chertsey House. How much did it cost?"

"Why don't you tell me?"

"I'm guessing one hundred and fifty thousand pounds."

Milton lowballed the value, knowing that it would have cost more, but knowing, also, that, if he was fortunate, they were about to enter into a negotiation. He didn't want to start too high.

Zharkov grinned. "Ten years ago, perhaps. Price goes up as years go by. Today's value, two hundred."

Milton had already checked, and he knew that that was about twenty-five thousand more than the property would fetch on the open market, but he wasn't about to dispute it.

"I'd like to buy the property."

"You?"

"That's right."

"You work in café. Now you want to be landlord?"

"I leave you to your business, Emil. Leave me to mine."

"You are funny man, Mr. Smith. How does man like you find money to buy flat for two hundred thousand?"

"Who said I was offering two hundred?"

"That is price."

Milton smiled. "No, Emil. It's not."

Emil's sunny disposition became occluded by irritation. "That is price, Mr. Smith. I do not wish to sell. If you wish to buy, you pay price I tell you to pay."

"I was hoping we could conclude this without the need for unpleasantness." Milton shook his head, making a play of his disappointment. "Are you sure that two hundred is your best offer?"

"Are you *threatening* me?"

"I suppose I am." He took out his phone, opened the media tab and selected the video he wanted to play. He passed the phone across the table. "Watch."

Milton had checked that the footage was clean and that it showed exactly what he wanted it to show. The tiny camera that he had hidden had recorded the moment where Dmitri and Pavel had come into the flat. Their faces were clearly captured. The microphone had picked up the conversation: the father's pleading for more time, Dmitri's threats, the shriek from the wife as her husband was struck, Ahmed rushing in to stand between his father and Dmitri. Everything had been recorded. Everything had been evidenced.

Milton watched Emil's face as the footage played. His brows lowered and came closer together, his eyes burned.

The footage stopped. Milton reached out and collected the phone.

Zharkov slammed his fist on the table. "You are blackmailing me?"

"This is just a negotiation," Milton said calmly. "I want that flat. I'm telling you what I'll offer for it. I have fifty thousand pounds in my bag. I'm prepared to give that to you, right now. In return, I want you to sell me the flat."

"*Fifty?* You are crazy!"

"That's not everything that I'm offering, Emil. It's fifty thousand, and I won't pass this to the police. A man like you can afford the best lawyers, and they could make it so that you had a way out of the mess that I could cause. But lawyers are expensive. And it would disrupt your business. So I want you to try to put a value on those things, too, and add them to the fifty. Do you think we're getting close to your valuation now?"

All of Emil's previous bonhomie was gone, revealed for the flimsy veil that Milton had known that it was. He glared at him without any attempt to disguise his fury.

"You are brave man, Mr. Smith, coming into my club and threatening me. People have been badly hurt for less. Killed for less."

"I'm sure they have. But you're wasting your breath. I'm

not frightened of you."

You should be frightened of me.

Milton didn't need to look to remember the locations of the weapons that were to hand: the glass on the table, the knife on the bar, the bottle on the bar, the corkscrew.

"You have deal," Emil said, finally. His face showed disgust; with himself, perhaps, for being backed into a position where he had no room to manoeuvre. "The money?"

Milton reached down, collected the bag and deposited it on the table. The Pole unzipped it and took out one of the bundles of banknotes. It was apt, Milton thought, that the dirty money that Higgins had hoarded was now being put to good use. Some would help Hicks and his family; the rest would help Ahmed and his parents.

"And the video?"

"I'll keep that. Just in case you think it would be a good idea to do something foolish."

"Not acceptable."

"I don't care. It's the only choice you've got. What's it going to be: yes or no?"

Emil must have realised that the files were digital and that Milton would have backups, and, after another moment of irritated contemplation, he spat a Polish curse and put out his hand.

Milton didn't take it. "Contact your solicitor and have him draw up the transfer documents for the house. I'll come back this time next week and we can sign them."

He stood.

"Why you do this, Smith? Why you put yourself in my business like this?"

"I've been wading through shit for the last week, Emil, and I've had enough of it. I want to do something good."

He left the money on the table, turned his back and, without a backward glance, walked to the door.

No one tried to stop him.

Chapter Sixty-Nine

MILTON WALKED through the supermarket and back outside into the darkening afternoon. He found the Volkswagen and set off. He needed to get back home. He wanted a shower, to wash the grime and muck from his body, and then he would have to start thinking about his shift at the shelter. He had missed a few nights recently. Cathy had been kind about it, but he didn't want to let her down or take advantage of her good nature.

The traffic choked up on Newham Way as he headed back to the west. Milton stared out at the long row of red taillights ahead of him, curving around the bend as the road turned through Beckton Park.

Milton saw the Nissan again as the traffic started to flow a little more freely. He had just passed through Beckton District Park; he signalled and exited the road at the junction with the A112, and then turned sharp left onto Tollgate Road. The Nissan signalled, too, and followed him off the main road. Milton flicked his eyes back to the mirror and saw a second car turning left, the three of them now heading east on Tollgate Road.

It was a two lane road that was hemmed in with 1950s terraced housing. The residents parked their cars in bays that alternated on the left and right sides of the road. The channel that remained in the middle was narrow, with only just enough space for both lanes of traffic to navigate easily.

Milton dabbed the brakes to allow the Nissan to draw a little nearer.

Milton recognised the driver.

He sped up a little, continuing ahead until he passed onto a stretch of the road that cut through the park he had seen earlier. There were metal railings on either side and then wide open spaces.

The Nissan's driver kept the distance down to twenty metres between the two cars.

Milton stamped on the brakes.

The driver behind him was too slow to react, and, although he managed to slow a little, it wasn't enough to prevent his car from bumping into the back of Milton's Volkswagen.

The second car that had turned off the main road was a Ford, a dowdy Mondeo that had seen better days. Milton recognised it: it was Alex Hicks's second car. He watched in the mirror as it pulled out and drove alongside the Nissan.

Richard Higgins didn't even have time to open the door and run.

Hicks raised a snub nosed Heckler & Koch MP5 submachine gun. He aimed across the cabin of the Mondeo and fired a contained burst through the open window. Hicks was close to the general, and he was an accurate shot. The spray of 9x9mm rounds blew out the window of the Nissan and perforated Higgins.

Hicks aimed and fired again.

The general slumped to the side until Milton could no longer see him through the mirror.

The engine still running despite the collision, Milton put his Volkswagen into gear and pulled away, heading east.

Chapter Seventy

THE SHOOTING of Richard Higgins made the news that night. Milton listened to it on the radio with some of the regulars in the shelter. While the police suggested that it was possible that the drive-by was connected to the story of the Westminster paedophiles with which Higgins was so intimately connected, there was no other clue to suggest what might have happened or who might have killed him. Milton wasn't concerned. There had been no witnesses that he had been able to see. The police had very little to go on.

It was one in the morning when Milton looked out of the hatch and saw the man waiting against the railings, his outline silhouetted by the streetlamp behind him. Milton waited until the shelter was empty and then opened the door.

Alex Hicks came inside.

"Evening, sir."

"I told you, Hicks, don't call me that."

Milton noticed that the younger man was walking a little gingerly, bent over very slightly to the left. The shoulder. His left hand was also heavily bandaged.

Milton sat down beside him. Hicks had been shadowing Milton for the last few days. They knew that Higgins had no idea where either of them lived, but it wasn't too much of a stretch to think that he would put two and two together and realise that Hicks had first seen Milton that night at the shelter. Hicks had telephoned Milton yesterday evening to tell him that the general was onto him. He had been outside the shelter when Milton arrived at the start of his shift and he had stayed in the area until the morning. Higgins was wily, and there had been no opportunity for Hicks to take him out then. Milton had led Higgins all the way home; it had been all he could do to stifle his instinct to shake him off, but he was the bait, and it was necessary. Hicks had been there, too—Milton had seen him—but the underground was unsuited to a quiet hit and the walk back to Arnold Circus had been busier with pedestrians than it usually was. There had been no opportunity for Hicks to put the general down then, either.

Hicks had reported what had happened. The old man had stayed outside Milton's flat for five minutes and then he had disappeared. Hicks stayed in the area, hiding out inside a flat in the tenement on the other side of the street. Milton had proposed it because he knew that it was unoccupied. The flat offered a broad view of Milton's building and its surroundings, and Hicks could observe from there without being seen.

And, true enough, the general had been back later in the morning.

"Was he following me all afternoon?"

"All the way to Beckton. God knows what he thought you were doing." Hicks paused. "Actually, what *were* you doing?"

"Never mind," Milton said. "I saw him. I saw you, too."

"Yeah, well," Hicks said, defensively, "you knew I was there. He didn't."

"No," Milton said. "He did not. You did well, Hicks. It was clean."

Hicks nodded with feigned indignation. Milton could see that his praise meant something to him.

Milton indicated Hicks's shoulder. "How is it?"

"Been better." Hicks smiled, a mixture of bitterness and rue. "I saw a friendly doctor I used to know from the Regiment. The general made a bit of a mess of it. Nerve damage, the scapula is chipped and he nicked the artery, too. All in all, I got lucky."

"And the hand?"

Hicks held up his left hand. It was dressed and wrapped in a bandage. "A little worse. Severed some tendons. Some nerve damage, too. I won't be able to use it properly again.

But, you know what, all in all? I reckon I got away with one."

"What did you tell your wife?"

"Haven't seen her yet. She's keeping the kids out of the way."

"You don't have to worry about that any more."

"No, I don't suppose I do."

Milton took out his cigarettes and offered the packet to Hicks. He shook his head; Milton took one of the cigarettes and lit it. "How is she?"

"Rachel?" Hicks shrugged. "No better and no worse."

"So how much do you need?"

"What for?"

"The treatment."

"A hundred thousand dollars."

"How much have you got?"

"About half."

Milton got up and went into the kitchen. He still had the second of the two sports holdalls he had brought with him today. He collected it and put it on the floor next to Hicks's legs. "There," he said.

"What's that?"

"Open it."

Hicks unzipped it and looked inside.

Milton watched him do it. "Higgins had a lot of money in the vault. There's enough in there for what you need."

"Seriously?"

"Money doesn't mean anything to me. I live a simple life. I'm not ambitious. And your family needs it. Take it."

Hicks turned and looked at Milton. His eyes were damp. "Thank you."

Milton got up and inhaled on his cigarette. "Don't make a song and dance about it," he said. "You're still an idiot."

Hicks stood, too, and wiped his eyes with the back of his jacket. "I know I am. I won't forget what you did."

"Like I said: forget it."

Hicks put out his hand. Milton took it and they shook.

"Go on," Milton said. "Fuck off."

Hicks smiled and, taking the bag in his uninjured hand, he opened the door and stepped down onto the street. Milton got up and watched him go. He didn't know whether he would see him again. Probably not.

Milton closed the door and crossed the room to change the radio to 6 Music. The DJ was holding a retrospective for The Bluetones, and 'Broken Starr' started to play as Milton reached over to fill the sink so that he could wash the dirty dishes. The fabric of his shirt was pulled taut, rubbing against his breast. He felt a prickle of discomfort and ran his fingers over the tight skin that reminded him of the fresh tattoo above his heart.

GET TWO BEST-SELLERS, TWO NOVELLAS AND EXCLUSIVE JOHN MILTON MATERIAL

Building a relationship with my readers is the very best thing about writing. I occasionally send newsletters with details on new releases, special offers and other bits of news relating to the John Milton, Beatrix Rose and Soho Noir series.

And if you sign up to the mailing list I'll send you all this free stuff:

1. A copy of my best-seller, The Cleaner (178 five star reviews and RRP of $5.99).

2. A copy of the John Milton introductory novella, 1000 Yards.

3. A copy of the introductory Soho Noir novella, Gaslight.

4. A free copy of my best-seller, The Black Mile (averages 4.4 out of 5 stars and RRP of $ 5.99).

5. A copy of the highly classified background check on John Milton before he was admitted to Group 15. Exclusive to my mailing list – you can't get this anywhere else.

6. A copy of Tarantula, an exciting John Milton short story.

You can get the novel, the novellas, the background check and the short story, **for free**, by signing up at http://eepurl.com/bLUP-5

IF YOU ENJOYED THIS BOOK…

…I would really, really appreciate it if you would help others to enjoy it, too. Reviews are like gold dust and they help persuade other readers to give the stories a shot. More readers means more incentive for me write and that means there will be more stories, more quickly.

ABOUT THE AUTHOR

Mark Dawson is the author of the breakout John Milton, Beatrix Rose and Soho Noir series. He makes his online home at www.markjdawson.com. You can connect with Mark on Twitter at @pbackwriter, on Facebook at www.facebook.com/markdawsonauthor and you should send him an email at mark@markjdawson.com if the mood strikes you.

ALSO BY MARK DAWSON

Have you read them all?

In the Soho Noir Series

Gaslight

When Harry and his brother Frank are blackmailed into paying off a local hood they decide to take care of the problem themselves. But when all of London's underworld is in thrall to the man's boss, was their plan audacious or the most foolish thing that they could possibly have done?

The Black Mile

London, 1940: the Luftwaffe blitzes London every night for fifty-seven nights. Houses, shops and entire streets are wiped from the map. The underworld is in flux: the Italian criminals who dominated the West End have been interned and now their rivals are fighting to replace them. Meanwhile, hidden in the shadows, the Black-Out Ripper sharpens his knife and sets to his grisly work.

The Imposter

War hero Edward Fabian finds himself drawn into a criminal family's web of vice and soon he is an accomplice to their scheming. But he's not the man they think he is - he's far more dangerous than they could possibly imagine.

In the John Milton Series

One Thousand Yards

In this dip into his case files, John Milton is sent into North Korea. With nothing but a sniper rifle, bad intentions and a very particular target, will Milton be able to take on the secret police of the most dangerous failed state on the planet?

Tarantula

In this further dip into his files, Milton is sent to Italy. A colleague who was investigating a particularly violent Mafiosi has disappeared. Will Milton be able to get to the bottom of the mystery, or will he be the next to fall victim to Tarantula?

The Cleaner

Sharon Warriner is a single mother in the East End of London, fearful that she's lost her young son to a life in the gangs. After John Milton saves her life, he promises to help. But the gang, and the charismatic rapper who leads it, is not about to cooperate with him.

Saint Death

John Milton has been off the grid for six months. He surfaces in Ciudad Juárez, Mexico, and immediately finds himself drawn into a vicious battle with the narco-gangs that control the borderlands.

The Driver

When a girl he drives to a party goes missing, John Milton is worried. Especially when two dead bodies are discovered and the police start treating him as their prime suspect.

Ghosts

John Milton is blackmailed into finding his predecessor as Number One. But she's a ghost, too, and just as dangerous as him. He finds himself in de ep trouble, playing the Russians against the British in a desperate attempt to save the life of his oldest friend.

The Sword of God

On the run from his own demons, John Milton treks through the Michigan wilderness into the town of Truth. He's not looking for trouble, but trouble's looking for him. He finds himself up against a small-town cop who has no idea with whom he is dealing, and no idea how dangerous he is.

Salvation Row

Milton finds himself in New Orleans, returning a favour that saved his life during Katrina. When a lethal adversary from his past takes an interest in his business, there's going to be hell to pay.

Headhunters

Milton barely escaped from Avi Bachman with his life. But when the Mossad's most dangerous renegade agent breaks out of a maximum security prison, their second fight will be to the finish.

In the Beatrix Rose Series

In Cold Blood

Beatrix Rose was the most dangerous assassin in an off-the-books government kill squad until her former boss betrayed her. A decade later, she emerges from the Hong Kong underworld with payback on her mind. They gunned down her husband and kidnapped her daughter, and now the debt needs to be repaid. It's a blood feud she didn't start but she is going to finish.

Blood Moon Rising

There were six names on Beatrix's Death List and now there are four. She's going to account for the others, one by one, even if it kills her. She has returned from Somalia with another target in her sights. Bryan Duffy is in Iraq, surrounded by mercenaries, with no easy way to get to him and no easy way to get out. And Beatrix has other issues that need to be addressed. Will Duffy prove to be one kill too far?

Blood and Roses

Beatrix Rose has worked her way through her Kill List. Four are dead, just two are left. But now her foes know she has them in her sights and the hunter has become the hunted.

Hong Kong Stories, Vol. 1

Beatrix Rose flees to Hong Kong after the murder of her husband and the kidnapping of her child. She needs money. The local triads have it. What could possibly go wrong?

In the Isabella Rose Series

The Angel

Isabella Rose is recruited by British intelligence after a terrorist attack on Westminster.

Standalone Novels

The Art of Falling Apart

A story of greed, duplicity and death in the flamboyant, super-ego world of rock and roll. Dystopia have rocketed up the charts in Europe, so now it's time to crack America. The opening concert in Las Vegas is a sell-out success, but secret envy and open animosity have begun to tear the group apart.

Subpoena Colada

Daniel Tate looks like he has it all. A lucrative job as a lawyer and a host of famous names who want him to work for them. But his girlfriend has deserted him for an American film star and his main client has just been implicated in a sensational murder. Can he hold it all together?

34817148R00216

Made in the USA
San Bernardino, CA
07 June 2016